PUCKING REVENGE

the revenge games

BRITTANÉE NICOLE

PLAYLIST

Moral of the Story - Ashe, Niall Horan

favorite crime - Olivia Rodrigo

The Man- Taylor Swift

Dog Days Are Over - Florence + The Machine

Till Forever Falls Apart - Ashe, FINNEAS

People Watching - Conan Gray

Romeo & Juiet - Peter McPoland

Hit Me Where It Hurts - Caroline Polachek

Green Light - Lorde

Radio - Lana Del Ray

Rest of Our Lives - The Light the Heat

Favorite Place to Go - Layup

I'm with You - Vance Joy

Feels Like- Gracie Abrams

I Don't Want To Wait - Paula Cole

You Are In Love - Taylor Swift

Heartbroken - Diplo, Jessie Murph, Polo G

It's Nice To Have A Friend - Taylor Swift

DEDICATION

To joy.
Because life is too short to not go after what you want.
And I want to smile while I do that.

And to goalie thighs. Definitely something to smile about.

CONTENTS

CHAPTER 1
Sara

Lennox: You looked hot tonight. Take any of those hockey players for a ride?

Me: LOL. No!

Lennox: Ahhh, this job is such a waste on you. Surrounded by all that testosterone and those thick thighs and you're probably sitting in your room wearing comfy pajamas watching Sweet Home Alabama again.

Me: Actually, it's How to Lose a Guy in Ten Days and I'm wearing leggings and a Bolts shirt.

Me: And I'm not by myself. Brooks is with me.

Lennox: Now there's a hockey player you should get under.

Lennox: Or on top of. Hell, maybe just sit on his face. Goalies are known for being good on their knees.

Lennox: Hellooo. Don't just ignore me.

> Lennox: Fine. I'm sorry. I know you have a boyfriend and you and Brooks are "just friends."

> Me: LOL. Sorry I was too busy laughing my ass off at your text. I showed it to Brooks and he went all quiet on me.

> Lennox: Aww, we broke Saint Brooks. Tell him it's okay, everyone loves a good boy.

> Me: He's not amused. I'm going back to the movie. Call you tomorrow.

> Lennox: Night, bitch.

> Me: Night, lover.

WITH A SMILE ON MY FACE, I set my phone face down next to me. I never know what kind of insanity Lennox will grace me with while I'm hanging with Brooks.

Lennox and I met in college, and I have no idea what I did with my life before she became my best friend. She's the loud to my quiet, the funny to my awkward, and the most loyal person in existence.

She's also stupid rich. The kind of rich that means she could never work a day in her life and still live in the lap of luxury. Instead, she's been trying out different career paths almost biannually since graduation. Like leasing a car. She works until she's sick of the job. Then she quits and moves on to something new. She could never waste her days away not working, and the idea of settling down and getting married is abhorrent to her. But she doesn't mind sampling every type of man she encounters.

I, on the other hand, would love to settle down and have a family. I'd love to find that person I can come home to at the end of the day and fall into easy conversation with. A person who's excited to see me. Who wouldn't force me to hide our relationship.

At least I scored my dream job. As a member of the PR team for the Boston Bolts hockey team, I get to travel across the country, attending games and handling press conferences. And I have Brooks. The best friend a girl could ask for.

As he does after most games, Brooks showed up at my apartment with to-go bags filled with dinner and dessert. Langfield Corp, the organization that owns the Bolts, also owns the building, and the majority of the guys on the team live here, as well as many employees who work behind the scenes. For some, it's a quiet place free of distraction where they can hunker down and stay focused during the season. For others like me, it's home.

It's just one more reason I love my job. Without the generosity of the Langfield family, I could never afford an apartment in Boston.

Sometimes, though, it feels a little like a college dorm. The older players and employees with families tend to live elsewhere, so the building is brimming with the younger guys and a few lucky staff like me.

"Puck bunnies hanging out on your floor again?" I tease.

Brooks's only response is a roll of his eyes. There is absolutely no reason for the man to live in this building. He could easily afford a penthouse in one of the nicest high-rises in Boston, but he wants to be treated like any other person on the team. Even if his family owns the entire franchise. Because Brooks Langfield is a good guy. Practically a saint. Hence the team nickname: Saint Brooks.

And because he's such a good guy, Brooks doesn't spend his nights out at the bar picking up girls like so many of his teammates. The things those boys do in this building, or in their hotel rooms during away stretches—sometimes their *shared* hotel rooms—are the kinds of things I often have to find creative ways to cover up.

I know far too much about who the guys in this building have slept with. Normally, I'm the one tasked with presenting the NDA a day too late.

I've never had to do that with Brooks. It could be that he handles it on his own, or that his family keeps it under wraps. His sister-in-law is my boss, after all. So it's possible she handles all Langfield transgressions to truly keep it in the family.

But somehow I don't think that's true.

Because more often than not, he can be found sitting with me, watching girlie rom-coms and making me smile.

"I can feel you watching me," he murmurs without dragging his focus away from Andie Anderson. On screen, she's walking up the steps wearing a yellow dress, giving Benjamin Barry a flirty smile.

With a grin, I throw a piece of popcorn at him. "You have *such* a crush on her. If she were single, you'd totally hit that, wouldn't you?"

Brooks coughs out a laugh. "*Hit that?* What are we, fifteen?"

A burst of joy rushes through me. "I mean, we can't all be old and distinguished like you."

He dips his chin and cocks a brow. "I'm only three years older than you."

"We're in completely different decades! You're in your thirties." I shiver dramatically. "Ew!"

"That's it." He launches himself at me, taking me down to the floor. Before I have a chance to escape, he digs his fingers into my sides, where he knows I'm ticklish.

I kick and squirm and try to fight back, but it's no use. The man is a six-five, two-hundred-and-twenty-pound beast. I don't stand a chance of stopping him.

I close my eyes and take the dead fish approach, letting my arms and legs go limp. It's a technique I always used with my brother. It never failed to make him laugh, and apparently it's just confusing enough to cause Brooks to pause.

"Sar?"

Rather than reply, I hold my breath and remain perfectly still.

"Oh fuck. Did I hurt you? Shit, shit, shit." He pushes off me, then he presses his fingers to my pulse point.

Unable to hold it in anymore, I burst out laughing.

"Asshole," he grumbles.

I open my eyes just as he's wiping a palm down his face and letting out a long breath.

"Aw, don't be mad at me, Brookie."

He scowls, rights himself, and leans back against the couch, his legs stretched out in front of him and crossed at his ankles. He's not a fan of that nickname. "Bet ya Kate would appreciate me," he grumbles.

"Thought her name was Andie," I taunt.

He shakes his head and cups his mouth with a hand to hide his laughter, but his eyes dance over that meaty paw. His hands are so freaking big and strong. Really, everything about him is.

I settle on the floor beside him again and snag a handful of popcorn. "You know, Lennox is single."

He eyes me without turning his head. "And?"

"You're single," I sing, tossing a piece of popcorn into my mouth.

"Ah, stop the presses. It's breaking news," he teases, his lips lifting adorably on one side.

"Come on. Don't you want that? Don't you see how happy your brother is now that he has a wife?"

Brooks's brother Beckett married my boss last year. I never thought I'd see the day when the grumpy guy would finally smile, but now that Liv is wearing his ring, he's genuinely happy all the time.

He dips his chin and picks at an invisible speck on his sweatpants. "Liv is special. Of course Beckett's happy."

"And Lennox isn't special? You got a problem with my best friend?"

Beside me, Brooks tenses. "No. It's just..." He sighs. "She's not who I'm interested in."

Oh. Things just got interesting. Even during the offseason, I never saw him with a woman. It's common knowledge that he doesn't date during the season, but from what I can tell, he doesn't date period.

Oddly, I find that comforting. He feels a bit like mine, and now

I'm feeling stupidly territorial. If he has his sights set on a woman, then there's a good chance he won't be hanging around much.

My stomach sinks. We spend the majority of our free time together and I'm not looking forward to giving that up.

Without him, the loneliness would be all-consuming. Especially since my boyfriend rarely has the time for me and insists our relationship remain a big, fat secret.

But if anyone deserves to be happy, it's Brooks.

I fold my legs and turn to face him. "Tell me about her. What's she like?" I edge closer and grip his bicep. "Do I know her? Is she nice? Will she like me?" When he doesn't reply fast enough, I duck my chin and whisper, "Does she like Lake?"

This is a trick question.

If she doesn't like Lake Paige, then we can't be friends. Because who doesn't like Lake? She's like the queen of pop. I live my life by the songs she writes. Not long ago, she caught her boyfriend cheating on her with her tour manager, so she dumped his ass. Then she got even by fucking his dad. Basically, she's my idol.

But—and this is a huge but—if she likes Lake, then this thing between Brooks and me, this friendship whose foundation was built around a mutual love of Lake Paige, will no longer be special. Because he'll share that love with this other woman as well.

Dramatic, maybe, but that's who I am. Deal with it.

My phone buzzes beside me, catching my attention.

SL: Just getting back. Come over.

When I look up, flipping the phone so it's face down on the rug, Brooks is zeroed in on it.

He clears his throat, and a flush works its way up his cheeks. "Sorry, I didn't mean to look. I've gotta go."

I grasp his arm and squeeze softly. "Wait, you never answered my question."

He drops his chin and blinks at our connection, so I release him.

"Yeah, you'd like her." He shakes his head and stands. "But it's nothing," he says, his shoulders slumped and his tone full of defeat. "She doesn't know I exist."

"Impossible," I say, picking the bowl of popcorn up off the floor and placing it beside the television.

Andie and Ben are now singing to one another. This scene always sucks me in.

It takes me a moment to pull my focus away from the screen. When I do, Brooks is already at the door, slipping his shoes on. "You're the best guy I know, Brooks Langfield," I remind him. "And my bestest friend."

He chuckles, his head lowered. "Yeah, after Lennox."

I roll my eyes. "Eh, you took me to see Lake Paige. And introduced me. You are totally winning the best friend contest."

Brooks beams as he opens the door. "Night, Sar."

"Night, Brookie."

"Good Morning, Boston, and what a good one it is! I'm Colton, and with me is my co-host, Eliza, and we're here to bring you the Hockey Report."

"Thanks for the introduction, Colton, and good morning, Boston. It's so great to be back in the studio now that hockey season is underway. Especially after last night's season opener, where our Boston Bolts took home a win."

"The boys looked great. Even the new guy. If you didn't tune in, we'll give you a quick rundown. Sanders has been traded, and Daniel Hall has officially taken over in the first line as a left winger."

"Yes, Colton. I think we all collectively held our breaths, waiting to see if Hall could measure up to Sanders. He left some big skates to fill after shooting the winning goal that led the Bolts to bringing home the Cup last year. From what we've seen so far, Daniel Hall's nickname, Playboy, may really be a nod to nothing other than his skills on the ice."

Colton laughs. "I'm sure plenty of young women in Boston would disagree, but number 18 certainly is a playmaker. And with War and the Leprechaun joining him on the line, Boston has a real shot at going all the way again."

"For those who are new to Boston hockey, Aiden Langfield, number 12, is the Leprechaun," Eliza explains. "And number 7, right winger Tyler Warren earned his moniker—War—because he's a fighter through and through."

"He definitely loves to stir it up since he took over the position after Fedir Rudenko retired and we love to see it," Colton drolls.

"Don't we ever. But the real star of last night's game against LA was Boston's favorite good boy and last year's Sports Illustrated Hockey Bachelor of the Year, Brooks Langfield. He is truly a Saint on and off the ice."

"He only let in one puck, despite the constant pressure in the crease. All in all, the team looks great. On defense, Bolts' Captain James "Gravy" McGreevey and Rowan "Slick" Parker were nearly unstoppable as well. It's going to be a great season, Eliza. Now stick around, folks. We'll be back after a word from our sponsor, Hanson Liquors."

CHAPTER 2
Brooks

"OH MY GOD. IS THAT—"

I turn my head and fight back a grimace. I should be used to it, the whispers and the stares, the pointed fingers, the ogling.

Yet it still sends a shiver of unease through me. Does anyone ever truly get used to being stared at like this?

Doubtful, because this attention isn't about my status as a hockey player—a fucking great one, at that—but because these teenage girls have seen me in my damn underwear on billboards all over town.

Coach chuckles as I slide into the bench seat across from him. "Can I get your autograph?" he teases in a high-pitched voice.

I roll my eyes and scan the menu. There isn't a chance in hell I'll get anything but my regular order—a six-egg-white omelet with sautéed veggies, turkey bacon, and whole wheat toast—but studying the menu means avoiding the stares that inevitably follow once the people around me realize that yes, I am *that* Langfield brother. Because not only am I on a billboard, but my family owns half of this city. So if my body doesn't do it for people, then odds are that my bank account will.

Despite the billboards and the notoriety my name brings, my persona as "Saint Brooks" makes me the most approachable of the

Langfield brothers. It's exactly what the man seated across from me raised me to be: a *saint*, as well as a great hockey player.

"Incoming," Coach warns.

In my periphery, a boy just a smidgen taller than our table shuffles up, and his mother follows close behind.

Donning the friendly smile I perfected years ago, I keep my focus locked on the little guy and patently avoid the eyes his mother is making at me. "Hi, big guy. Whatcha got there?" I point to the kids' menu he's clutching. It's been colored and is covered in some foreign substance I'm doing my best not to think about. I'm really hoping I can avoid touching it.

"Can I have your autograph?" the boy says, darting a glance back at his mother.

I survey her quickly, just to see if she's pushing the boy to approach me. When she catches on to the attention, she offers a flirtatious smile.

No, thank you.

It's not that I have anything against moms, but I loathe people who use their kids as props. Probably because, for years, my siblings and I were often displayed as shiny props for our parents.

With my focus back on the kid alone, I sign what I discover is a syrup-covered menu. When I'm finished—and realize my hand is nice and sticky—I say goodbye to the little boy while expertly ignoring his mother's attempt to offer her number. Then I turn back to face the man who actually raised me.

Coach married my Aunt Zoe when I was five. My younger brother and I, the perfect props, were ring bearers in the wedding. The morning before the *I do*s, Seb and all his groomsmen took to the ice for a skate.

Maybe he was trying to impress my aunt, or maybe he liked us. Either way, Coach asked if Aiden and I could join in. And that's the day I fell in love with hockey.

Coach played for the Bolts at the time. He wasn't a star, but he was on the ice, and to the majority of us players, that's all that matters. My family, of course, owns the team, and that's how he met my aunt.

From the moment I stepped onto the ice, I was filled with a power I'd never experienced before. And when I looked up and discovered one of his bigger friends gliding straight for me, my life flashed before my eyes. Not in the sense that I thought I was going to die, though. In that moment, I intrinsically knew exactly what to do to stop him from getting the little black object past me.

The save was epic. For a five-year-old, that is. The guys all cheered and bragged about me for the rest of the day. A few weeks after the wedding, Coach showed up and brought me down to the rink. And then he showed up again.

My father had no time to haul me back and forth to early-morning hockey practices, but Coach made sure I got there. When I wasn't practicing with my team, I was watching the Bolts play. I grew up in that arena. There wasn't another place on earth I felt more comfortable. Not then, and not now.

This man across from me is the person I have to thank for it all. He saw me that day, saw my potential and nurtured it. And he's been doing it every day since. He's one of the best guys I know.

"You look tired," Coach says, brows furrowed as he studies me.

"Feel fine."

"Hope you weren't out all night like the other guys. You know you have to set an example—"

I pick up my glass of water and tune him out. This speech is one I could recite in my sleep. Yes, I'm Good-Boy Brooks. I don't need to be reminded of that reputation and all it implies.

The nickname makes me cringe, but it's fitting.

"Was in bed early. No clubs, no bars. Don't worry, my virtue remains intact," I grit out.

The sting that comes along with that last part is a little sharper than it's ever been. Not dating never bothered me until I met Sara. Now it's all I think about.

Am I saving myself for her? Possibly. Which just means I'll die a virgin, because the girl doesn't see me like that.

The waitress appears, thank God, and we give her our orders. Once she walks away, my uncle dives into talk about our plan for practice today and tomorrow's game.

This is what gets me up and moving on mornings like this. Not because I love forcing myself out of bed early on practice days to meet up with him, but because he wants to go over game strategy with me. My opinion matters to him. I've spent my life striving to get here. Making him proud is truly the only way I know how to thank him for investing in me the way he has.

Once we've polished off our breakfast and gone over his plans, we stand, both smoothing out our suits—my uncle would never approve of wearing something as pedestrian as a pair of jeans out in public, even if it's to the damn greasy spoon we've frequented for years—and head out into the crisp October air.

The beginning of the season always brings such promise. We're the defending Stanley Cup Champions, so there is a lot riding on these first few weeks. A lot to live up to. Especially, since the team has changed in some big ways—making the line-up look almost unrecognizable from the past year. We even got new jerseys and a new plane. But our team is young and hungry. There's no reason we can't do it again.

"You walk like an old man," Aiden chirps, rushing to catch up to me on the way to the locker room.

I eye him. Yeah, I'm older than he is, but I've also got a couple of inches on him and a shit ton more muscle. "I'm in better shape than you."

"Impossible." With a grin that splits his face, he pulls his shoulders back and slaps his stomach. "Washboard abs, baby. You could do push-ups on these things."

I choke out a laugh. "Pass."

He shrugs. "You're missing out. Speaking of missing out, why didn't you come out last night? We don't even have a game today."

Gravy wraps his arm around my shoulders and pulls me close, jostling me as he does. "Because he was hanging out with his Sar Bear, eh?"

"Shut up," I groan, my chest going a little tight at that sentiment. My Sar Bear. If only.

War, the right-wing instigator on our team and my best friend, holds open the locker room door as we file through. "Your brother was no better. Aiden spent half the night on the phone with Jill."

"Did not," Aiden whines. Then he lets out a long sigh, his shoulders slumping. "She just gets nervous because of how you idiots act when you're out."

I roll my eyes. Jill sucks. Not that I'll ever tell Aiden that. Guy needs to figure that out himself. Hopefully soon, because if this goes on much longer, I can only see things going one way. He'll marry her, and once the dust settles from the ridiculously lavish wedding, she'll cheat on him. Then she'll take him for half of what he's worth. But it's his life. I can't fix everything for him. He wouldn't listen even if I tried.

There are four of us Langfield brothers. Beckett and Gavin are several years older than me, but Aiden and I are close in age. He's been following me around since he was old enough to skate, so we've always been tight. Playing for the same team and spending almost every waking minute of every day together only adds to that.

But he's a lot. Youngest brother syndrome or something. Even if he's not the baby. That title belongs to our only sister, Sienna.

As we're hitting the lockers, my phone buzzes.

Beckett: Want to come over for dinner?

Aiden: Fuck yeah!

> Me: Sure, what time?

> Gavin: What did you do?

> Beckett: Why do you assume I did something? Can't I just want my brothers to come over and hang with my family for dinner?

> Gavin: No.

Aiden lets out a laugh beside me, and I frown at my phone as the texts continue to come in.

> Beckett: Fine. Liv is less likely to kill me with you guys there.

> Gavin: And I repeat, what did you do?

> Me: On second thought, I'm pretty sure I have plans.

> Aiden: I'll be there. I love to watch Liv put you in your place.

This time I snort, and Aiden grins. The kid lives to make people smile. He and Beckett are polar opposites in that respect. I love my oldest brother, and he's always gone out of his way to take care of us, even when he was a kid, but he's an asshole to just about everyone but his wife and kids.

> Beckett: I bought a dog.

Aiden sucks in a breath beside me.

Me? I'm imagining Liv's reaction. My balls shrivel at just the thought.

Last year, my brother was forced to move into a crumbling brownstone with her and her three best friends *and their seven kids* in order to fix a PR nightmare.

Every one of us knew Beckett was in love with Liv—and had

been for years—before they got married in Vegas. Everyone except Liv, that is. As head of PR for Langfield Corp, she has this eerie way of seeing and preparing for every situation and eventuality. Beckett's attraction to her was her one blind spot.

They may have gone into the marriage to fix Beckett's image, but the moment she became his wife, he made it clear that his feelings were real. Then he proceeded to purchase every house on the block where she lived with her friends. Now they all live side by side in individual brownstones, though they're still raising their kids as one large, nontraditional family unit. It's strange, but it works for them.

Liv is one of the coolest women I've ever met. She's down-to-earth, and she doesn't let Beckett get away with anything. Not to mention she has all of our backs. Not because she's the head of PR, but because she's our sister. I love her to death. But when she's pissed off... Shit, Beckett is lucky he got a dog, because he'll be living in the doghouse for a while.

> Gavin: Without Liv's knowledge?
>
> Beckett: <Sends pic of dog> look at him. He's so ducking cute. What was I supposed to do? Seriously, Gav. I need you to have my back. I need a story. Give me something to work with here.

I screenshot the entire text chain and send it to Sara.

> Sara: Awe, that puppy is so cute! But yeah, Liv is going to kill him. I'd pay to see what she does to him tonight.

> Me: Why don't you come with me?

Those three dots that signal she's responding dance on the screen, then disappear. When they don't reappear and no message comes through, I slide the phone into my locker. I don't have time to wait for Sara to make a decision. I have to get to practice.

As we make our way out to the ice, my heart trips over itself. Because there, standing beside Coach, is Sara. Her smile is wide and her eyes are bright. The girl is a breath of fucking fresh air in a space that often smells like gym socks and moldy food.

Or maybe that's just McGreevey beside me. He blames American food. I blame the Canadian's obsession with ketchup.

He nudges my side, and I finally remember to breathe.

It's always like this.

Chest aching, lungs seizing, lightheaded, and feet floating an inch off the ground.

Will it ever *not* be like this?

Her blond hair is up in a ponytail, highlighting her high cheekbones and sleek jaw line. She is stunning. Blue eyes, creamy skin, button nose, and that goddamn smile.

As soon as she spots me, her eyes light up. "Looking good, Brookie!"

I roll my eyes and shake my head, mouthing, "Cut it."

As we approach, I nod a hello to Coach, but my focus remains on Sara. "What are you doing here?"

"Came to see my favorite guys practice for a bit before I head up to the office." Her eyes dance. "Although after what you told me about Beckett, I may hide out here for a bit. Hope he doesn't tell her while they're at work."

"Can't believe you're walking so easily after Brooks had you awake all night," Daniel Hall chimes in. Kids a menace. He's obviously earned the *Playboy* nickname.

I'm glaring at him as Coach blows his whistle. "Enough fucking around. On the ice."

With a wink at Sara, I push off the door to head to my spot in the crease.

Coach's voice stops me halfway there. "You know the rules. No fucking the staff."

My stomach sinks, and I quickly turn to Sara.

She looks as shocked as I do. Her mouth in an O and her eyes as big as saucers.

She doesn't deserve any of the shit spewing from my teammates' mouths or from Coach's.

Dammit.

Heart lodged in my throat, I lick my lips, determined to clear this all up. "We didn't—"

"Drop and give me fifty." Coach skates up close, his jaw clenched tight. This hard expression is one I've seen plenty over the years, but never directed at me. "Go near her again, and you'll be riding the bench for the rest of the season."

What the hell?

He skates away, and all I can do is gape. Does he really think I'd break any of his damn rules?

Regardless, I'll do exactly what he says. As it is, the guys think Aiden and I get special treatment because of our last name. The last thing I need is for my teammates to be up in arms, claiming that I think I don't have to listen to Coach.

In reality, he goes harder on us than everyone else, clearly over-correcting for perceived nepotism.

It's bullshit. Aiden is the highest scorer on the team, and it's rare for anyone to get a goal by me. We're both fucking good at our jobs. *That's* why we're here. The Langfields are as competitive as they come. If Gavin, who took over the hockey side of Langfield Corp from our dad, didn't believe we could perform, he'd have us on the damn bench himself.

"Is there something wrong with your hearing?" Coach hisses. "Should we have the doctor come take a look at you?"

Without hesitation, I drop my stick to the ice, then I follow. And I count. Loudly. "One. Two..."

CHAPTER 3
Sara

"WHAT THE HELL WAS THAT ABOUT?" I whisper shout at Sebastian as he stalks back my way.

He just humiliated Brooks for no good reason.

Arms across his broad chest, he turns back to the ice. He doesn't look in my direction, though it's obvious his next words are meant for me. "Thought you were tired last night."

"I was." I'm fuming. The rink is cold, but suddenly, I want nothing more than to tug off my jacket. "You texted me at midnight. I'm not some fucking booty call who's waiting around, ready to perform at all hours of the day."

"But you were awake enough to hang out with Brooks."

I scoff, fighting the urge to round on him and cause a scene. "You're acting like a child. Brooks is my friend. That's all we are."

"Remember that next time I call. Don't waste your time hanging out with boys when you can spend time with a man."

The laugh that escapes me is bitter and a little too loud. And this time I can't help but turn to him. "Ha. Because you're acting like such a man right now. Forcing your nephew to do push-ups on the ice because he played with your toy."

He glares at me, his brow pulled low and his chest heaving. "Watch your fucking tone. And stay away from him."

Suddenly, standing between Beckett and Liv when she discovers he bought a dog sounds much more appealing than watching practice. "You don't get to tell me who I can and cannot hang out with." I spin on my heel and stomp away, annoyed beyond belief.

I falter when Sebastian's warning hits me. "But he'll be the one to pay for it."

Hours later, I'm still fuming, though I'm also filled with a perverse excitement, knowing I'm actively disobeying Sebastian.

The knock on my door comes at exactly five o'clock. When Brooks says he'll do something, he does it. I, on the other hand, am still jumping around in my bedroom, tugging a pair of jeans up my legs. My hair is still a mess and my makeup is only half done.

"It's open," I holler from my bedroom as I button my jeans.

His footsteps signal his entry, along with a heavy sigh. "How many times have I told you to keep that locked?"

Peeking out from my bedroom, I shoot him a devilish grin. "I knew you were coming over."

He's hovering near the door, always the gentleman, ensuring my privacy. He'd never just wander into my bedroom. "You live in a building full of horny hockey players."

"Who believe you've staked a claim on me." I bat my eyes and shoot him a wide, innocent smile. Yes, every one of them believes we're more than friends. No, I don't mind. Langfield Corp has a no-fraternization policy, and this keeps me from having to shut any interested guys down.

Because the last thing I want to do is risk my job. I love what I do. And more importantly, I *need* this job.

Seb and I have kept our relationship discreet, obviously, and he's promised that my job is safe either way. He divorced Brooks's aunt years ago, but he's still close to the guys, Brooks especially, and he worries it'll upset them to know he's dating. He's not giving them enough credit. Brooks doesn't judge people. That's just not who he is. And he loves his uncle. He'd want him to be happy, regardless of what that looks like.

Although, right now, I don't give a shit if Seb is happy. In fact, I'm tempted to text him a picture of Brooks and me just to piss him off. He thinks he can tell me who I can and cannot be friends with, but he seems to have forgotten who he's dating.

Brooks stares me down, hands on his hips, but when I just keep smiling brightly, he drops his head and gives it a shake. "You're a pain, you know that?"

"That I do." I turn back so I can finish getting ready and holler over my shoulder. "Does Liv know she has an extra ten people coming to dinner?"

Brooks laughs. "Not likely. Knowing Beckett, he didn't tell her."

I toss my blond hair up in a high ponytail and coat my lips in a layer of gloss. In front of the mirror, I give them a good smack and inspect my reflection. With a quick glance at my outfit, which consists of jeans and a mocha sweater that hugs my curves—perfect for the fall vibe I'm rocking since it's pumpkin season and I'm basic like that—I head out to the living room.

Brooks is typing furiously on his phone, his smile wide, when I exit my bedroom. He's sporting his usual man bun. It's pulled back neatly, though the few rogue curls that always try to sneak out are already making their escape. The man has, hands down, the best head of hair in Boston. It's chocolate brown with natural highlights, and every time he turns those damn green eyes on me, I almost melt on the spot. My best friend is simply gorgeous. And far too humble.

In short, he's the perfect man.

"Texting your new girlfriend?" I plaster a grin to my face and do my best to keep my tone even.

I'm not jealous, exactly. He asked me to go to dinner with him, not her, so clearly, he's still making time for our friendship.

Brooks frowns, his dark brows drawing low. "Who?"

"The girl you told me about?"

He blinks, and his eyes clear in understanding. With a subtle nod, he slides his phone into his pocket. "Nah, just the boys. They're taking bets on how Liv will kill Beckett." He holds out his hand. "Ready to go?"

That's another thing I love about my best friend. He's so affectionate. That's probably why his teammates think we're together. Brooks is always touching me. It's never sexual. He keeps every touch appropriate. Like now. He slips his palm against mine and leads me out the door.

Growing up, I never experienced this kind of affection. My mother was always working, and my father dipped out before I turned two, so I spent the majority of my childhood alone.

Meeting Lennox in college was like hitting the lottery. From that first day, she took me under her wing and forced me out of my shell.

When I met Brooks, I swore I'd found the person who completes me. There was a moment when we first met where I thought maybe we would be more than friends, but then I found out about the no-fraternization policy, so I put him in the friend zone. Fortunately for me, Brooks is the best kind of friend, always making time for me.

My heart squeezes in my chest, making it a little hard to breathe. I really hope this new girlfriend doesn't ruin it for me.

"Sorry about this morning," Brooks says when we reach the car.

"This morning?"

"With Coach and the guys." He clears his throat and slides his hand from mine so he can set it on the small of my back as he opens the door. "I talked to them, by the way. They won't be making comments anymore."

I let out a soft laugh as I climb up into his truck. The thing is massive. It's a souped-up F-150 in Bolts blue. It's the only loud thing associated with Brooks. He so often flies under the radar, but the people who live between here and the arena know when Brooks pulls onto the road.

"You didn't have to do that. I can handle myself, Brookie."

He glares at me like he does every time I use that nickname. And I use it a lot. The man is so even and collected. I like getting a rise from him.

He shuts my door, rounds the hood of the truck, and climbs in beside me.

"Coach, on the other hand…" I hedge, keeping my teeth clenched tight to hide my hurt.

Seb was an asshole this morning.

What will Brooks think when he finds out we're together? It's going to be difficult enough admitting I lied to him about who I was dating, but when he realizes that he was punished because his uncle is a jealous asshole, he'll probably be even more upset. He won't get angry. Brooks never gets angry, but he'll be hurt. And that's so much worse.

"That's on me too. I talked to him after practice. Made sure he knows nothing's going on." He grasps my hand again and squeezes. "Don't worry, your job is safe. We all know you'd never risk it for a man."

The laugh that bubbles out of me is strained. He's right, I wouldn't risk my job for a man. I need this job. *Without it…*

I shake the thoughts from my mind. It's not worth stressing about. I've got this under control. No one will find out about Seb and me until there is something worth finding out about. We're new. And I have no doubt that when that time comes, I can talk to Liv. She'll help me ensure I can have it all. The man, the job, the security I've always craved. It's not about the money, though money does provide security. Only people who have truly lived without it can understand just how much that really matters.

At this moment, I don't care much about my relationship with Seb anyway. If he keeps acting like a two-year-old, the only people he'll have left to play with will be the boys he coaches.

When Beckett and Liv's brownstone comes into view, a bolt of excitement courses through me. Maybe it's juvenile, but I love watching the two of them together. Beckett was such a grumpy ass before he convinced a drunken Liv to marry him in Vegas. Before that fateful night, he'd secretly pined for her for years, while she'd spent her days rolling her eyes at him.

And now he's a ball of mush in her presence.

It makes me giddy.

Brooks shakes his head at me and chuckles. He always does that —laughs at my ridiculousness.

But I love making him smile, so I don't intend to curb my insanity any time soon.

"Come on, Sar. Let's go watch the show."

The front door of the brownstone beside Beckett's opens, and out walks Cortney Miller, his wife, Dylan, and their daughter, Willow.

I wave a hello as I hop out of the truck, and Dylan shoots us a surprised look. The redhead is Liv's best friend. Until recently, Dylan and Liv, along with their two other best friends, lived together.

From the way Beckett talked about the place, one would think it was a house of horrors, but the house at the end of the block doesn't look bad to me. It's beautiful and well-kept, just like the other three brownstones.

"What are you guys doing here?" Cortney shakes Brooks's hand, then angles in and presses a kiss to my cheek. Cortney Miller, former catcher for the Boston Revs—the baseball team owned by the Lang-fields, along with the Bolts—is now their general manager. He and Beckett spend far too much time together. Not only do they work side by side every day, but their wives are best friends, and they live next door to one another. I've even heard rumors of an interior door from one house to the other, though I haven't seen it yet.

I'm not sure how Cortney puts up with the grump. He's a giant with long blond hair, and he's one of the friendliest people I've ever met. Dylan, from what I can tell, is super chill. They're the antithesis of Beckett, but maybe that's why they get along so well.

Unable to fight the smile spreading across my face, I peek over at their six-month-old daughter. She's all rosy cheeks and smiles, with red hair like her mother.

Brooks grins. "Beckett has a surprise for Liv, so he asked us to come by for moral support."

I laugh. "Pretty sure he thinks that as long as there are witnesses, she won't kill him. Is that why you're heading there too?"

Dylan shakes her head, her golden eyes dancing with glee. "No, Liv has something to tell Beckett. She's worried he might lose it. I guess we'll be there for moral support too."

My stomach sinks. What the hell could Liv have done wrong? "Everything okay?"

With a laugh, Dylan runs the pendant she's wearing back and forth along its chain. "Oh, the universe has this covered. It will be fine, right, baby girl?"

The little girl babbles up at her mama, her lips glistening. God, she's adorable.

Cortney whisks Willow from her mother's arms. She snuggles into his shoulder, tugging at the long blond locks that he's so famous for.

"I'm not sure the universe is ready for Beckett Langfield to get this news, but after what he put me through, I'm dying to watch the events unfold."

Still confused, I follow the two of them up the steps to the brownstone, but I turn at the sound of a vehicle slowing in the road. A large black limo van pulls up to the curb, but rather than a limo driver behind the wheel, it's Beckett.

That's strange. Before he married Liv, he treated his prized Bentley with more love and care than any woman, yet he's cruising around in an oversized van?

A loud laugh escapes Dylan, and she slaps a hand to her mouth. "Maybe he already knows." The words are muffled, but her eyes are bright.

Beckett jumps out and hustles to the back of the vehicle. He hauls the rear door open and helps the most adorable dog to the side-walk. Its fur is golden, and there's a white patch over its eye.

With a leash in one hand, Beckett holds a finger up and shoots a scowl at Cortney. "Not a word, Man Bun."

Dylan throws her head back and full-on guffaws. "This is going to be so good."

Brooks drops to his knees and grabs for the puppy. "What's the little guy's name?"

My boss, who looks like a grumpy, well-groomed Henry Cavill and is dressed in a navy-blue suit, smiles proudly. "Deogi."

"D-O-G?" I can't help the confused frown that takes over my face.

"Yeah, Deogi."

Brooks, who's still kneeling, laughs as he looks up at his brother. "You can't name your dog *Dog*."

Beckett frowns. "I didn't. I named it Deogi."

"Oh my God. Someone stop the insanity," Cortney grumbles behind me.

Dylan shuffles forward, still grinning, then sighs. "I really can't wait for Liv to see this."

Behind the sleek van, Gavin pulls up in his black Bugatti. This man is as ridiculous as Beckett used to be when it comes to his car. He constantly refers to it as his baby in an almost creepy way.

The passenger door flies open, and Aiden jumps from the front seat. He springs off the sidewalk and throws himself down next to Brooks. "A dog!" His eyes are saucers as he looks from Brooks to Beckett to Gavin and then back to the dog again. "Can I get one?"

Brooks throws out an arm and pushes him over. "You control you, bro. Do what you want."

Aiden collapses on one side, but he doesn't look away from the dog. He's still all heart eyes and giant smiles.

"He's not getting a puppy," Gavin grumbles, rounding the hood of his car.

It's impossible not to smile in the presence of all four Langfield brothers. I truly love them. Sure, they write my paycheck—Gavin more so than the rest, since he manages the hockey division of Langfield Corp—but when they're all together, they're hysterical.

"Come on," Aiden whines, popping back up on his knees and nuzzling the dog.

"We do travel for like 70 percent of the year," I offer. If I have to pick a side, I'm going with Gavin. Staying in his good graces is always priority number one. Paycheck signatures and all that.

Brooks just shakes his head and gives me a charming smile, then turns back to the dog. There he is, laughing off my ridiculousness again. But this time all I'm doing is stating a fact.

Gavin claps Beckett on the back. "Cute dog. Can't wait to see Finn's reaction."

"It'll probably be like Aiden's." Beckett cocks a brow at his youngest brother, who's got his face buried in the fur of the dog's neck.

"Hey," Aiden whines, pulling back. "Are you calling me a child?"

"If the shoe fits," Gavin mutters, heading up the steps. "Let's get this show on the road. I'm starving. What are we having for dinner?"

The front door swings open, and Liv's six-year-old son appears. He's dressed in camo pants and holding a Nerf gun in front of his chest.

Beckett points at his little boy. "Gun dow—"

Finn drops the brightly colored weapon on the porch with a clatter and launches himself down the stairs, where he scoots in between Brooks and Aiden. "Whose dog?"

Beckett crouches low and holds the dog's collar so he can't jump on Finn. "Ours, Huck. What do you think?"

"Really?" he screeches. He's up again, and then his little arms are circled around Beckett's neck and squeezing him tight.

Beckett, miraculously, remains in his crouched position, still holding the dog, and now his son. "Yeah, let's go find your mom, okay?"

Finn takes off first, and we all follow. The second he's over the threshold, he screams, "Mom, Winnie, Addie! Bossman boughts us a dog!"

The foyer is tight as we all shuffle in. Aiden is bouncing on the balls of his feet, still as ecstatic as Finn. Beckett is half carrying the dog, who isn't sure about following along with our obnoxious crowd. Gavin heads straight to the living room, pointing toward me. "We definitely need a drink for this."

Brooks presses a palm to the small of my back and guides me forward and out of the craziness. "You seem far too excited to be here," he teases, his breath warm on my neck.

The big family thing is still a novelty to me. When I was a kid, it was just Mom and me. Then, when I was in high school, my brother was born. After that, she was home even less. Her days were spent shuttling him to doctors' appointments and therapy or working so she could afford to take him to those appointments and therapy.

More often than not, I was home watching television while my brother hung out in his crib. My friends were Monica and Rachel or Pacey and Joey on *Dawson's Creek*. When he graduated from the crib, I spent my days keeping him entertained in ways that wouldn't wear him out. To this day, my eye still twitches any time I see a puzzle.

The chaos of a big family like this is enthralling. I don't quite understand all the intricacies, but like Gavin, I'm predicting an evening full of entertainment, so a drink sounds perfect.

"You did what now?"

We've all filtered into the living room when Liv appears, with their youngest daughter Addie in tow. Addie is four and since the day I met her, I've never not seen her in anything but pigtails. Liv pulls up short, and her eyes go wide when she catches sight of the audience.

With a lip caught between her teeth, she scans us, then her attention falls to the dog. For a long moment, she doesn't move. Then, without a word, she closes her eyes. Knowing Liv, she's taking deep breaths in for four, then letting them out for four. It's what she does at work. At least when Beckett is around. I've never seen anyone get under her skin quite the way he does.

"Meet Deogi," Beckett says, holding up one end of the leash. The other end is still clipped to the puppy that's now letting out the cutest little playful growls and wrestling with Finn.

Gavin spits out his drink. "He named the dog *Dog*?"

"What did you do?" Liv's hands are on her hips now.

Winnie, Liv's daughter, appears at the bottom of the stairs. Like her little brother, the ten-year-old instantly drops to the floor, her grin wide. She's Liv's mini me, with brown hair and brown eyes, but she's got a dusting of freckles across the bridge of her nose. And, if I'm not mistaken, the braces are new. Poor kid, I've always been told those things suck. We couldn't afford them, so I have an imperfect smile, but what can ya do?

Beckett moves closer to Liv, his voice soft. "We got married because of a dog."

"Because you ran over a dog," Gavin calls.

Turning to Brooks, I cover my mouth to keep from laughing. His green eyes are bright and full of humor.

"I didn't hit the dog," Beckett calls back, though he doesn't turn away from his wife. "Charlie did."

Their driver.

Gavin snorts. "That's not what the papers said."

"Enough," Liv cries, craning her neck to look around her husband. "Gavin, why did you let him get a dog?"

Gavin's eyes go wide, and this time I can't hold in the giggle bubbling up inside me. Clearly, he didn't expect to be put in the hot seat. He cocks a brow at Beckett, then shrugs and tugs on the sleeves of his suit jacket. He leaves us all holding our breath in anticipation for another long moment before he lets out a heavy sigh.

"He was stuck at the farm, Liv." Behind the bar, he uncorks a bottle of Jackson pinot noir and snags a wineglass, no doubt to give him something other than Liv to focus on while he straight-up makes up stories.

Beckett nods. "Yes, the farm." The words are tentative. Like the rest of us, he probably doesn't know where Gavin is going with this.

"What farm?" Liv demands.

"The one on Blackstone." A smirk teases Gavin's lips, like he's really settling into his story. He holds out the glass of wine and raises his brows at me, so I shuffle closer and accept it.

It's at this point that I realize he means the shelter. The team did a photo shoot with puppies at that particular one last season. They raised quite a bit of money for new equipment and supplies for the shelter, and they brought a lot of attention to the place. Within days, almost every dog had been adopted. We have another event planned next week.

"Anyway, Beckett was all 'the dog is not staying at the ducking farm.' He was shouting and yelling and making a scene. The volunteers there were confused about the ducks. They didn't understand that your husband has just lost his mind and doesn't curse anymore." Gavin takes a deep breath. "So they handed him the dog."

This guy is good. Even I'm starting to believe this all really went down, when I know firsthand that Gavin was just as shocked to see the puppy as Liv.

Liv shakes her head and turns to me. "He bought a dog," she mouths, her eyes wide and her face ashen.

I hold my glass of wine out to her. She needs this more than me. Although she might need something stronger.

She bites her lip and spins back to her husband. "Beckett, there are too many of us already. We can't add a dog to the mix. Five kids *and* a dog?" She closes her eyes again. This time she tips her head back and counts out loud. "Breathe, one, two, three."

Dylan has now taken up residence next to her, rubbing her shoulders and murmuring soothing words.

Beckett shakes his head. "Livy, we've got plenty of room. And we only have three kids."

Liv's eyes snap open, and she zeros in on him. Instantly, the modicum of calm she found is gone. Her chest rises and falls, and her nostrils flare. "No, Beckett. Five."

He holds up a hand and counts the kids off on his fingers. "Bear, Huckleberry Finn, and Little One. Three." Those three fingers are still in the air, like he's using the prop to emphasize his point.

Liv smiles. "Five."

He spins and frowns at Cortney. "What did you do? If you upset Dylan again, I'll kill you."

Dylan steps in front of him and pats him on the arm, giving him the most serene smile I think I've ever seen. "She's not talking about my kids."

It hits me then, why Liv asked Dylan and Cortney to come over, and my heart flips in my chest.

Beckett still hasn't put the pieces together. "Medusa and the shining twins are not moving in here! We just got our own space. I'll talk to Enzo. They'll work through it. Surely she's figured out how to apologize by now."

I'm lost now, but I think Medusa's his nickname for another one of his wife's friends.

Liv silences him by cupping a hand over his mouth. Then she grasps his wrist and presses his palm to her stomach. "Not our friends' kids, Beckett." She says each word slowly, her brows raised like she's urging him to pick up on the meaning behind them. "*Our kids.*"

Beckett blinks half a dozen times, then drops his focus from Liv's face to where she's holding his hand against her stomach.

Brooks nudges me, distracting me from the scene. His green eyes swim with warmth and happiness as it hits him too. He's going to be an uncle again.

"Our kids?" Beckett rasps.

Liv nods. "We're having twins, Bossman."

While Beckett stands there dumbstruck, the house erupts. Gavin lets out an ear-piercing whistle in celebration. Beside me, Brooks claps, and Addie joins in, grinning up at him. Aiden throws his arms around Liv and lifts her off the ground. Winnie and Finn are both hopping up and down, asking a million questions. There's joy in every corner of the room.

After Beckett has finally come out of his shock, and he's stolen a quiet moment with his wife to perhaps celebrate, I wander over to congratulate her, and she pulls me in for a hug.

"Why are you all here, anyway?" She glances at Brooks, then focuses on me again.

"Oh, Beckett wanted support when he brought the dog in, so he texted the guys."

"And you just so happened to be with Brooks when that text came through?" The smile she's wearing is full of teasing, like maybe she's under the impression we're more than just friends.

"Liv..."

She ducks in close and squeezes my arm. "Your secret is safe with me."

I clasp her wrists, searching for the words to explain that there's no secret, but then it dawns on me that there is, in fact, a secret. It's just not what she thinks it is. If she's under the impression that I'm dating Brooks, and she's okay with it, then it shouldn't bother her if it turns out that I'm actually dating another person within the organization. Say, the coach...

If I wasn't so mad at Seb right now, I'd probably text him.

But since I am, I settle at the table and ask Liv a thousand questions. Then I listen to her chat with Dylan about the joys of pregnancy and children and families. Though they make it clear not every aspect is picture perfect, she wears a soft smile all night.

And don't even get me started on Beckett. The man's chest is puffed out, and he's beaming.

When my phone lights up on the table in front of me, I immediately put my hand over it—a habit I've acquired since my secret relationship began. Subtly, I ease it into my lap and unlock the screen.

SL: Come over.

I roll my eyes. This guy has got to be kidding me.

> Me: Not home.

> SL: Where are you?

Of its own volition, my mouth turns up. My heart picks up its pace too, because I'm about to piss him off, and I'm enjoying the prospect of it far too much.

> Me: Hanging with Brooks.

With that, I silence my phone and slide it into my back pocket. I refuse to let him ruin anything else for me today. When I look up, Brooks is watching me from the bar. Around him, his brothers are chatting and laughing. He winks and holds up his glass, the universal sign for *Do you want another drink?*

I smile and excuse myself from the ladies. Tonight has been a good night, and I'm going to enjoy it with my best friend.

CHAPTER 4
Brooks

AS WE STEP into the elevator in our building, Sara suggests we hang in my apartment rather than hers.

I'm surprised by the request. I thought she'd be exhausted. She was up late last night, and the insanity that occurred tonight at Beckett's house even had Finn and the puppy passing out early. And all of that aside, we never go to my apartment. We always hang in hers. And I'm normally the one inviting myself over.

So I'm a little thrown. Especially when she ducks her chin and tucks a strand of hair that's escaped her ponytail as she asks, like she's suddenly shy around me.

"You want to pick a movie?" I drop my keys into the bowl by the door and head to the kitchen to grab drinks. A Powerade for me because I need to hydrate for practice tomorrow, and a bottle of water along with a glass of red wine for Sara because she likes to have one before bed.

"Um, let's get another episode of the Creek in," she says, tugging at the blue Bolts blanket I leave draped over the back of the couch just for her. The woman is always cold.

I settle beside her and hold both the water and the wine out to her. Unsurprisingly, she grabs for the wine with both hands.

With a chuckle, I set the water on the table in front of us. "Make sure you drink that before bed, or you'll have a headache tomorrow."

"Whatever you say, Brookie." She pulls her legs up under her and gives me a wicked grin.

Blowing a breath out through my nose, I grit my teeth. When she talks like that, I want to pull her over my lap and spank that teasing smile right off her lips.

But I'm the good boy, so I push those thoughts out of my mind and stretch my legs out on the ottoman in front of me, crossing one ankle over the other, while she starts up the teenage drama. "Remind me of what happened during the last episode."

It's been over a week since the last time we watched this show. She's been on a romantic comedy kick lately.

"It was the one where Pacey bought her the damn wall. God, I just love him. It was so obvious they were always endgame."

I let out a big sigh and drop my head back. "Sar, if you want me to watch the show, you can't keep telling me what happens in the last episode."

She sips her wine unapologetically, her eyes dancing. "I don't understand how you never watched this. It's insane to me."

"You're younger than me. How did you watch it?"

She sighs as she curls further into herself. "Reruns. And I had a lot of time, Brookie."

This time the nickname doesn't even faze me.

Sara has only offered me glimpses of her life outside of Boston. Hell, I barely know anything about her life outside the Bolts. For a woman who lives out loud and unapologetically, she's notoriously quiet when it comes to personal matters. But from what I've gleaned, she had a lonely childhood.

While I have an abundance of siblings, I understand the feeling. Most don't get the sentiment, but constantly being surrounded by people can get lonely too. So I reach over and pull her closer.

Her wine sloshes dangerously close to the rim of her glass, and she gasps, bringing her other hand to it to hold it steady. "If I spill on your couch, I don't want to hear it."

"Shut up and cuddle me, Sar."

Her response is a soft chuckle that reverberates against me. Then she does just that, settling her head on my chest and stretching her legs out across the couch.

When my phone vibrates in my pocket, she tries to pull away so I can reach it, but I band one arm around her so she can't shy away, then dig the device out awkwardly.

> Beckett: Thanks for tonight. Appreciate you guys being there.
>
> Gavin: Proud of you, bro. You're already one hell of a father to Liv's kids. Can't wait to see you with your own.
>
> Aiden: I have tears in my eyes. That was probably the nicest thing you've ever said. Say something nice to me.
>
> Beckett: Thanks Gavin. Wouldn't be here without you pushing me, though.
>
> Gavin: Nah, you woulda figured it out eventually. Just would have driven Liv crazy for a few more years.
>
> Aiden: Cool, you're just ignoring me. Hey Brooks, you ever gonna chime in?

I shake with laughter as their texts pop up, one after another, then hold the phone down in front of her so she can read them all as I text a response.

> Me: Excited for you, Beck. You're gonna be great with twins. Agree with everything Gavin said. Aiden, you're a good boy.

> Aiden: I'm not a ducking dog.
>
> Gavin: <image of a duck>

Aiden: I meant *fucking dog*

Gavin: Dog fucking, that's low even for you.

Beckett: Duck, what the hell did I start? I'm going to bed. Don't forget dinner tomorrow night for Dad's 70th.

Gavin: You bringing the baseball team?

Beckett: Duck you. It'll just be Livy and the kids and me.

Gavin: And that makes…?

Aiden: Tell Finn to bring his game boy.

Gavin: You're a toddler.

Aiden: Finn is six. That makes me at least six.

Sara erupts in laughter. The sound of it and the absolute glee in her expression make my chest squeeze. "Oh my God. I seriously love your brothers."

I arch a brow at her and press my lips together.

"Don't worry, Brookie. You're my favorite."

I squeeze her hip in response, and she squeals, pulling away.

"But seriously. They are so fun."

"You should come tomorrow."

She shifts so she's sitting cross-legged beside me and tilts her head, like she's surprised by the suggestion. "To your dad's seventieth?"

"Not as a date," I add. I don't want her to get the wrong idea. Then she'd definitely shoot me down. "But as my friend. You had fun tonight, right?"

With a soft sigh, she sets her wineglass on the table, then gets back to cuddling. This time she rests her head in my lap and smiles up at me. I might like that smile a bit too much. "Yeah. I really enjoy spending time with your family."

"Then come."

She nibbles on that bottom lip of hers, considering.

I force myself to look away. It's what I always do when she does something that makes me want to kiss her. I have no poker face when it comes to Sara. It's impossible to hide the longing that hits me like a punch to the gut when she pulls that lip between her teeth or when she laughs or gives me one of those soft smiles. It's better this way. Safer. Because she certainly isn't looking back at me in any sort of way.

"Okay, I think I will. If you're sure."

"I'm sure." I point to the clicker, signaling that she should start the show, but I continue to keep my gaze averted. Two seconds after she hits Play, I'm talking again. "You going to tell me why you wanted to come back to my place?"

She glares up at me. Sara hates when I talk during movies or shows, but it's virtually impossible not to. I never run out of things to say to her. Why waste that time zoned out on a screen when I could be listening to her adorably insane ramblings?

When I drop my chin and stare at her, refusing to cower, she relents. With a huff, she rolls her eyes. "Got in a fight with the boyfriend. Don't feel like dealing with him tonight."

My stomach sinks at the mention of the other man in her life. The one I like to pretend doesn't exist. I'm not sure why she's hiding him or allowing him to hide her. All I know is that if I were dating a girl like Sara, I'd make sure the world knew she was mine.

I use one finger to gently sweep a piece of hair from her face and swallow thickly. Her blue eyes hold so much hope. As if she's counting on me to respond in a way that will make her feel better.

Wanting to say the right thing, to be the person she needs in this moment, weighs heavily on me, even as I keep my tone light. "You can always come here. Always." I don't look away, and I don't stop stroking her hair. I want her to feel just how sincere I am.

The softest smile stretches across her pretty face. "You're the best, Brooks. One of the greats." With that, she shifts onto her side, but she keeps her head in my lap. "Now be quiet and fall in love with Pacey with me."

I lean back and let out a chuckle, determined to enjoy this angsty teen drama with my favorite person.

Problem is that with her in my arms like this, Pacey is not the one I'm falling for.

CHAPTER 5

Sara

SOMETHING IS POKING me in the goddamn eye. "Stop," I whine, pushing it back. Whatever it is snaps back at me, hitting me in the nose. What the fuck?

Forcing my eyes open, I growl and grasp the object that had the audacity to smack me in the face. I've got my fingers curled tightly around it when the fog of sleep releases me. My heart lurches, and I gasp in extreme horror, because holy hell, I am *groping* my best friend's *oversized woody*.

"What the fuck?" Brooks rasps above me.

At the sound of his voice, I pounce from my position. Only I forget to drop said over engorged cock.

Brooks yelps as I pull him with me. "Let go of my dick," he says slowly, his brows pulled low and his jaw clenched tight.

I splay my fingers wide and yank my hand back, gaping in shame. "I'm—oh God—I'm so sorry. Is your penis okay?"

Adjusting himself with one hand, he winces. "You had me in a vise grip. What the hell, Sar?"

I'm going to die of embarrassment. I slink off the couch, all but melting into the fabric and onto the floor—slowly, as if maybe he'll forget I was even here—and consider army crawling my way to the door.

"What the hell are you doing?" His voice is less raspy, like he's more awake. He's bent in half, eyeing me where I lie on the floor.

I can only imagine how ridiculous I look, in a heap below him, my hair a wreck and my mascara probably smudged, since he poked me in the eye with his damn monster dick.

"What am I doing?" I slap a hand to my chest. "What *the hell* do you have in your pants? You should be required to have a goddamn license to carry that thing."

Brooks's expression is blank, and he's silent for one second, then two. The silence drags. *Three, four, five.* And then it happens. That glorious laugh escapes him. It's deep and rumbles all the way up his chest. It's the kind that makes his face all squishy because he's so overly happy.

And it's because of me.

Despite my utter mortification, I can't help but beam. It's impossible not to when his green eyes are so full of joy. Brooks sticks his hand out, and when I grasp it, he hauls me to my feet. With a satisfied sigh, he clasps my waist and guides me until I'm seated on the couch. Then, with a shake of his head, he stands and steps away.

My smile morphs into a frown. "Where you going?"

"To get a coffee for you. Then I need to go take care of this monster so I don't scare you any further."

"Take care of it how?" My lungs seize at the same time my stomach flips. The mental picture that instantly materializes in my head is one I have to shut down quick. "Let me leave before you start moaning and shaking that thing. It's probably like a machine gun, going off in all directions."

Brooks steps into my space and crouches. His face is too close to mine—is the man not grossed out by morning breath like the rest of the world?—but at least it's not his dick. "Sara, take a breath."

I shake my head and press my lips together tight.

"What are you doing now?" He's trying not to smile, but he's doing a terrible job of it.

"Morning breath," I murmur, only letting the corners of my lips move.

Brooks heaves himself up and lets out a deep bellow as he walks away. "God, you're my favorite person."

A little lightheaded from holding my breath for so long, I inhale deeply and slump back on the couch. "Right back at you. What time is it, by the way?" I pull my phone from my pocket and tap the screen. It's filled with missed call and text notifications. They're all from the same person, so without responding, I slide the device back into my pocket. Not dealing with him right now.

"Six. Sorry I can't do breakfast or anything." He moves around the kitchen gracefully as he prepares the coffee. "I've gotta shower and head to the arena for practice."

I sit up straight and grin. "Your one-night stand etiquette needs some work. Is this how you treat all the ladies? Poke them in the eye with your monster cock, then kick them to the curb without food?"

Brooks's cheeks are pink when he wanders my way with a coffee mug in hand. "Yeah, Sara. This is exactly how all my nights go." He holds the mug out to me. He's already doctored the brew just the way I like it, with lots of creamer. "But since you're my best friend, I'll throw in a coffee for you."

I tip my head back and grin. "See? Who said being friends with you didn't come with benefits?"

He shakes his head. "Let yourself out when you're done. Pick you up tonight at six?"

Oh, right. The birthday party. Shit, Seb will definitely be there. As I consider the situation, the warm smile on his face morphs into a mask of nonchalance.

"If you still want to come. No pressure. Just let me know." He backs away, then spins and heads for his bedroom.

Dammit. My stomach knots at the thought of hurting his feelings. "Six it is!" I call out. "Sorry, still seeing stars from that cock of yours."

He shakes his head and disappears behind his bedroom door, letting out a deep chuckle that blankets me in a comforting warmth.

Much better. Brooks Langfield's laugh is a national treasure. It must be protected at all costs. That smile too.

I slide on my shoes, and with my coffee in hand, I step out into the hall and close the door behind me with a quiet click. I'll bring the mug back tonight. As I turn and bring it to my lips, a dark figure appears in the hallway.

I swear the kind of eerie music that signals something bad is about to happen plays, coming to a crescendo as the figure steps closer. And the shriek that forces its way out of my mouth makes even my ears ring. Coffee splashes over the side of my mug, scalding my hand and wrist, as well as dousing my shirt in the hot liquid.

"Fuck!"

The looming shadow steps into the light then, and he makes no move to help me. No, Seb stands stock-still, his jaw hard and his eyes narrowed. "What the hell are you doing coming out of Brooks's apartment at six in the morning?"

With a huff, I pat down my wet shirt and mimic what would be a normal conversation if he wasn't such a massive dickhead. "*You okay, Sara? No, Seb. I've been scalded because you scared the fucking shit out of me.*"

Unamused, he grits out, "Answer the question."

"You're being an asshole." I take a slow sip of what's left of my coffee.

What the hell is he even doing here? He lives a few floors above Brooks—right next door to me, of all places—so it doesn't make sense for him to be down here if he's headed for the arena. And clearly, he is. He's already dressed in a suit, salt and pepper hair perfectly slicked back, blue eyes angry.

Does he smile? If so, I can't even conjure an image of what it looks like right now.

"And you're being a slut. You think this is going to make me claim you? Make me want to go public? Because if that's the game, then you've already lost. Hate to break it to you, but you're going to be miserable when you realize I'll never do that."

My heart drops to the floor. More than anything, I want to knee him in the balls, but I keep my composure and use my words instead. "Excuse me? Never?"

He sighs. "Not when you're acting like this."

"And how is what I'm doing a problem, Seb? I fell asleep on the couch while watching a movie." I throw an arm out and point at Brooks's door. "Nothing happened."

With a deep breath in, I search for the composure I normally reserve for handling PR for the team, but it appears to have gone missing.

"If you think that calling me a slut and threatening to keep our relationship a secret indefinitely will stop me from spending time with my best friend, then I'm pretty sure you're the one who will be 'miserable,'" I echo his words, my tone nothing but disgust and fury. *Fuck him.* "Because that's never going to happen."

"You're acting like a child." He takes a step closer. "Remember who you work for."

"Oh, I remember. Olivia Langfield is my supervisor, and I answer to Gavin Langfield. Remember him? What about Beckett? I answer to him on occasion too. Or did you forget about your other nephews, since you're so focused on the one I'm spending time with?"

His only response is a glare.

That's when his words really sink in. *Remember who you work for.*

"Wait a second." I hold up a hand and pull my shoulders back. "Are you threatening my job? Seriously? You swore it was safe. Promised that nothing that happened between us would affect it."

When he still doesn't speak, I shake my head. How could I have been so wrong about this man?

"We are *so* done."

Even as I say the words, my heart pounds so hard I worry I'll crack a rib. Panic claws at me. I can't lose my job. Without it, I can't afford my brother's medication.

My mind is still racing out of control when Seb grabs for my arm.

On contact, my skin crawls, pulling me back to the moment. "Touch me again, and I'll be filing a complaint with HR, Mr. Lukov."

That's all it takes for him to release me and step back. "I could hear you hollering about my star goalie's cock all the way out here. Engaging in a sexual relationship with a player is a fireable offense, Ms. Case." He fists his hands at his sides and pulls himself up to his full height. "I won't remind you again. Stay away from my players or find yourself another job." Without waiting for my reply, he straightens his suit jacket and spins on his heel. Then he's striding down the hall, head high and arms pumping.

Me? I'm glued to the spot, shaking.

He couldn't. He wouldn't.

Holy fuck. Would he?

I still can't wrap my head around my interaction with Brooks this morning, but I'm positive of one thing: my relationship with the man storming away from me is over.

CHAPTER 6
Brooks

"WHY DO you look like you got laid last night?" War elbows me in the ribs as we step into the locker room. His next words are spoken in his native French Canadian and under his breath.

When I get a look at Aiden, I don't need to understand them to get his meaning. My brother is standing by his locker, naked as the day he was born, chin tucked to his chest, staring at his dick.

What the hell is he doing?

McGreevey claps me on the back, forcing my eyes off my brother's dick. Thank God. "Sar probably kept him up all night again, War."

At the mention of Sara, a smile splits my face. She was absurd this morning. In a good way. "Maybe if the two of you focused on your own sex lives, you'd be smiling too."

Aiden spins. Now he's got his dick in his hand. "Is it possible for a woman to run out of orgasms in her lifetime?"

"What the fuck are you going on about?" I turn to my locker to avoid getting another eyeful of my brother's junk.

"Jill said—"

"That's problem number one," War mutters. "Listening to anything that woman says."

McGreevey scowls at War, then turns back to Aiden and takes on a kinder tone. "Jill said what?"

"That because of the piercing, I give her too many orgasms. Said she needs an entire month off from sex to recover."

He steps closer to me, dick still in hand. "What do you think?"

Channeling Beckett, I give him my best *what the fuck?* glower and stare him down. "I think you should put your dick away."

Aiden, unfazed, merely turns his attention to his next target. "War, you use your dick a lot. Have any of the women you've hooked up with ever told you it's too much?"

It's three solid seconds of silence before all three of us start laughing so hard tears stream down our faces.

"Did you just ask War if a woman has ever told him his dick is too much?" I choke out between heavy breaths.

War wipes away his tears of laughter. "Only every one."

"Saint, see me after you get changed!" my uncle barks.

Instantly, my good mood vanishes, my stomach twisting in knots.

"Fuck," War mutters. "Someone is in a mood again. What the hell does he care who you screw, anyway? He's got an unhealthy obsession with your sex life, Saint." He roughs a hand through his hair and looks over my shoulder.

"Aiden, what the fuck are you looking at on your dick? Put that thing away!" Coach adds.

Without a word, my brother snags a pair of boxers from his locker and tugs them on, thank God.

War looks back at me, his head tilted like he's still waiting for me to explain my uncle's mood.

I duck and rub at the back of my neck. War is well aware that I have no sex life, so this is all just shit talk. Regardless, I don't like the insinuation.

"I didn't mean it to come out like that before. I'm not sleeping with Sara. We're *just* friends."

Finally clothed, Aiden bounces on his toes and spins in our direction. "Brooks doesn't even look at women during the season. He's definitely not screwing around with Sara."

McGreevey shakes his head and grunts. "Season is long as fuck. I have no idea how you do it."

"Easy when the woman he wants is taken," Aiden says, rifling through his practice gear.

I shoot him a glare, silently telling him to shut the fuck up, but my brother just smirks and pulls on his jersey.

No, it's not a secret that I have a crush on my best friend. The entire team knows it. But I'm trying to keep it from being obvious to her. And after her confession about things being rocky with her boyfriend—the stupid asshole who makes her keep their relationship a secret—I'm feeling a little less certain about how to handle things tonight.

Should I flirt with her? We've always been affectionate with one another, so last night's cuddling wasn't out of the ordinary. Though we've never fallen asleep together. That was obvious by the way she acted when she woke up in my lap. I have to cover my mouth to hide the smile that sneaks through at the memory of her insanity.

And then I remember how it felt to wake up with her hand wrapped around my dick. It's like my brain stopped working from that moment forward.

Screeching about how I'd poked her in the eye—please, it's not like my cock has a mind of its own. With her, maybe it does, and I'll admit that it's large enough to stab her and do some damage, but that's not what happened.

What happened was that Sara did what she always does when she's feeling vulnerable. After her confession last night, she woke up in my lap and decided to act like a lunatic rather than owning up to her feelings.

Or maybe I really did just poke her in the eye with my massive dick.

But the way she kept talking about my cock? And the feel of her fingers wrapped around it? Let's just say she thoroughly fucked with my head.

"If you're done gossiping," Coach gripes as I all but plow into him on my way out of the locker room.

"Shit." I grasp his shoulders and right him.

I've got a good three inches on him and at least forty pounds of additional muscle. My uncle isn't small, but more often than not, I'm the biggest guy around.

"What the hell was Sara doing coming out of your apartment this morning?"

My head snaps up, and I have to keep myself from staggering back in surprise. The better question is, how the hell does he know that? Did he say something to her? Shit, I hope not. It was bad enough that he acted how he did yesterday.

"We're friends. We fell asleep while watching TV." I sidestep him and head for the ice. The conversation is getting me heated, so it's best that I walk away.

He grips my shoulder and pulls, halting my movements completely. "You can't give her what she deserves."

With my eyes closed, I take a deep breath to steady myself and to keep from lashing out. My uncle means well. He's been open with me about the regrets he has when it comes to his career. But I'm not him.

When I know I can control my tone, I respond. "We're just friends."

"Look at me," he says, his voice quieter.

Pressing my tongue to the inside of my cheek, I huff and finally turn to face him. "Yeah?"

"Your father never had time for you kids because he was busy with work. I was happy to step in and help you become the player you are." He roughs a hand down his face. "You can't do this and have a family. Not when you're playing at the level you're playing. She deserves better than that. You know you can't give it to her, so don't lead the girl on."

Grinding my teeth, I give a single nod. He's not wrong about how difficult it would be to live this life and have a family. It's why I didn't make a move on Sara when she started working with us last year. Yes, she's amazing. And could I see a future with her? Yeah, she's the only person who's ever made me question the damn pact I made with myself when I went pro.

But I grew up coming in third to my father's other responsibilities. I won't make that mistake. This life isn't easy, and in order to give it my all, hockey has to be my primary focus. That means a family will have to wait until after I retire. Coach is also right about Sara. She deserves the undivided attention of the man she's with. She deserves someone who will put her first. I can't be that person.

As much as I hate this lecture, Coach is saying all the things I need to hear. Sara's relationship status at this moment doesn't matter. Neither does how she feels about me. If, by some miracle, she ever sees me in the way I see her, I couldn't be with her. Not while I'm still playing. And I'd never ask her to wait for me.

"Now get on the ice and give me a hundred. I told you to stay away from that girl. You went against my instructions, and now you have to deal with the consequences."

His words are like a damn slap. One minute, he's talking to me like he cares, and the next he's playing stupid games. I storm toward the ice, pissed off again.

The man may be able to force me to listen to him while I'm on the ice, but tonight, I'll be walking into the party with her on my arm. And I'll gladly pay for it with another hundred push-ups tomorrow.

CHAPTER 7
Sara

"DOES THIS LOOK OKAY?" I shift the phone so Lennox can see the slinky silk dress I'm wearing. It's a deep cranberry color, and I've paired it with a pair of nude suede heels she lent me.

When I texted Lennox this morning and mentioned the party tonight, she had her personal shopper deliver these items. She has more money than she knows what to do with, and no matter how much I beg her not to spend it on me, she does anyway. She says it's her love language and to let her love me. You can only say no to that girl so many times.

She raises her brows and smirks. "Seb is going to die when you walk into the party. The man will be claiming you and eating out of your hand by the end of the night."

My stomach sours. "Ugh, that is so not what I'm going for."

Lennox gapes and moves to her phone. "Wait, what?"

With a sigh, I pick up the phone, then I slump against the bed. "We're done."

"What happened?"

"He was being a dick about my friendship with Brooks. And it wasn't the cute kind of jealousy. He made Brooks do push-ups on the ice in front of the whole team yesterday. And from what I heard, he did it again at practice today. A hundred of them. He's being an ass."

"Wow, Seb sucks."

I laugh. "Yes, he does. And that's not even the worst of it. This morning, he accused me of playing games and told me that if I thought this would make him 'claim' me, then I was sorely mistaken. That it would never happen."

"Dick."

"And then he made a veiled threat about my job."

Lennox goes rigid, and I swear flames burst in her eyes. "He wouldn't do that to you. If he even considers it, I'll fucking string him up by the balls."

My heart takes off again, just like it did this morning when he made that comment. Losing this job—and in turn, losing the ability to afford Ethan's medication—would mean my mom would have to choose between his meds or her rent. It's unfathomable.

"What was I thinking, even getting involved with him in the first place? And how the hell did I let him sweet talk me into believing he was this good guy? He made me think he cared about me. That my job was safe." I pinch the bridge of my nose to stave off the tears threatening to well. "I figured that since he was older, I could trust him. That he could be my safe place. I confided in him about my family. I haven't even told Brooks about Ethan, yet I poured my heart out to this guy? What the hell is wrong with me?"

She shakes her head, her eyes practically glowing. "*Nothing.* Nothing is wrong with you. You're perfect and beautiful and kind, and you go out of your way for the people you care about. You worked your ass off to put yourself through college, all while working multiple jobs so you could send money to your mom. I lost count of the number of nights you didn't come out because you refused to let me pay and you wouldn't dip into any of the money you'd worked so hard to earn." She huffs a breath. "So don't you dare criticize yourself. I won't hear it."

I fall back against the pillow and bang my head against it softly. "What if I lose this job? The guy is unhinged. He's in his fifties, yet suddenly, he's acting more immature than half the hockey boys who streak down the hallways of my apartment building."

Lennox chuckles, her blue eyes dancing. "God, I miss you."

"When are you coming home?" I whine. I need her more than I realized.

She looks out her window, probably enjoying the view from her New York City apartment. I'm sure it's incredible. "I'll try to come up one night next week. What's your schedule look like?"

Flopping over to one side, I scan the calendar I keep beside my bed. I'm never sure where I'll be from one week to the next. I go where the team goes, and they're always on the road. "Looks like we're in town next weekend. Then we're on the road for ten days."

"Then I'll plan to make my reappearance in Boston before you leave."

"Thanks, love. I could really use a friend."

"You've got the best one." She grins. "We'll figure this out, babe. Please don't stress. You know I've always got your back." She turns serious then, her tone deepening and her eyes pools of sincerity. "Ethan will never go without medicine, and you will always have a roof over your head."

I twist my lips. I'm grateful for her, but we both know I'd never accept her handouts.

"Speaking of friends," Lennox says, brightening again. "Maybe you should use Saint Brooks and that hot dress to show Seb what he's missing."

"Fuck him." I honestly could give two shits about Sebastian. He *will* lose his mind when he sees me on Brooks's arm tonight. But the last thing I want is to put Brooks in the line of fire again. The man has been nothing but a good friend to me, yet he's been punished repeatedly. "Besides, Brooks did mention a girl the other night."

Lennox sits up higher on her bed, her phone screen wobbling. "Oh yeah? I don't remember him ever dating anyone for long."

"I always forget that you grew up with them."

She drops her chin and inspects her manicure. It's her silent way of saying she doesn't want to discuss something. And despite being an open book, her relationship with the Langfields is never something she's willing to divulge.

I was shocked when she called me up and told me they were hiring. After college, I couldn't afford to live on my own, and my mother needed every extra dime we had to take care of my brother, so I moved back to North Carolina. When Lennox showed me the ad for the open PR position with Langfield Corp and suggested I apply, I immediately dismissed the idea. The pay looked great, but the cost of living in Boston was far, *far* out of my budget. Then she showed me the fine print. The job came with housing.

I didn't understand why they would provide housing until I moved into the building and suddenly found myself surrounded by Neanderthals. The Bolts needed a babysitter for these idiots.

I do get a little reprieve during our very short offseason. Most of them have apartments or houses in their hometowns, so they tend to take time away, and I get a little break.

My days and nights can get a little crazy, since I'm expected to be available to put out fires at all hours, but my housing is free, and the place is gorgeous. One other major incentive back then was being in the same city as Lennox. Though that didn't last long. Now she's in New York, and with my travel schedule, even when she's in town, it's hard to see one another.

The doorbell rings, pulling me back to the moment. I sit up on my bed with a groan. In the little box on the screen where my image appears, I can see that my hair is now a mess. "I gotta go."

Lennox promises to visit next week, and then we're disconnecting.

I holler that the door is open, then focus on fixing my messy hair. Dammit. After all the time I spent curling it, I'll probably have to just pull it up.

"I'm going to start locking you in from the outside," Brooks grumbles from outside my bedroom door. He hasn't appeared. He's being gentlemanly again, probably concerned that I'm not decent.

"Come in, Brookie. I'm dressed."

He ambles in, and my breath goes shallow at the sight of him. God, this hockey boy cleans up well. Brooks is always in a suit—when the team travels, before games, and more often than not when he steps out of this building—but that's business Brooks.

This Brooks, who's propped up against the doorframe, arms crossed, black suit straining across his muscles, crisp white shirt with a burgundy tie—because, of course, he asked about my dress color so we could coordinate—is every woman's fantasy. He's dangling a to-go cup I imagine is filled with coffee in front of him as he scans me from head to toe. His green eyes are darker than usual, like a Christmas tree in the forest, or at least what I imagine one would look like. I've never actually gone out into the forest to pick my own tree.

"You look beautiful." His tone is warm, his smile lazy.

"You clean up pretty nice yourself, Brookie. That for me?" I take a step closer and make grabby hands for the coffee.

He pulls it back and tuts. "Not if you keep calling me that."

With a laugh, I snag the cup from him and bring it to my lips, my eyes never leaving his as I do. When the flavor hits my tongue, there's no holding back the moan that escapes me. "Pumpkin spice. It's like you know me or something."

Brooks chuckles and dips his chin. "Sure do. And I learned early on that pumpkin spice is the key to your heart."

I point to myself and lift my brows in a *who me?* kind of gesture.

His response is a smirk and a pointed look at my bed. It's covered in a burnt-orange quilt, and front and center is a pillow that says *Pumpkin spice is my spirit animal.* It is fall, after all, so it's fitting. I love decorating and only just switched out my seasonal decor. It makes my little apartment feel homey, and for a girl who grew up without that kind of warmth in her life, these little things hold a lot of meaning.

With another sip of coffee, I spin around so I can finish getting ready. When I catch my reflection in the mirror, I let out a frustrated breath. It's confirmed. My hair is a wreck. "Sorry, I was on the phone with Lennox, and I lost track of time. Let me just throw my hair up, then I'll be ready to go. We still have time, right?" I snatch my phone from the other side of the bed and tap the screen to check.

Brooks shrugs and sits on the edge of my mattress. He's so big he makes my queen-size bed look minuscule. "No rush. The party doesn't start until seven."

I snap my head up and frown at him. "Then why did you tell me to be ready before six?"

The smile that breaks out across Brooks's face is devious, like he's about to zing me. "Because you're always running late."

"Rude," I quip, though he's not wrong. "I just like making an entrance." I spin back to the mirror and scan the surface of my dresser for a hair tie.

Brooks's gaze warms my back so thoroughly I don't have to look to know he's watching me. "You sure do," he rasps.

I give him a shy smile in the mirror. "You trying to tell me something, big guy?"

"Big guy. Hmm, I like that a hell of a lot more than Brookie."

Laughing, I pull my hair into a loose ponytail and arrange a few curls so they frame my face, then I set it with spray. "There, how does that look?" I ask, spinning toward him.

He shrugs. "I think my hair looks better, but that'll do."

I roll my eyes, though he's not wrong. He's got his hair back in that damn bun again. The long hair makes him look just a little less perfect. Like it's his one fuck-you to the world. Only Brooks doesn't think like me, so he probably doesn't keep his hair long to spite anyone. He's Brooks. Good-Boy Brooks. Saint Brooks. Always polite and respectful. Holding doors and making room for others. He probably says thank you when he comes.

The second that thought pops into my head, my mind conjures

an image of Brooks with one hand on his monster cock, grunting out a thank-you as he lets loose, spurting everywhere.

I giggle, and my face warms. Did I really just picture Brooks coming? *Holy hell, Sara.*

"What are you laughing at now?"

I cup my mouth to quell the glee escaping me. "Sorry." I shake my head, but I can't catch my breath.

"Sar."

"Fine." I pull in a deep breath and compose myself. "I was just... well, you're always so polite. I was thinking that you probably say thank you when you come."

For a long moment, he doesn't move. His green eyes rove over me, but his lip doesn't even tick up. There's nary a smile nor a grunt. No, Brooks is staring at me like I have seventy-five heads.

"Well, that joke went over like an old man's toot."

He continues to stare at me without giving away a hint of what he's thinking.

"Okay, let's go." I snag my purse from my dresser, flip the light switch, and head out my bedroom door with my coffee cup in hand. In the living room, I set my coffee on an end table and pick up the cream faux-fur shawl Lennox also had delivered.

Brooks appears at my back, startling me, and lifts my ponytail. With a gentleness that seems impossible for a man his size, he smooths my hair out over it, then he leans in close. His lips are a whisper against my skin, causing a full-body shiver to rock me.

Then with the slightest brush against the shell of my ear, his voice all gravel, he murmurs, "If you ever saw me come, the only person who would be saying thank you is you."

A half hour later, I'm still tongue-tied and a little shocked. My best friend has a dirty mouth, and I never knew it. Fortunately, I'm easily distracted, and the sights and sounds that accompany a seventieth birthday party for one of the wealthiest people in Boston is quite the distraction.

Brooks didn't share any details about the party other than to tell me that I'd want to dress up. Preston Langfield is one of the wealthiest men in the world, so that was a given.

With what I know about the man and his status, I was prepared for a party to end all parties, so I'm ill-prepared when I step inside a tiny Italian restaurant and find only one long table set for about twenty people.

"Where are the other tables?" I whisper as Brooks guides me toward the bar where his brothers are congregating. His palm is warm on my back, giving me a semblance of peace despite how out of sorts I suddenly feel.

My trepidation dissipates when I get a look at the rest of the Langfield men. God, every one of them is gorgeous in his own right. The suits they've chosen showcase just how beautiful they are.

Like Brooks, Beckett is rocking the hell out of a black suit. He has an arm wrapped around Liv's waist. She's tucked into his side, but her attention is fixed on Finn, Winnie, and Adeline, who are coloring at a small table in the corner.

Gavin's suit is navy, and the shirt beneath it is light peach. As we get closer, his laughter echoes across the small restaurant.

Beside him, Aiden is grinning, obviously the source of Gavin's entertainment. His horrible girlfriend, Jill, is beside him in a far too revealing green dress that matches his tie. His suit is navy as well but has a slight pinstripe design.

Aiden's personality is loud. No matter where he is or what he's doing, it explodes from all directions, his mouth, his smile, and his clothes. The epitome of a little brother, he's screaming for attention at all times, yet this outfit is muted, reserved.

"I don't think I'll make it through this night without wine," Liv mutters as we approach.

I give her a sympathetic squeeze, but I'm shooed away by her overprotective husband.

Beckett pulls her back into his side in a gentle move so at odds with his domineering personality. "Don't hug her too tight."

Liv rolls her eyes and pats his chest. "Beckett, your babies are safe and sound inside my body. Neither your penis nor Sara's arms are going to penetrate them."

Brooks snorts beside me and Gavin spits out his drink. "Holy fuck, Liv."

From the corner, Finn shouts, "That'll be a thousand bucks, Uncle Gav!"

With a scowl, Beckett digs his phone out of his pocket. He mutters under his breath as he taps on the screen, then he holds it out to Gavin. On the screen, he's pulled up a QR code. "Use duck or pay the price."

Without so much as a flinch, Gavin pulls out his own phone and scans the code. "I'd prefer to pay the fine to keep my manhood, thank you very much."

With my lips pressed together, I scrutinize one brother, then the other. What the hell is happening here?

Only when Brooks squeezes my hip do I realize he still has his arm around me. He angles in until his lips brush against my ear. "What can I get you to drink?"

A shiver racks through me, so I pull my shawl tighter around myself, cursing the cool October air. "Um, something fruity, please."

I'm not much of a drinker. I'll have a glass or two of wine, or maybe prosecco at brunch with Lennox, because boozy brunches are a Sunday ritual when she's in town. Otherwise, I stick to cocktails with little umbrellas.

Like I said before: basic.

Brooks smiles down at me, probably internally chuckling at my general basic bitchness, then asks the bartender to make me something sweet that will match my dress.

Beaming at him like he's the damn sun, I finally let myself relax. Sure, he and his brothers each have enough money to buy a small country, but they're some of the most down-to-earth people I know, and I've rarely met anyone more genuine. I should know this by now, yet I still let myself get worked up over their status. With a deep breath in, then back out, I let the rest of that apprehension go and settle into the moment.

The guest of honor arrives, and suddenly, it's a frenzy of birthday hugs and kisses all around.

Brooks's mom greets me with a big smile. "Sara, you look stunning. I'm so glad you came."

Monroe Langfield exudes wealth and privilege. She's in her late sixties, though one would never know it. Barely a wrinkle dares mar her face, and her posture and figure rival that of women half her age. Obviously her genes are superior. Just look at the children she and Preston produced. Even so, this kind of perfection isn't natural.

No judgment here, though. She's always been lovely to me, and more than anything, I respect a person's kindness and the way they treat the people around them.

Behind her, the youngest Langfield, Sienna, appears. She's a fashion designer and recently starred in her own reality show. For months, a crew followed her around in Paris, documenting the release of her latest line. The paparazzi have been relentless, so it's no surprise that she arrived with a big man in a traditional black suit at her side. His expression hard as granite, he sweeps the room from one side to the other, then back again, as if he's making sure we're all safe.

"Wow. Your sister is a big deal," I mutter to Brooks as he hands me a cranberry-colored drink with a sugar rim. I covertly lick at the sweetness and savor the taste while everyone's attention is fixed on Sienna. Celebrity status or not, the baby of the family is a treasure that none of the guys can ever get enough of.

Brooks's deep rumble sends the loose tendrils framing my face fluttering. "That's not a bodyguard. That's Garreth Hanson." He steps up beside me and holds out his hand to the oversized blond man. "Didn't know you'd be here. You in Boston for a bit?"

Garreth takes Brooks's hand, his scowl softening a fraction and his shoulders easing.

Beside him, Sienna's smile falls. "Don't be too charming to him, Brooks. We don't want him to think we *want* him here."

With another boisterous laugh, Gavin pulls his sister in for a tight hug and presses a kiss to her cheek. "You giving our best friend trouble?"

Garreth looks down his nose at Sienna with a smug purse of his lips. "Trouble. That's like her middle name."

"No one said you had to follow me around like a shadow," she shoots back with a sharp glare.

"Actually, he did," he grumbles, pointing to Beckett.

Beckett lifts his chin, not the least bit ashamed. "And that's all your fault, Sienna. You fire every bodyguard I hire. Let one of them stick around, and I won't sick my friends on you."

I cup a hand over my mouth to stifle my laughter when Liv whirls on her husband and smacks his arm. "Beckett Langfield!"

He shrinks just a little, but he still holds his hand out to Garreth and rumbles out a greeting.

Wildly entertained by the little spat between siblings going on, I sip my drink and take in the room. Near the door, Monroe is hugging a woman who is close to her age. She's equally gorgeous and equally flawless, and she looks more like Sienna than any Langfield I know. I nudge Brooks and angle in close. "Who's that?"

The smile that splits his face is full of fondness, and his eyes warm at the sight of her. "That's my Aunt Zoe." He clutches my hand and practically tugs me along with him as he makes a beeline for her. "Seb's wife."

The earth shifts below my feet, and I stumble as Brooks continues dragging me closer. Unfortunately, when the ground cracks open wide, it doesn't swallow me up like I'm suddenly wishing it would.

His wife?

My stomach drops and then does a somersault. Or maybe it's my heart.

"Wife?" I ask, unable to hide my shock. I can only imagine the horror on my face.

Brooks stops and frowns at me in confusion. "Yeah," he says, drawing out the word. "Aunt Zoe. When I was a kid, she and Seb were like my second parents. Come on, I want you to meet my other favorite woman."

Though my heart has lodged itself in my throat, I force a smile to my face. Surely, he means Seb's ex-wife. Seb isn't still married.

That's what he told me. They separated years ago. We had a whole conversation about it.

Right?

Behind the two gorgeous older women, Seb appears, and all the blood drains from my face. Like everyone else, he's decked out in a dark suit that stretches taut over his broad shoulders. His smile is wide as he claps Preston on the back and wishes him a happy birthday.

Then, to my horror, he grasps Zoe by the hip and hauls her to his side. She tips her chin up and smiles with nothing but love in her eyes. When he dips low and presses a quick kiss to her lips—the easy, familiar kind that makes it obvious they do it all the time—my lungs seize in my chest.

"Sorry I'm late, baby," he says, wearing a warm smile. "I wanted to pick you up myself, but my meeting ran over."

I'm going to throw up.

Brooks, clueless to the living nightmare I've found myself in, squeezes my hand and tugs me forward. "Don't worry, Coach should be chill tonight. He's always in a better mood around my aunt."

"Aunt Zoe, I have someone I want you to meet."

At Brooks's words, his aunt and Seb turn. That's the moment when I think I officially die. Seb's smile falls when his focus lands on me, and he goes rigid when he notices the way Brooks is clutching my hip.

"This is Sara." Brooks gives me a gentle squeeze. "Sara, this is my Aunt Zoe."

The woman's smile is genuine, and her blue eyes light up when she takes us in. "It's so nice to finally meet you, Sara. I've heard only lovely things from Brooks."

That comment knocks me back a step, but I recover quickly and plaster what I hope looks like a smile to my face. Because this woman knows all about me, yet I've never heard a peep about her. "Well, Brooks is the nicest guy I know. I'm not sure he could say a mean thing if he tried, so don't believe everything he's said."

With a light laugh, Zoe pulls Brooks in for a hug. He accepts it with a warmth so genuine it makes my chest ache.

Beside her, Seb is watching me, his blue irises like ice and his jaw hard, like he's pissed at me. The attitude is rich coming from him. He'd begun to show his true colors this morning, and in this moment, I see him for what he really is: A liar and a cheater. The epitome of selfishness and deception.

I look away first. He doesn't get to make me feel bad for being here. He doesn't get to make me feel anything at all.

Asshole.

The need to run overwhelms me. I need to get out of here. Brooks is going to hate me when he finds out what I've done. How could I be this person? How could I have slept with a married man?

Seb made me a home-wrecker. God, I hate him.

"Excuse me," I murmur to Brooks, heart beating wildly against my ribs. "I'm just going to freshen up in the bathroom."

He nods but turns back to his family quickly. Sienna has appeared, and she's launched into a story about her time in Paris.

My ears are doing that buzzing noise that happens when a person's heart is beating so loudly everything sounds like an echo. I practically trip as I stumble out of the room full of people who would hate me if they knew what I've done.

Once I'm safely locked in the bathroom, I dial Lennox. This can't seriously be happening. As I wait for her to pick up the phone, I assess myself in the mirror. Is it possible that I look different now that I know? An hour ago, I looked like the fun-loving best friend, and now, the woman in the mirror looks like nothing more than a liar and a cheat.

He made me a mistress.

My burgundy dress feels cheap against my skin. My mascara is smudged. With a deep breath in, I swipe at the black below my eyes.

Do not let him see you cry.

"Hey, babe." Lennox's upbeat voice echoes off the tile walls in the bathroom, almost like it's taunting me.

"Hey." My voice is the exact opposite, full of nothing but brokenness and defeat.

"What's wrong?"

"He's married," I sob. There's no stopping the tears now. Damn him. "He's fucking married."

"Who's married? Brooks?"

The sarcastic laugh that escapes me is harsh in the small space. "Good-Boy Brooks would never do something like this. Fuck, he's going to hate me, Len. He's going to fucking hate me."

"Take a deep breath and start again," she urges. "Who's married?"

I snatch a paper towel from the dispenser and wet it as I take a deep breath. "Sebastian. He's still married to Brooks's aunt. She's so damn adorable, and he seemed smitten with her. How could he be so sweet and swoony with me for all these months and have a wife he adores at home?"

My heart cracks open at the image that hits me then. Zoe at home while Seb was with me. The idea makes me sick. Hockey season is long. We travel constantly. But even during the offseason, the coaching staff is working, so Sebastian was around all summer. *Where the hell was his wife?*

"Holy shit," Lennox mutters.

"Yeah. What the hell am I going to do?" The tears have stopped, but the pain in my chest hasn't dulled. I'm not even upset about Sebastian. In my mind, we were over when he called me a slut and threatened my job this morning.

Growing up, I was nothing more than an afterthought. My mother tried so hard but my father got a new family and despite my mother's attempts, he often forgot I existed. From the time I was old enough to understand, I promised myself that I'd never allow that to happen again. If I'm not considered a priority, then that person has no place on my roster. It's that simple.

And no one tells me what to do.

It's only been hours since our blowup outside Brooks's apartment, but it's not Seb that I'm upset over. It's Brooks. It's the Langfields. It's my job.

"Oh my God. I'm going to lose my job."

"You are not going to lose your job. If that asshole tries to get you fired, I'll go to law school and sue his ass."

Despite the utter devastation coursing through me, a laugh bubbles out of my chest. My best friend would so do that. "It would take too long," I remind her. "I need this job, or I can't stay in Boston, Len."

Ethan's face appears in my mind, and the devastation turns to anger.

"I've gotta go." I've already been in the bathroom too long. It's time to come up with an excuse and get out of here. I can't possibly sit at a table across from Sebastian and his wife.

Just...no.

"Okay, call me as soon as you get home so we can plot his murder."

Leaning over the vanity, I use the damp paper towel to blot at the skin under my eyes. "You mean my job search."

"No. I said what I said."

I laugh. "I love you."

"Love you too, babe. Remember: you did nothing wrong. You walk out of there with your head held high. We've got this."

I hang up feeling decidedly like I don't have this at all. With no other option but to face the Langfields, I toss the paper towel, determined to get this over with. But when I open the door and find Sebastian standing on the other side, blue eyes cold and angry, I wish I'd just stayed inside.

CHAPTER 8
Brooks

I ADORE MY SISTER, I really do, and because I rarely see her, I tend to hang on her every word. But tonight, I'm not paying attention to a damn thing she's saying. My focus is fixed solely on my best friend, whose got my head all sorts of fucked up. She disappeared in a rush and has been gone for too long, likely because I had to go and make things weird today.

Her comments about my status as Boston's good boy—that because I'm a gentleman, I wouldn't know what to do in the bedroom —hit a nerve.

Even if that insinuation isn't totally off.

But I took it too far. Did I really tell Sara that if she ever heard me come, she'd be the one saying thank you?

My stomach sinks. Because yeah, I did.

What the fuck was I thinking?

The moment I pulled her close to introduce her to my aunt, she went rigid. *I did that.* I made an inappropriate comment, and in turn, I made my best friend uncomfortable with my touch. All because I have a goddamn crush that I can't get over.

I have to fix it. Not that I know how, but I can't handle knowing that my actions have caused her discomfort.

With my sister and aunt distracted by a story Aiden is telling, I head toward the back of the restaurant so I can find Sara and apologize.

When I step into the hallway and find Coach crowding her, his face a mask of anger and his chest puffed up like he's doing his best to intimidate her, another emotion takes over.

Rage bubbles up, instantly threatening to spew out of me.

After our conversation at practice and the subsequent push-ups, I had no doubt that he'd be pissed when I showed up with her tonight. Maybe I should have told him she was coming, but honestly, we're just friends. She can't be my girlfriend, I get that, but I can damn well be her friend.

If he's laying into her now, telling her to stay away from me, I'm going to lose it. He has no business saying anything to her. If he's got an issue, then he and I can deal with it.

I move closer, ready to step between them and take the brunt of his anger.

With the way he's crowding her personal space, neither of them notices my presence.

He's looking down his nose at her, wearing a haughty sneer. As I take another step, I fist my hands at my sides, willing myself to keep my anger at bay. My blood boils.

My uncle's tone is pompous. "So this is about Brooks?"

At the sound of my name, my heart lurches.

Sara scoffs and tips her chin up. Despite his stance, she doesn't cower. "It's certainly not about you. You made it clear this morning that we would always be a dirty little secret. Now I know why. So no, I don't care who you do or don't sleep with."

My heart officially stops when her words register.

Sara said 'we'. They're a 'we'? Sara and my uncle? No way. He wouldn't do that to my aunt. To me. He's Uncle Seb. The best man I know. The man who made me who I am today.

"She's my wife," he grits out.

Sara lets out a sound that might be a growl. "Do you hear yourself? One minute, you're divorced, and in the next, she's your wife." She pulls herself up a little taller. "Which is it, Seb? I'm sure she'd be thrilled to discover that you've been fucking her nephew's best friend for months." Her eyes are wild as she flings out her arms, completely unhinged.

My stomach turns so violently I think I might actually be sick.

My uncle steps in so close he's got her cornered against the wall. I have to take another step toward them to hear his next words.

"Keep your voice down before someone hears you," he hisses. "You have no room to talk. Suddenly, you're dating Brooks and showing up to *my* family party to announce your relationship? All because I wouldn't make our relationship public? You don't have real feelings for him. You're using him."

Those words are like a knife to the gut. For my whole life, I've put this man on a goddamn pedestal.

Be courteous, Brooks. Always smile, Brooks. Family comes first, Brooks. Always be a professional, Brooks. Be like me, Brooks. Not like your father. Don't date someone you work with, Brooks. You can't have it all. Don't date until you retire. Hockey has to come first. You can't give Sara what she needs.

I've taken this man's word as gospel. I've idolized him and worked to be like him every day of my life. And he's been out cheating on his wife, lying to my best friend—*the woman he knows I've been crushing on since the day I met her*—and treating her like a dirty little secret.

And she's been dating him behind my back.

He's the one she's been sneaking around with. The man she wasn't ready to introduce me to.

The lies hurt. The betrayal *hurts*.

But when Sara's voice breaks, that hurts more. "Brooks is the best man I've ever met. I would never—"

Before I know what's happening, my feet are carrying me down the hall. Rage courses through me as I take in every detail of how he's pinned her against the wall. I move so quickly that they still haven't registered my presence when I step up beside them and pull Sara to me.

Startling, she snaps her head toward me. Her blue eyes are watery and full of anguish as they find mine.

My chest aches with the need to take all the pain away. To rid her of the guilt and shame that are so clearly eating at her. I stroke her cheek with my thumb, and despite the devastation wreaking havoc on me, when I speak, my voice comes out surprisingly steady. "Hey, Pumpkin. You okay?"

Sara blinks rapidly, stunned, her lips parted and her expression a mix between confusion and fear.

Come on, crazy girl, I silently plead with her. *Play along.* She's the queen of acting like a lunatic when she's feeling vulnerable. This should be second nature.

"They're bringing out the appetizers, and we both know how you love your apps. Didn't want my girl to miss out on all the good ones." I cup her chin and hold her steady so she only sees me.

Fuck my uncle. Fuck the tears brimming in Sara's eyes. *Fuck him* for what he's done.

Tipping close, I ghost my lips over hers. It's not even a kiss, but fuck, does it feel good. I've been desperate to get my mouth on hers since the moment I first heard her laugh. "Come on. Food's getting cold."

Those beautiful blue eyes glisten, and her lip wobbles. I swear to Christ, if she cries, I'm going to punch him in the face.

I brush my cheek against hers and bring my lips to her ear. "Breathe, Sar." The words are quiet, meant only for her. "I got you."

When I pull back, she's got that bottom lip trapped between her teeth, but she's nodding and slipping her palm against mine.

That's all the confirmation I need. Without bothering to look at my uncle, I tug on her hand, ready to head back to my family.

My uncle clears his throat and calls after us. "There's a no-fraternization policy. She'll be fired when word of this gets around."

I freeze but keep Sara's hand tight in mine. My teeth are

clenched so tight my jaw aches, and the anger coursing through me is molten. But I don't turn around when I respond to him. "It's a good thing my name is on the arena, then." Ready to deliver the final blow, I finally glare at him over my shoulder. "*Not yours.*"

His jaw practically falls to the floor. Never in my life have I spoken back to this man. I've worshipped the ground he walks on since I was five years old. More than anything, I've wanted to make him proud. To do so, I've followed his every directive without argument, including staying away from this woman.

That. Ends. Today.

Tugging her along with me, I head back toward the party. When she squeaks, I squeeze her hand. "*Not a word.* We'll talk later, but until we get home, not another word."

She sucks in an unsteady breath, and I close my eyes, willing myself to calm down.

"Just follow my lead." It's a challenge to keep my tone calm and the volume of my voice low. I leave it at that, because anything else I say right now will come out wrong. The last thing I want to do is make her feel worse, so for now, I trudge back to the table, my new girlfriend by my side, ready to tell the entire world to fuck off.

CHAPTER 9
Sara

BROOKS PULLS out my chair and holds out a hand, motioning for me to sit. Thank God the cocktail hour appears to be over and the guests are settling around the table, because my ability to stand is severely compromised right now.

The saying about going weak in the knees must have been coined by a woman whose best friend went feral for her.

That's what just happened, right? I don't know how else to explain it.

Brooks literally lost it on his uncle. He claimed me. Caressed me. Kissed me in front of the man.

But why? I'm not even sure if he knows the truth of what happened between Seb and me. If he did, he'd be kicking me out, not pulling me close.

It's obvious by his protectiveness that he heard *something*. But what? And how much? And what the hell is his plan?

Brooks settles in the chair next to me and grasps my hand. It takes a second for him to extricate it, since I'm wringing both of them in my lap. But once it's free, he tugs it up and onto the table with a loud *thwap*, drawing the attention of the guests near us.

Across from me, Liv licks her lips and eyes me. She's obviously fighting a smile, but her dark eyes are wide and filled with joy. I'm not sure what the hell I'm even supposed to do with my face. Five minutes ago, I was crying in the bathroom. Now my best friend is claiming me.

His words from earlier hit me. That comment about me being the one to say thank you if I just so happened to witness him come. In this moment, I believe it, because he is something else.

Who is this man and what happened to Saint Brooks?

My tongue feels too big for my mouth, and it's like I've forgotten how to use my body parts. I can blink, but that's about the extent of control I have over myself. My nose is itchy, but I don't dare scratch it with the hand Brooks has practically glued to his own.

When the server comes around to fill our water glasses, Liv smirks. "Hey, Brooks. You think you can let go of your girl's hand long enough so that she can fill her water?"

Brooks drops his chin and assesses our hands, like he's surprised to see that he's still holding me so tight.

With a sigh, he peels his fingers from mine. "Sorry. Here." He picks up my glass and hands it to the server.

I take the opportunity to scratch my nose in case Brooks grabs for me again.

Seb saunters into the room, head held high, buttoning his jacket. He only hesitates when he takes in the open spots at the table. One next to his wife, and the other closer to our end of the table.

For a second, I think he's going to sit near us, and my stomach bottoms out. Blindly, I grasp at Brooks's hand and then lean into his arm.

"You okay?" His tone is soft, the anger that laced every word only moments ago all but gone.

"Yes, thank you."

He shifts in his chair and takes me in, his green eyes studying me like he's seeing me for the first time, as if he's cataloging every inch of my face. Then he cups my cheek and strokes my face reverently with his thumb. "Thank you."

My breath hitches, and tears burn at the backs of my eyes at his gentleness. "For what?"

Angling closer, he dips his chin and holds my gaze. "For being here. For staying."

"You're my best friend. You told me to follow your lead." I swallow past the lump in my throat. "I trust you."

Something about those words must settle him, because his forehead hits mine, and he closes his eyes as he takes a deep breath.

Across from us, Gavin chuckles. "Well, that's one way to announce a relationship."

Brooks huffs a breath of a laugh and opens his eyes. This time when he focuses on me, there's a spark there, something akin to joy. A knowing glint in his emerald irises. Like he's looking forward to whatever he's going to do next.

It's impossible to look away from him, even as he does just that. He turns, though his forehead still slightly kisses mine, and clears his throat.

"Figured that since everyone would be here tonight, this would be the perfect opportunity. Ya mind if we steal a little of your thunder, Dad?"

Oh my God. What is he doing?

I don't have a clue what's going on, but my heart trips over itself, and a smile consumes me, unbidden. Because this version of Brooks is fun. He's always calculated, always thinking five steps ahead. Always in control. But for the first time, he seems like he's enjoying his calculations.

Preston shakes his head, but he's wearing a knowing smirk. "It's about damn time."

Beside him, Monroe sits straighter and beams. "Couldn't be happier for you both."

Confusion washes over me at their reactions.

What the hell?

Beckett grins and loops an arm around Liv. "I'm going to take credit for this one."

"You take credit for the relationships of every person you know." Gavin groans. "Please explain to me how you could possibly have led these two together."

Beckett sits up taller and drops his forearms to the table, settling in. Oh, here we go.

"You tried to force me to admit my marriage to Liv was fake by asking her to travel with the hockey team. You remember that, right?" He glares at his brother. "And I put my foot down, because I'm amazing. I told Liv she was staying home, and that decree led to Sara taking over the hockey team."

Beside him, Liv rolls her eyes and chugs her water, probably pretending it's a big glass of wine.

"She's worked with us long enough to know that we Langfield men are the best of the best, so naturally, she already knew she needed to get one of her own. Since Brooks is only slightly less good-looking than me, it makes sense that she'd fall madly in love with him once they started working so closely together."

Beaming, Beckett scans the group. The rest of the guests are wearing expressions that range from amused, with smirks and twinkling eyes, to annoyed, with pinched brows and frowns.

Finn is the one to break the silence. "You're silly, Bossman." He holds out a fist, and Beckett taps his against it, taking it as his tacit agreement, it seems.

Then Beckett is back to assessing us all, waiting for confirmation of his theory with his brows raised.

Aiden's the next to speak. He pushes back in his chair and huffs. "No way is Brooks the second best-looking Langfield. That distinction goes to me."

I surprise even myself when I laugh. These freaking Langfield men. Aiden isn't even arguing for the title of best-looking Langfield brother. He just allows Beckett to maintain that status.

Honestly, all four brothers are drool-worthy in their own ways. I just happen to be partial to the man beside me. Always have been.

There's just something about those goalie thighs. Not to mention the messy bun and friendly smile.

"Actually, it was Uncle Seb who brought us together," Brooks says, squeezing my hand like he's silently urging me not to panic.

Sebastian straightens in his chair, smoothing his tie, and his wife, completely oblivious that a cheating scoundrel sits beside her, perks up. "Aw, hunny. Have you been keeping secrets?"

A sarcastic laugh puffs from my lips. Eyes wide, I slap a hand to my mouth quickly and cover it with a cough.

Without missing a beat, Brooks picks up the water in front of him and hands it to me. He waits until I've taken a slow sip, then lets out a steady breath. "'Fraid so, Aunt Zo."

"Well, don't keep us waiting," Sienna begs, picking up her wineglass and holding it out toward her brother.

Beside her, the grumpy man leans back in his chair and scrutinizes us. The clarity in his expression makes me wonder if he can see through this whole façade. If so, he seems like the only one. The rest of the people here, minus Seb, are wearing smiles and watching us eagerly.

"Recently, Uncle Seb reminded me that the people in our lives are what's most important. Not our careers or accolades, but the relationships we have. He really got me thinking, and that's when I realized that I didn't need to wait to have everything." He squeezes my hand and focuses on me, and I swear to God, I feel the words as he says them. "Because she's right here." With a sweet smile, he brings my knuckles to his lips and plants a soft kiss there, never looking away.

My heart flip-flops in my chest, and I think I swallow my tongue.

"Aw, Seb. That's beautiful," the cheater's wife says. Or at least I think that's what she says. My hearing may be out of whack since my heart is beating so loudly the energy coursing through me could power a Lake Paige concert right now.

Brooks doesn't say things he doesn't mean. Until this moment, I truly didn't believe he possessed the ability to lie.

I was so, so wrong. This man must be an expert-level liar, because he even has *me* believing that he thinks I'm his everything.

"Too bad we're going to have to move Sara to another department," Seb says, stealing the air from my lungs.

As if he actually gives two fucks. He's not nearly as good at lying as his nephew is. How am I just now noticing this?

Gavin frowns, swirling his glass of whiskey. "Why would we have to do that?"

Brooks sits up straighter. As he does, he grips the seat of my chair and pulls me closer. "Yeah, what's the issue, Uncle Seb? Last time we chatted, you didn't have a problem with Sara being involved with someone on the team."

My stomach sinks. *Apparently he heard everything.*

I swear I'm on a goddamn roller coaster. My heart has gone from light to aching to shattered tonight.

Brooks knows about Seb and me, yet he looked me in the eye and told me it was all okay. See? The man is possibly the most talented liar I've ever met, because there's no possible way he's okay with what I did.

"She can't handle PR for you if you're dating, now, can she? Not when she's part of the story." Seb has his elbows planted on the table and his fingers steepled. His full attention is fixed on Brooks, like I'm not even here.

Liv laughs. "I suppose I should resign, then, since my biggest pain in the ass—er, client"—she waggles her brows at Beckett—"happens to be my husband."

Beckett doesn't even growl. The man just grins at her. It's so weird seeing him so relaxed and okay with Liv's teasing. Even after his overconcern about his wife being hugged too tightly, I think the pregnancy has made him even more relaxed.

He throws his arm around Liv and tugs her close. "She's right. And if anything directly involving Sara pops up, Liv can handle it, just like Sara does for us when it involves Liv."

Liv winks at me. "I've got your back."

I lick my lips and force a smile. She wouldn't if she knew about the real scandal.

All these people who are jumping to defend my job would be chasing me out of the city of Boston if they knew what I was to Sebastian.

I hate what he made me.

As if Brooks can feel my self-loathing, he squeezes my hand and presses his lips to my forehead. Then he turns back to his uncle. "We're a team, and teams stick together. Right, Seb?"

I don't hear Seb's response, because Brooks has lowered his forehead again. He's watching me intently, those green eyes full of all sorts of secrets.

I want to unravel every one. I want to know what he's truly thinking. But part of me is scared to death that I won't be able to handle the truth when it all finally comes out.

CHAPTER 10
Brooks

Gavin: Sara okay? She seemed off tonight.

Aiden: Sara's perfect. She's dating a Langfield. There's nothing better.

Beckett: For once I agree with Aiden. But also, what Gavin said. It was hard for Liv when the media circus hit. Even though they're trained for this, it's a lot. Tell her Liv is here to talk if she needs anything.

I CAN'T HELP but gape at my text messages, my heart in my throat. My brothers are being...weird. Not Aiden. He's being Aiden. Thank fuck. But the other two are way too fucking perceptive for my liking right now.

I pocket my phone because I have no idea how to respond. My mind is spiraling, and for now, I need to focus on channeling a calm I don't feel. In about five minutes, Sara and I are going to have a very real conversation, and the last thing I want to do is lose it on her.

After dinner, when we got in the car and were finally alone, she wrung her hands in her lap and shifted so she was facing me. It was obvious she was collecting her thoughts, but I held up my hand, silently begging her to wait. I needed the fifteen-minute drive to decompress.

My time is up, though.

Outside her apartment door, she turns to me, though she keeps her attention fixed on the floor between us. "Do you want to come in?"

I got so used to touching her in the restaurant that it's killing me not to now. It was all for show, and it was only a few hours, but now my fingers itch to pull her hair out of that ponytail. I ache to press her against the door, cup the side of her neck, and hold her in place while I kiss the stress right out of her.

She was sleeping with your goddamn uncle.

That thought is the bucket of ice water I so badly need to get my head on straight.

"Yeah." I clear my throat. "We need to talk."

She nods, and with the key in the lock, she lets us both in.

Walking into her space for the first time since the bomb dropped feels different. I peer into every corner, survey every inch of this place, with a new awareness. Are there pieces of him here? Did he sit in my spot on the couch? Did he kiss her up against the door the way I've fantasized of doing? Was he here living every moment I've ached to share with her while I sat alone in my apartment only a few floors below, completely oblivious to it all?

"He's never been here." She slips off her shoes and shuffles to the kitchen.

Damn, she's so fucking perceptive. At least when she wants to be.

When she returns, she's taken her hair down, and she's carrying a bottle of peanut butter whiskey and two glasses. Holding them aloft, she smiles. It's not her real smile. She's nervous. And feeling guilty. I hate that, but I can't erase her guilt. Can't ease it either. There are still too many things to talk about before I know how to proceed with her.

She pads back in my direction. "Figure we might need this."

A little lightness seeps into me then, because even when she does shots, they're so her. Full of sugar and sweetness. This is Sara. She doesn't have a devious bone in her body. She didn't seduce my uncle knowing he was married. There's no question about that. If there was even a hint of doubt in my mind, I wouldn't be sitting here.

She sets the glasses on the coffee table and unscrews the cap from the bottle. Scooting to the edge of the couch, she pours the whiskey, but her hands shake so badly, the bourbon sloshes over onto the table.

I put my hand over hers, steadying it. "Let me."

With a long sigh, she hands me the bottle, then slumps back against the couch. Her messy blond curls fall like a curtain around her face, hiding her eyes. The burgundy silk of her dress folds against her chest as she slides her legs beneath her and turns in my direction.

I hold out her shot, and when she takes it, the feel of her warm fingers against mine has me pulling away and throwing back my own shot quickly.

"How long?" The question escapes me as I'm refilling my glass.

"We're diving right in, I see." She's zeroed in on her full shot glass, lips and hands trembling.

"Need to rip the Band-Aid off, Sar. Let's get it all out now, and then we don't have to talk about it again."

Her eyes meet mine. "During the playoffs," she breathes. "But I didn't know he was married, Brooks. I swear to God, he told me he was divorced."

With an elbow on one knee, I turn toward the dark window and take a deep breath. That motherfucker. "He married my aunt when I was five. I always thought I was so lucky to witness a love like theirs. To be his nephew." The words are bitter and sharp as I release them, like shards of glass tearing at my lungs.

Beside me, Sara sniffles, garnering my attention. Her eyes are welling with tears again, and as they crest over her lashes, she swipes them away quickly.

I sit up straight and bat at her hand gently, using a thumb to wipe at the fat tear forming on her lash line before it can hit her skin again. Tender. Soft. "I'm sorry he lied to you."

She shakes her head, and a sob breaks free of her chest. "Why are you apologizing? If I'd just talked to you, if I hadn't listened to him and agreed to sneak around, I would have known the truth a long time ago."

"Love makes people do stupid things," I whisper.

Her lips twist at that word—*love*—but she doesn't deny it, and another piece of my heart splinters.

I remove my hand from her face and run it through my hair, pushing away the pain so we can get through this.

"Why did you act like you were my boyfriend tonight? Why did you come to my rescue after you found out about what I've done? You must hate me." Sara licks her lips and finally takes her shot, though she keeps those teary blue eyes trained on me as she does.

My elbows fall to my knees as I consider her question. Really think about it and try to recall what I was thinking. But the truth is, I wasn't.

"I know you, Sara. You would never knowingly have an affair with a married man. But the truth is, I didn't think before I acted. When I saw my uncle in your face, when I heard the way he was speaking to you, I reacted." I take in a deep breath and tug my hair out of its tie. "Since I was a kid, my uncle has preached about what I need to do in order to be successful. I've always listened and worked hard to obey his every instruction. He was my idol. My entire life, I've done everything he's told me to do." Anger surges up inside me at the memory of his disapproving look at practice this morning. "He told me to stay away from you—that I should avoid relationships—but he never had my best interest in mind. He convinced me to stay away because he wanted you for himself. He took the fears I've held on to since childhood—the hurt that came every time my parents put work above me and my siblings—and he used them to keep me from being honest with you."

She nods as a tear slides down her face. I don't brush this one, though. I don't trust myself to touch her when we're both this raw.

"And what would you have told me if you were being honest?"

I close my eyes to steady myself. The alcohol is making me woozy. Now is not the time to admit to feelings I'm not sure still exist. When I open them again, I force myself to look at her. "Nothing."

She winces, though she tries to cover it with a heavy breath. "So what happens tomorrow?"

I'm still lost in the flash of hurt that hit her at my words. "Hmm?"

"Will you tell your brothers it's over? That you suffered from temporary insanity?" Her red-rimmed eyes go steely, wary. "I should probably start looking for another job." She wrings her hands and slips her legs free.

Chest still aching, I frown. "What? Why? You did nothing wrong."

She stands and paces to the kitchen, then turns back. "I can't work with your uncle every day. Especially once he realizes you were just showboating. The two of you will get past this. He's *your family*. I'm just—" Her voice cracks, and she swallows thickly. "I'm just the mistress."

My world tilts at the way her voice breaks, and I'm moving again without thinking, pulling her into my chest and raking my fingers through her unruly hair. I grip it firmly and tilt her head so she's forced to look at me. "You are not *just* anything. You're not a goddamn mistress, or a dirty secret. You deserve to be paraded around. Celebrated. And that's what we're going to do."

Breathless, she stares up at me. "What?"

"Let's do this, Sar. Be my girlfriend. Let me show my uncle how you should be treated. Let me show everyone, including you, how you deserve to be treated."

She lets out a bewildered laugh. "Brooks, I literally ended things with your uncle *today*. I'm not ready for another relationship."

I throw up my shields before her words can touch my heart and scramble for a way to convince her to try this with me. "It wouldn't be real. Just—let's get a little revenge. Show him what it feels like." I bend my knees so we're eye to eye and capture her attention. "Would it be so awful to have to pretend to be mine?"

Sara's eyes soften, and her palm finds my cheek. I hate how I want to lean into it. "No, it wouldn't. Not at all, Brooks. But I don't deserve it."

There goes my heart again, aching for her. How can she believe that about herself? "Maybe you don't think you do," I argue, "but don't I deserve it? Please, I need this. I need..." I blow out a breath and press my forehead to hers like I did at the restaurant. "He needs to pay. I can't tell my aunt what he did. The last thing I want to do is hurt her. But...he can't just get away with this." My words sound as desperate as I feel, but I'm not above begging when it comes to Sara. "Do it for me, Pumpkin."

A puff of a laugh escapes her. "That nickname, Brooks."

My heart lifts just a little, enough that I find myself grinning. "Like it? Honestly, it just slipped out. I can try other names. Sugar? Sweetie pie?"

She smiles up at me, the first one I've seen from her since Seb stepped into the restaurant earlier, and she loops her arms around my waist, melting against my chest. "You really want me to be your fake girlfriend?"

No, I want her to be my real everything, but I can't exactly say that. "Yes."

She pulls back and studies me, her brows pulled low. "How would it work exactly? I work for the team. Won't that cause complications?"

"Like my brothers said, it's fine." I brush a strand of hair from her forehead. "If it involves us, Liv will handle it. But you know me. You haven't had to handle a single scandal for me yet."

"That's because you're Good-Boy Brooks. What you're talking about doing now is very un-good-boy behavior."

With a low growl, I haul her to me again. "Good. Then maybe you'll stop with that fucking nickname."

She laughs and pinches my side. "Aw, you want a new nickname, Brookie?"

In retaliation, I tickle her stomach.

She loses it, practically going limp and tumbling toward the ground, but I catch her.

"Keep it up, and I'll show you how very bad I can be." Holding her tight, I go for her stomach again.

Sara sucks in a breath and grasps my hand before I can tickle her. She looks up at me and bats her lashes in a way that practically makes me melt. Then she pops up on her toes and whispers, "First you'll have to catch me." Then she pushes off me and rushes to the other side of the room.

A warmth spreads through me as she bounces around on her toes, watching me like she's trying to predict which way I'll go, her blond curls dancing with every move. The cranberry silk of her dress strains against her curves in the most perfect way as she shifts from foot to foot. God, she's gorgeous. And she's finally fucking smiling. Really smiling.

"You really want to play?" I taunt, taking one step closer.

She stands still and taps her finger against her chin. "Hmm, yup!" Then she scurries around the couch, headed toward her bedroom, but I've got longer legs and a determination to win.

Once I've got both hands on her waist, I lift her off the ground and pull her to me. The way her legs continue to move even as her ass is glued to my hips pulls a bark of laughter from me.

"Nice try, Pumpkin. Now give me a new nickname, or we'll be doing this all night."

With a groan, she drops her head back against my chest. "You gotta give me more time to think."

Her proximity, the feel of her in my arms, her body pressed against mine, momentarily steals all my sanity, and I find myself dipping in close and sliding my nose up the curve of her neck, inhaling her sugary-sweet scent.

The softest sound escapes her throat, barely a moan. It's not a sound I'm familiar with, and I'm dying to hear it again. So I do it a second time, then nip at the bare skin of her shoulder.

"You have until tomorrow." I release her and take two big steps back. If I don't get out of her apartment, I'll do something I can't come back from. Like pin her against the wall and taste other parts of her.

Sara spins, her jaw unhinged. "You're leaving?"

I swallow past the lump in my throat and give her one subtle nod.

"Okay," she says, drawing out the word. "So we're dating?" Her voice is low, unsure.

"Yup."

She tilts her head and pulls that bottom lip between her teeth. "For how long?"

I keep walking backward until I hit the door. "Till my uncle quits."

"What?" She presses a palm to her chest. "He's never going to quit."

"He will if we play this right. I saw how he looked at you." I take a deep breath and ignore the ache in my chest. "You weren't just a fling for him."

I hate to admit it, but there's no way he didn't have real feelings for her. How could he not care about her? She's perfect. And as much as it hurts, I have to believe he did. Because if he cheated on my aunt with a woman he didn't really care about, just because he could, well, there's no way I can reconcile that with the person I thought he was. But if he did it because he fell for Sara? I still can't condone it or even forgive him, but I can understand it.

At least a little.

"What about you?" she asks, crossing her arms over her chest and lifting her chin, suddenly bolder than she's been all evening.

I lean against the door and grasp the knob. "What about me?"

"The girl you told me about. Won't this be a problem for her?"

This fucking girl. God. "I don't date during hockey, Sar."

She nods. "Right. But you said—"

"You're my only girl." I pull up to my full height and shut her down. "Stop worrying. The only thing you should be concerned about tonight is what you'll be calling me when you fake scream my name."

She throws her head back and laughs. "God, with a mouth like that, I should start calling you dirty boy."

I wink and pull the door open. "Now we're talking. Night, Pumpkin."

"Night, Brooks."

CHAPTER 11

Sara

GAME DAYS ARE my absolute favorite. The boys swagger everywhere they go, cocky as shit. The energy levels in our apartment building and at the arena are high. Even the office is abuzz with an excitement that pushes the day along.

On game days, I don't have to be in the office until later in the day, since I cover the press and deal with the players long after they exit the ice for the night. The days are long, but every moment is charged with excitement.

It makes it impossible not to love my job.

A job that has given me so much more than money to help my family. It gives me a purpose. Not to mention, I'm damn good at it.

And I really freaking don't want to lose it.

Liv steps into my office, phone in hand, not quite paying attention to me as she taps out a message on the screen. She's dressed in all black, as usual, and her dark hair is pulled into her signature bun. "What time you heading to the arena?"

"I'll probably head that way in half an hour. Need me to handle something here first?"

Liv looks up from her phone and smiles. "No. I'm going to the game too."

"You are?"

Liv never comes to the hockey games. She's normally at home with the kids in the evenings, per Beckett's orders. Though the orders are really suggestions, and only because he's so obsessed with making her happy. For years, he expected her to travel with him and the Revs for every road stretch. It wasn't until they were "fake married" that he realized how much she was missing out on with the kids. Once he was hit with that reality, he encouraged her to promote me. Now I handle the hockey team travel, and my counterpart, Hannah, handles the baseball travel.

"Yup. My kids are sleeping at Dylan's, so Beckett and I are having a date night at the game." She steps farther into my office and lowers her voice. "Rumor has it that Ford and Lake are going to be there to watch Daniel play."

Oh my God. I'm not trying to faint, but Lake is literally my idol. I know we've already been over this, but seriously, I love her.

"You do realize I hate you right now," I whine.

Liv laughs. "Why don't you hang in the owner's box with us tonight? You don't actually have to sit with the boys during the game. There's no way the press is coming near them while they're playing."

She's right, and I can't even believe I'm saying this, but... I shrug. "I want to be there for Brooks."

Liv's smile is so bright it hurts to look at. "I need the full story one of these days. I always knew he had a crush on you, but you seemed kind of oblivious to it. What changed?"

Her words have me holding my breath. *Brooks had a crush on me?* That's news. Brooks and I are close, but outside of the last twenty-four hours, he's never so much as flirted with me.

"Honestly," I say, going for nonchalant, "he went all caveman on me and declared me his. I didn't have much say in the matter."

Sticking as close to reality as I can feels like the safest bet, and even though we're pretending, those words are more like the truth than anything else I could admit. Over the last two days, I've discovered a whole other side of Brooks, and I don't hate it one bit.

Liv brings a hand to her heart. "Those Langfield men. Am I right?"

"Yes," I huff a laugh and check the time on my computer screen. "You are most definitely right." Standing, I run a hand down the front of my shirt to smooth it out. "On that note, I'm going to freshen up before heading to the arena." I hold up my phone. "Text me when you're with Lake."

"You got it, babe." She heads for the open door but turns back at the threshold. "And Sara?"

I pull open the top drawer of my desk, ready to grab my toiletry case, and look up at her. "Yeah?"

"Enjoy yourself tonight."

In the bathroom, I run into Hannah, who I thought had already headed home for the day. When the baseball team isn't playing and she isn't traveling, her workdays are shorter, just like mine are when the Bolts aren't playing. If the Revs were playing tonight, there's no way Beckett would be going to the hockey game. Also, the offices, which are located directly between the stadium and arena, are always buzzing on game days. Our side of the office, the hockey division, has been a madhouse all day, but the baseball group is basically MIA.

When Hannah whips a jersey out of her oversized purse, her presence makes more sense.

"Ah," I say. "I see you heard Lake was going to the game."

She grins and tugs the jersey over her head. "Is it that obvious?"

I set my makeup case on the counter beside her. "And you're wearing Daniel Hall's number."

A pink flush creeps up her neck and into her cheeks, and she ducks her head, fiddling with the hem of her jersey.

"Hannah!"

She looks away from me. "Shh. He's a good player, that's all. And it'd be weird to wear one of the Langfield jerseys. Like, how do you pick one? They own the team."

I shrug. I hadn't considered wearing a jersey, but suddenly the idea of showing up wearing Brooks's number sounds like a fantastic idea. It's what a real girlfriend would do. And as a bonus? It would really piss off Seb.

"Can I sit with you?" she asks, interrupting my train of thought.

I drop my lipstick into my makeup case and prop one hip up against the counter, facing her. "You realize Lake will be in the owner's box, right? I'm sitting with the team."

Hannah nods, her lips pressed together. The hope in her eyes is impossible to miss.

Oh shit. The girl has a crush on the new star. She may only be twenty-six, but he's twenty-three. The Bolts recruited him while he was still in college. He helped us win the Cup last year while getting his degree online.

"All right. Let's head to the game." I zip up my bag and tuck it under one arm, then turn for the door. "Oh." I whip around so fast the ends of my ponytail whack me in the face. "Since you'll probably hear all about it when we get there, I might as well tell you now. I'm dating Brooks."

With that, I rush out of the bathroom, leaving her shrieking in excitement after me.

Not gonna lie, this is kind of fun.

It's not hard to come by a Langfield jersey. Especially number 13. Brooks, unsurprisingly, is a fan favorite.

Normally I wear a suit to the games. I keep it professional like the team does before and after every game. Tonight, I'm in jeans. The casual clothing will totally piss Seb off, but it won't make him nearly as angry as the number emblazoned on my back.

I almost said no when Brooks suggested the revenge dating scenario. A ploy like this is typically beneath him. The man is so buttoned up and proper and, well, good. The revenge plan is something Lennox and I would have cooked up in college, but these days, I've risen above that kind of pettiness. Or so I thought.

When I waltz down the hallway outside the locker rooms, decked out in a blue jersey over a long-sleeve white shirt, I can't contain the huge smile that consumes my face knowing how pissed Seb will be.

"Case! What are you doing wearing Langfield's jersey? You know you'd look so much better with Warren on your back."

I spin around, ready to hit the right winger with a witty come-back, and almost stumble over my own feet. Just outside the door leading to the locker rooms are War, Aiden, and Brooks. It's the way Brooks is standing, I think, that short circuited my brain—feet planted wide, hands in the pockets of his dress pants. Or maybe it's how his suit strains against his shoulders as he studies me. Lips parted—like he too has lost his words—green eyes darker than I've ever seen them and laser focused on my tits.

Stupefied, I drop my chin and follow his gaze. *Oh.* It's on the jersey. Definitely the jersey. Why would he be looking at my tits?

"Turn around." The command he grits out sounds like sex talk-ing. Like literal sex just dripped down my leg and spoke those words.

With a thick swallow, I scan the hall to make sure he's talking to me, unable to believe my sweet Brookie would use that tone with me.

Aiden's lips twitch, and War's gaze bounces from me to Brooks and back again.

Brooks? He's frozen in place, like I've ensnared him in a trap I didn't know I'd set and he's tracking my every movement. My every breath.

He moves closer, and the wide hallway narrows. With every step he takes, the space continues to shrink and my body heats another degree.

"I said turn around, Pumpkin." There it is again, that tone full of nothing but sex.

Holy fuck. My best friend has a sex operator voice.

Would he be up for recording himself for me? Ugh. I'll have to ask later, because he's so close I can see the way his chest is heaving with every breath.

"It's like you want to be punished." His voice is softer now, but not any less alluring.

With one hand, he grasps my wrist and tugs me closer. Then he steps around me, his dress shoes clicking on the concrete floor. His grip is tight but not painful as he circles me, still holding me in place. Then his free hand is between my shoulder blades, his heat soaking through the jersey into my skin. He slides it down my back slowly, warming me as he goes, until he grips my hip.

"Fuck, you look good with my name on your back," he rasps against the sensitive skin of my neck, sending goose bumps skittering down my spine.

The gentle kiss that follows is so surprising I suck in a breath.

Is it possible the oxygen is restricted down here below the arena? I'm suddenly dizzy. Overheated.

I pinch the fabric of my jersey and pull at it, desperate for air. "God, did they turn up the heat in here?"

Aiden covers his mouth to muffle a laugh.

War is watching us with wide eyes, like we're a damn circus act. "It's freezing down here. It's always freezing down here." He shakes his head. "What the fuck is going on with you two?"

Brooks tightens his hold on my hip and pulls until my back is flush with his chest. "She'll only be wearing Langfield on her back from now on."

Holy shit. Who is this man? I twist at the waist, since he's yet to release his hold on me, and come face to face with the cockiest fucking smirk I've ever seen. "Enjoying yourself?"

"Immensely," he mutters.

I cough out a laugh. "Good. Didn't know I'd make you so happy. Figured it'd piss Seb off."

Brooks exhales a loud breath, and his shoulders drop. "Right. Yeah." He finally releases me, and when he steps away, I'm hit with a shot of cool air.

"I gotta go get changed. See you out there." Then he's wandering off, past his brother, his demeanor a little less cocky than before.

Aiden watches him go too, then focuses on me. He's wearing a frown that doesn't at all fit his happy-go-lucky attitude. My stomach sinks when he gives his head an almost imperceptible shake.

Shit. What did I say?

"Show's over. Get changed!"

I practically jump out of my skin at the sound of Seb's sharp bark, but I steady myself quickly.

"Ms. Case, I don't think we have any PR concerns right now. We'll see you after the game."

With the biggest smile I can muster plastered to my face, I spin on my heel. "Just saying hello to my boyfriend and wishing the guys good luck."

Sebastian is wearing a game-day suit, black with a royal blue tie, like always. His dark hair is tousled like he spent the last hour pulling on it. Or maybe his wife did. "Girlfriends aren't allowed in the locker room, Ms. Case."

With a wink, I saunter past him and point to the name on my back as I go. "This one is."

CHAPTER 12

Brooks

I TAKE my time gliding out onto the ice for warm-ups. War is already glaring at New York's lineup, likely scrolling through his mental list of their weaknesses. He loves to taunt. Loves to throw people off their game. More than anything, he loves to fight.

I don't get to fight anyone. Not that I've ever felt the rush to punch an opponent in the face. I play for the thrill of the game, the rush of a save, the sound of a rowdy crowd when I stop a puck. I like bringing pleasure to those around me.

Today, all the excitement that comes with the game is missing. And I'd really like to fight someone.

"Brooks, drop and give us a hundred!" Coach bellows without even looking up from his iPad as he sits on his end of the bench.

"What the hell has gotten into him?" War groans, tossing his head back. "He's been riding your ass all week."

Aiden shakes his head and does a fucking spin in front of me. "He's taking this Sara thing to the extreme." His voice is quiet enough that I'm the only one who hears him.

I drop my stick to the ice and go down with it, then grunt out a loud *one*. I keep up the loud counting as I go, and when the crowd behind the net counts along with me, I know this will be all over social media tomorrow. Asshole wants to make me a monkey, then I'll play along for now.

I finish off my set, and when I hop to my feet, the crowd cheers. Half a dozen women in the section ask if I'm single or beg for my number. Even more turn around and show off the number 13 on their backs.

With a polite nod to the stands, I turn to the bench and zero in on the only girl who's ever made my pulse race at the sight of her wearing my jersey.

Sara with my number on her back and my name across her shoulders is quite literally the hottest thing I've ever seen.

Would have been hotter if she'd actually worn it for me.

She smiles and waves at me. Behind her, Coach is glowering, so I tap my fingers against my heart and point at her. That goddamn smile, the most beautiful sight in the world, grows wider, and her cheeks go rosy pink.

Parker skates up and stops short, spraying me with a bit of ice. "I know that look."

I shake my head but don't take my attention off Sara. This guy has no room to talk. He fell in love with my sister-in-law's roommate last year. On the nights she came to watch him play, he could barely walk straight, let alone stay up on his damn skates.

"Just focus on New York and keep them out of my goal."

With a grin, he skates off to get into position.

Tonight's game is a big one. Boston and New York will never not be rivals in any sport, but the personal connection here adds even more pressure. Seb's brother's kid plays for New York, and much like I'm known as the saint, Vin is known as the asshole. He's intentionally gone after Aiden on the ice multiple times. Only reason he hasn't come for me is because I never get in fights.

Nothing he can say will draw me out of my net. He knows it too, so for the most part, he leaves his jabs for after the game. As if dealing with his dirty plays on the ice isn't enough, Coach forces us all to meet up for a late dinner or a drink when the game's over. For years

I've done my best to be kind, to bite my tongue when he mutters insults out of Seb's earshot. He wouldn't dare be a blatant asshole in front of our uncle. He wouldn't want him to know what a huge disappointment he is. But if Seb steps away to use the bathroom or to order another round, it's guaranteed his true colors shine.

He's a winger, an instigator like War, but not nearly as good on the ice, and he's far more volatile.

The moment the puck drops, I clutch my stick and zero in on the game. War gets control almost immediately and rushes forward, darting past New York's center and right winger. Vin is right on his heels, slicing with his stick at the back of War's skates.

"Where's the fucking penalty?" I groan as he knicks him.

War shoots him a warning look, his gaze sharp, but Vin has never been good at heeding sense. He slices at War again, and this time he makes contact with the back of his skate, and War goes down.

The penalty is called, but it's too late. War is already up, tossing his stick and gloves, fists up and ready for the fight. Thirty seconds in, and Vin's already up to his dirty tricks. This is gonna be a long night.

The period ends zero-zero and our guys are dragging. I skate off the ice and when I get to the tunnel, tugging at my helmet, Sara is already holding a bottle of water out to me.

"Thanks." With a long breath out, I tip my head back, then I pour the water down my throat. Next, she comes at me with a towel, like she's going to swipe at the sweat on my face and neck. It may be cold in the arena, but between the compression shorts and shirt, my gear, and all the hustling I do, I burn up during the games. Before she can get close, I duck out of the way and reach for the towel. I have no doubt that I stink already, and I don't need her anywhere near me in this state.

She dodges me and pulls the towel into her chest. "All the guys smell horrific, but not you. You always smell clean. How is that possible?"

I frown at her, but when she pushes closer, I don't shy away this time. With a sweet smile, she wipes at my face. It's weird being cared for, being touched so openly, but I don't exactly hate it. In fact, I might like it too much.

When she's finished, she pulls back, assesses me, then angles in again and presses her lips to my cheek. "There, now you're perfect."

This time when she backs up, I hover where I am and stare at her like an idiot. She only smiles back, looking all sorts of pretty, with a big smile on those pink lips. Each time she inhales, my jersey tightens slightly over her breasts, killing a few more of my brain cells.

The guys are all shuffling past us, heading toward the locker room. Despite the way it felt as if time has been standing still, it's been mere seconds, and I'm already wishing I could stay with her rather than head to the locker room with everyone else.

"There's a reason puck bunnies aren't allowed back here, Ms. Case," Coach says.

Those words—*puck bunnies*—shake me from my impure thoughts and instantly send me into a rage. Hands gripping my stick in front of me, I glare at him. "What did you just say?"

His smug smile doesn't falter. He can't even imagine a world where I'd stand up to him. "You heard me. If she's going to act like your girlfriend, then she should be sitting with the WAGs." He points back toward the arena.

With smoke billowing out of my ears, I stalk toward him, all sense gone.

Most of the guys have disappeared to the locker room, but the ones who are still here go silent, though the arena is still buzzing.

"The only reason you're not on the ground right now begging me for mercy is because I care about Aunt Zoe," I grit out. "But this is your one and only warning. Keep my girlfriend's name out of your mouth, or you'll be missing teeth the next time you open it."

I shove past him, knocking him into the cement wall with my shoulder. Whatever he hoped to accomplish with that little comment has surely backfired, because now the whole team knows we have a problem. And when it comes down to it, my fucking last name will always be synonymous with this team, whereas his could easily be erased.

The assistant coaches, including Fitz, the goaltending coach, are all gaping. But not one of them says a thing.

I stalk past War and head to the locker room, knowing I need to get my temper under control. Adrenaline may have me ready to fight, but I need to save it for the ice.

War rushes to catch up to me and grabs my shoulder. "You and I are going out after the game, and you're gonna tell me what the fuck is going on with you and Coach."

I suck in a deep breath and shake my head. "Forget it."

"The whole team is watching. McGreevey may be the captain, but that's only because you can't be. We all know you're our leader. And if there's trouble between you and coach, you need to fucking figure it out. The guys are only going to follow one of you."

"They should follow him," I grunt. "He's the coach." I glance back in the direction of the rink, where Seb is having a heated discussion with Fitz. People are already starting to talk. To worry. The plan is working. "For now, at least," I mutter under my breath.

We win the game two-one, and War practically drags me out of the locker room with threats that he'll talk to Gavin if I don't tell him what the hell is going on. Fortunately, when we step out into the hallway, Sara is waiting, ready to lead me to the press. I've never been so excited to answer rapid-fire questions in my life.

I grin at War and slap his shoulder. "We'll catch up later." With that, I'm striding toward Sara.

"Sar," he hollers. "Drag him out when he's done."

With a laugh at my best friend, I drop my head, but I don't slow.

My fake girlfriend falls into step with me, giving me a sideways glance. "You okay?"

I slide my hands into my pockets to keep from reaching for her. "Why wouldn't I be?"

"Oh, I don't know, because you almost got into a fistfight with your coach tonight."

Brow cocked, I study her, but I don't stop moving. "He can't talk to you like that."

Sara's lips twist to the side in a small smile, and she reaches for my arm, looping her hand within it.

"What are you doing?" I dip my chin and take in the way her hand looks against the dark fabric of my suit.

She bites her lip. "When you go all protective boyfriend like that, it turns me on, and since I can't kiss you, I'll take what I can get."

My heart trips over itself at her words. Fuck, this girl and her honesty. She has no idea what she does to me. Not an inkling that the idea of her lips on mine, the fact that she's even thought about it, makes me want to pin her against the wall and claim her.

Press be damned. Career be damned. My entire life plan, including waiting until I retire, be damned.

But one look into those beautiful blue eyes swimming with mischief has me backpedaling. Because my uncle may be an asshole, but he was right about one thing. She deserves better than that.

She deserves better than me.

"Oh, by the way, Lake is here, so when we're done with the press, we are totally going out."

Clasping the hand she still has wrapped around my arm, I suppress a groan. I can't deny her. Because while she's mine, I'll give her every damn thing she asks for, and hanging out with her favorite singer is definitely not negotiable.

If only her favorite singer wasn't married to the father of one of my teammates. I can guarantee that wherever we end up, War will be there too, and he's not going to let go of his little quest to get to the bottom of what's going on with me.

CHAPTER 13

Sara

THERE'S a secret bar that can only be accessed from beneath the arena and the baseball stadium down the block. Naturally, the Langfields own it. Its purpose, obviously, is to allow the players for both Boston teams a place to cut loose and relax away from the prying eyes of their fans and the media.

During the first month I lived in Boston, the guys on the team talked me into coming out with them, but since that night, I've rarely been here. The unspoken rule is that in order to be here, you have to be invited by a player. This is where they come to relax, so more often than not, they don't invite guests. That fact makes it the perfect place for the Langfields to hang with Ford Hall and Lake Paige tonight.

"I can't believe we're really here." Hannah is practically vibrating with excitement next to me while we wait for our drinks at the bar.

Every inch of this place is covered in sports memorabilia: Black and white images of past championships. Souvenirs from world series games played at Lang Field. Even the picture of the Bolts players on the ice with the Cup after last year's win.

A sense of quiet respect reverberates in this space. It's only underscored by the low din of the music, the dimmed lighting, and brick walls.

I bump her shoulder and take in the small crowd that's gathered. "It's incredible."

Brooks, who disappeared along with his brothers when we arrived—probably to discuss the fight with his uncle, which was impossible to miss—is back, cool and calm as always.

Me? I'm the opposite of cool and calm. My body is on fire, and I didn't suit up and play a hockey game. I didn't come within inches of getting into a physical altercation. And I wasn't forced to do one hundred push-ups on the ice in front of thousands of fans.

After all that, how is it possible that he can look so at ease? So perfectly put together and handsome? So unaffected?

Hannah grins up at him. "She looks good in your number, Brooks."

He eyes me over the rim of his lowball glass as he sips his whiskey, the epitome of calm. When he brings the drink back down, he lifts one brow. That's the only reaction the comment gets from him. "That she does."

When Hannah turns to accept her drink from the bartender, I nudge Brooks with my elbow.

"Are you upset that I'm wearing your jersey?"

"Upset?" He frowns. "Not in the slightest."

Maybe he isn't now, but he was. Before the game, when I bumped into him outside the locker room, he went from almost possessive to aloof in the blink of an eye. I want to know why. "You just seemed...I don't know, put off by it."

He shakes his head and blows out a breath, moving into my space. "The last thing I am is put off by the sight of you in my jersey, Pumpkin. It's just..." He fingers the blue fabric, pulling at the bottom of it. "I'd prefer it if you were wearing it *for* me."

Confused, I tilt my head and study his resigned expression. "Who else would I be wearing it for?"

"You said you were wearing it to upset my uncle."

Ah, that's what this is about. The worry gnawing at me eases as my stomach does a little flip. "Oh, Brookie baby."

He glares at me. Apparently he doesn't like that nickname either.

"I did wear it for you. Because *you* want to piss your uncle off." Pressing closer so only he can hear me, I pop up onto my toes and whisper, "This revenge isn't for me, Brooks. I wouldn't be doing this if not for you."

Any feelings I had for Seb dissipated before I found out he was married. The relationship was over the second he tried to tell me who I could be friends with. I don't need revenge. What I need is for my best friend to be happy. If revenge will do that, then so be it.

"Really?" He watches me from beneath furrowed brows. Though his tone is guarded, he gently cuffs the back of my neck and holds me in place. I'm significantly shorter than my monster of a best friend, but like this, we're practically nose to nose, like he's holding me up by my neck. Or maybe he's just leaning down into my space. It's hard to tell when all the oxygen has left my brain with his lips this close to my own.

What the hell is happening right now, and why am I licking my lips wishing that I could be licking his instead?

"It's you and me, Brooks. You're all that matters."

His green eyes bounce between mine, as if he's searching for a lie. He won't find one. I don't tell them. If I didn't want to be here, I wouldn't be. I don't do things unless I want to, and I'm honest to a fault.

There isn't even a hint of sugarcoating going on here. Not when I'm in this state. Right now I'm too consumed with trying to figure out why the hell I'm literally aching for him to press closer. Why I crave his heat and the feel of his hard body against mine.

"You know what's funny?"

The sound of Hannah's voice so close sends a jolt of shock through me. Blinking rapidly, I suck in one heady breath, then another, willing my brain to come back online.

Brooks's grip on the back of my neck eases incrementally, but he remains focused on me for a long moment before finally releasing me and turning to face Hannah. I feel the loss instantly. It's like the power went out just as the best part of the movie began, and it's one that I don't know the name of, so I can't cue it up again to discover how it ends.

It's silly that I feel that way, but the panic of it almost claws at me.

"What's funny, Han?" Brooks grasps my hips and tugs me so I'm standing directly in front of him.

It's hard to focus on their words when his thumb has slipped just inside the waistband of my jeans. It's not even moving, and I'm acutely aware of every indent in that damn piece of flesh. I have to focus on each breath in and back out to remain conscious of the conversation.

Hannah shakes her head. "For months, you've been getting texts from SL, so I assumed the man you were dating had those initials. But all along, it was Brooks. I never put the pieces together."

My stomach knots, and I cough out an uncomfortable laugh. "Oh, that is funny."

"It's because I was her secret lover," Brooks says without pause.

Fuck, he's so good at thinking on his feet. Goalies really do work best under pressure, I guess. But I'm more impressed by the BS he just pulled out of thin air than I am by any of his saves tonight. Quite frankly, it's tied with the moment he almost knocked Seb out in the middle of the game, and that's saying something.

Hannah smacks my arm and grins. "Oh my God. You two are so adorable. Seriously, the cutest!"

For a moment, guilt over the lie swamps me. In general, I have little issue with what we're doing because it makes Brooks happy. But watching as Hannah, a woman I consider a friend, turns practically giddy over our 100-percent fabricated romance sends a streak of unease down my spine.

And yet...as I burn up beneath my best friend's thumb like this, I'm not sure I've felt more right in a long, long time.

"You guys want to play pool?" Hannah tips her head at the group behind us.

The Halls are here. They've settled in with Beckett and Gavin. Liv is stationed on a bar chair with a water in her hand. Beckett is hovering beside her, as if he's protecting her from the crush of a mosh pit rather than the two dozen chill patrons in the not so crowded bar.

I nudge Brooks and nod in their direction so he can see what I'm seeing. His brother really can be so damn adorable when it comes to Liv. I can't wait to see how much more aggressive that protectiveness becomes as her pregnancy progresses.

Brooks nudges me back gently. "Maybe in a bit. My body is kinda beat from the game. I might sit for a minute, but you should go play."

Hannah's brows are high on her forehead as she watches me, waiting for my response.

Though she's probably silently hoping I'll be her wing woman, I'm desperate to get back to the conversation Brooks and I were having. I want to get the power turned back on and cross my fingers that the movie from earlier will pick up right where it left off. Ya know, in that moment when Brooks almost kind of maybe might have been thinking about kissing me.

"I'm gonna hang too," I tell my friend. "Go play."

Hannah doesn't put up a fight, and a moment later, she wanders over to Liv. She's really itching to hang out with Daniel Hall, and if I wasn't so invested in finding out what's going through Brooks's head, I'd be searching for a bag of popcorn to snack on while I watched that interaction play out.

At this moment, though, I want nothing more than to focus solely on the man who's settling in a seat at the bar beside me.

The slow way he lowers himself and the grimace that flashes across his face make it obvious he's in pain.

I hop up onto the stool beside him and drop one elbow to the lacquered bar top as I swivel to face him. "You always this sore after a game?"

Brooks sips his whiskey and shrugs, his attention fixed on the variety of bottles behind the bar. "It's nothing."

Lips pursed, I eye him. "Maybe your girlfriend should give you a rubdown when you get home."

That makes Brooks choke on his whiskey. "Fuck, Pumpkin." He pounds his chest with a fist and gasps for air.

I giggle, bringing my drink to my mouth. It's a pumpkin martini that seemed to magically appear when I turned around. Brooks is always seeing to my needs in that way. "This is delicious."

Lips tugged up on one side, he shakes his head and turns away.

"So are we going to talk about earlier, secret lover?"

Brooks hums, still studying the fascinating bottles of liquor behind the bar, it seems.

Commotion from the entrance has me turning, and when I catch sight of Sebastian walking in with his nephew Vin, I scowl.

"Seriously?"

Brooks follows my line of sight and stiffens. On instinct, I scoot closer to him, and he surprises me by turning until he's facing me and widening his thick thighs. Then he pulls my stool so I'm wedged between his legs. His heavy hand lands on mine, and he tugs my fingers into his and squeezes.

I'm not sure if his natural inclination is to protect me from Seb, or if he's doing this for show. Knowing Brooks, he's being protective.

The thought sends a wave of relief over me. I lean my head against his chest and sigh, letting my shoulders ease a bit lower.

Still holding tight to my hand, he drapes his free arm over my shoulder and pulls me even closer, if that's possible. The feel of his strong chest, the sound of his steady heartbeat, and the smell of him— all man and musk from his shower gel—coax my body to soften against him further. I've never been quite as comfortable as I am when I'm in his arms. His thumb scrapes softly against my shoulder as he whispers "I got you, Pumpkin" into the top of my head.

What he doesn't understand is that I don't need protection. What I'm doing here, and what I did at the game tonight, is all for him. But if it makes him feel better, then I'm okay with letting him believe he's my superhero. For now, at least.

And while I'm a girl who likes to stand on her own two feet, even I can admit that it's nice being taken care of for once.

"Thought only Bolts and Revs players could come in here," I mutter.

I don't know why I'm surprised that, once again, Seb is breaking the rules. The man has zero moral compass. Why would a little hockey code mean anything to him?

"And our friends and family. Vin is Seb's family." Brooks's tone is dark and resigned. Obviously he doesn't love that fact, and who could blame him? Vincent Lukov is an asshole.

When the two men stop to say hello to Gavin and Beckett, I consider pushing Brooks up so that we can disappear before we have to deal with an awkward encounter, but I swear that as the guys step farther into the room, the arm draped over me gets heavier, holding me in place. Like Brooks wants this awkward interaction. Like he's claiming me.

The prospect is thrilling. And to be honest, it's fucking hot.

It's like standing beside a bomb and watching the seconds tick down. Anxiety plagues me as the guys turn toward the bar. The feeling is so visceral it forces my leg to bounce while simultaneously causing my stomach to sink. They head in our direction in what feels like slow motion. Seb raises his head slowly as he comes closer. It's like we've been transported into one of those movies full of aliens with laser eyes. Any second now, I expect him to start shooting us.

"Dammit, where's Will Smith when we need him?" I mumble.

Brooks snorts, the reaction jostling me. "What are you going on about?"

With a squeeze of his hand, I will my nerves to steady. "Ya know," I squeak out. "*Men in Black.*"

Seb's attention is fixed on me as he slides his hand into his pocket.

My brain must malfunction in that moment, because that little move has me pushing myself against Brooks and screaming "bomb!"

The bar is loud. It's full of people, and music filters through speakers throughout the space. But it's not *that* loud.

The second the word is out of my mouth, every eye is locked on me, so, naturally, that's when the stool beneath me slips. As I'm going down, I grab for the first thing I can find.

"Oh my God, Brooks!" I gasp at the appendage I'm clinging to. "Your dick is hard!"

Why am I talking so loudly? And why am I gripping my best friend's dick?

"What the fuck is wrong with you?" He's looming above me, his tone frantic and his face a mask of confusion. He wiggles his thumb, tugging at my hand and garnering my attention.

Ohh. My hand is wrapped around his *thumb*. So *not* his dick, after all. With a grunt, he hauls me onto his lap. The movement sends my stool clattering to the ground.

Through the whole debacle, the rest of the man's body doesn't move. His damn thumb muscle lifted my entire body. What in the hell are they feeding these hockey players?

"Is that your wallet, or are you just happy to see me?" The tease escapes from one side of my mouth.

His expression is dark as he bands his arms around me and pulls me close. "You've lost your ever-loving mind, Sar. Fucking gone."

Maybe he's right, because over the course of the last two days, I've developed an unhealthy obsession with Brooks's dick. Maybe if he let me take a quick peek at it, this fascination would end. I shift on his lap and suck in a breath, ready to suggest just that, but before I can, Seb and Vin appear beside us. Vin is wearing a grin, but Seb is scowling.

"Your girl all right?" New York's asshole asks the question, but there isn't a hint of concern on his face. No, it's all pompous amusement.

When Brooks replies, his tone is eerily calm, but he doesn't look away from me. "My girl is perfect. Right, Pumpkin?"

I nod like a bobblehead. I'm still all over the fucking place, but I figure the silent response is better than talking at this point. God only knows what would come out of my mouth if I did.

Seb snorts. "She's certainly flexible."

"Excuse you." I push off Brooks, despite the way he's clinging to me, and press into Seb's space, head held high and shoulders back. "Who do you think you are?"

Seb's bored expression only irritates me more. "I was only commenting on how gracefully you landed that fall."

Vin turns to the bar to order his drink, but Seb keeps his smarmy smile fixed on me.

"And you're good at bouncing from one man to the next."

I raise my hand, ready to slap the smirk off my ex's face, but before I can, Brooks is beside me, looming over his uncle, his fist prepared to do the heavy lifting.

Suddenly, Tyler is here too, with one hand on Brooks's arm, he stops things from escalating. "Whoa, buddy. Let's go for a walk."

I suck in a breath as I watch Tyler drag Brooks out the door. Then my lungs seize as I realize we're in public. My eyes scan every inch of the bar. Fortunately, not a soul is looking in our direction. It appears that no one but Tyler saw what happened.

I let out a long breath then, only to hold it again when I realize I'm still standing next to the jerk who's still acting all smug, like Brooks is the one in the wrong.

I'd love to smack that cockiness right off him, but I quickly remember that the best revenge is happiness. *Mine and Brooks.*

With my chin held high once more, I snatch my purse from the bar and shoot him a glare. "You're not worth it, but I sure as hell found someone who is." Then I stomp off with my dignity in tow.

CHAPTER 14
Brooks

"DUDE, WHAT THE FUCK WAS THAT?" War asks as he drags me out of the bar by my lapels.

I turn around and heave a sigh of relief when I catch sight of Sara. When she skitters to a stop in front of me, I haul her to my chest and rock her back and forth. "You okay?"

She sighs against me, then tips her head back. "No beating up coaches, thirteen. I need you to keep your job so I can keep mine."

I heave a relieved breath at the annoyed frown on her face. It means she's not overly upset about my uncle's asshole remark. With a kiss to her forehead, I tuck her into my side, then lead her down the underground hallway that'll take us back to the arena.

"Yeah, you're going to have to start talking," War says, keeping pace with us.

"Brooks was defending my honor," Sara replies, leaning forward to look at War.

I shake my head and hold her tight. She doesn't take the blame for this. When men make bad decisions, they're to blame. Not the women who stand beside them.

"Just working through some shit. It will be fine."

War eyes me, squinting like he doesn't believe me, but he doesn't push as we continue on toward the player's garage.

"See you back at the apartment?" I ask as we approach our vehicles.

War grasps my hand and pulls me in for a hug and a clap on the back. Then he leans down and kisses Sara's cheek. "Nah, I'm heading out for a bit."

"Don't forget we have to be at the shelter first thing tomorrow," Sara reminds him.

War runs his hands through his dark hair. Women love his bad boy persona—I happen to know it's all bullshit. He's one of the nicest guys I've ever met, but he plays it up with the tattoos that peek out from the collar of his suit and both sleeves. His ice-blue eyes scream mischievous devil, and his chiseled jaw has been broken in more than one fight.

"Eh, Ava will assume I'm going to be late anyway. Why disappoint her? Admit it, she told me to be there half an hour before the rest of the team, didn't she?"

I laugh and hit him with a light punch to the gut. "Be nice to her. She's a good girl."

Tyler scoffs. "Yeah. If you want to call the devil an angel, be my guest." With a wave of his hand, he turns toward his car. "See you in the morning, lovebirds."

I open the door for Sara, but instead of climbing in, she turns to face me full on. "What's with him and Ava? She's so nice."

Ava heads up VIP relations and charity work for the team. She's one of only a handful of females who live in our building, so she and Sara are close.

"All I know is that they don't get along." I rest a hand on the small of her back and guide her up into the truck. "He didn't show up to an event she set up for us last year, and she was not happy."

Once Sara is settled and is pulling her seat belt across her torso, I shut her door and round the back of the truck. As I go, I pull in a few deep breaths. The adrenaline rush that's kept me going for the last few hours is fading fast, and the weight of today's events is beginning to hit me.

I almost punched my coach today. *Twice.* It's true that he can't fire me, but it's not okay for me to be getting into fistfights with the man who leads our team. He needs to be gone. Quick. It's the only option.

"Why didn't Tyler show up at the event? He was obligated to be there. Charity events are written into your contracts. I can understand Ava's anger if he blew it off. She works hard to set them up for you guys and make sure they work with your travel schedule." Sara goes on about the issue facing War and Ava, completely unaware that I'm having a mini panic attack beside her.

"We need to take things up a notch," I blurt, my heart racing again and my palms sweating. "I can't keep getting into fights with him. It's not good for the team."

Sara studies me, her expression full of concern. "You don't have to defend me, Brooks. I've done nothing wrong, and I'm a big girl. I can handle his little slights."

As I exit the parking ramp, my grip on the steering wheel tightens, along with every muscle in my body. I'm so wound up, I'm about ready to snap. "No one, I don't care who they are, can speak like that to you."

"You're taking this whole boyfriend thing very seriously." Sara lets out a breathy laugh. *"Don't mess with my girl."* Her tone is teasing, and she puffs out her chest and swings her arms in front of her in what I guess she thinks is a mockingly manly way.

"You're my friend. *My best friend.* My feelings on the matter have nothing to do with a pissing match. This is about making sure you're being treated with respect."

Does she not get that? Does she really think my anger has more to do with some macho man thing than her happiness and well-being? Fuck that.

"I've gotten into exactly zero fights in my life." I face her as we come to a light to emphasize my point. "*Zero.* I'm not a hothead who gets up in arms when someone says shit to me."

She blinks a few times, like she's letting my explanation sink in, and nods. "Okay."

With her lip caught between her teeth, she fiddles with the hem of her jersey for a quiet moment. When the light turns green, I continue toward home.

After another block or so, she speaks again. "So, what can we do to push your uncle over the edge?"

My brain is a jumbled mess of terrible ideas. Kissing her in the middle of the packed arena. Fucking her so he can hear us. They are neighbors, after all. They share a wall and everything. I mean, really, what will it take for him to disappear? Should I propose?

Sara interrupts my crazy. "Come over for dinner tomorrow. He's right next door. We can play board games or have a karaoke competition. We both know how loud my singing gets. He'll definitely know we're hanging out."

Right. Because those are normal ideas. Unlike mine. What kind of sane person comes up with things like *fucking my best friend against the wall until I make her scream so loud my asshole uncle knows precisely who she's with?*

I clear my throat and nod. "That works."

Once Sara is safely inside her apartment, I head back to the elevator, glaring at my uncle's door as I go. I hate that his apartment is right next to hers. It used to be one more reason I looked up to the man. His choice to live here with his players during the season.

The building is beautiful, but the units are all relatively small. He could easily afford a condo or a brownstone like Beckett's, yet an apartment here was good enough for him. I thought that was another thing the two of us had in common. Nice things are great, but I'm a simple guy. I don't need a penthouse like Gavin's. My love of the game and a healthy respect for the people in my life are what I've always strived for. Coach taught me that. It's the image he always portrayed and the one I've worked my whole life to emulate.

Now I see his reasoning in a new light. Did he choose to stay in this building because it made it convenient to cheat on my aunt? They own a gorgeous house on the water in Florida, and that's where Zoe lives year-round. Seb stays there often during the offseason and travels to visit her between games the rest of the year. I thought it showed dedication. To her and the team. Now I know better, and it only makes me hate him even more.

Part of me wants to move out of the building tonight. Leave all the memories behind. But that would be giving in. Giving up. And I don't give up. Never have.

I've spent my life being expected to remain steady under the toughest conditions on the ice. I've perfected the ability to stay focused under any kind of pressure. If anyone has trained for the next few months, it's me.

When my key turns in the lock too easily, I frown down at the doorknob. Why is my door unlocked? I'm meticulous in a lot of my routines, and I wouldn't give Sara a hard time about always leaving her door open if I was in the habit of doing the same.

With a sigh, I push the door open. I can't say I'm surprised when I find all the lights on and my younger brother bent over in front of my fridge.

"Don't you live somewhere else?"

Aiden jumps, smacking the back of his head inside the open fridge. "You scared the shit out of me." He rubs at his head and turns on me with a scowl.

I drop my bag beside the door and toe off my shoes. "Excuse me for scaring you in my own damn apartment. Why the hell are you here? You didn't even come out for drinks after the game."

If I had to label one of my teammates as the stereotypical partier, it would be Aiden. He's always the fun one. The good time. Yet tonight, he skipped out on celebrating a win over New York, a win he definitely deserved praise for. And that makes zero sense.

He leans against the kitchen counter and takes a long swig of the beer he pulled from the fridge. It's from a six-pack of a special malted brew I bought at a local brewery Sara and I had dinner at a few weeks ago. I grab one for myself and settle against the counter opposite him, then stare him down, waiting for an explanation.

"Jill and I got into a stupid fight. I rushed home after the game to talk to her, but she'd locked me out."

I cross my free arm over my chest and tuck my hand under the opposite bicep, then take a pull off my beer. "It's your apartment. Don't you have a key?"

"She dead-bolted it."

I hide my laughter with another swig. "Musta been a doozy of a fight."

He sighs, his shoulders slumping. "That's just it. I don't even know what she's mad about."

Lose the girl. The words are on the tip of my tongue, but a comment like that will only add salt to his wounds. Aiden must see something in his girlfriend that the rest of us don't, because from where I'm standing, she's nothing but toxic.

"You can sleep on the couch." I tap my beer against his, then wander toward my room. Now that I'm home, my exhaustion has hit like a freight train.

"Can't you go stay at your girlfriend's? Then I can sleep in your bed."

My steps falter as I hit my bedroom door. The image of waking up with Sara has me smiling. That image quickly morphs into a memory, and I have to hold back a laugh. I did wake up with her yesterday. And then she acted like a complete psychopath. After that incident and the way she latched on to my thumb at the bar, I'm beginning to realize that's her thing. She acts like a lunatic when she's off-kilter. And she's obsessed with my cock.

"No." I leave it at that. I don't have the mental energy to come up with an excuse as to why I won't rush upstairs and sleep in Sara's bed. I close the bedroom door, muting his whining, and chuckle.

Fucking Aiden.

"Good Morning, Boston. Eliza here, with my co-host, Colton, ready to bring you the Hockey Report."

"Thank you, Eliza. Not so sure it's a good morning for everyone in Boston, though."

Eliza hums. "Yes, while our Boston Bolts pulled out a win last night, it was an ugly one."

"And you aren't just referring to the game," Colton interjects.

"Nope. I think we're all more interested in what was going on off the ice than on it. There's a video trending this morning that shows a skirmish between Coach Lukov and Boston's favorite goalie, Saint Brooks, who didn't appear very saintlike."

"No, Eliza, he did not. In fact, it appears he shoved Coach Lukov. It isn't clear why or what was said, and he wasn't benched for it."

"You don't bench Brooks Langfield," Eliza deadpans.

"If he was in the wrong, any coach would be well within his rights to bench him. Though if Coach Lukov was in the wrong, that could explain why Brooks continued to play. We can only hope to get more insight into the reason behind the spat between uncle and nephew."

"That's the problem with working with family, Colton."

"She's my sister, ladies and gentlemen. She's teasing. She loves working with me."

"Sometimes," Eliza jests.

CHAPTER 15
Brooks

"DUDE. You couldn't even bother to wait for me?" Aiden pulls up beside me, panting like he had to run to catch up to me.

War strolls in behind him, hands casually stuffed in his pockets and an easy expression on his face.

Tucking a strand of red hair behind her ear, Ava sighs and consults her clipboard as she steps closer. "Now that everyone is here," she says, pointedly looking at War, "the goal is to get these babies adopted. Word that you're here working the adoption event has been all over social media, so there will be a long line of people. Most of them will show up for a chance to meet you, so try to focus on the animals. The only people allowed in the building will be those who have filled out an application to adopt, so that should help keep things moving smoothly." She taps her pen against her lip and bites down on it, surveying us. "Marginally, at least. Aiden," she says, pointing her pen at my brother, "you're with McGreevey. Parker, you're with Warren, and that leaves you with me, Brooks."

I head her way but pull up short when McGreevey whines. Our team captain earned his status and then some. He's not a whiner. Yet when I turn to him, his face is puckered and he's backing away from my brother.

"No fucking way am I dealing with this one. Why the fuck do you smell so bad?"

A rumbling laugh works its way out of me and echoes around the mostly empty space.

"Because," Aiden groans, pointing at me, "that one locked me out of his bedroom."

"You have your own apartment." I scoff. "And if I'd left my door open, then you would have gone through my shit and taken one of my shirts."

When we were kids, Aiden was notorious for stealing my clothes. I still don't understand why. I've always been at least a couple of sizes bigger than him.

"Don't know the story behind why you're staying at Brooks's place, and I don't want to," McGreevey mutters. "Brooks, he's related to you. That makes him your problem. Parker, you're with me."

The two married men are always pairing up. Not that I blame them. If I had someone waiting for me at home, I'd ditch the single guys too.

Heck, I do it more often than not anyway so I can hang with Sara.

"Who the fuck am I with, then?" War grumbles.

Ava lets out another aggravated sigh. "Me, apparently. Just— don't talk, and maybe we'll make it through the day."

I have to hold back a laugh at the sass coming from the normally sweet woman.

War, on the other hand, drops his head, lets out a string of curses, and follows behind her.

Aiden steps closer, and his rancid scent envelops me.

I throw an arm over my nose and mouth to keep myself from passing out and shoot him a glare. "Did you not shower after the game last night? You fucking reek. I'm going to have to have my couch power washed."

"I showered. I just—" He pulls on his neck and gives me a sheepish look. "I didn't have a fresh pair of socks, and apparently the ones I found in your laundry basket weren't as clean as they looked."

"You're fucking gross. You went through my laundry?" This is exactly why I lock my bedroom door. The guy has no boundaries.

He shrugs and lifts his chin, going for flippant now. "Whatever. We're at a damn animal shelter. The piss smell in here will overpower it anyway. And they're your socks." Without a glance back, he heads down the hall where the rest of our group disappeared.

Begrudgingly, I follow, doing my best to breathe through my mouth only. It's going to be a long morning.

CHAPTER 16

Sara

"ANY CHANCE you could pause the game and actually look at me while we're talking?" I tease.

My brother doesn't even bother to look away from his gaming screen when he rolls his eyes.

I'm running late for work, but I couldn't leave home without checking in. Not after all the panicked messages my mom left last night. According to Ethan, she's out picking up breakfast now.

When he answered, I immediately put it on FaceTime so I could see him for myself. While he's barely looked at the screen, I can tell by his posture and his tone that he's feeling good. To anyone else, he looks like a typical twelve-year-old boy who's more interested in the game he's playing on his Nintendo Switch than in what his big sister has to say.

He licks his lips and leans in closer to his screen. "Sorry, Sar. Just need to block this puck."

My brother has a crazy obsession with hockey, and because of his multiple sclerosis, this is probably the closest he'll ever get to the ice.

He hisses a *yes*, then finally turns his attention to me. "You look tired."

I snort a laugh. "Thanks. Appreciate the brutal honesty."

"Hey." The grin that splits his face is blinding. "Someone's gotta tell you the truth."

"You feeling okay?"

His expression sours, and his eyes go dull. "I'm fine."

"Mom sounded—"

"Like Mom," he interrupts. "I'm fine, Sara. Seriously. You know how dramatic she is."

He's not wrong. My mother sent me a dozen messages last night, each one more panicked than the last. When I got home and picked up the phone I'd forgotten to take with me that morning, my stomach had plummeted.

I never go anywhere without my work phone since I handle the majority of social media requests for the team, but I often forget my personal device.

It was late, so rather than immediately calling my mother back and potentially waking her up, I listened to her messages, figuring they'd make it clear whether I should. By the time I got to the last one, I knew everything was fine.

My brother's reaction to his new trial medication was normal, according to the doctor, and a sign that it was working. Pediatric MS, while a devastating diagnosis, is manageable. As long as I can pay for treatments, Ethan's medical team is hopeful that he'll go on to live a long life.

I study my brother, his posture and expression, the light in his eyes, discerning whether he's really okay or downplaying his pain and other symptoms to keep me from worrying. It's tempting to hop on the next flight home so I can see for myself, but the airfare is stupid expensive, and my credit card is officially maxed out.

I could go to Beckett for a loan. Or Liv. They've been nothing but generous, and over the last several months, they've become more than my bosses. They're my friends. But it's too damn embarrassing to admit that even with my extravagant salary and the free apartment, I'm unable to handle my bills.

Besides, the team is headed to North Carolina in a few weeks, so I'll see him then.

"Fine. But don't be too hard on her. She's only dramatic because she loves you."

Like a typical twelve-year-old boy, Ethan rolls his eyes and huffs. He knows it, even if she drives him crazy.

I lean closer to my screen and pause until I'm sure he's looking at me. "And I love you."

He gives me a half smile. "Course you do. What's not to love?"

This kid. I can't help but laugh. "All right, I've got to head to work. Tell Mom I called."

"Will do." Without waiting for me to disconnect the call, he picks up his Switch. That little bit of normalcy forces some of the tension still plaguing me to ebb. He's going to be fine.

Exhausted and late, I hustle to the employee entrance of the office building at Langfield Corp. Before I reach the doors, Beckett, Liv, and Gavin stroll out. Beckett is holding a leash, and Deogi is traipsing after them.

"Perfect timing," Liv croons. Her cheeks are rosy and her eyes are bright. She's wearing her hair down today. For the first several months I worked for Langfield Corp, I never saw her without it pulled up into a bun. Now, with the way it falls in soft waves around her face and paired with the black leggings and an oversized burgundy sweater, she's the epitome of relaxed.

"Where are you headed?" I crouch so I can greet their pet too. "Hi, Dog. How you doing, buddy?"

Beckett lets out a gruff sigh. "It's not Dog. It's Deogi. Say it with me. Deee-oh-giii."

Beside him, Gavin snorts, his eyes twinkling.

Still scratching behind the pup's ears, I peer up at Beckett. Despite his ridiculousness, he's wearing his signature serious face. The man isn't messing with me. No, Beckett Langfield doesn't joke around.

"Why the duck are you looking at me like that?"

Gavin laughs harder and grasps my upper arm to help me to my feet. "We're on our way to the shelter. When you weren't at your desk, I figured you'd already headed over with Brooks."

Shit. Even after our talk with War last night, I'd forgotten about the event. My brain is officially scrambled. At least I decided on pants today rather than a skirt.

It's mayhem when the Langfields' limo pulls up to the event. Once we've all exited, Beckett looks at every other animal as if it's inferior to Deogi, and Liv rolls her eyes the whole way into the building because her husband is so absurd. I adore them.

Before Beckett married Liv, I feared the man. He was constantly grumpy and snapped at his employees regularly.

It's obvious now that he was a hungry dog, and Liv was a treat dangled just out of his reach day in and day out.

Now that he can touch her and kiss her any time he wants, it's like he's getting a steady stream of dopamine.

"I really think it'd be better if you took Deogi back to the house," Liv says gently, trying to coax her husband to leave. "This is a lot for him."

Giving her the kind of warm smile that still surprises me coming from him, he presses a kiss to her forehead. Then he grabs a chair from against the wall and drags it over to us. "Just sit here with him and make it look like you're the happiest woman in the world. Show all the people here what they're missing out on because they don't have a dog."

Liv bites back her smile, and I giggle. The man is completely serious.

"Okay, baby," she says, placating him. "I can do that."

Gavin nudges me. "Looks like your boyfriend and his dog have quite the line."

I follow his line of sight until I spot Brooks and Aiden crouched down in front of a group of kids. His long brown hair is pulled back, and a green sweater stretches across his muscles, making his emerald irises pop. The dark jeans he's got on are worn perfectly in all the right places and molded to his thick thighs. Damn, I can't keep my eyes off my fake boyfriend. When he scoops a tan and white boxer into his arms, my chest warms and butterflies take flight in my belly.

"Man, I have no idea how I missed it," Gavin says beside me, though it sounds like he's speaking from inside a fishbowl.

"What?" I ask, but I don't turn to look at him. I'm fixated on the genuine smile on Brooks's face. And when he laughs with the kids surrounding him and his eyes crinkle, it's like a shot to the heart.

"We all knew he had a crush on you, but until now, I never noticed that you look at him in the same way."

That snags my attention. I whip around and gape at Gavin. That's the second time one of Brooks's family members has mentioned him having a crush.

"It's a good thing." Gavin gives me an encouraging smile, like maybe he senses my confusion. "There's no one better. Seriously. You're in good hands."

He's right about that. There is no one on earth as kind and caring as Brooks. Allowing that thought to settle me, I nod and turn back to the show the hockey players are putting on by simply existing.

Ava is hugging her clipboard to her chest and glaring down at War, who's sitting cross-legged on the ground with an oversized mutt in his lap, commanding the attention of half the room. The man is pretty, that's for damn sure. And every time he peeks over at Ava, his blue eyes dance with mirth. He loves pissing her off.

McGreevey is chatting with fans, along with Parker, whose wife is with him. When the tiny woman with dark hair cut in an asymmetrical style spots Liv, she heads our way. She's one of Liv's former brownstone roommates, and the two have been friends since college. After I give her a quick hug, I head toward Brooks and Aiden.

"You guys having fun?" I open my arms and angle in to give Aiden a squeeze hello, but I'm stopped when large hands find my hips and pull me back. "Excuse me!" With a huff, I whip around and glower at my giant of a best friend.

Brooks doesn't let go of me, even after I've maneuvered around to face him. "Believe me," he chuckles, "I'm doing you a favor."

Aiden shakes his head and drops to his haunches to love on his dog some more.

With my hands on his biceps, I step in and tilt my head back. "Want me all to yourself, secret lover?"

His chest shakes with silent laughter. "No. My brother stinks. I'm seriously protecting you."

I peer over my shoulder at Aiden, then turn back to face Brooks. He cups my jaw and rubs his thumbs over the apples of my cheeks, taking me in and cataloging every inch of my face. "You sleep okay?"

Nuzzling into his hands, I tilt my face down to hide the dark circles under my eyes. "Just tossed and turned for a bit. How are the adoptions going?" I step in close, and when he releases his hold on my face, I lean my cheek against his chest and listen to his steady heartbeat. God, if I stayed like this, I'd probably fall asleep. He's so warm. Somehow, he manages to be both firm and soft, and he smells so damn good.

"Pretty good." He tugs at my ponytail. "Although Aiden's scaring people away. Maybe I should keep you by my side. You're pretty and you smell like fall." His voice is pure affection.

Forcing my eyes open, I tip my face up to take him in, eager for a glimpse of the smile I know he's wearing, and am greeted with a kiss to my forehead. It's innocent. Something I'm sure he's done before. But this time it feels like more than just a friendly kiss. The rumble in his chest makes it feel possessive.

That thought has me scanning the room for Seb. But as far as I can tell, he isn't here.

I shake off the thought. Brooks is just a friendly guy, and like I said, he's probably kissed my forehead a dozen times or more since we met. That move wasn't out of the ordinary.

For the next three hours, we work the lines of people and play with dogs of all ages. When my phone vibrates in my pocket and I pull it out to find my mother's name flashing on the screen, I sneak outside to take the call. Unfortunately, service is terrible, so when I answer, I get nothing but silence. I immediately call her back, but it goes straight to voicemail.

Slumped against the brick building, I curse my stupid phone service.

"Come on, Livy. It's Friday. You know what that means," Beckett says as he and Liv walk out of the building, hand in hand, with Deogi trotting along beside them, tail wagging and tongue lolling out of his mouth.

I raise my hand, ready to call out to them, but snap my mouth shut when Liv says, "You're not putting it in the butt tonight, Mr. Langfield."

Holy fuck. I really wish I'd made a damn noise the second they stepped outside. Holding my breath, I press back against the bricks and will myself to become one with the wall. I even close my eyes. If I can't see them, then they won't see me, right?

"You know what you calling me Mr. Langfield does," he purrs.

He fucking purrs. I swear.

Ermygod.

When I hear the sound of a car door opening, I let out the breath burning my lungs, hopeful that I'm in the clear. Except before I can open my eyes, a heavy weight settles over my shoulders.

"Can the two of you stop talking about butt stuff? You're freaking out the head of my PR team."

Cringing, I pry one eye open and peer up. Gavin is giddy as he grins down at me.

Groaning, I whack him in the stomach with the back of my hand.

He makes a loud *humph*, but an instant later, he falls into a fit of laughter.

"Don't worry. They were already in the car when I yelled that." He straightens and smooths out his suit jacket. "But seriously, can they get a room?"

I drop my head back against the brick, ignoring the way it tugs at my hair, and blow out a breath. How do these things keep happening to me? First I'm poked in the eye by Brooks's cock, and then I make a scene at the bar. Now I've accidentally become a voyeur while a married couple talk dirty to one another. The Langfields are going to think I'm a pervert with really weird fetishes.

Like really weird.

The door beside us opens again, and this time Brooks and Aiden appear.

"Want to do something for dinner?" Aiden is asking as they step out onto the sidewalk.

"No, I have plans." Brooks's face lights up when he spots us, but in an instant, his jaw goes rigid and his eyes narrow on where Gavin's arm is still draped over me.

Oblivious to his brother's sudden shift in mood, Aiden continues, "I'll just hang at your place, then."

Brooks stomps our way, his expression getting harder with every step he takes. "Don't you have somewhere you can go?" he asks Aiden, his tone gruffer than I thought he was capable of.

Beside me, my boss shakes with laughter, then steps away. "God, you're so easy to rile up." He slides his hands into his pockets and rocks back on his heels. "Aiden, why don't we leave the lovebirds to themselves? You can have dinner with me."

Brooks slides a palm down his face. "I can't believe I'm saying this, but I can't in good conscience let him go with you. The man fucking reeks."

Aiden glares at Brooks and stomps his foot like a little boy.

Gavin laughs, moving closer to his baby brother. "So go home and shower, you idiot."

"Jill kicked me out." The poor guy hangs his head, and my heart aches. It's rare to see the silliest of the Langfield brothers anything but chipper.

Gavin holds up his hands and quickly changes direction, backing up toward the street. "I'm not touching that with a ten-foot pole. Aiden," he commands, pointing a finger, "break up with Jill. She sucks." Then he turns his attention our way. "Brooks, I swear I wasn't hitting on your woman. Sara, great job today. No more butt stuff, okay?"

With a wink at me, he spins on his heel and practically skips down the block, probably reveling in the knowledge that he just kicked up a full-blown shitstorm.

"Butt stuff?" Aiden hisses.

"Dude, read the room and go the fuck away," Brooks snaps in a way I rarely witness. The man is always so easygoing, but apparently his vast well of patience has run temporarily dry.

"I swear I didn't offer to have anal sex with your brother."

It takes everything in me not to smack myself when those words are the ones my brain has chosen to spit out.

And from the scowl he shoots me, he doesn't appreciate them either.

"Or any kind of sex," I explain, because obviously that elaboration is so much better. "Not even oral."

"Oh my God," Aiden mumbles, dropping his head into one hand. "Stop while you're ahead."

I really, really should. The smelly man is right. But the blank stare on Brooks's face is freaking me the fuck out, and when I'm freaked out, I can't control the words that spew from my lips. "Not that I'm opposed to butt stuff. It's just—I wouldn't do that with your brother. *Obviously.*" I let out an exasperated breath, trying to convey how ridiculous that would be.

Brooks only blinks. Shit.

Aiden at least has the courtesy to grumble. "Any chance you can teach me how to use the washing machine?"

I bite my lip and look between the two men. "Um, sure."

"We're busy," Brooks grits out. "Stop making plans with my brothers."

With an awkward laugh, I grasp his wrist and tug. "I never made plans to do butt stuff with Gavin. I swear it."

Brooks slides a palm down his face and groans. "Please stop saying butt stuff."

"It's a totally normal thing to do, Brooks."

Shoulders slumping, he peeks at me from between his fingers, but he doesn't respond.

I hold up my hands. "Fine. No more butt stuff. Aiden, meet me in the laundry room in thirty minutes."

CHAPTER 17

Sara

Lennox: Guess who's coming home tomorrow and can come to a game with her bestie?!

Me: Really? Shut up!

Lennox: Want to hang before? I fly in late tonight, so I can head your way tomorrow morning.

Me: Yes. I have so much to tell you.

Lennox: Let me guess: Brooks finally confessed his undying love for you?

Me: Why does everyone keep acting like this is a thing?

Lennox: Ha! He did!

Me: No. But I don't want to get into it over text. I'll tell you all about it tomorrow.

Lennox: Okay, babe. Just remember, a good man always lets a lady go first.

Me: It's not like that.

Lennox: Oh I said that wrong, a good man always lets a woman COME first. Make sure Brookie baby knows that.

Me: Goodbye you pervert!

Lennox: Love you!

LAUGHING, I throw my phone onto the bed. No wonder I say such ridiculous things all the time. My closest friend literally has no shame. For the first time in hours, I'm hit with genuine relief. Because Lennox will be here tomorrow. I need her more than I realized. She's the only person I've ever completely opened up to about my family, about this job and what it means to me, and about my friendship with Brooks.

She knows everything about me. Or she did. But then Brooks and I started this fake dating thing. It's not something I want to explain over text. The tangled web I've found myself in requires a face-to-face explanation. From her responses, it's clear she already has the wrong idea. Brooks and I are just friends.

His horrified expression when I mentioned butt stuff this after-noon is proof enough of that. Or his reaction to the way I grabbed his finger and mentioned his hard cock yesterday. Or the way he couldn't get away from me fast enough when I screamed about his monster cock poking me in the eye. Yeah, he could not be less interested if he tried. Not that I can blame him. I'm insane.

I can only imagine how demure and perfect the woman he really has feelings for is. She's probably my exact opposite.

I slip off my work clothes and toss my hair up into a ponytail.

Then I turn on the shower, making sure to crank the knob all the way to scalding, all the while considering what type of woman would catch Brooks's eye. What is his type? In all the time I've known him, I've never so much as seen him flirt with a woman.

Standing under the spray, I run my hands over my torso, hissing when I brush over my nipples. Shit, just thinking about Brooks has me turned on. What sort of crazy is that?

With my lip caught between my teeth, I eye the dildo that's suctioned to the shower wall. *I really shouldn't.* Fake dating Brooks is one thing, but fucking myself in the shower while I think about him?

Heat pools low in my belly when I remember waking up and discovering his cock pressed against my cheek. I glance at the dildo again, running my tongue over my teeth. Is it possible he's bigger than that? I grip it with my hand, fisting it and sliding along its length. I close my eyes and focus on the ridges and the girth. Yup, it feels about the same as what I remember from the fleeting moment I had his monster cock in my hand.

My heart rate picks up, and I grip the length tighter, then—oh my God, I'm jacking off my shower dildo while picturing Brooks.

Groaning, I stare at it, then my gaze wanders to the shower head, then back to the dildo. Fuck it. I'm never going to make it through dinner with him if I don't take the edge off. Not with the way my imagination has taken off.

But I absolutely, positively will not think of him while I do it.

I tip forward at the waist and position myself perfectly. Then I shuffle back an inch, then another. I'm absolutely not thinking about the ease with which Brooks knocked out one hundred push-ups on the ice or the way his body looked lowering and raising without a tremor, his thighs not even quaking, as I slide back until the dildo is deep inside me.

"Ah, Brooks," I murmur, heat and desire coursing through me.

In the next second, my heart lurches. *Shit, shit, shit.*

With one hand braced against the wall and the other grasping the shower head, I work myself back and forth, taking it slow and keeping the stream of water aimed exactly where I need it. That's when I give up all pretense. There's no denying that it's Brooks's mouth I'm imagining on my clit, his head between my thighs. And when I come faster than I've ever come before, it's his name on my lips.

"Okay, now you add the softener."

War snorts beside me. "The Leprechaun is always soft, Sar. He doesn't need any help in that—"

Aiden's fist is connecting with Tyler's arm before he can finish the sentence.

"Ow!" War yells. He follows it up with a slap to Aiden's shoulder, then another and another. Aiden retaliates, and in seconds, they've reverted into preteen boys engaged in a slapping match.

"Incoming!" Daniel, crouched inside his wheeled laundry basket, flies through the space. It's a mystery how a six-foot, two-hundred-pound hockey player can squeeze into the thing, but he's headed straight for us, so I dive out of the way. Just in time, too, because in the next second, he knocks both Aiden and War down like they're bowling pins.

"Watch it," Brooks growls, looping an arm around me and pushing me behind him. "You almost took out my girlfriend."

I press my lips together to suppress a smile as all three guys gawk at the big brute. This is the first time he's claimed me in front of his friends, and that simple sentence alone makes me think I may need another round in the shower before dinner.

What the hell is happening to me?

"Aw, Saint. We're just playing." Daniel is propped up against the wall across from us, still inside his basket. He clutches the edges and squirms, trying to wiggle his way free, but his efforts are fruitless. All his movements do is cause the basket to roll one way, then the other. He throws an arm out for balance and shimmies again. When the basket tips, and he has to grab the wall to stay upright, he slumps back in it. "Can one of you help me?"

"No," Brooks says. His mouth is downturned and his brows are low. What is going on with my best friend? He's always the happy one, and we're watching Daniel Hall trying to wiggle his way out of a wheeling laundry basket. This is comedy gold.

I slide my phone out of my back pocket so I can get a shot of the buffoon around Brooks's massive shoulders. "Say cheese, Playboy!"

Hamming it up for the camera, he gives me his famous lopsided grin.

I've never been into younger men, but I guess I can see the appeal. His father, though? *God*, I can understand why Lake went after Daddy Hall. Ford is one hot dad.

War gets to his feet and offers Aiden a hand. "Let's get Leprechaun's laundry going. I'm starving. Dinner?"

I tuck my phone back into my pocket and step out from behind the protective wall of muscle still hovering in front of me. "Brooks is making dinner."

War waggles his brows. "Oh, Saint is pulling out all the stops. I'm coming over."

From his cart, Daniel is still huffing and puffing. "Is someone gonna help me out of here?"

Brooks clasps my hand and tugs. "No. Come on. We're late."

I dig in my heels and pull him back. It's not easy. The man is double my size and acting like a stubborn bull all of a sudden. "We're staying in. Who cares if we have dinner a little later?"

He clenches his jaw in response. God, angry Brooks is hot.

"You getting hangry?" I tease, pressing my hand to his cheek, hoping he'll relax.

On contact, his lids fall shut, and he pulls in a breath so deep it feels like he's sucked all the air from the room. His green eyes flutter open and lock on me for an instant, then he turns his attention to the men behind me. "Order a pizza. Sara can help you finish with your laundry if she wants, but then I'm making dinner at her place. No third wheels allowed."

"Aw, you want me all to yourself." I try for a light, teasing tone, but my heart is tripping over itself. Maybe he really did steal all the oxygen, because suddenly I'm lightheaded.

Brooks grasps my chin with his thumb and forefinger and watches me so intently it feels like an examination. His thumb brushes once, then twice, against my bottom lip before he murmurs, "Yeah, so what if I do?"

My swallow is heavy. I lick my lips, tracing the path where his thumb just ghosted.

Brooks shifts imperceptibly closer, leaving barely a breath between us, his pulse fluttering at the hollow of his throat.

"Yes!"

At Daniel's cheer, I jolt and dart back. Brooks does the same.

Aiden is laughing as Daniel finally stumbles out of the basket. The basket itself clatters to the ground loudly.

But War? His focus is trained on Brooks and me. His lips are parted in surprise and his eyes are wide. He looks like his thoughts mirror mine. I'm pretty sure Brooks almost kissed me. And nothing about the tension between us during that moment felt even remotely fake.

CHAPTER 18
Brooks

Me: Anyone want a roommate?

Beckett: Way too many people live in my house, so I love you, but duck no.

Gavin: I'm afraid to ask.

Aiden: Fuck you bro. I'm locking you out.

Gavin: LOL! OH, now I get it. Jill kicked Aiden out and now Aiden is cramping Brooks's style.

Aiden: Thanks for the play by play of my life dickhead.

Gavin: It was for Beckett. By the way, Sara now knows that your wife likes anal.

Beckett: Mention my wife and anal again and we're going to have a problem.

Beckett: Seriously, Aiden, run while you can. But get your own place. Brooks finally got the girl of his dreams. Don't ruin it for him.

Me: Well this has been…enlightening. I'm going to make dinner for "the girl of my dreams" now. Aiden, if you lock me out I'll be sure to tell everyone about your fear of bunnies.

Aiden: Fuck you. It's their damn eyes.

Gavin: I agree. Bunnies' eyes can be very scary. Especially when they're on their knees.

Aiden: You sick fuck.

Me: LOL No. Aiden is afraid of real bunnies.

Aiden: I'm coming up for dinner.

Me: You show up at this door and I'll punch you.

Beckett: Are we done here? Liv is giving me non-scary eyes and I'd really like to enjoy it.

Gavin: Dude, what the duck? Do you want me to picture your wife like that?

Beckett: Picture my wife like anything and I'll tell our brothers what you're really afraid of…

WHILE I'M interested in the secret fear Beckett is alluding to, the oil in the pan is crackling, signaling that it's time to put the chicken on the skillet. When I was a teenager, Aunt Zoe insisted I know how to prepare at least three meals. According to her, the knowledge would come in handy when I went to college, where I'd no longer have access to a whole host of staff like I was used to.

What I discovered when she taught me those three basic meals was that I really enjoyed cooking. In college, I cooked for the team once a week. It was a bonding activity.

Though I have no interest in having my teammates over while I hang with Sara tonight, it wouldn't be a bad idea to start up weekly dinners with the Bolts. I considered it years ago, but Coach talked me out of it. Convinced me to use that time to focus on the game.

At this point, I could give two shits about his opinion. And since I found out about Seb and Sara, things with the guys have felt a little off. This might be the perfect way to make sure we stay in sync as a team, and it wouldn't require including Coach in the activity. Not to mention cooking has always been soothing for me. Maybe it will help me get focused again.

I hate that my anger at Seb is affecting other parts of my life. I'm grumpy—which is so my oldest brother's MO, not mine—and I'm snapping far too much. Even War looked surprised at my outburst in the laundry room.

Or maybe he was reacting to the way I was staring at my best friend's lips like they were my salvation. God, I was practically panting for a taste.

We need rules. A set of parameters to remind me that what we're doing is for show. That my feelings for Sara have to remain on lockdown. I can't forget that the way she was looking at me down there—all heart eyes and soft smiles—wasn't real.

"What are you making?"

Her voice startles me, and the chicken slips from the tongs with a splat. The hot oil pops and hisses, singeing my skin.

"Fuck." I jump back and shake out my hand.

"Jeez, you know how much those hands are worth?" Sara yells, eating up the space between us. In a heartbeat, she's standing in front of me and tugging on my burned hand so she can inspect it. While she examines my almost microscopic injuries, I study her. Her vibrant blue eyes, her tiny nose, the wisps of blond hair that have escaped her messy updo.

When she brings my hand up and presses a kiss to my wrist, I suddenly understand why little boys always ask pretty girls to kiss it better. That simple gesture instantly takes away the sting. Probably because I can focus on nothing but the sensation of her soft lips on my skin and the electricity that arcs through me at the contact.

"I'm going to get the Neosporin. Step back from the stove. You're too important to the team to risk those hands on me."

As she walks away, her burnt-orange sweater falling off her shoulder and her perfect ass on display in a pair of black tights, I can't help but imagine my hands on every inch of her.

> War: What the hell is going on with you and Sara?

> Me: We're dating.

> War: So that's why coach was pissed?

> Me: I'm handling it.

> War: We have a game tomorrow. You need to lock that shit down before then. You know I love Sara, but this is your career.

My stomach sinks. Dammit.

Outside my brothers, War is my best friend. We went to college together and roomed together while we played in the NCAA. After two years, we were both called up to the NHL. We've been playing hockey together for over twelve years. Other than Aiden, there isn't a soul in the world who understands quite how much this game means to me.

If I could tell him the truth, he'd be devastated over my uncle's betrayal, just like I was. He respects him as much as I used to. Looks up to him. While he probably deserves to know what's going on, not only with Coach, but with me, Sara deserves her privacy more. She's putting her ass on the line for me, and she's mortified, because even though Seb lied to her, she was still the other woman.

And if the guys found out, they'd look at her differently. And then she'd probably start looking for another job. If she did that, I'd lose her. And I can't lose her.

I don't know how the fuck to respond to War, so I don't. He doesn't text again, thank fuck. He knows me well enough not to push it.

"C'mere."

Sara's soft voice startles me again. It's becoming a habit, getting lost in thoughts of her.

She's standing before me, Neosporin in hand. Still in my head, I let her take the lead.

"Lennox is coming to the game tomorrow. I kind of want to sit with her. Think Gavin would mind?"

I clear my throat and pull back so I can check on the chicken. It's crisping up nicely, and this time I concentrate on my movements when I turn it over to keep the oil from splashing.

"Not a problem. We have family seats too, if you'd rather sit there."

She ducks her head and blushes. "Yeah, I don't think that would be appropriate."

"Why? You're my girlfriend."

Her eyes go wide then, so I rush on, hoping to smooth things over.

"At least to everyone else."

"Yeah, but your mom sits there. I don't—" She shakes her head and looks away from me. "I'd rather sit near the team. That way I can still do my job. I just thought I could have Lennox there too."

"Whatever you prefer. Are you, uh..." My face goes hot, but I push through and ask the question. "Are you going to wear my jersey again?" This time I'm the one who looks away. I take the opportunity to slice into the cucumber I plan to add to the salad.

"If that's okay with you. I could wear Aiden's number if you'd prefer."

Instinctively, I clutch the knife handle and squeeze. It slips when I press down a little too violently on the cucumber.

Sara lets out a light laugh beside me. "Jeez, you're too easy to rile up." She pokes me in the side, then holds out a hand, silently urging me to give her the knife. When I do, she bumps me out of the way with a hip and takes over. "Who knew Saint Brooks had a jealous streak? If I wore Aiden's number, at least it would still be your last name on my back."

I blow out a breath and fold my arms across my chest, watching the smooth way she slices the cucumber into chunks. "The only number you'll wear is mine, understood?"

She peers over at me, batting her lashes dramatically. "Perfectly. Now, instead of worrying about which number will be emblazoned above my ass, how about you focus on those noodles? They're boiling over."

In the next instant, the telltale hiss of water dripping down the sides of the pot and onto the burner fills the kitchen. With a grunt, I spin and simultaneously turn down the heat and lift the lid off the pot.

I'm back to impersonating grumpy Beckett, but Sara is still laughing at my jealousy.

She's right to laugh. I've never been a jealous man. Especially when it comes to my brothers. But Sara is the exception. For everything. And she's the one person I won't share.

"We're playing in North Carolina next month. You going to visit your family while we're there?"

Across from me, fork midair, Sara pauses for a heartbeat, then shoves the food into her mouth. After she takes her time chewing, she picks up her glass of red wine. I've got a game tomorrow, so I opted for water, but I poured myself a small glass of wine too so she wouldn't feel awkward.

"Yeah, I'll stop by and see them during the day."

"Want me to get tickets for them? I could probably get your brother down on the ice before the game too."

Sara drops her attention to her plate and shakes her head. "No. They're not big hockey fans. No need to waste the seats on them."

"They're your family, Sar. You could spend more time with them if they came to the game, but if you don't think they'd enjoy it, that's fine. Will I get to meet them?"

She looks at me when she shakes her head this time, wearing a tight smile. Clearly, she doesn't want me to meet them.

I try not to let that truth claw at me. Yes, this relationship is fake, but we've been friends for over a year. Why is she so against me meeting her family?

"I just—I don't want to have to lie to them about us. But I don't want to tell them the truth either." She brings her glass to her lips again, but she can't hide the way her eyes dull as her fake smile slips. "My mom would be so disappointed if she found out about the affair."

I cup her hand on top of the table and squeeze. "You did nothing wrong."

"Intentional or not, I slept with another woman's husband."

It takes everything in me not to flinch when those words escape her. If I give away the disgust that hits me every time I think about her sleeping with my uncle, it will only make her feel worse. So I take in a deep breath, school my features, and rub my thumb over the back of her hand, focusing on how warm and soft her skin is rather than the images of these hands anywhere near my uncle.

She tips her glass and downs the rest of her wine in one go, then she pulls my glass toward her. "You're cute pouring yourself a glass so I wouldn't feel awkward."

With a laugh, I lean back and watch her. The wine has left her cheeks rosy. God, she looks so damn pretty sitting across from me. "True, you've done far more embarrassing things than drink wine by yourself."

She rolls her eyes and tilts her head. "Ha ha. You are *so* funny, Brookie baby."

I grunt at the annoyance stabbing me in the gut. "I thought we settled the nickname thing."

She licks her lips. Her tongue is stained red from the wine, making her that much more alluring. "Oh, you want me to call you secret lover?"

My dick hardens on the spot. I try to drag my focus away from her mouth, but the sexy smile she aims at me makes it difficult.

"Should I scream that tonight while I come? Make sure your uncle knows it's you who's taking me to the edge."

"Fuck, Sar." I'm at full mast instantly, and the pain in my chest is so acute I worry I'll need her to call the team doctor.

She stands and steps toward me, never taking her blazing blue eyes off me. "Or should I yell your name? Or maybe number thirteen?"

I clutch the edge of the table to keep from reaching out for her as she saunters past me. With a hum, she stops behind me, then her lips are grazing the shell of my ear. "Is that what the bunnies yell when you make them come?"

"Sara," I grit out, my knuckles going white. If I let go now, I'll reach behind me, pull her over my lap, and spank her ass for turning me on like this when she knows damn well I can't do anything about it.

"Oh, right," she whispers, her lips ghosting my neck, sending goose bumps rippling across every inch of my skin. "You don't fu*ck* during the season."

The way she says it, enunciating the *ck*, makes my balls tighten. I want her so goddamn bad I might lose it.

"Brookie it is, I guess."

Sara's warmth disappears from my shoulder, and she shifts behind me, as if she's going back to her spot. Without giving myself time to second-guess the move, I grab her wrist and tug her close. I slap her hand to my chest, making sure her palm is flat against my beating heart. The move is so fast her body collides with my chair and her head snaps back. When she steadies herself, her cheeks are flushed and her eyes are bright.

"You'll call me Saint when you come, because I'm a goddamn saint for not spreading you across this table right now and eating you until you forget all those goddamn nicknames you love teasing me with."

Sara gapes for a moment, her lips parted and her chest heaving, but she's finally speechless. Then she blinks once, twice, three times, and lets out a light laugh. "Saint it is."

CHAPTER 19
Brooks

IT ISN'T until I'm standing in front of my door after having said goodnight to Sara that I realize I don't have my keys. Though I wish he'd go home, Aiden is likely still here, so I ring the doorbell. When he doesn't answer, I bang on the door, but I'm met with only silence. When I call him and he doesn't pick up, I let him know just how annoyed I am in my message.

Fuck.

My next attempt is War, but he doesn't pick up either. It's already after ten, and because of Coach's curfew, they shouldn't be out, which means they're likely already asleep.

Double fuck.

With a long breath out, I spin and stuff my hands into my pockets. I've been gone a whole five minutes, so Sara is definitely still up. When I reach her door, I knock.

"Coming!" she shouts.

She doesn't immediately open the door, so I try the knob. Sure enough, it's open. "Sorry, Sar. Lost my keys and Aiden locked me out." I close the door quietly behind me and scan my surroundings, trying to determine where I might have set them down. "Mind if I hang on your couch until—"

"Yes, Brooks!" she shouts from the other room. Her tone is breathy and strange and followed by a loud bang.

"You okay?"

"Harder, Brooks. You can do better than that."

I can?

Scratching at my jaw, I assess her bedroom door. What the hell is she talking about? I step closer, hoping she can hear me. "Sar, do you want me to come in there?"

"Yes! Yes!" she screams.

The urgency in her response makes my stomach flip. I turn the knob, not really sure what to expect, and curse when I find Sara kneeling on her bed, hands on the headboard and completely bare from the waist down.

"Yes, Brooks. Harder. Right there, baby." She rattles the headboard and throws her head back with a moan.

It takes me a minute to figure out what I'm actually seeing. My jaw is on the floor and my heart is racing as I realize that this is real life. Sara is really in front of me, straddling a dildo, bobbing up and down, bare ass rocking.

And she's shouting *my* name.

Glued to the spot, all I can do is watch. "Holy fuck."

She whips her head my way, her blond hair flying, and her eyes go wide. "Oh my God, Brooks," she screams. "I'm going to come!"

The torment on her face makes it clear that she's mortified, but also that she can't really stop it.

Clarity falls over me like a shroud in that moment. I have two options. I could turn around and walk out that door. If I do, she'll forever be weird around me. Or I could say fuck it and make sure she owns it.

There's no way in hell I'm missing this, so the decision is pretty easy. "Show me, Pumpkin. Show me how beautiful you are when you come."

She closes her eyes, and a deep flush steals up her neck and into her cheeks. She's embarrassed. I hate seeing that expression on her face, so I stalk toward her, determined to ease her suffering.

"May I?" I point to her mattress and lift a brow.

She nods but makes no other noise.

The bed dips when I press one knee to it, then the other. Slowly, so as not to scare her off, I slip in closer, taking in the supplies she has spread out. A bottle of lube is on its side beside her, along with two more toys.

"Can I touch you?" My entire body trembles in anticipation, but my voice is miraculously steady.

When she nods, I push the hair that's fallen forward out of her face and press a kiss against the spot where her sweater's fallen off her shoulder. Cinnamon and sugar dance on my tongue. God, she's the sweetest goddamn thing I've ever tasted.

The most enchanting moan escapes her throat. If the press of my lips to her shoulder elicits that kind of sound, I can't wait to see what else I can do.

"Can I use the wand, Pumpkin?"

Another jerky nod.

I pick it up and turn it on, relishing the way it vibrates in my hand.

Her legs are still spread wide over the dildo, so I take advantage of the access to her inner thigh and press the wand to the sensitive skin there.

She shudders, and goose bumps cascade down her legs.

I angle in closer and bring my mouth to her ear. "Fuck, Sar. Your ass is insane. If you were really mine, I'd be counting down the seconds until I could fuck it."

"Oh God, I'd want that," she whimpers. They're the first words she's spoken since the moment she saw me standing in her doorway, and they leave me hard as a rock.

"Now's not the time to go quiet on me. I want the whole building to hear your screams. We'll use a plug next time so we can fill all these holes, but right now, you just have the wand and my hands. What do you want?"

"The wand in my pussy and your finger in my ass."

I slap her ass cheek and have to clamp down on my lip at the way it jiggles in response. Fuck, she's perfect.

I set the wand down and slide my hands beneath her shirt and up her sides, stopping at her ribcage, where I caress her warm skin. "That's my good girl. And what about these tits, Sar? Can I touch them while I get you off?"

"Please," she begs.

I slide one hand between her thighs and remove the dildo. "You're fucking dripping."

Sara looks at me over her shoulder, her lips parted and her eyes hazy. It takes everything in me not to take her mouth and kiss her. That act would be tame in comparison to what I've done up until this point, but it feels like crossing a line, and my sense of self-preservation is strong.

If I kiss her while she's naked on the bed and soaked for me, I don't think I could stop myself from kissing her everywhere else. Or from licking that sweet cunt. From sliding inside it.

And then I'd be done for. She'd own me, and I'd break my own damn heart, because I don't own her.

"Your words do this to me, Brooks. And the way you're touching me. It's you who makes me this wet." Her words, said in that throaty rasp, are so damn intoxicating. The sexy tease that she is, she fucking knows exactly what she's doing. Damn, is it a turn-on that she isn't shy when it comes to sex. That she enjoys it. That she asks for what she wants and then fucking takes it.

But even more than that, I like being the one who gives it to her.

When I slide my middle finger inside her, she clamps down on me and hisses.

"Yes. Please, more." Finally over the blip of embarrassment that hit her, she rocks her hips back and shakes that perfect ass.

"Grab the wand, Pumpkin. I want you to fuck that pussy for me while I play with your tits."

I need both of my hands on her for a moment. Need to squeeze her delicious tits, to play with her nipples. Hands splayed along her warm skin, I work my way up her thighs. I pause at her hips when she hasn't made a move for her wand. The look she shoots me over her shoulder is pure heat. And without another second of hesitation, she grabs the toy from where I left it between her knees.

Good girl. It's like she can read my mind.

I love that she's obedient. I would have bet my life savings that she'd be nothing but sass in bed. But no, she's completely surprised me by allowing me to be dominant here.

Pressing gentle kisses against her shoulder, I glide my hands across her tits. I take my time rubbing and tugging on her nipples. All the while, she writhes in front of me, fucking the wand just like I asked. Her moans get louder when I bite down on her shoulder.

"That's my girl. Let everyone hear what a good little bunny you are for me. Fucking your toy because I told you to. You're greedy for my cock, aren't you?" I murmur into her skin. "You're gonna have to get used to it. I won't let you have it yet."

"*Yet,*" she pants.

My dick is like granite, and my mind is a mess of lust and need. I clamp my teeth on her shoulder and breathe in deep to quell the urge to touch myself, just to relieve the pressure. "Needy girl. You feeling empty?"

"Stop teasing me and give me those damn hands." Her words are loud this time, so I reward her with a slap to one ass cheek. In response, she screams. The sound goes straight to my balls. Fuck. She does exactly what I want, all without being told. So I reward her again with a slap to the other cheek. Then I shift back and smooth both globes with my palms.

"Since you asked so nicely." I swat the wand away and slide two fingers inside her. Slowly, I fuck her, pulling almost all the way out before sliding back in to the knuckles. When I pull out again, I fully intend to slip those wet fingers back and play with her other hole, but at the sight of her arousal coating my skin, I can't resist the urge to taste her. I remove my hand with a groan and bring my fingers to my mouth.

She arches back, her focus locked on my hand as I lick my fingers. "Holy fuck, that's hot."

"Fuck, Sar." I moan, swiping at one finger. "I want to feast on you. You taste so goddamn good."

I slip my fingers inside her again, and this time, once they're coated, I brush them against her tight hole. She relaxes for me, then leans forward and opens wider. My vision goes hazy as I slide my thumb inside her and dig my fingers into the flesh of her ass.

"Right there, Brooks. Right fucking there," she pleads.

"Not going anywhere, Pumpkin. Keep teasing yourself with that wand." Brushing kisses across her neck and shoulder, I circle her throat with my free hand. With a final nip to her skin, I bring my mouth to her ear. "Now fucking scream for me."

Sara shatters in my arms, shuddering and trembling. She continues to fuck her wand while I play with her ass. Cheeks flushed and body covered in goose bumps, she chants my name over and over, all while banging the headboard against the wall as loud as she can. It's the most perfect fucking sight. I'm leaking inside my jeans just waiting for the moment I can get home and replay our night with my hand wrapped around my cock.

When her body goes limp, I press one more gentle kiss against her shoulder. "You were perfect." Gently, I release her and support her as she slumps to the mattress. Then I head to the bathroom to clean up.

When I come back, Sara is curled up with her head on her pillow and her sheet pulled up to her chin, wearing a lazy smile. "Not gonna lie, Brooks. You've got me completely spent."

I let out a low chuckle and hang my head between my shoulders. I can't look at her right now. She's too beautiful. Too perfect. More than anything, I want to sink down on the bed next to her, pull her close, and hold her all night.

But that's not in the cards.

I point to the door. "I'm going to sleep on the couch."

She jackknifes up, and the sheets fall down a bit. Before I get a glimpse of her gorgeous tits, she slaps a hand to her chest, holding the sheet to her body. I try to hide my disappointment. I've had her breasts in my hands, and I've felt them beneath my fingertips, but I've never laid eyes on them.

"I can take care of you if you want. I feel—"

I shake my head and wave her off. "I'm good. Seriously. I'm used to the no sex during the season thing."

Really, I'm used to the no sex at all thing, but she doesn't need to know that. Right now, it feels harder than ever to abide by that rule. Probably because my gorgeous best friend has never been naked and offering to pleasure me before.

"Brooks," Sara chides.

"Sar," I mimic.

She closes her eyes and falls back against the pillow with a sigh. "Fine. I'll just get all the orgasms, and you can continue to watch."

"Not the punishment you think it is, Pumpkin."

With a giggle, she settles on her side. "Night, not so secret lover."

"Good night, Sar."

As I'm crossing the threshold into the living room, she calls for me. "Why are you sleeping on my couch?"

"Aiden locked me out."

"Brooks," she says, rolling to her back again. "You have a game tomorrow. You're not sleeping on the couch. Come here." She pats the mattress beside her.

I don't move from my spot at the door.

"Seriously, you can fuck my ass with your fingers, but you can't cuddle me? We cuddle all the time."

I let out a deep sigh and rub at the back of my neck. "It's because I fucked your ass with my fingers that I now can't cuddle you."

"No." The single word is said with such force, so defiantly, it nearly knocks me back.

I swallow past my confusion. "Excuse me?"

"No. I don't agree to those terms. We're best friends first. You promised nothing would get weird. So get in this fucking bed and cuddle me, or I'm not speaking to you again."

Amused shock ricochets through me. "You're serious?"

She juts her chin, arms crossed over her chest, gaze angry and determined.

My heart doesn't know whether to hide away or leap in my chest, but I shuffle back to the bed. "Fine. But no talking about my hard cock in the morning."

With her sheet clutched to her chest, she scoots over, making space for me. Though trepidation has replaced the bravery that hit me when I first stepped into the room, I stand beside the bed and slip off my sweater and the T-shirt underneath, then my jeans. When all that's left is a pair of black boxers, I slide in beside her.

Head on the pillow, I pull her close.

"You're really pretty, Brooks," she whispers, settling her cheek against my chest.

My heart is galloping with so much violence, its pounding rhythm will probably keep us both awake.

Even so, I press a kiss to her forehead and close my eyes. "Go to sleep, Pumpkin."

CHAPTER 20
Sara

THE MOMENT I wake up I wiggle my ass against Brook's very obvious erection. "Is there a tree in this bed, or are you just happy to see me?"

He groans and clamps down on my hip to still my movements.

"What do you call morning wood that wakes you up?"

"Sara."

I laugh. "No. Alarm cock."

He nuzzles into my neck. Then, with a growl, he nibbles at the place where my neck and shoulder meet.

I yelp and push back into him further. "You want me to take care of that? We could give your uncle another show this morning."

"How is it that twelve hours ago, you were the hottest fucking thing I've ever seen, but right now you're driving me nuts?"

I hum, tucking away those words—*hottest fucking thing*—to analyze later. "It's impressive, isn't it? A real talent. But you know what else I'm talented at? Sucking cock. You should let me show you." I attempt to spin in his arms, but he tightens his grip. "Brooks!"

"*Saint.* We've been over this. I'm a goddamn saint for not flipping you over and fucking you senseless for the way you're rubbing your sexy little bare ass against my very erect, as you've pointed out, penis."

"Oh my God." Laughter bubbles out of me, and I throw my head back on the pillow. "You just said penis. So technical." I take a deep breath to calm myself and peek over at him. Then, channeling my inner sex kitten, I whisper, "Please, Saint. Fuck me with your erect phallus."

He huffs and glowers at me. "Are you done yet?"

"Stick it between my silky folds and puncture my vagina."

His face screws up in a look of pure revulsion. "What the fuck kinda dirty talk did you and Coach partake in?" He palms his forehead. "Never mind. Don't answer that."

I laugh. "Nah. I got the terms from the romance books I read. You'd be surprised by the words people use to describe their nether regions." I wiggle against him again and rest my head on my pillow. "Thanks for not getting weird on me after last night."

Brooks snuggles into the space between my shoulder and neck. "You're weird enough for the both of us."

"True." I hum.

As silence falls between us, I replay last night. Unlike some of the books I've read, Brooks has no problem with the dirty talk. Fuck. His words are now the official soundtrack to all the images in my spank bank.

I clear my throat, hoping the action also clears away the lust that's just started to swirl inside me. "You nervous about the game tonight?"

"Nah. But I should get moving. I have a lot to do."

The clock on my nightstand reads 6:55 a.m. "What in the hell do you have to do at this hour?"

"I start every morning before a home game at the diner."

Oh, hockey players and their superstitions. I didn't grow up around hockey. Until I was hired by Langfield Corp, I'd never watched a single game. Early on, when I mentioned that to Liv, she slapped a hand over my mouth, peered over her shoulder, and told me never to repeat it.

So then I went in the opposite direction and told Brooks and the guys that I'm a rabid hockey fan. When they questioned me, I swore I knew all the ins and outs. That resulted in me having to look up every little thing he and his friends talked about.

Why I didn't just come out with it and tell the truth—that I'm a regular, everyday girl with some knowledge but not a ton—is beyond me. It probably has something to do with how I turn into a whack job when I'm nervous. I just start talking, and sometimes I talk myself right into a corner.

"Would you want to come to breakfast with me, Pumpkin?"

The question throws me for a loop. Partly because I was in my head again, but also because I've never gone to breakfast with him before a game. Wouldn't my presence interrupt his ritual? I wiggle my way to my other side so I can face him. "Are you sure that's wise?"

Brooks clears his throat and takes a deep breath. "Sar, you're currently naked in my arms."

With a grin, I peek down. "Well, look at that. Spoiler alert, I don't wear clothes to bed. Why bother? You've already been near my ass."

His laugh is like a hit of serotonin, instantly relaxing me. When I woke up, I silently panicked, sure he would act weird about last night.

Maybe we can have fun while we're faking things. I certainly wouldn't mind returning the favor. My best friend is hot. And last night, he proved that he's not just a pretty face. The man knows what he's doing with those fingers. And those thighs? God, I can only imagine what they're capable of. The power in that tight, toned body. The stamina.

Suddenly salivating, I lick my lips and eye his ripped chest. In the middle of my perusal, his dick thumps against my belly. Instantly, heat pools in my core, and I have to bite down on my lip to hold back a groan.

"Okay," he says, his voice tight. "I'm getting out of bed."

He releases me, but this time I'm the one clinging to him. With more strength than I knew I possessed, I push him onto his back. Then I straddle him so that he'll have to throw me if he wants to move. His hands fall against the mattress and he fists the sheets. "Sar, you're fucking—"

When he doesn't finish the sentence, I wiggle atop him. "I'd like to be fucking, but someone won't let me."

His focus lowers inch by inch from my face to my chest. He swallows thickly, his Adam's apple working, then he drags his gaze back up to my face again, wide-eyed and heaving, as if he shouldn't be looking at me. The sheet has fallen and I'm bare as the day I was born, completely on display and not ashamed in the least. What's there to be ashamed of? I have great tits. He should stare.

"You're fucking gorgeous, Sara."

Butterflies take flight in my belly at the awe in his tone.

"The most beautiful woman I've ever seen." He focuses on me as he confesses, his full attention locked on my face. Like he really wants me to hear his every word. He's so damn respectful, even when he's literally talking about how gorgeous he thinks I am while I'm naked and straddling him.

This man is a gem.

"Fine, I'll go to breakfast with you." I dismount quickly, throwing one leg over him, and hop off the bed. At the bathroom door, I throw a look over my shoulder and find him staring at my ass.

With a saucy wink, I give it a little shake, then continue on my way.

Twenty minutes later, dressed and with my hair pulled back in a ponytail—tight on the top but curly in the back, to change things up—I'm damn proud of how put together I am. It's not even eight a.m. on a Saturday, and I'm ready to walk out the door. I'm patting myself on the back when Brooks walks into my apartment wearing a goddamn navy suit.

"I thought we were going to the diner."

He holds the door open and nods for me to exit. "We are."

"Brooks Langfield," I chide, digging for my keys so I can lock the door. "Not once in the time I've known you have you acted like the cajillinoaire you are until this very moment."

He frowns and runs his palm over his hair, smoothing the already perfect style.

I spin and take off toward the elevator. "No one wears a freaking suit to the diner."

"I wear one every time." He eats up the distance between us with his long legs, and in three strides, he's walking beside me.

I don't say anything while we wait at the elevator bank, but I keep my focus trained on him. He'll figure it out if I give him a minute.

It doesn't take long before he goes ramrod straight in acknowledgment, and half a second later, he drops his head forward and sags. "I wore a suit every time I went to breakfast *with my uncle.*"

I step closer and tug on his lapels, forcing him to look at me. "If you *want* to wear a suit, that's okay."

His eyes fall shut, and he grimaces like he's in pain. "It's like I'm unlearning everything I was ever taught. I've been doing it forever. Putting on this suit, walking into that diner. Fuck, we were like gods. But we treated everyone with respect. Or at least I thought I did. Maybe—"

I lift on my toes and press a finger to his lips. "You've always been the best person in every room. He didn't make you that way." I tug on the fabric again. "But neither did this suit. Choice is yours. You get to choose who you want to be now. And I won't judge your decision. Swear it."

He lowers his forehead to mine. For a long moment, we stay like that, me holding on to his suit jacket, his head resting against mine, like he's literally leaning on me for support. "I think I'm going to change."

"Okay."

He presses a kiss to my nose, and my heart trips over itself.

"What other pregame superstitions do you have?"

We're sitting in the back, mostly out of view of other diners. When we walked in, every person we encountered greeted him warmly. The waitress's smile faltered for only a moment when she caught sight of me. She recovered quickly and was nothing but pleasant when she waved us back to Brooks's usual spot. On our way there, customer after customer said hello, shook his hand, and wished him good luck tonight. One or two even hollered *you bringing us the Cup again this year?*

As we sat, me facing Brooks and him facing the restaurant, he was at ease, like this was an everyday occurrence. I, on the other hand, itched and fidgeted, certain that every person in the place would be watching us through the entire meal.

Is this how his life is all the time? Normally, we hang out in one of our apartments or at the Bolts' bar, where regular fans can't congregate. It didn't hit me until this moment that I've never really witnessed his day-to-day life.

"I'll go for a jog when we get home. When it gets too cold, I hit up the gym so I can run on the treadmill. Just to loosen my legs up a bit. Nothing strenuous. Plus, running helps clear my head. I take a nap in the afternoon, followed by sitting in my apartment in the quiet, visualizing the game." He peels back the paper ring holding the napkin and silverware together. "The plays I'll make. I walk through every scenario and consider the ways I'll block the puck. Then music an hour before the game."

My chest aches with affection at his sincerity. "Do you have a playlist?"

One side of his mouth ticks up, and he pulls his phone from his pocket. He knows me so well. He knows how nosy I am and that I'm itching to see the songs he's put together. Without a word, without a single instruction or warning about what I can or can't look at, he slides the device across the table to me.

God, he's such a good guy. One day some woman is going to be incredibly lucky to have him.

And for just a moment, I'd like to practice Brooks's visualization tactics and imagine scratching her eyes out.

The waitress appears beside us, and I order pumpkin pancakes with candied walnuts and extra whipped cream. When she slides her pad into her apron without taking Brooks's order, I frown at her, then at him.

"Don't you have to order?"

The woman hovering at the end of the table shakes her head. "Six egg-white omelet with sautéed veggies. A side of turkey bacon and whole wheat toast. And a glass of orange juice and black coffee."

My face sours. "That's—"

Brooks laughs and splays one hand on the sticky table in front of him. "You know what? She's right. Make it a bacon and cheddar omelet, breakfast potatoes, and rye toast."

The waitress blinks a couple of times, but she nods quickly and yanks her order pad from her apron again. "Of course, Brooks. I'll put that right in."

I bite my lip to contain my glee. Because Robotic Brooks is breaking down. He doesn't need to change. He's the most incredible man. But he should be living his life for himself. Not for Seb.

He deserves to make choices based on what he wants, not who his uncle molded him to be. The important parts of Brooks won't change, regardless of what he eats or how he dresses.

The good, kind human he is, the funny guy who makes me smile even when I'm feeling down, has nothing to do with his uncle. He didn't create the man who snuggles me whether I'm naked and in bed or in sweats and eating sweets on the couch.

"Pretty proud of yourself right now, aren't you?" he teases, his green eyes warm and the skin at his temples crinkling with happiness. He's dressed in a gray Henley now. The way it stretches across his chest is doing funny things to my insides. Especially now that I know what it's like to sleep on the expanse of it. Even though he's covered in muscles—literally ripped in a way I didn't think was humanly possible—he's soft too.

All of North America knows what Brooks looks like in nothing but his underwear, since he's modeled quite a few varieties on billboards and in magazines. But to be pressed up against his warm, smooth skin, to hear the steady heartbeat beneath those muscles— that's a whole other level of hotness.

"Just like seeing my best friend relaxed, is all. Speaking of rituals...I need you to do me a favor."

He arches his brow and tips forward.

"Pull off a shutout tonight."

With a snort, he falls back against the booth's cushion. "Sure, no problem."

Smiling, I slap the table in front of me. "Come on, I need you totally focused on this. When you're doing your visualizations, do not visualize a single puck going through those thick, beautiful thighs of yours."

"Thick, beautiful thighs, huh?" He sets his forearms on the table. "Is this from another one of your books?"

We're beaming at one another now. In our own little corner at the back of the diner, I'm the happiest I've been in who knows how long.

"Pfft. Work with me here."

He leans forward again, ducking his head a little. "Okay, Sar. But for the record, I never visualize any puck making it into my net."

Satisfied with his answer, I lean back and cross my arms over my chest. "Good."

Pushing his lips to one side, he regards me, studying every inch of my face. "That's all? Good? Ya gonna tell me why you want a shutout tonight?"

I lean in close, dropping my forearms to the table to match his posture. "Because," I whisper, tamping down that glee again, "then you'll be forced to give me an orgasm the night before every game."

CHAPTER 21

Brooks

"WELCOME TO THE JUNGLE," War mouths along with Axl Rose, spinning to snatch up his compression shirt.

We're in the locker room, getting ready for the game, our game-day playlist in full swing now.

Daniel, who's playing an air guitar, falls to his knees, head banging as he goes.

The laughter that escapes me echoes even over the earsplitting music. This is exactly what I need to get me out of the funk I've been in—my boys. Coach normally leaves us alone while we suit up, but he'll be in here soon enough to give his pregame talk.

I can only guess he'll pull me aside and give me hell after the sounds Sara made against his bedroom wall last night. A chuckle breaks through me when I'm struck with a memory of the look on his face when he stepped inside the diner this morning. For an instant, he lit up, but just as quickly, his bright expression fell. Probably when he realized I wasn't wearing a damn suit. Then the look went murderous. That was the moment he noticed that I wasn't alone in the booth he and I normally occupy. He turned right around and stormed out, leaving Sara unaware of the entire encounter.

Maybe it's wrong, but knowing he was uncomfortable fills me

with a sense of satisfaction. My goal is to make him as uncomfortable as possible until he has no choice but to leave. As the Guns N' Roses song comes to an end, every guy in the room starts snapping. We all know precisely what comes next.

Not yet in his skates, but already donning his uniform and socks, Aiden jumps up onto the bench and starts his a cappella version of Flo Rida's "My House." Like he does with any song he sings, Aiden comes up with his own lyrics, and he raps the words rather than singing them.

> *"Welcome to the Bolts' house*
> *Brooks will take the net now*
> *My wingers never slow down*
> *War will take you out*
> *Welcome to the Bolts' house*
> *Parker gonna show you how*
> *We got the best defense now,*
> *and then War gonna take you out*
>
> *Sink the puck in the net, I like it wet.*
> *Block the puck, Saint, we are the best*
> *Wipe the floor with the other team*
> *Yeah, you know the fans will scream*
>
> *Gravy's in the back*
> *And Playboy's by my side*
> *Yeah, War gon' attack*
> *And Slick gon' spin in*
> *Welcome to the Bolts' house."*

By the end, we're all singing along and breaking it down, the energy in the locker room out of control. Aiden isn't team captain, but he might as well be. He may drive me fucking nuts half the time, but he's a leader, and he beats to his own damn drum.

The guys come to me when they need a steady head to help work through shit, but on the ice, Aiden's a natural leader. His skill is unmatched.

For a moment, I allow myself to get caught up in how proud I am of him. And how grateful I am that I get to play hockey with him.

"You okay?" War turns, putting his back to the rest of the guys who are now tying up their skates and bullshitting with each other.

I blow out a breath. "I'm good, man."

The second my shoulders relax, my uncle enters, and his steely gaze immediately finds me. I don't allow myself to tense up again. Instead, I drop to the bench and lace up my own skates, wanting as little interaction with him as I can get.

All that matters is the game.

Sara's request from this morning filters into my mind, so I close my eyes and go back to visualizing. Tuning out all the noise. I wouldn't mind a repeat of last night, and if she wants to use my hockey superstitions as an excuse to let me touch her again, then I'll happily get on board with that.

CHAPTER 22

Sara

"DAMN, girlie. Brooks is going to come in his pants when he sees you wearing his jersey."

With a squeal, I spin around and throw my arms out.

Lennox launches herself into my arms, her platinum blond hair swinging back and forth in its high ponytail as we sway from side to side, holding tight to each other. Her sugary scent permeates the air, hitting me with a dose of pure elation.

"You smell like a candy shop."

She pulls back, grasping my biceps, and shimmies her shoulders. "Thanks. I snagged the bottle and the lotion as my last F-U when I left the spa."

"Wait." My stomach flips over. "I thought you loved that job?"

Until this moment, I thought Lennox was still working for a nationwide chain of upscale spas. She traveled to each one to help them pick their stock.

With a huff, she throws her head back. "I did. But then I may have told Janine that she swallowed too many kids, and that's why everything that comes out of her mouth is childish. HR wasn't a fan of that."

I snort. "You did not."

"Sar," she says, popping one hip, "she sucked. You know it takes a lot to get me to that point."

I tip my chin down and scrutinize her, my lips pressed into a straight line.

She holds up her hands and takes a step back. "Fine. Okay, I'm always like that. I can't help it if I'm incapable of lying. You see this face?" She moves one pale pink nail in a circle in front of her. "It conveys all my thoughts, with or without my permission."

With a laugh, I turn back to my mirror. We need to leave for the arena in ten minutes, and the nerves are starting to eat at me. I still haven't decided whether to tell Lennox the truth or stick to the fib that Brooks and I are really dating.

I trust her with my life and every one of my secrets, but Brooks and I haven't discussed the idea of cluing her in to the ruse, and if I do so without checking in with him first, it feels like I'd be betraying him. That is the last thing I want to do, but I don't know if I can openly lie to my bestie.

"You look..."

She taps her finger against her chin and circles behind me, taking me in. I focus on my reflection and finishing my makeup, but her scrutiny is like a physical touch. It's impossible to ignore the way she's studying me.

"You got laid."

"No I didn't." The words escape me far too quickly. Before they're even out, I realize I've made a huge error.

"Oh." She nods. "You're right. You didn't." With a step closer, she lifts one brow. "But you did have a male-induced orgasm."

She's eerily good at this game. In college, she could tell a girl exactly what she'd done the night before, down to which hand the guy used to get her off. I'm not sure anyone would call it a talent, but it's certainly a skill she's perfected.

I cover my mouth with a palm to hide the way my lips tip up as she pushes even closer.

"And he used a toy." In my periphery, her eyes go wide, and she clings to my arm. "Oh my God. He touched your ass."

"How the hell do you do that?" I huff out an annoyed sigh and spin so I can stare her down. "It was Brooks. We're a thing now, so don't be weird about it."

With an ear-piercing squeal, she throws her arms around me. "Oh, thank fuck. I was nervous it was Seb doing the ass stuff, and honestly, Brooks is so much hotter."

"And nicer. That's the important part, Lenny. He's a nice guy."

"With huge hands. That's gotta mean—"

I slap a hand over her mouth. "Please do not start talking about my boyfriend's dick."

I can feel her smile beneath my fingers, and her eyes light up. It's impossible not to grin right back at her.

"You're really happy," she says when I pull my hand away, going all mushy on me.

I have to look away before I admit the truth. Yes, I am really happy. And unfortunately, it's fake.

"'Scuse us. We're just going to see her boyfriend." Lennox steps right up in front of the security guard, hands on hips.

Behind her, I shake my head and flash my badge. My best friend is ridiculous. She's done that to every person we've seen.

"Hey, Sar," he says with a chuckle.

"Evening, Stu. How are Laney and the baby?"

In response to my question, he pulls out his phone and taps the screen, then turns it toward me. His chest puffs out a bit as I take in a picture of his new baby.

"She's adorable. Hope she's sleeping for you."

"She's an angel," he admits, wearing a soft expression so contradictory to his size and the security uniform he's wearing. "Enjoy the game."

"Oh, we will. Her boyfriend is going to dedicate a goal to her," Lennox says.

Stu squints at her, but he's polite and keeps his mouth shut.

With a groan, I shake my head. "She's joking. She grew up watching hockey. She knows goalies don't score goals."

Lennox shakes her head. "Of course I know that. But now that he's your boyfriend, I'm pretty sure Saint Brookie can do anything he puts his mind to."

I pull her by the elbow, waving bye to Stu. "Tone it down. Remember, I'm working *right* now."

"Technically," she drawls, "you work after the game. When it's time to deal with the press. Attending the game is a perk."

I drop her elbow and sigh. She's not wrong. It's why Brooks told me to sit in the WAG section tonight.

"Just be good when we go down to the ice. I want to check in with Gavin before the game. Then you can go back to being your obnoxious self."

Grinning, she loops her arm through mine and rests her head on my shoulder. "It's so good to be home."

"You don't live here." I drop my head to hers and soak in how good it feels to have her with me, even if it's temporary.

"Boston will always be my home." Her tone is wistful. It's so unlike my always loud and extreme friend, it gives me pause. When she gets quiet, it means she's really in her feelings.

"You can stay with me whenever you want."

She snuggles closer. "No, you need space to boink your new boy toy."

"Oh my God. Who says boink?"

"It's like the new *it* saying. I read it in *Jolie*."

"You did not. *Jolie* would never print that garbage."

"You're right." She laughs as I push open the gate to the team bench. "But we could totally make it a thing. Especially now that you're the future *Mrs. Brooks Langfield*."

I suck in a sharp breath and then choke on my own saliva only to find every man in the vicinity staring.

The boys are already on the ice, thank God, so the number of people is far smaller than it could be. Just outside the bench area, chaos ensues as spectators crowd the glass, trying to get a good look at their favorite players before they're forced to take their seats for the game.

Of course, Seb didn't miss Lennox's loudmouth insanity or my choking, and he stands with his arms crossed, eyes narrowed to slits. I swallow past the lump in my throat and pull my shoulders back. I won't let him intimidate me.

Next to Seb, Gavin is dressed in a suit and watching the guys on the ice, completely oblivious to my predicament.

"Be good," I whisper to my best friend.

She swallows her smile and nods.

"Hey, Gavin. Seb." I keep the words clipped and my tone professional.

Gavin gives me a warm smile, but Seb's expression remains dark.

"Puck bunnies aren't allowed on the bench."

Gavin reels back and swivels his head, blinking at Seb. Before he can speak, I take control of the conversation. "Not here to distract Brooks. Just making sure Gavin doesn't need anything before Lennox and I find our seats."

Gavin brightens at the mention of Lennox. "Oh shit." He laughs. "If it isn't Lennox Kennedy all grown up."

She lowers herself in a ridiculous curtsy, and his smile grows as he pulls her in for a hug.

"Aiden know you're here?"

Her smile falters for a half a second, but then it's back and as bright as ever. "No. We didn't really keep in touch."

He nods, but his smile remains. "You should come by the bar after. I'm sure he'd love to see you."

"Oh, I go wherever this girl goes." She thumbs in my direction.

His lighthearted demeanor evaporates, and the look he gives me is full of sincerity. "Make sure you're there."

"Of course," I squeak. I consider this man a friend. He's easy to be around. But suddenly, I'm breaking out in a cold sweat under his attention.

Brooks skates over and pulls up his mask. "Hey, Pumpkin. Hey, Lennox."

"Oh my God. He calls you Pumpkin." Lennox splays a hand over her heart. "Gavin, did you hear that? He called her Pumpkin!"

Gavin stuffs his hands into his pockets and rocks back on his heels. "That he did. Good luck, Brooks. Looking good out there."

Seb breaks into the conversation, all glowers and sharp words. "Enough fooling around, thirteen. Drop and give me a hundred."

Brooks grits his teeth, his jaw going rigid, but he doesn't dare fight Seb. Even as Gavin looks back and forth between the men, wearing a confused frown.

Once he's tugged his helmet off, Brooks drops his stick to the ice and follows it down.

As he begins his count, women on the other side of the glass hoot and holler, and by the time he hits twenty, a crowd has formed.

Brooks pauses then and lifts his chin and hits me with a grin. "Hop on, Pumpkin. I could use a more challenging workout."

Without hesitation, I throw a leg over the boards. Seb grasps my elbow but releases it quickly when Gavin pulls him back. "Let her be. The crowd is going to eat this up."

Cheeks heating at all the attention, I settle my ass on my man's back. "You sure about this, thirteen?"

He chuckles, glancing at me over his shoulder. "If it means getting close to that ass, then absolutely."

Laughter rolls through me as he takes me up and down, all while Seb stews behind his iPad. After twenty push-ups, he snaps up straight and storms away.

Daniel and Tyler skate circles around us, spinning and dancing with one another like figure skaters, making the scene even more ridiculous. The crowd is almost deafening as they count along with Brooks.

When we reach one hundred, Tyler stops in front of me and offers me a hand. I take it and let him haul me to my feet. Once I'm steady on the ice, he skates backward, dipping his hand as if he's my knight in a shining hockey uniform, and then Brooks hops up with ease, like he isn't covered in a thick layer of pads and wearing knives on his feet.

"Thanks, Pumpkin." Brooks hauls me into his arms and I lace my fingers around his neck, wrapping my legs around his hips. It's a challenge because of his bulky goalie uniform, but I make it work and hold on for dear life as he skates in a circle, then beelines for the boards. Once he's deposited me beside Lennox, he pulls back and winks. "Enjoy the game."

"Get me that shutout," I taunt, blowing him a kiss.

Then he's gone, skating back to where he left his stick and helmet. He scoops them up and continues on in the direction of the goalie coach, who's waiting for him at the net.

"Holy shit. That was hot," Lennox says beside me.

"Agreed," I murmur, still focused on my fake boyfriend. After that interaction, I don't ever want to look away.

Aiden skates by then, and beside me, Lennox straightens. A wide smile takes over her face, and she waves. The happy-go-lucky brother of my fake boyfriend, a man I've never seen so much as frown, is like a deer in headlights. Eyes wide and jaw slack, he barrels into the glass with his arms and legs spread like a starfish.

The arena erupts in sharp gasps and shouts. Gavin is up and over the boards in seconds, followed by the team's medical staff.

Holding my breath, I look from Lennox, who's covering her mouth with one hand, to the ice, where Aiden is sprawled out flat on his back and being tended to. When he's finally on his feet with his hands out in front of him, as if assuring the small group surrounding him that he's fine and they should back off, I finally breathe.

"Holy shit. You literally took that man's breath away."

Lennox is silent. No quippy comeback or sassy *of course I did*.

I've never seen her so out of it. Nervous, I cling to her hand and squeeze. "He's okay, babe. The guys get slammed into the glass all the time."

She nods woodenly. "Yeah, it's just..." She licks her lips and follows his every move. "It's been a while."

She isn't talking about how long it's been since she's seen a hockey game. No, those simple words have a different meaning entirely. Eventually, she'll tell me. And I have a feeling this is only the beginning.

"Holy shit, I think they're gonna get a—"

I slap a hand over Lennox's mouth, and every one of the women in the box with us hisses.

If there's one rule in hockey, it's that you don't mention the shutout before it's happened. Hockey players aren't the only people who are superstitious about the game.

There are two minutes left in the final period, and as Lennox almost pointed out, Brooks hasn't let a single goal in. I broke out in a cold sweat on our way to the WAG box tonight. Before now, I've only ever dealt with these women when there were PR issues or in passing at family events. Our interactions have never been anything but cordial, but they've been few and far between and surface level. Tonight, I've spent hours surrounded by them, and the idea that they might not accept me as one of them makes nausea roll in my stomach.

Not that I truly am one of them, but still, I want them to like me.

It's a silly personality flaw of mine. I want to be liked.

"And that's what we call a hat trick." McGreevey's daughter Emma Cate sits up straight a few seats down as the crowd goes wild.

Moments ago, War was skating down the ice at lightning speed, keeping tight control of the puck. Florida's defensemen charged after him, and like the moves were choreographed, War scooped up the puck and launched it to Aiden. Without missing a beat, he slammed into the defensemen, laying him out, then immediately blocked the other defensemen, all without slowing, so that Aiden had a clear shot. The move was so fluid the goalie had no hope of stopping the goal.

Leaning forward, I plant my elbows on my knees and look past Emma Cate's mom to where she's sitting. "The toss is the hat trick?"

Her little sister Riley shakes her head. "No. Three goals by the Leprechaun."

Lennox's laugh is bubbly. "I can't believe they still call him that."

McGreevey's wife, Becca, smiles over her shoulder at us. "He's certainly Boston's lucky charm."

With a soft hum, Lennox keeps her attention locked on Aiden. He's currently taking his victory lap.

"There's still another minute," Emma Cate reminds me.

I bite my thumb and will my nerves to settle. Am I that obvious? The women surrounding me figured out real quick that I didn't know all that much about the game. When my secret was out, they were nothing but kind, rather than judgmental like I'd expected. From that moment, the girls jumped in to describe the intricacies of each play using terms an average person like me can actually understand. Coulda used them when I started this job.

Florida is flying down the ice in front of us. The urge to close my eyes before their player takes the shot is almost overpowering.

I have no idea how Brooks stays so calm under the pressure when he's tasked with keeping that tiny puck from making its way into that huge net, all while men with sticks and sharp objects strapped to their feet fly at him from all directions.

Parker and McGreevey are both defending the net, but Florida's center dodges them left and right until he's charging toward Brooks. McGreevey goes for the puck but misses. Then it's Parker's turn to try. But the center pushes Parker into Brooks, and they both go down, leaving space for the puck to soar past them and into the back of the net.

The smaller Florida crowd loses it, cheering and clapping and stomping like mad, and the goal is added to the score.

"That's bullshit!" I scream along with the crowd, my blood pressure skyrocketing. "Hey, ref. Where's the call?"

Brooks gets up on his skates, and like he can hear me, his head snaps in my direction. Then he points at me, heaves his shoulders up and lets them fall in an exaggerated shrug.

"Sar, look." Lennox slaps my arm, and when I turn, she's pointing to the Jumbotron hanging over the rink. The screen is split in two, and on one side, the camera is focused in on Brooks, who's still turned toward me. My image is plastered on the other side. My face goes so hot, my flush is visible on the screen.

I bite my lip and tip my chin, but quickly look back up and own it. Sliding to the edge of my seat, I blow Brooks a kiss and give him a broad smile. "You did great, thirteen!" I holler. "The refs are blind!"

"Oh my God. You guys are so adorable," Becca says. She leans closer and grasps my wrist. Then she peers over her shoulder at her daughters. When she turns back to me, she tips in even farther. "Have you surprised him in nothing but the jersey yet?"

My heart stutters in my chest. "Um, no. Is that a thing?"

She nods and swats the leg of the woman sitting directly behind her. "Sara is asking if the jersey with nothing else is a thing."

Lennox smirks. "I remember those days."

I nudge her, my interest totally piqued. "If the way Aiden slammed into the glass when he saw you is anything to go by, then he remembers them too."

She throws her head back and laughs. Down near the team, she went rigid beside me, but in the last couple of hours, she's loosened up. This Lennox is the woman I know inside and out.

"You coming out tonight?"

She shrugs. "Maybe."

The Bolts win the game four to one. Despite narrowly missing the shutout, I'm excited to see Brooks. Maybe a little too excited.

Last night was probably a fluke, a one-time insane situation that he has no plans to repeat. Yet butterflies flutter violently in my belly as Lennox and I make our way toward the team room. This sensation isn't lust, even if I wish it were. No, what's happening inside me, low in my core and behind my ribs, is something I've never felt. While a stream of nerves runs through my veins, it's overpowered by the lightness and excitement powering through me at just the thought of seeing Brooks. Of imagining the sheepish smile he'll give me.

Our reunion will have to wait, because now that the game is over, I have work to do. I leave Lennox with McGreevey's wife in the team room, then head toward the door so I can ensure the guys make it over to where the press is waiting.

I'm halfway across the space when Jill barrels into the room, a whirlwind of drama, her blond hair swinging, all caked-on makeup and too-tight clothing. "Oh my God. Where's Aiden?"

As Aiden's longtime girlfriend, I would expect her to know that after a game, he heads straight to the locker room to shower, then over to talk to the press. It will be a while before he's here.

Resigned to dealing with her since I seem to be the only staff member nearby, I approach. "Need something, Jill?"

Her shoulders relax when she notices me. "Thank God it's you. I need to see Aiden."

"You know the drill," I say, keeping my tone friendly, even if I want to roll my eyes. "He has to shower and talk to the press."

"He has a concussion! They never should have let him play. Did you see how badly he hit the glass during warm-ups? He was probably distracted because I kicked him out. I rushed over here as soon as I saw it."

Tipping to one side so I can peer around her, I check the clock on the wall. "It's after nine. Warm-ups were at six."

She huffs. "It took me a while to get here."

"You live five minutes from the arena."

She huffs, and I swear she lifts her foot like she's going to stomp it, but then she straightens and fists her hands at her sides. "Are you going to go get him for me or not?"

This time I can't fight the eye roll. With a subtle nod, I stalk out the door and stride toward the locker room. I do my best to stay out of this space, especially after a game when there's a good chance of seeing someone's ass. The guys pay little attention to who walks around. They just go about their business because there are women wandering through at all times. Trainers and support staff and such. Despite how hard I try to avoid it, I end up here pretty frequently.

When I step inside, I cover my eyes, hoping not to get an eyeful of anybody's junk. "Aiden, your girlfriend is here."

Rather than Aiden, Tyler is the one who replies. "Saint, your girl-friend is here."

I've still got a hand covering my face, so my heart leaps into my throat when I'm suddenly airborne. There's a strong arm banded around me, then I'm tossed over a meaty bare shoulder. I have to pull my hand away to brace myself on the muscular back as the man carrying me runs around the locker room like a loon.

I squeeze my eyes shut and squeal. "Get me out of here!"

"War!" Brooks's tone is pure anger.

Tyler must be the one carting me around in a fireman's carry. The warning does no good. In fact, it only makes the right winger move faster.

On instinct and out of pure self-preservation, I open my eyes. I need to prepare myself in case Tyler falls. Not that it would do me a whole lot of good. If he goes down, I don't see any way to save myself from going down with him.

With my cheek pressed against him, I try to make sense of the spinning room. Every person I lay eyes on is wearing nothing but a towel. It's disconcerting, but not nearly as bothersome as the towel scratching against my skin. Because if I'm not mistaken, it's the only barrier between my face and War's ass. "Tyler Warren, I am going to tell on you!"

I ball my hands into fists and bang against his ass, but he only laughs louder. Bracing my palms against his lower back. I turn to get a look at the other side of the room. The first thing I see is Brooks, brows pulled low and mouth set in a snarl, darting for us. He grips his towel with one hand and reaches for me with the other.

My stomach flips, and not just because I'm upside down. No, it flips because I'm envisioning that towel falling to the floor. The view from here would be *spectacular*.

"I got him, Sar!" Aiden lunges forward.

As he does, Tyler darts left, and instead of grabbing Tyler's arm, Aiden fists his towel.

Lungs seizing, I watch as he holds the towel up in front of him. A bolt of terror zaps me in that moment, because as War moves, my head bounces off his hairy ass. "My head is on his ass. My head is on his ass!"

The room goes silent, all but a single ridiculously loud snort, and not a single person comes to my aid. Not even Brooks. In fact, when I push up, making sure my hands are planted on War's back and *not* his ass, one man has the back of his hand thrown over his mouth, stifling laughter. *Brooks* is losing it.

My damn fake boyfriend is trying—and failing—to stop from laughing. The rest of the guys are still silent, eyes wide as they look from him to me and back again.

"Put. Me. Down," I grind out with a pinch to War's ass.

And as if my face bouncing off War's stinky rear end wasn't bad enough, when I'm upright again, the first thing I see is Seb. He's in a dark suit, hair slicked back, with his arms folded across his chest, glowering at me.

Fuck my life.

CHAPTER 23
Brooks

"BROOKS, when Florida scored, you didn't seem nearly as upset as we'd expect. Not when you were so close to a shutout. Can we assume that's because of the woman in the stands you pointed at?"

I'm not at all surprised by the question from the reporter in the back. The guys have been ribbing me about it since we got off the ice.

I was pissed. But they're right. Somehow looking up and seeing Sara wearing my jersey, screaming her head off, eased that anger. Made me smile. The girl is nuts. Certifiable. And if she asked me to, I'd join her in a straitjacket. I'm fucking obsessed.

I arch a brow at her now. She's standing off to the side, overseeing as usual. When she doesn't direct me to stay quiet, I look back to the reporter and go with the truth. "What can I say? I'm crazy about her."

"Could you give us her name? How long have you been dating? Is it serious?" The questions hit me one after another, each from a different reporter around the room.

Naturally, that's when Coach steps in front of me. "No more questions. We'll see you in Denver."

Sara worries her lip and tilts her face down.

He kept her a secret. Hidden from the light.

Fuck it.

I make a beeline for her. I don't have to answer the question to show the world exactly who she is and how proud I am that she's mine.

Her eyes are wide as I approach, that lip still caught between her teeth, but there's a hint of a smile on her face and a pleased blush creeping up her neck. I pull her against my chest and cup her neck with both hands, caressing the underside of her jaw with my thumbs. And then I dip down and press my lips against hers.

Sara makes a surprised little yelp, and my dick jumps. She doesn't pull away, *thank fuck*, and when I deepen the kiss, she sighs into my mouth and melts against me.

I didn't mean for our first kiss to happen in front of a room full of reporters *and* while we're both technically working, but I couldn't wait a second longer.

I slip my tongue between her lips and tease hers, and that's all it takes. She smiles against my mouth, and then she's kissing me back. Her soft lips, the taste of her, sugary sweet just as I knew she'd be, make this the best kiss of my life. Not that I'm surprised. Sara's the best thing to ever happen to me. A year ago, my days were nothing but gray skies and ice and hockey pucks. Dull and monochromatic. But with her crazy one-liners, her taste in music, the truly insane things that happen to her and the way she reacts, and her damn smile, she's brought a rainbow of color to my life.

When she pulls back, I follow, pressing kiss after drugging kiss against her mouth. Sweet little nips at her lips because I truly can't get enough.

She giggles and pushes against my chest, her blue eyes shining with wonder. "Everyone is staring."

"Good. Then they know you're mine. Come on, crazy girl. Let's get out of here before I get carried away and give them a completely different kind of show."

I tuck her beneath my arm and guide her out of the pressroom, head held high.

When we pass Gavin, he pats me on the shoulder. "Great game tonight."

"Thanks." I turn my attention back to Sara. "We going out?" It's the last thing I want to do, but since Lennox is in town, Sara will want to hang out with her.

She blinks up at me, lips swollen and parted. I should kiss her more often. "Um," she finally says, like she's finding her voice again. "Lennox left after Jill made a scene. So that's up to you."

"Do you *want* to go out?"

She nibbles on her lip and shakes her head. "No. Not really."

I jostle her gently, forcing her even closer to me. "What do you want to do?"

"I think I might want to kiss you again," she breathes out. She tips her head back and studies me, an adorable crease between her brows like she's surprised by her admission.

My cheeks burn in response. I'm just as surprised, and my damn heart is tripping over itself. So I push her up against the wall in the hallway outside the pressroom. It's loud out here. Voices echo off the cinderblock walls as reporters mill about, hoping for a player to go rogue and give a statement.

I'll do them one better.

My girl can't tell me she wants a kiss and not get one. Anything she wants is hers for the taking.

"Just one more." I dip down again, brushing my lips against hers. It's quick and so gentle it can barely be considered a kiss. But I have a lifetime of practice when it comes to restraint, so I release her and fist my hands at my sides to keep myself from touching her. If I don't back away now, then I don't know that I can stop the freight train of desire barreling through me.

Standing with her in public like this is addicting. Knowing others are watching when I kiss her only spurs me on. Shit. Just the thought of taking it further, touching her in other ways regardless of who's around, is far too appealing.

With one deep breath, I rein in my errant thoughts and rest my forehead against hers with a sigh, willing my heart to settle. When I pull back and take her in, her eyes are glassy and her breaths are coming heavy.

"Let's get you home, Pumpkin."

"Did you have fun tonight?"

We're riding the elevator up to my floor because Lennox is staying at Sara's.

It's been a long, long day, but as soon as Sara settled in my pickup, it's like she got a second burst of energy, talking a mile a minute, giving me a play-by-play of her night.

"It really was amazing." She clutches her hands to her chest. "And that little stunt you pulled?" The hum she lets out is pure delight.

"Which one?" I tease. I pulled a few tonight, and I couldn't blame even half of them on my uncle.

"The push-ups with me on your back." She sighs, her body practically melting beside me. "You should have heard Seb after that. He was fuming."

"He didn't do anything to you, right?" I press closer, inspecting her like there's any way I would have missed an injury. I know better, but it doesn't stop me from checking. If he left any marks, they're the invisible ones, and the emotional scars are what I'm truly worried about.

She pushes me back with a laugh. "Nah, a little name calling never hurt me."

A shot of anger rushes through me. "He called you a name?" I'm standing too close again, my hands balled into fists at my sides.

She rolls her eyes and lets out a little laugh. "Puck bunny."

How is it that she can let that roll off her back so easily while I'm seething on the inside? She's not a fucking puck bunny. And honestly, I hate that term.

"You're not a puck bunny. He can't call you that."

The elevator dings, and when the doors open on my floor, she grabs my hand, pulling me forward. "I know that. Seb's words don't faze me. I know exactly what we are. You're my best friend."

Those words don't touch what we are. Sure, she's my best friend, but so is War. I sure as fuck don't have this overwhelming compulsion to push him down on my bed and devour him.

My relationship with Sara transcends friendship and lust. It transcends every feeling I've ever had for another person. I'm in so far over my goddamn head I can't see straight.

As we walk down the hall hand in hand, her warmth seeps into me and spreads through my body, settling me. Maybe I'm finally seeing straight. Maybe we both are. When she tips her head up, giving me that coy smile of hers, the smile she's shared time and again, I finally see all those moments between us for what they really were. Whispered secrets, reassurances sometimes veiled in teasing or sarcasm, full conversations held without words in a language entirely our own.

But despite all that, there's a piece of me I haven't shared with her, and I'm tired of hiding it. I want to tell her exactly how I feel. As we round the corner to my apartment, I tug her closer, eating up the space between us until she's just a breath away. "Sar, you're so much more than just my—"

"Oh, thank God!"

I'm knocked back at the sound of my brother's shout down the hall.

Sara's eyes go wide, and she spins toward him, pulling back a step.

Aiden jumps up off the floor in front of my apartment door. "I swear I've been sitting here waiting for you guys for hours."

"You okay?" Sara drops my hand and moves closer to him.

What the hell?

"Am I okay?" he bellows. "No, I'm not okay. How the hell do you know Lennox?"

Moving to Sara's side, I glare at my brother. "Watch it."

Aiden runs his hands through his curly hair. It's still damp from his after-game shower, and it's a wild, tangled mess. He's in a suit, but it's rumpled and so unlike Aiden. The kid always looks sharp. He may be a clown off the ice, but he's always a well-dressed clown.

"Sorry." He lets out an exaggerated sigh. "But seriously, Sar. How do you know her?"

With a low grunt, I tilt my neck one way, then the other, hoping to release the tension that's suddenly taken over. With Aiden here, there's no way Sara and I are going to have our big talk tonight. It kills me, but it's pretty clear that I won't be getting another taste of her either. Not yet.

I shake it off and step up to my door. Once I've got it unlocked, I hold it open for Sara. She gives me a quick inspection as she passes, but her brow is furrowed and her shoulders are tight. Dammit. She's uncomfortable. When Aiden crosses the threshold, I slap a palm against his chest to stop his movement. "She's her best friend. Be kind."

Aiden winces and pulls on the back of his neck. "Yeah."

I drop my keys in the bowl by the door and slide off my shoes, then rest my hand against the small of Sara's back and lead her to the couch. "Want something to drink?"

"A beer would be great," Aiden replies behind me.

"Get your own drink." With another glare at him, I slip out of my suit jacket and drape it over the back of a chair at the kitchen counter.

He scowls. The dude is more surly tonight than I've ever seen him.

Sara, thankfully, seems to have relaxed a bit since she settled in on the couch cushions. "I'm fine."

When I turn back to Aiden, the defeated slump of his shoulders tugs at my heartstrings. "You're buying me another six-pack," I grumble. I head to the fridge and snag a pumpkin beer for Sara and two lagers for Aiden and me.

I hand Sara her beer, top already off, and she rewards me with a sweet smile. As I settle beside her, Aiden drops into the chair across from us and slumps forward, dropping his elbows onto his knees and holding his beer loosely in front of him. "Is she dating anyone?"

"Fucking A," I grumble.

Sara lets out an uncomfortable laugh and pushes her hair behind her ear. "I'm not sure if I should answer that. Maybe you should talk to her."

With his elbows still planted on his knees, he lifts his head. "Does she talk about me?"

"Oh my God." I take a swig of my beer and marvel at the insanity before me. "What the hell is going on with you and Jill?"

Aiden straightens at that question. "Nothing. I just—"

"Then go home to her."

The way he deflates makes me feel like an ass.

Sara grips my thigh, silently signaling me to go easy on my brother, but now that she's touching me, I can't focus on the man falling apart on the other side of the room. All my focus has been rerouted to my dick. I clear my throat and mentally scold myself. If I can keep the train on the tracks and get Aiden's head on straight quickly, then I can—

"I'm going to let you two talk," Sara says, instantly killing my mood.

With that statement, any hope that this night could end with my hands on her has evaporated. She squeezes my thigh again and angles in close. Her sweet scent envelops me as she pecks my cheek. "Great game tonight, Saint."

Every cell in my body is screaming for me to stop her. Hold her hostage.

"Thanks, Sar." Aiden, the idiot, is completely oblivious to his status as a major cockblock.

She stands and smiles at my brother before I can formulate a sentence. "I'm gonna take this for the road." She brings her bottle to her lips. "Don't want to waste a perfectly good pumpkin beer." She winks at me.

All I can do now is hold back my groan and accept that there is no salvaging this night.

"Breakfast tomorrow?" I scramble for a reason to see her as I stand and follow her to the door. It's stupid. We're headed out on the road in two days, and unlike the rest of the guys, my girl travels with us. I *will* see her again.

And she's my Sara. We're going to see one another. We always do.

She winces. "I've got plans. But I'll see you on the plane on Monday?"

Monday? What about tomorrow night?

Of course I don't say that. Don't even ask what her plans are. She'll probably be hanging with Lennox, since they don't get to see each other much. And it's not really my place to ask, is it?

Fuck, I'm a disaster.

"Yeah, of course. Monday." I itch to touch her, to pull her close and hold her. To relive the kisses she so easily gave me only an hour ago. And fuck it, I don't have the wherewithal to stop.

Threading my fingers in the hair at her nape, I pull her close, and when she fists my shirt and smiles, I press my lips to hers. Like earlier, she lets out a surprised little yip. And just like that, I'm obsessed with the sound. Then she slides her tongue against my lips, seeking more.

"Fuck, crazy girl." I pull back a fraction and fill my lungs, then I dive back in for another kiss.

"Shit." The word is low, almost imperceptible, as she pulls back. Licking her lips, she studies me, scanning every inch of my face. "Shit."

"You already said that," I tease softly. Then I go back for more, gently brushing my lips over hers one more time.

When I step back this time, her eyes are hazy, and a slow grin spreads across her face. She blinks once, twice, then she offers a small wave and takes a step backward, toward the door. In true Sara fashion, she stumbles over her own two feet, but she quickly rights herself. With a shake of her head and a little laugh, she spins, and then she's gone.

Shit is right.

"Good Morning, Boston. I'm Colton, and this is my co-host, Eliza, and we're here to bring you the Hockey Report."

"Good Morning and thank you, Colton. I think we all know what we'll be talking about today."

"No, Eliza, I think our hockey fans would prefer to talk about the actual game more than the news you're thinking of."

Eliza laughs. "Please. You gossip more than I do. Before the show started, you—"

"Don't finish that sentence, or I'll tell Mom you complained about her lumpy mashed potatoes last Thanksgiving."

Eliza hisses. "I'm going to kill you, dear brother. And Mom, I loved your mashed potatoes. They were perfect. Ignore him. Now, as I was saying, what we all really want to talk about is the news that Brooks Langfield is in love!"

Colton chuckles. "He didn't say that. Give the poor man a chance. When asked about the woman he brought out on the ice during warm-ups, he said, and I quote, 'I'm crazy about her.'"

"So who's the lucky lady?"

"He didn't give a name, but there are reports that he was seen kissing the head of Bolts' public relations after the press conference, so chances are she's the one," Colton surmises.

"If not, he'll have some explaining to do. In the meantime, the Bolts are heading to Denver next. They'll be on the road for the next two weeks, so if she's his good luck charm, then we're in luck, because she travels with the team."

"Thank God for that." Colton laughs. "Now can we talk about hockey?"

CHAPTER 24

Sara

"WHEN WILL YOU BE HOME?"

The only reason Ethan is asking is because my mother is driving him nuts. He knows as well as I do that she'll turn her desperation on me the moment I walk through the door. Then he'll have a reprieve.

I turn my phone so that Ethan can see the team calendar pinned to my bedroom wall. Each of our trips, including the one to North Carolina in four weeks, is listed clearly. He knows when I'll be there, so the question is unnecessary. The kid follows the Bolts' schedule like he works for the team. He knows all the guys' stats and loves to tell me who's playing well and who could use some work. Not that I share that information with them, and not that I have any control over the roster or decisions that aren't directly related to PR.

"Soonish. You know that."

Ethan groans. "Wish I could come stay with you. Your apartment is empty half the time anyway, since all you do is travel."

I laugh. "I doubt Mom would let you move to Boston, but nice try."

"She barely lets me go to the bathroom alone, so yeah, that's a solid no." He heaves a sigh. "You going to see Josie today?"

"It's Sunday and I'm in Boston, so you know it."

"Can you FaceTime me when you get there?"

"Will do." I nod and give him a smile. "Okay, I'm going to get in the shower. I told Ava we'd meet her at ten."

Lennox walks out of the bathroom, towel wrapped around her body and her platinum blond hair dry.

"Love you, kiddo. Say hi to Lenny." I toss her the phone, then head toward the bathroom while she wanders out into the main living area.

Lennox and I have a busy day planned. While I typically enjoy having a quiet day at home after a Saturday game, I need the time with my best friend so that I can get my head screwed on straight when it comes to Brooks.

Last night threw me. Even more than the night before. The orgasm delivered by Brooks fucked with me, that's a given, and I've been aching for him to touch me again.

But when he kissed me in front of the press? When he claimed me *in public and in private?* My world flipped upside down, and it still hasn't righted itself.

I feel like I'm floating. My stomach has flipped more in the last twelve hours than it did when I spent the day riding roller coasters as a teenager. My heart skips a beat when I so much as think his name, let alone remember the way he smiled as he said "just one more" before he kissed me again.

Butterflies. That's what Brooks Langfield gives me. Fucking kaleidoscopes of butterflies.

Thirty minutes later, we're dressed in jeans and sweaters and heading into the bakery to grab goodies to bring to the hospital.

"Extra pink ones, please," I remind the woman behind the counter.

"Josie's favorite," Ava says softly, a wistful smile on her face. "I brought her chocolate the other day. You should have seen the way her face fell. Won't be doing that again."

I laugh, and my heart tugs at the thought of her trying to hide her disappointment.

Josie is all feisty sweetness. Her personality is a contradiction to the frail body she's trapped inside. God, what I'd do to see her outside those hospital walls, running and playing like other kids her age.

My brother has spent more than his fair share of time in a hospital bed, and every time he's admitted, it breaks my heart, but Josie's always stuck inside those beige hospital walls. The bland canvas depresses me within minutes each time I visit her. I can't imagine being a virtual prisoner inside them. It's why we brighten her room in any way we can as often as we can. Ava gets over there more often than me because I travel with the team, and the heartache of Josie's situation hits her the hardest.

"You sure she won't mind if I come with you?" Lennox is loaded down with a cardboard drink tote filled with hot coffee and a bag of snacks for the nurses.

We've got donuts and hot chocolate for all the kids on the peds floor, and a special pink donut for our Josie girl.

Ava snorts, her red hair swinging as she tosses her head back. "She'll have you roped into bringing her treats for the next year." With a hum, she eyes Lennox's black boots with the red heel. "Actually, she'll probably ask for something with a little sparkle from you."

I grin. Josie does love sparkles.

We deliver the coffee and treats to the nurses' station in the peds unit. A group of them, all dressed in pastel scrubs with animals printed on them, are chatting and working on charts, but they light up when we approach. Ava's the regular here, but she includes me in her Sunday tradition as often as I can make it happen.

When Gavin discovered her visits, he insisted we use the Bolts' expense account to spoil the kids and the nurses. He's one of the good ones.

All the Langfield men are.

And now I'm back to thinking about Brooks. So much for this distraction.

"She's having a good day," Maria says as she takes the donut boxes from Ava. Maria has been taking care of Josie since the day she was admitted.

When she was diagnosed with Hodgkin's Lymphoma at the age of four, she was living with a foster family. The diagnosis is a serious one, though her chances of survival are high. From what I've been told, her foster parents had plans to adopt her. Yet after she arrived, they only visited once, then they vanished.

I can't imagine the emotional damage that must have done to the sweet thing. To not only be poked and prodded and forced to take medication that makes her feel terrible, but to then have the only parents she's ever known walk out? It's inconceivable.

Ava met her shortly after she started treatment. She planned a charity event over Christmas for the Bolts and spent a good deal of time here then. She's been coming back weekly for the ten months since. For the last few months, I've joined her as often as I can.

"Any word from the social worker?" Ava asks.

Maria shakes her head and frowns, her wrinkles deepening. "Not easy to place a sick child."

Ava squeezes her fists at her sides and lets out a sharp breath through her nose. She loves coming to see Josie, but each visit breaks her a little more.

I hand off the hot chocolate to Lennox and wrap my arm around her shoulder, then I lead my friend in to see the little girl we're all in love with.

"I need your help."

Ava is always quiet after leaving Josie, so I suggested brunch and mimosas at Lucy's. It's a hipster spot in the Seaport district. It's also near the outdoor shops at Faneuil Hall, which is where we're headed next.

"Anything, babe," Lennox says, bringing her mimosa to her lips.

Ava's cheeks are almost as red as her hair from the champagne, and she finally seems to be perking up.

"Seb made a comment about me being a puck bunny yesterday."

Ava and Lennox are the only people I confided in about my relationship with the asshole. Until yesterday, I'd never kept a secret from Lennox. I still don't like the idea of not filling her in on the fake relationship business Brooks and I have going on, but I haven't had time to discuss it with him.

Ava, on the other hand, discovered what was going on when she saw me leaving his apartment late one night and put two and two together. Thankfully she came to me first and promised to keep it to herself. Like me, she had no clue the bastard was married. When I found out, and after I ended things with him, I filled her in. Ava is as good a friend as they come, so I have no doubt that she can be discreet.

"Asshole," Lennox mutters.

"Right. That's not news." I shrug and stab a strawberry with my fork. "But I want to show him that I don't care. That his taunts don't bother me and that I'm happy."

"You are happy, right?" Ava asks, head tilted and scrutinizing me, like if she focuses hard enough, she'll find the answer in my expression.

My response is easy. "Brooks is the best man I've ever known. I don't miss Seb at all."

The worry lines on Ava's face ease, and she smiles. "He's a great guy."

"He is," Lennox agrees. "Back to the cheater. We need a little something to stick it to him." She taps her red-soled foot on the ground and hums. Then her face lights up, and she throws her head back with a cackle. "I've got it. We need a Bolts' beanie. Do you have one?"

Once we've finished brunch, I guide the girls toward the shops, and Lennox fills us in on her plan. And, oh my God, I knew I asked the right person. As always, Lennox's brain is downright devious.

CHAPTER 25
Brooks

Beckett: I need Sara.

Gavin: No

Beckett: This isn't up for debate. Liv has morning sickness.

Gavin: You have Hannah.

Beckett: Hannah is Hannah. I need someone to be Liv for me.

Me: Bro, that's weird.

Beckett: Not like that. Don't be an idiot.

Aiden: You can't have her. I need Sara

Gavin: What the hell do you need Sara for? And why aren't you on the damn plane? We're leaving in five.

Me: None of you can have Sara.

Gavin: Watch out boys. Brooks was never great at sharing his toys.

> Me: Sara is not up for grabs. She's a person.

> Gavin: Yeah, your person.

WHEN I STEP onto the plane, I zero in on my brother and shoot him a glare. He's settled in beside my girlfriend, fingers laced across his abdomen and one ankle crossed over the opposite knee, like he's ready for takeoff.

"Move," I grumble.

War, who's a pace ahead of me, snorts. Then he continues down the aisle of the team plane.

Gavin tips his chin up, brows lifted. "Excuse me?"

"Please," I add. I'm grumpy. I'm never grumpy, but I haven't seen Sara since Saturday, and I'm feeling territorial. Like I want to put my hands on her and physically fight off my brothers when they try to steal her attention from me. It's slightly pathetic. I know. Okay, it's really pathetic. And they were sure to point that out during Sunday night dinner at my mom's yesterday.

A squeak beside Gavin snags my attention, and for the first time, I really take Sara in. She's watching me with wide eyes and parted lips, clearly shocked by my insanity.

"Where's Sara?" Aiden stumbles onto the plane, curly hair a disaster yet again. "I need to talk to her about—"

When his words cut off, I spin to face him.

He's frozen at the front row, his hands on the seat backs on either side of him. I follow his line of sight, and for the first time realize that Lennox is sitting across from Sara and Gavin.

Blowing out a breath, I home in on Gavin, ready to ask him what the hell is happening here, but behind me, Aiden heaves. I spin, and sure enough, he cups his mouth and does it again. What the fuck?

"Shit." Gavin is up and out of his seat in a flash, hustling down the aisle toward our baby brother. On his way, he nods at the group of medical staff seated near the front. "Let's get him checked for a concussion again."

Once they've ushered Aiden to the back of the plane, I stuff my bag into the overhead compartment, then settle in beside Sara in what used to be Gavin's seat. "Hey, Lennox."

There's a cup of coffee on the table between us that I'm almost certain belongs to Gavin, so I slide it across the surface so it's in front of the empty seat beside Sara's best friend.

"He okay?" Her focus is fixed on the closed door at the back of the plane where Gavin disappeared with Aiden.

"He probably ate something he shouldn't have. Kid is always having too much sugar."

The laugh that escapes her is forced. She knows Aiden, so she probably realizes it's more than that.

"You joining us for the trip?"

Sara answers this time. "Yeah, Gavin said she could stay with me since she's off this week."

My stomach sinks, but I force a smile to my face. With Lennox staying in Sara's room, I doubt we'll have any time to spend alone. I always bunk with Aiden, even though we could easily afford our own rooms. The rest of the guys double up, so regardless of our last name, we do too.

Honestly, most of the time I don't mind. Like me, Aiden doesn't sleep around. He's faithful to Jill, and before they started dating, he was a serial monogamist. Most nights, we watch TV and go to bed early.

One of these nights I'll have to make an exception. Maybe put Aiden and Lennox together. That would certainly be interesting.

"You okay?" Sara edges in closer and squeezes my thigh. My entire body relaxes at her touch.

I lean back against the seat and let my head loll to the side. "Yeah, Pumpkin." My smile is all genuine affection. "Just needed my hit of sweetness this morning."

She bites her lip and presses a kiss to my jaw. "That work?"

I tip her chin up so her lips are a breath from mine. "That how you kiss your boyfriend?"

Her smile grows, and pink stains her cheeks. "You trying to tell me you want a real kiss?"

"Yeah, Sar. That's exactly what I'm saying. You going to give it to me?"

We watch each other for a beat. I'm sure my smile is just as dopey as the one she's wearing. Then, *finally*, she leans in and fuses her plump lips to mine.

I slide my hand from her jaw to her nape and thread my fingers through her hair so I can angle her up for an even better kiss.

The connection is broken all too soon when she eases back with a heavy breath. "Shit."

I chuckle and kiss her once more, soft and sweet, then force myself to sit back in my seat. But I take her hand in mine as I do and hold it on my lap.

"Nice seat." Gavin drops into the row across from me and picks up his coffee.

"Aiden okay?" Lennox asks.

I'd honestly forgotten she was here. Whoops.

"Yeah, they think it was something he ate. But if you notice any concussion symptoms, Brooks, you better tell me."

"Got it." I dip my chin. I don't always love taking orders from my older brothers, but in this capacity, Gavin is my boss, so I'll always defer to him.

He shifts in his seat and focuses on the woman beside him. "Now tell me what you've been up to since high school, Lennox."

"Did she say anything to you on the plane?"

I kind of want to kill my brother. He hasn't stopped asking about

Lennox since we entered our hotel room. We have an early morning tomorrow, and I have a game-day ritual to follow, only he's already fucking with it. Sara should be sitting on my face right now, and I should be nowhere near Aiden's whiney ass.

"No." I unlock my phone, breathing through the mounting frustration.

He flops over to his side and huffs. "It's weird, right? Her being best friends with Sara?"

"It's only weird if you make it weird." Holding my phone overhead, I pull up Instagram and scroll mindlessly. "You dated in high school. And I thought you and Jill were serious."

"We are."

My annoyance ramps up another notch, and I let out a humorless laugh. "Then why are you so worried about Lennox?"

"I'm not worried about her. It's just weird. And it's weirder that you don't think it's weird."

"Whatever you say."

Snatching the remote from the nightstand, he sits up and aims it at the television. When he finds SportsCenter, I go back to scrolling, thankful that he's finally stopped talking.

Sara: Ready for the game tomorrow?

Me: Not really. I was promised a certain ritual, and after one game, it's already been abandoned.

Sara: You didn't get a shutout. Figured you wouldn't want a repeat of that night at the risk of losing another one.

Me: We dominated that game. And all this means is that we have to try another position. You know what coach always says. Practice makes perfect.

The dots on the phone dance, then disappear completely, and my stomach lurches. Shit. Did I push too hard?

Just as I'm considering how to play it off, the dots are back. Then a message appears.

> Sara: We both have roommates. There's no privacy.

> Me: Privacy is overrated. Meet me at the hot tub?

I'm already up and out of bed, confident she'll say yes. Sara isn't an overthinker. She's also not shy.

"Where you going?" Aiden tracks me as I shuffle over to my suitcase and pull out my board shorts.

"Gonna go get in some laps and then hit the hot tub to relax my muscles. My quads are still tight from Saturday's game."

Aiden swings his legs off the bed. "Cool, I'll come."

I point at the bed. "Lay back down."

Hands thrown up, he follows the command, but he's wearing a bewildered frown. "What the fuck?"

I sigh. "I'm meeting Sara up there."

"Is Lennox going?" He sits up again, his palms pressed to the mattress on either side of him. "Did she say she doesn't want me to be there?"

"Oh my God, dude. Dump Jill and talk to Lennox." I swat at him with my board shorts. "This is pathetic. No, Lennox is not coming. I'm going to spend some time with my girlfriend. *Alone*. Okay?"

One side of Aiden's lips quirk. "You really don't share well."

Ignoring him, I stomp to the bathroom to change. When I'm finished, I grab a key card from the table, and then I'm gone without another word, anxious to get up to the roof to see my girl.

CHAPTER 26

Sara

"I'M GOING to meet Brooks up at the hot tub." The second his text came through, I was up and rummaging through my bag.

The first time I went away with the team, I didn't pack a suit, and of course, Liv, my new boss who I was so desperate to impress, invited me to the spa, then asked if I wanted to join her in the hot tub. Without a suit, all I could do was sit on the edge and soak my feet. I vowed never to forget a suit again.

For this trip, I packed two.

A lot of the guys like to swim laps during the season. It's a good workout and easy on their joints, so the powers that be who book lodging always put us up in five-star resorts equipped with pools. And where there's a pool, there is often a hot tub.

I typically start my days doing laps when we travel. I've yet to hit the pool or hot tub at night, because the guys tend to take over, and I prefer to stay out of their way.

"God, I'm so jealous," Lennox whines. "It's been forever since I've gotten some."

I stand up straight and whip around, gaping at my best friend. "Really?"

From the day I met her, Lennox has been a big proponent of sex. An equal opportunist, if you will. She doesn't believe in relationships. In college, she was always going on about how they'd only lead to heartbreak.

After their brief interaction yesterday, I'm curious about whether that philosophy has something to do with Aiden.

Did he break her heart? Or was she the one who did the breaking? If I was a betting woman, I'd put my money on Lennox. More than once, I've watched her run when a man got too close, like she was determined to leave before he could.

"I think maybe I want more."

Her confession should have bowled me over, but my mind is muddled with thoughts of Brooks. There's no room left to pick apart that confession. "Wow, this is serious coming from you, and I feel like I really wanna dedicate a lot of time to that discussion."

Lennox laughs. "Go up to that pool, or your boyfriend is going to kill me. Did you see him almost take out Gavin this morning? Boy's got it bad for you."

Damn if the feeling isn't mutual. Not only is he taking up all the free space in my brain, but he's taken up residence in my heart too.

I change quickly and slip on a pair of sweats over my bathing suit. Then I grab a Bolts sweatshirt and the beanie the girls and I had made.

"Oh!" Lennox laughs. "Saint Brooks isn't gonna be able to help himself when he sees you in that."

I smirk. "I'm counting on it."

When I open my door, I come face to face with Brooks, and the smile that crosses his face when he gets a look at me makes my heart float in my chest.

He spreads his arms out wide and pulls me against him. "Fuck, I missed you." His low, rasping tone sends goose bumps skittering down my spine.

I tip my head so that he can get a good look at my beanie and give him a wicked grin.

He pulls back and holds me at arm's length. "Where the fuck did you get that?" With a laugh that echoes down the hallway, he tucks me under his arm and drags me down the hall.

"Oh, I had it made." I loop an arm around his waist and hustle to keep up with him. "Think Seb will like it?"

He slows a little, and with a roll of his eyes, he presses a kiss to my forehead, right below the space that says *Brooks's Bunny* across my hat. "I don't really give a fuck what he likes, but no, I don't think he will."

"How's Aiden feeling?"

"Other than being whiny as fuck, he's fine."

I squeeze him tight. From the moment I met this man, he's been easy-going. Hard to rile up. So much so that he's rarely bothered by his insane brother. Lately, he's been gruff and short with everyone but me. I don't like it.

"Brooks?" I stop short.

He follows my lead and stops in front of me. "Yes, Pumpkin?"

"I don't want him to change you."

Green eyes darken as he studies me. "Who, Aiden? Please. He's harmless. He'll be fine."

"No. I don't want Seb to change you. I don't want what we're doing to change you. His lies hurt. I get that. And I can understand that you might feel betrayed. But remember: he didn't betray you. He betrayed me. He betrayed his wife.

"And he didn't make you into the man you are. You did that all on your own. I don't wanna see you change because of something that quite frankly doesn't involve you."

He lets out a bitter laugh and pinches the bridge of his nose. "Considering that he fucked with two of the most important people in my life, Sara, I'm going to disagree with you there. It does affect me."

For a long moment, neither of us speaks. His jaw is like granite as he considers me, but his eyes are swimming with hurt. Finally, he lets out a brutal sigh of defeat. "I'm trying not to let it. I hear you, and I promise I'll do better. The last thing I want is to hurt you."

With a low groan, I drop my head to his chest. "It only hurts me because my Brooks, the one I've adored since the moment we met, is not this angry guy who's been stomping around and snapping at his friends and relatives."

"I'll do better, Sar. I promise."

I sigh, hoping he can hold himself to that. But I'm not sure he truly gets what I'm saying.

Maybe what I'm asking for is impossible. Maybe, after what he discovered about the man he always held on a pedestal, a piece of his happy-go-lucky innocence has been shattered. And maybe there's no putting it back together. But I'd hate that to be true.

It doesn't change how I feel about him, and it definitely doesn't affect the respect I have for him. He'll always be the best person in the room, hands down. But I want him to also be the happiest.

Brooks holds open the door, and I step out into the cold Denver air. It's beautiful out here. The sky is filled with more stars than I've ever seen in Boston. They glitter against the dark sky, lighting up the mountains in the distance. The low rumble of the hot tub to one side of the pool calls to me with promises of soothing my achy muscles.

I tug on Brooks's arm, ready to jump right in, but he's rooted to the spot, his attention on the lit-up pool.

"Come on, big guy. I'm cold!" I abandon him and jog to the hot tub. I grab two towels as I pass a big stack of them, then toss them onto a chair nearby and kick off my shoes.

That's all it takes to get the big brute moving. In an instant, he's hovering behind me as I undress, standing so close I elbow him as I reach for my waistband.

"What are you doing?"

"I don't want him to see you."

I don't even ask who the *him* is. Whether it's a stranger or his uncle, my answer is the same. "Yours are the only eyes I want on me, Saint. Do you like the view?" I peek back at him and drop my sweats.

He groans, his eyes heating as they eat up every inch of my body.

I wink. "That's what I thought." Once my sweatshirt joins my pants on the lounge chair, I dip a toe in the hot water.

Now that I'm in nothing but a swimsuit, the cool air sends goose bumps rippling over every inch of my skin, so I make quick work of slipping into the water. I scoot along the bench until I'm centered over a jet, then settle back.

Brooks, who's back to being broody, even after our discussion, finally shucks his shoes and rips his shirt over his head. He's so tense, every one of his abs is like a solid rock, and I swear I can feel the stress rolling off him.

"If you don't start smiling, I'm going to start removing more clothes until I make you smile."

That makes him pause. With his hands fisted at his sides, he takes a slow breath. Then he raises his eyes and looks at me. "You're playing with fire, Sar."

"No, Brooks. I'm playing with you." I kick one leg out, sending water splashing in his direction. "Now come in and play back."

The man moves so fast I don't have a moment to react before he catapults into the hot tub, completely soaking me. He goes all the way under, and when he surfaces, he's wearing the easy smile I love.

I throw myself at him, wrapping my arms around his neck and my legs around his waist.

Squeezing my thighs, he shuffles back and drops into the seat so that he's facing the mountains. In this position, I've got a clear view of the pool. Sure enough, Seb was the one doing laps. He's now standing beside a lounger, toweling off, a scowl on his face.

Brooks grasps my chin and turns my face so he's all I can see. "Eyes on me, Sar."

I smile. "What else shall I put on you?"

He slides his hand down to my hip, then both make their way to my ass. He caresses my skin with his thumbs, and I wiggle against him in response.

Damn. He's so fucking hard beneath me.

I'm dying for the moment he finally lets me see what's beneath these board shorts.

"Thinking we should try something different tonight." He nuzzles my ear, then ghosts his lips over the sensitive skin just below it. "You want to ride me until you come, crazy girl?"

I laugh at the nickname he uses sparingly. Almost like it slips out when he's not scheming. When he's not faking. When it's only about us. And I kind of love that.

Heat pools low in my belly as I splay my hands against his hard chest and get to work exploring. "Fuck, your muscles are insane." The ridges have their own peaks and valleys. He's a masterpiece. Cut from stone.

Brooks curls forward and drops an open-mouthed kiss to my collarbone, then he moves to my neck, dipping his tongue in the hollow of my throat.

I arch back, giving him access to explore my body and discover other places to lick. The move forces me to grind against his hard dick, and bolts of electricity streak through me. Desperate for another hit, I roll my hips over him again and again.

"I'm so wet." I try to keep the words between us, but I'm quickly losing control of myself.

With a grunt, he grasps my hips and pushes down, then works me over him so I feel every blessed inch of him.

"One day you're going to let me slide inside you." It's not a question. We both know it will soon be a reality.

"God, I wish you would now. I'm dying to taste your cock."

He silences me with an aggressive kiss. Warm water sloshes around us, leaving us both slippery as we find the perfect rhythm. His fingers grip my hips so tightly I'll have beautiful bruises tomorrow.

I claw at his chest, unable to get enough of him.

Of the feeling of him beneath my fingers.

Of the way he tastes.

Of the grunts that slip from his throat every time I glide along his cock.

Panting, I arch back and take him in, dazed and so close and yet not anywhere near where I want to be.

I'm lost in the moment, but not so far gone that I don't feel the presence looming beside us.

In my periphery, Seb stands over the hot tub. I don't pay him any mind. I'm too busy riding Brooks like I'm at Six Flags.

"Get the fuck out of here." Brooks's gruff voice startles me, disturbing my rhythm.

Seb doesn't fight him. With a huff, he stalks off.

The moment the door shuts behind him, Brooks is dragging me up onto the edge. "Fuck, I need you."

The sting of the cold air barely registers. I'm too lost in the feel of Brooks as he slides his palms up my thighs and forces my legs apart.

"Can I taste you, Sar? Bet you made a mess all over this suit."

"Please," I beg, shamelessly pulling my bathing suit bottoms to the side.

He nuzzles against me, dragging his lips against my swollen sex. "Holy fuck, you're perfect."

"Tongue, Brooks. I need your tongue."

It's obscene, really. We're on the pool deck of a swanky hotel in Denver. Moments ago, my ex stood beside us and stared us down. Anyone could walk out and see me spread wide while Brooks eats me. Including his fans and people we work with.

And I couldn't give a fuck. I've never been so turned on. Never been so needy for an orgasm. For another person.

He swipes his hot tongue against me, and I fucking purr. Never in my life have I purred. Until this moment, I didn't know I had the ability.

"Oh my God, that feels..." I'm so delirious I can't even finish my sentence. Warmth spreads through my body despite the cold air. My legs tremble, and a tingle makes its way up my spine. "I—*shit*—" I babble, making absolutely no sense.

"I love kissing you."

I tip my head down, finding his hooded eyes on me.

He presses another kiss against my clit, so tender and sweet, but in an instant, he's sucking and flicking it with so much intensity a cry rips from my throat.

"Everywhere, Sar. I love kissing you everywhere." Determined to prove his point, he slides his tongue between my ass cheeks.

Whimpers are all I can manage as I squirm at his touch.

With his fingers splayed over my clit, he rolls figure eights that have me practically bucking off the edge of the tub. He simply holds me down with one heavy hand pressed to my belly until I'm crying out and coming apart for what feels like an eternity. Above me, the stars blend together until all I see is white light.

When I've come down, I'm nothing but limp arms and legs and heaving breaths. Brooks straightens my bathing suit bottoms, then he pulls me back into the hot tub and holds me so my back is flush against his chest, his arms locked tight around my torso.

I tip my head back and look up at him. He's wearing the old Brooks smile. It's easy and a bit cocky. "Proud of yourself?"

He chuckles and presses a kiss to my forehead. "Satisfied."

I try to spin around, but he splays a hand over my stomach, just like he did when he ate me out, holding me in place.

"You'd be more satisfied if you let me suck your cock," I argue.

He groans. "Another night. Right now I want to sit in the hot tub with my best friend and hear all about how the last few days have gone."

"You missed me, didn't you?"

"Yeah, Sar. I fucking missed you. Now tell me about your day."

"Good Morning, Boston. Eliza here, with my co-host, Colton, and we've got today's Hockey Report."

"Hello, Boston. Eliza, I don't know about you, but I'm feeling like a kid at Christmas. Last night's game was incredible. The Bolts have been unstoppable. The season was off to a shaky start, but if the last four games are anything to go by, they're going to be playing for the Cup again."

"I think you're right, Colton. Though New York is looking just as strong. As is LA. But we've got the Langfield brothers. If I were Seb Lukov, I'd be feeling pretty good with those two on my team."

"Did you see that trick shot Tyler Warren sent to Daniel Hall? The Langfield brothers may be well known, but they're not the only stars. With the way Hall slapped it into the top corner of the net, there was no way Danner could have stopped that puck. I don't know about you, but I couldn't even find the puck. Not until the play was over and it was time for faceoff at center ice."

Eliza sighs. "It's a great time to be a Boston fan. That's for sure."

CHAPTER 27
Brooks

Beckett: I'm still trying to find the puck, Gav. ESPN is showing the play over and over again. One hell of a win. Congrats boys.

Aiden: Shot was sick.

Gavin: I've watched it six times. I can't find it.

Me: Flew past his left shoulder. He was too low when Hall slapped.

Gavin: Ha! And that's why I pay you the big bucks.

Beckett: Boy is cocky now that he's got a girlfriend.

Aiden: He's nauseating. All the kid does is smile and shoot heart eyes at Sara in the stands.

I SLAP Aiden on the back of the head as I walk past his locker.

He whips around and crows. "What? You know it's true."

"What's true?" War has a towel wrapped around his waist, black hair spiked back. He's clearly got something going on tonight. The man usually towel dries his hair and lets it remain wild after games.

"That Brooks is like a smiley oaf now. Bet you his brain chants *Sara, Sara, Sara* throughout the whole game."

War's genuine laugh makes me smile.

"Whatever. I'm happy." I snag my towel from the bench and whip it at him. "Maybe if you talked to Lennox, you could be happy too."

Aiden sighs and looks away. "I have a girlfriend," he grumbles. "A girlfriend I *love*."

I don't buy it for a second, but I also don't want to get involved with my brother and Sara's best friend. Since we started fooling around, my mind's enough of a mess. I don't need to add to the insanity.

My phone lights up with another text. Instead of my brothers, it's Sara. Just the sight of her name makes my heart stumble over itself.

Sara: Coach's office. Now.

I turn so my back is to my locker and scan the guys around me to make sure they can't see my screen, then I type out a quick reply.

Me: Playing with fire there, Sar. Don't I have to be in the pressroom in like ten minutes? And don't you have to be there now?

Sara: I got Hannah to cover for me. Don't make me wait, Saint.

Saint. That's all it takes. Fingers trembling, I button my shirt. Then I slip my jacket on, and I'm gone. Within three minutes, I'm throwing the door to the office open, head held high and shoulders back. The sight in front of me—Sara kneeling on the desk, legs bare, wearing my jersey, offering only a slight tease of what's beneath—steals all the breath from my lungs.

Slamming the door shut so that no one else can get a peek at this perfection, I stalk toward her with only one thing on my mind: how quickly I can make her come.

"Crazy girl, what are you doing to me?"

Blue eyes dancing, she drops her hands to the desk and dips low, keeping her ass in the air, looking like a damn tiger ready to pounce. The move sends the trinkets on Seb's desk scattering. An award of some kind clatters to the floor. I don't know which one, because I can't look away from her. I'm solely focused on what she'll do next.

"I heard hockey players have a thing about their girls dressed in their jersey and nothing else. And since I didn't get the reaction I wanted the first time I wore this, I thought I'd test it out. What do you think? Is this doing it for you?"

My cock strains against my navy-blue dress pants in response. "Yeah," I say on a rasp. "I think I need to see it from behind. I wanna get the full effect of the number and the name on your back."

Sara licks her lips. "I was hoping you'd say that. Get over here. Sit your ass in your uncle's chair and fuck my pussy with that delicious tongue."

I whip around and lunge for the lock, but I freeze when Sara hisses.

"Leave it."

"Sar." I shoot her a look over my shoulder. "What if he walks in?"

"Then he'll see his goalie doing something he never could."

Heart pounding right out of my chest, I turn on my heel. With a deep breath in, I stalk toward her. I squeeze my hands into fists at my sides and release them, desperate to feel the smooth skin of her ass.

She tracks my movements as I round the desk, even peering over her shoulder as I roll the leather chair forward.

I grasp her hips, relishing the way her soft skin gives under my hold. "And what's that, Sar? What can I do that he couldn't?"

She laughs. It's throaty and devious and so fucking sexy. "So many things, Brooks."

I kiss the back of her thigh and take in a deep breath through my nose.

She hums in approval. "But what I was referring to was make me come. Only you've been able to do that."

My heart beats out a fast rhythm against my ribcage, and pride surges inside me. I may not be experienced, but I'm dedicated. And a bit of an overachiever. Working to make Sara come over and over again is not a hardship. It's my new favorite activity.

After that first taste of her in the hot tub, I'm certifiably obsessed. Over the last two weeks, I've eaten her every chance I can get. I even snuck her into the back of the plane and played with her perfect pussy while Aiden serenaded the team with Taylor Swift songs. She got off twice. Once during "Shake It Off," then again during "Wildest Dreams."

This view—royal blue against her skin, the number thirteen on her back, and Langfield scrawled between her shoulder blades— might be my all-time favorite. Especially when it's paired with her ass in my face and her smile aimed in my direction.

She's a vision. Every dream I've ever had. The only woman I've ever wanted everything with.

Digging into her flesh with my fingers, I spread her cheeks and survey my new heaven. I angle in close, being sure each of my exhalations hits her skin, and watch the goosebumps pebble. But I don't immediately give her what she wants.

Head thrown back, she moans. "Please, Brooks. Be a good boy and lick me."

My cock swells further, threatening to tear a hole right through my slacks. I smack her ass cheek. Hard. Instantly, I'm leaking. The redness that blooms on her creamy skin might be the hottest thing I've ever seen. "Don't tell me how to make you come."

This moan is louder. Maybe loud enough for a person walking by to hear. She arches her back, pushing her ass closer to my face and putting that gorgeous glistening pussy on full display.

Shit. The temptation to give in is strong. But I push it down deep, determined to torment her.

"I should leave you here, wet and begging for me, while I go to the press conference. See how good you can be for me. See how wet you are when I get back. You'll probably drip all over his desk just thinking about my tongue."

"Yes," she whispers, desperate now.

I smack her other cheek, leaving a matching mark. Then, because I can't help it, I kiss the welt I left behind, then run my tongue against it.

"But I'd much rather talk to the press with your cum on my tongue. Yeah, I think that's what I'll do."

I don't make her wait any longer. I keep my hands on her ass, spreading her even wider, and slide my tongue through her slit from front to back. "So good, Pumpkin. So fucking sweet and delicious."

Pushing back, Sara rubs against my face, chasing her release, loud and unapologetic. "Make me squirt all over his desk."

Fuck, now I really am going to come in my pants. Can I do that? Can I get her to squirt? "Fuck, Sar." I drop my head to her ass cheek and close my eyes, willing myself not to explode in my pants. "Tell me what to do. I'll be your good boy. I promise."

"You always are." Her voice is soft and full of praise, at complete odds with the filthy words coming from her mouth. "Give me two fingers, Brooks."

I obey, watching the way she sucks my fingers into her warmth. Blood rushes in my ears at the thought of what it will feel like when it's my cock. How good she'll feel wrapped around me. Tight. Hot. Once I fuck her, I know I'll want to live inside her.

The guys think she's all that's on my mind now? Once I get to feel this tight cunt wrapped around me, hockey will be a distant memory. Filling her. Listening to her soft whimpers and moans. There won't be room for other thoughts in my mind.

"You're so tight, Sar. So fucking warm. My cock can't wait."

"Yes, Brooks. I can't wait for you to fill me. I'm dying to feel every ridge as you work your way inside. You'll fill me so full I won't be able to breathe. You're big. I could tell when I rode you in the hot tub."

That's as close as she's gotten to my dick. I'm not ready for more yet. Still haven't gotten my fill of eating her, playing with her, teasing her. And the instant I sink inside her, whether it's her mouth or her pussy, she'll own me.

I'm a fool. Because whether I've been inside her or not, she already does.

"Now curve your finger. Then put your tongue back where it belongs."

"Here?" I tease. Then I slip my tongue between her ass cheeks and lick my way up.

She moans like the dirty girl she is, loving the feel of my tongue pressed against that tight hole. "Oh fuck. Yes, Brooks. Right there."

I work my fingers in and out, making sure to curl them as I do, and to slide my tongue all over. Her ass, her pussy, back and forth until she's crying out, desperate for more.

More than happy to please, I give her a thumb.

"Holy shit, yes," she pants.

I push my thumb deeper, stretching her tight asshole, all the while fucking her cunt with my fingers. When she goes over the edge, her body milks me, sucking me deeper. In response, I curl my fingers and press harder.

I'm rewarded when she christens the desk with her cum.

Holy shit. My hunger for her is nowhere near satiated, so I dip back in and lick her up and down until she's begging me to stop.

"Please, Brooks. It's too much. Too sensitive."

Eyes closed, I lap at her once more. Then I pull back, drop my arms to the leather armrests of my uncle's chair, and admire the view. Sara, spent and still on her knees, face pressed to the desk, chest heaving, legs wide, my jersey bunched up. Her blond hair is a wreck, and her skin is glowing.

But it's always her smile that gets me.

When she slides off the desk and turns it on me, blue eyes the color of turquoise waters on a sunny day, pure happiness aimed in my direction, that's when I know I'll be walking out of this office a happy man.

Everything else is just icing. But Sara happy because of me? That's the damn Stanley Cup.

CHAPTER 28
Brooks

"DO IT AGAIN." Fitz turns up the music and motions for me to get back into position.

Now that I don't spend my mornings before games going over plays with my uncle, I need some new rituals. I asked my goalie coach to work on drills with me before today's game.

I'm keyed up. Touching Sara is the most incredible thing I've ever experienced, but without finding my own release, I'm edging closer to bursting. With any luck, these drills will quell the torturous ache plaguing me.

"You're dropping your shoulder too early," Coach calls from off the ice.

I take a deep breath, set on tuning him out. But Fitz is watching me, his hands on his hips, waiting for me to acknowledge Seb.

I stand taller and get back into position. Then I run the drill.

"Again," Seb shouts.

Fuck him.

Thirty minutes later, I'm more keyed up than when I started, and now my shoulders are sore from all the anger I'm holding inside. I glide off the ice, keeping my focus set on anything but my uncle.

Only he doesn't understand how not interested I am in his feedback.

"It's clear you should have gone to bed early instead of hanging out with your friend."

I stomp forward on my skates, ignoring him.

"At least I kept her hidden when I got her naked. You have her splayed out like a hooker everywhere you go. Thought I raised you better than that."

I don't stop to check our surroundings, whether we're being watched. Hell, I don't even toss my stick. I just turn, and with all the force I can muster, channeling all the anger and tension that have been coursing through me, I punch the man I once considered my mentor straight in the fucking face.

The force of it knocks him to the ground. He hits the floor, sprawled out on his back, his head smacking the concrete.

I stand over him, one finger pointed at his face, rage tunneling my vision. "You speak a fucking word about her again, and I will step on you with my goddamn blade and end your life."

I don't wait for a response. I don't even see him. He might be bloody. It's possible he's completely fine, though that's doubtful. With blood whooshing in my ears and my heart pounding out of my chest, I stomp off and don't look back.

As soon as I hit the locker room, I toss my stick and smack the wall, desperate for an outlet for all the anger burning me up.

"Hey!" War yells. "What the fuck, man?"

At the sound of his voice, I deflate. Shoulders slumped, I heave myself against the wall, panting, but I can't find it in me to respond.

War hovers in front of me, a concerned frown marring his features. "Breathe, Brooks. Breathe." He instructs me to inhale and hold it while he counts to four, then he tells me to exhale and counts again.

I obey, focusing on his voice, using it to anchor me to the moment.

When my vision clears, I tip my head back. War is still standing in front of me, but now he's holding out a bottle of water.

My energy is sapped. There's no fight left in me. I honestly have no idea how I'm going to play tonight. I chug the water, then duck my head. The angry heat that fueled me has now turned into embarrassment. My face is hot, my chest tight. Dammit. Why do I let him affect me like this? I can't continue to work with him. Especially after his comment today. But he isn't any closer to leaving. If he doesn't, then should I? Do I have it in me to quit the team?

"You need to talk to me." War's voice leaves nothing up for discussion.

He's right. I need to talk to someone. So I slide to the floor and hang my head. When he settles next to me, the words pour out. I tell him everything. My uncle's betrayal. Sara's devastation. The fake relationship. All the very real feelings that are now fucking with my head.

"Do you think she feels the same way?" He studies me with real concern in his eyes.

I run my hands through my hair. "I have no fucking idea. But as much as I hate him, Coach isn't even wrong. If someone had seen her —" I shake my head. What the fuck was I thinking fucking around with her in public?

War nods. "You've always held a torch for the girl. Don't—" He lets out a long breath and shifts so he's facing me head-on. "This could just be sex for her, Brooks. And she's your friend."

My heart pangs at the thought. "My best friend," I retort.

War's response is an arched brow.

"Okay," I laugh, feeling a fraction lighter and thankful for the levity. "You're up there too."

"But you don't want to fuck me," he drolls.

Another wave of anxiety has me doubling over. "I know what you're saying. It's just—when I'm around her, God, she's everything, War. Everything I've ever fucking wanted. And now I'm allowed to touch her. Allowed to kiss her. How am I supposed to stop?"

He drops his head back against the cinderblock wall. "You need to talk to her. Figure out where she stands before you go any further.

I've never seen you like this, man." He roughs a hand down his face. "You're the most levelheaded guy I know. Hell, you're probably the only virgin hockey player in the entire league."

I cough out a laugh and swipe my hand over my mouth. "NHL and NCAA more likely."

War smiles. "That's my point. What's going on between you and Sara means something to you. You need to make sure it means something to her too." His smile falls, and his tone turns more serious than I thought he was capable. "And you can't knock Coach out again. Even if he deserves it."

I drop my elbows to my knees and slump. He's not wrong.

"Just take a breather. Focus on the game tonight. Not on what's going on off the ice."

It's a lot easier said than done, but he's right. The only thing I can do is get my head in the game and play.

CHAPTER 29

Sara

Me: Good luck tonight. I'll be the girl in your jersey screaming your name.

Me: Haha that was a joke.

Me: Tough loss. You slipped out while I was still with the press. Want to meet up somewhere?

Brooks: Sorry. I'm tired. Gonna get some rest.

Me: Oh okay. Of course. Lennox invited me to stay at her apartment when we're in New York, but I thought I'd stay at the hotel. That way we can have some privacy. Thoughts?

Brooks: You should stay with Lennox. You never get to spend time with her.

Me: True. Good Point. Okay. Well, get some rest. I'll see you on the plane tomorrow.

"Good Morning, Boston. I'm Colton, and this is my co-host, Eliza, and we're here to bring you the Hockey Report."

"Sorry, Colton. I don't have it in me. I'm depressed after last night's game. The team on the ice last night was not the team I've been watching for the last six weeks."

"It was brutal. Brooks Langfield practically stepped out of the crease and pointed toward the net, inviting the puck in."

"And New York is looking better and better as the season goes on. We'll have to see how they do against our boys this week. Chicago skated circles around the Bolts' defense, and their record is nowhere near as good," Eliza whines.

"New York is definitely a team to watch."

CHAPTER 30

Sara

"THAT WAS A TOUGH ONE." Lennox leads me through the tunnel in New York where the fans dressed in blue exit in a somber horde. New York beat us four-one. The entire team, including Brooks, played terribly.

He's played like shit for the last two games, and other than the moments after games when I'm herding him and the team in for questions with reporters, he's barely spoken to me. Even in those moments, he avoids eye contact, and he doesn't dare touch me.

On the plane, he sat with Tyler and Aiden like he used to without a word to me. All I got was a slight nod before he was settling in and losing himself in conversation. When we landed in New York, he suddenly had plans with his goalie coach. It felt an awful lot like he was avoiding me.

I'm losing my goddamn mind.

"You sticking around?" I ask her outside the locker room.

Lennox shakes her head. "Nah, I'm going to head back to my apartment. You coming to my place or you headed back to Boston?"

Despite Brooks's attitude, I've made the best of the time I've had with my bestie. But the team is headed back to Boston tonight, while she'll be staying in New York.

She says it's time to start her job hunt. All week I've tried to convince her that this would be the perfect opportunity for her to move back to Boston. If Aiden wasn't in the picture, I think I may have been successful, but since that moment he slammed into the glass at the sight of her, she's been spooked. She's hidden it well, but I can see the underlying disquiet that's plaguing her. Clearing the air might help, but they've yet to talk. I'm not sure if that's because of her or him, and I'm not pushing. I'm dealing with enough relationship drama myself.

"I really need to talk to Brooks."

Lennox eyes me. "Yeah, if not for your sake, then you need to do it for the Bolts. The guy is falling apart on the ice."

I cross my arms over my chest and roll my eyes. "That has nothing to do with me."

At least I hope not, but with every passing day, I'm a little more concerned that it does. Is Brooks staying away from me because I'm bad luck? He's a stickler for rituals and shit like that, sure, but if he's pushing me away because of a goddamn superstition, then I'm really going to punch him in the face.

Either way, if I head back with the team tonight, I can visit with Josie tomorrow. Time with her is guaranteed to brighten the shadows that have enshrouded me this week, and I know she looks forward to it too.

"Don't be a stranger," I beg her, pulling her in close.

Once we part, I head to the pressroom. New York is dealing with the media first, so I lean against the door and watch each of them give their wrap-up.

"Vin, you've never scored more than one goal on Brooks Langfield. Tonight you scored three. What happened?"

When Vin gives the reporters a cocky smile, the anger that rushes through me is enough to make the edges of my vision go red. I have to turn around and walk out so I don't launch myself across the room and beat him up myself.

I could tell them what happened. The team was a mess. Brooks's head wasn't in it. He was just a second too slow, and with the speed at which the puck travels on the slick ice, a second is practically a lifetime.

As I'm leaving the room, my focus snags on a familiar face in the back corner. Jill. *Why the hell is she here?*

She wasn't in the WAG box tonight, and the woman never comes to home games, let alone away games. But here she is. She's beaming in a black dress and black thigh-high boots with a red scarf around her neck.

Is she wearing New York colors?

No. There's no way.

For a long moment, I watch her. She's intently focused on the front of the room, and the smile on her face is full of affection. I follow her line of sight and discover that it leads straight to Vin. What the hell?

"They ready for us?" Tyler is waiting for me just inside the locker room, showered and dressed in his game-day suit. He, along with Aiden, Brooks, and Seb, will have to answer for the Bolts' lackluster performance.

"Almost." My mind is spinning. Should I mention my suspicions about Jill to him? Should I ask about Brooks?

I'm still considering when Brooks breezes past me without so much as looking my way.

The pain that explodes in my chest at the utter disregard is so harsh I have to suck in a breath to keep from doubling over. "Excuse me," I whisper to Tyler, fighting back a string of curses. Then I turn to go after Brooks.

Before I can make it to the door, Tyler grasps my elbow and pulls me back into his chest. "Give him some space, Sar."

I spin and pull my shoulders back, glaring at his hand.

With a grunt, he releases me and takes half a step back. "He had a bad game."

No shit. I lift my chin and zero in on him. "That doesn't give him an excuse to be a dick."

Tyler's blue eyes soften. "It doesn't." Then he arches a brow. "But everything else—" He sighs, his shoulders slumping with an invisible weight. "He's spiraling, and he's just trying to get his bearings. As his *friends*, it's our job to have his back. And if he's a dick? Then we should remember not to take it personally. He's just working through some shit."

I press my tongue to the roof of my mouth to stave off the tears pricking the backs of my eyes. Fuck. Brooks told Tyler. My stomach sinks at the thought. What exactly did he tell him?

"Well, *as his girlfriend*, Tyler, it fucking hurts." I clear the emotion from my throat. "You may be okay with it when he acts like a dick, but I'm not. So if you'll excuse me, it's time I called him on his shit."

Instead of arguing like I expect him to, Tyler studies me with his lips quirked up on one side. Then he shakes his head and lets out a surprised laugh. "Yeah," he says, rubbing a hand over his mouth. "Maybe it is."

I don't have a clue why he's so smiley, but I don't have time to consider the reasons. I have another hockey player to put in his place. So with a nod, I stomp off in search of Brooks. When I find him, he's standing outside the pressroom, his attention on his phone.

To quell my anger, I take in deep breaths as I approach. The sharp tapping of my heels on the concrete floor announces my arrival.

He snaps his head up, and his eyes soften for a beat. His hair is still wet from his shower, but it's back in a low bun. A navy-blue pinstripe suit strains against his thick shoulders as he pockets his phone and stands taller. He dips his chin and takes a deep breath. When he focuses on me again, it's like he's secured the shutters over his heart. The warmth in his eyes that's always been all but permanent is absent, and his mouth is fixed in a straight line. He's emotionless.

"What the hell is going on?" My voice quivers. I keep my head held high, but an acute pain radiates through my entire body. I'm at a loss as to how to fix what's wrong between us.

For days he's been nothing but cold. For days he's pushed me aside like I'm his dirty little secret. It's Seb all over again.

Brooks wasn't supposed to be like this. He was supposed to be safe.

He studies me, his gaze remaining cool. "What are you talking about?" With a glance over my shoulder, he huffs. "Played like shit, got reamed by Coach. Now I'm about to go talk to the media, where they're going to go on about how I couldn't stop a puck even if it was slow rolling into the net."

The sigh that escapes me is pure exhaustion and anger. "I could give two shits if you let in seventeen goals, Brooks. I'm talking about us."

His jaw ticks, but he keeps his focus locked on something just behind me. "What about us?"

"You're acting weird. I thought—" I shake my head and look away, willing myself to keep my composure. Whatever I thought was obviously wrong. It's clear our connection was only physical for him. But God, it hurts. So much more than when I discovered Seb's betrayal, even. Because this is Brooks. Because I thought our friendship mattered more to him. "Forget it." I take a step back, suddenly desperate for a moment of privacy to pull myself together.

Brooks clutches my shoulders and spins me against the wall, essentially creating a shield between me and the world with his body.

I can't hold back the gasp that escapes me at the abrupt move.

"You thought what?" His voice is quieter now, his expression a fraction softer.

"Am I bad luck?" I slump back against the wall. "Is that why you won't come near me? Or did I do something wrong?"

With a groan, he drops his head back. When he straightens again and focuses on me, the old Brooks is there. Eyes warm, face full of nothing but affection. He angles forward, like he can't get close enough, and cups my face. "No, Sara. You did nothing wrong."

"Then why are you pushing me away?" The ache in my chest flares. "Why are you acting weird?"

"Because we shouldn't have done what we did. *I* shouldn't have done what I did. Of course I'm acting weird."

I try to step to one side, to put distance between us, but he doesn't let me go. "You can't be serious right now. You promised nothing would change. Now that we've hooked up, you ignore me?" I lick my lips and drop my chin, focusing on one of the buttons on his shirt, willing my heart not to crack. "I need this job, Brooks. You're the face of the team. No matter what you do, you'll be okay. Your spot here is secure. But I'll be heading back to North Carolina with nothing. I *need* this job." I force myself to meet his gaze, despite the tears blurring my vision. "I don't think you understand just how much."

His face twists in anguish. "Never, Sar. No matter what happens, never. Your job is safe." He huffs out a breath. "Fuck, I'm fucking this all up."

I scan his face, searching for the meaning behind his words. Trying to reconcile the man I thought Brooks was—the kind, loyal, caring guy he's portrayed for the year we've been friends—with the asshole who's been giving me the cold shoulder all week.

All I come up with is a whole lot of nothing. "Yeah," I sigh. "You are."

With a low groan, he rests his forehead against mine. He takes several shallow breaths and watches me. I can't take my eyes off him either.

"Believe me," he says, his voice low. "I'm the one at risk here."

"What does that even mean?"

He shakes his head against mine. "Just know that you'll always have a spot with the Bolts. And more than that..." He takes my hand and lifts it to his chest. His heart pounds beneath my palm. "You'll always have a spot here. You have nothing to worry about." The warm breath that leaves his lips sends the hairs framing my face fluttering. He uses one finger to brush a few stray strands from my temple, then settles his palm against my cheek. "I'll do better."

I cover his hand and lean into his touch. "I'm so confused. You haven't so much as looked at me since we were in your uncle's office."

Swallowing past the lump in my throat, I force myself to ask the questions I don't really want the answers to. "Did I push you too far? Is that not what you want? Are we just friends? Please." God, I hate how desperate I sound. Even so, I don't stop. "I need to know what's going on between us."

Without my permission, a tear crests my lashes and slips down my cheek.

Brooks's face crumples, his lips turning down and anguish overtaking his features. He swipes at the tear with his thumb. "No crying, baby. I'm sorry. No, we're not just friends. But what happened in the hot tub—what happened in Seb's office—that should have been just for us. You're not a fucking prop, Sar. I all but fucked you in front of my uncle on the pool deck. Anyone could have seen. Taken photos. Anyone could have walked in and caught us in that office."

"But I liked it," I hiss. "I know I'm not a prop. I orchestrated the damn thing in the office." My heart clenches in my chest so sharply I suck in a breath. "I need to know that I didn't force you to do something you didn't want to do. Because that's how I feel. God, Brooks, I feel like I seduced my best friend, and now he's realized I'm the horrible person his uncle says I am. The slut. The bunny." Another tear escapes, then another.

Brooks's grip on my cheek tightens, and he steps closer, so we're chest to chest. "No—"

Beside us, the facility assistant appears, startling us both. "Press is ready for the Bolts."

CHAPTER 31
Brooks

Me: I need an excuse for why we can't go to mom's for dinner tomorrow.

Aiden: I got nothing.

Gavin: Everything okay?

Beckett: Already done. Finn broke Dad's whiskey decanter with the Nerf gun last time we were there.

Me: Tell that kid I'll buy him whatever he wants this week as a thank you.

Beckett: Yeah, no. We don't need any more animals in this house.

Gavin: Oh, you know you miss Junior.

Beckett: I can't wait until you have kids.

Gavin: LOL never happening. You are having more than enough kids for the rest of us.

Beckett: Duck you.

> Me: I'm coming over tomorrow. I need advice.

> Aiden: Finn does give great advice.

> Gavin: Aiden, you're an idiot. Brooks, I'll ask again. You okay?

> Me: No.

> Aiden: I'll be right over.

> Beckett: Let him be. I'll see you all tomorrow? We can take DOG to the park with Finn. And Brooks, you can snuggle Addie. She makes everything better. If that doesn't help, then we can make friendship bracelets with Winnie.

I SHAKE my head and read that last text again. It's insane to think that's who my older brother has become. And yet, beneath the hard CEO persona he wore for so long, he's always been caring and attentive. And he's always been so damn aware of what the people around him need.

For most of my life, I thought my uncle had taught me to be a good person, but the more distance I put between myself and him, the more I see that the lessons that really shaped me all happened at home.

Maybe Sara is right. Maybe Seb had nothing to do with the parts of me she loves. He molded me into the athlete I am, sure. But the nice guy, the one who smiles at everyone, the guy who genuinely enjoys life? I can still be him in spite of Seb, not because of him. And more importantly, I think I want to be that guy for Sara. And for me.

> Gavin: Ha! So you admit you named him DOG? And cuddles with Addie sound perfect. I'm in. Brooks, call me if you need me.

Aiden: Same.

Me: Thanks guys. I'll see you tomorrow.

"And that, Uncle Gav, is how you tie the bracelet off." Winnie holds up the blue and gray beaded bracelet that says *Best Uncle.*

I snatch it from her hand before Gavin can accept it. "Thanks, Bear," I say with a cheeky smile. Beckett gave her the nickname when he met her, and it stuck.

We've been through the whole list of Beckett's suggestions. We spent the afternoon at the park letting Beckett's mutt of a best friend chase the squirrels while Finn chased him. I got in some good snuggles with Addie before she went down for a nap, and now bracelet-making time is over.

Liv and Dylan are in the kitchen making dinner. Dylan's husband Cortney is snuggled up with his baby girl on the couch, and Beckett is set up in his favorite armchair. The two of them are chatting baseball. The season is over, but they're already making plans for next year.

Aiden has disappeared with Finn and Liam, Dylan's teenage son. I don't even want to know what kind of prank they're planning.

Finn jabbered on about how he took over as king of pranks when they moved out of the brownstone from hell—Beckett's words, not mine—and Liam shot Beckett a look. Probably because of the curse the six-year-old so naturally uttered along with his declaration.

Beckett shook his head. "I already paid Finn for that slip. I'm not paying you because he repeated it."

Winnie giggles, her freckled cheeks going rosy. "I'll make three more *Best Uncle* bracelets. But I'll use fire colors for Uncle Dec's."

I bite back a groan. I always forget that there's another uncle to contend with. Liv's brother still lives in their hometown and is the local fire chief.

Winnie darts out of the room and clomps up the stairs, probably in search of more beads.

Thankful for the break from bracelet-making, I slump back in my chair at the dining room table.

"You gonna tell me what's going on?" Gavin doesn't look away from the bracelet he's making. Oddly, this one says *Peaches*.

"Might as well call the rest of them in so I don't have to tell this story seventeen times." I push back and balance on two chair legs, then I let out a whistle. "Beckett, can you come here?"

Cortney stands, cradling his sleeping daughter on his chest. "I'm going to put her down and see if Dylan and Liv need help with dinner." He winks at me, then heads out. The man has an uncanny ability to read the room, so I have no doubt he understands my need for privacy. I appreciate it. I need their advice, and in order to get it, I'm going to have to open up. But I'd rather keep the details of the situation in the family.

Sara's relationship with Seb is her secret, not mine, so I avoid that issue and stick to the ones that involve me. I explain how Coach caught us fooling around and how I got into a fight with him over it. I keep some of the details vague, since Seb's official story is that he tripped and fell and that's why he's sporting a broken nose.

The way Gavin's eyes narrow on me makes it clear he's reading between the lines, but I continue on.

"Anyway, I didn't handle it well. After the fight with Seb, I pulled back. He never should have seen her in that position. I shouldn't have put her in that damn position. And now she's worried that her job isn't secure. She was upset and afraid that she took things too far with me. And because of the way I acted, she's worried that she'll be left in the cold."

Gavin lets out a low whistle.

"I'm speaking to my brother, by the way," I say pointedly. "Not to the owner of the team or her boss."

Gavin juts his chin. "That's a given. As your brother, I love seeing the two of you together. And as your boss *and* hers, I'm all for it. The fans love it too. Obviously we'd all prefer that you're dressed when we see you together, but I think Beckett's with me when I say that sometimes it's hard not to get caught up in the moment and do stupid things."

Beckett smirks. "I never do anything stupid."

"Conning your drunk employee into marrying you in Vegas isn't stupid?" Liv asks as she walks into the dining room.

"No. It was the most brilliant thing I've ever done." He pats his lap, signaling for her to join him.

With a laugh and shake of her head, she slips into the seat beside him. He, of course, tugs her closer and rests a gentle hand on her stomach.

Gavin clears his throat and plants his elbows on the table, steepling his fingers. "This shit with Seb—it gonna be okay?"

"Not if he keeps treating Sara like she's a puck bunny," I say, clasping my hands on the table in front of me.

Liv sucks in a shocked breath. "He said that?"

"He did," Gavin answers for me. "I heard it the night she ended up on the ice while Brooks did push-ups."

Beckett grimaces. "And you didn't say anything to him?"

Gavin waves his hand. "Sara glossed over his comment. She called Lennox over, and I got distracted. But obviously shit like that doesn't fly. What does he have against her?"

I lower my head and survey my *Best Uncle* bracelet. Dammit, I hate lying to my brothers, but I refuse to spill Sara's secrets. "He thinks she's a distraction."

"Is she?" Beckett asks.

I tip my chin up and glare at him. "Yes. Just like Liv is for you." Then I turn to Liv and soften my tone. "A good distraction. I can do my job and have a girlfriend. I just, ah—" An annoyed breath escapes me. "I'm screwing it up with her. Seb said those things, and then War meant well, but something he said got in my head. And...I don't know. I just figured a little distance would be best. Give me a chance to clear my head. But now she thinks I don't care about her."

Beckett nods. "Open communication is key. As are dates. That's always been my rule."

"Yup," Liv agrees, sitting straighter. "Friday night date nights. They were his requirement when we were fake married."

"It was never fake," Beckett grumbles. "See that ring on your finger? It's been there since the day you became my wife."

She presses her lips together but can't hide her smile. "I love riling him up."

Squinting, I assess my oldest brother. "So you forced Liv to go on dates with you, and that's how you got her to fall for you?"

Beckett's face darkens, and he pitches forward. "Watch what you're suggesting."

Liv laughs beside him. "Yes. It was his only rule. I had many."

I arch a brow. "Any good ones?"

"He had to watch the kids on Thursdays. No PDA. No kissing."

Head tipped back, I bark out a laugh. "Those are awful."

The growl that Beckett lets out practically rattles the table. "Telling me."

Liv smiles. "Not awful. Because when he did all those things, I knew that he genuinely wanted to. That it wasn't just a PR stunt to him."

Beckett weaves his fingers with Liv's and squeezes her hand. "I always wanted you."

"I know that now, baby." She bumps his shoulder with hers. "I didn't know it then, though. And it was hard to believe. We'd worked together for years, and he never said anything."

"You were married," Gavin quips, but he quickly slams his lips shut when Beckett glowers at him.

"You want to show Sara you care about her?" Liv asks, keeping the conversation on track.

"Yeah, this week was stressful for me, and I didn't handle it well. I think she took it personally."

"I did too." Gavin scoots in closer, back to steepling his fingers in front of him.

Liv frowns at him with a disapproving look she usually reserves for her husband.

He holds up his hands. "What? It's my damn team that's playing like shit. I take it personally."

Aiden snorts from the doorway, then saunters in and drops into a chair across from me. "Then throw on a pair of skates and get out on the ice. Score the damn goals for us."

"Or block them," I challenge.

Gavin shakes his head. "I'm just saying that I get where Sara is coming from. You are all broody motherfuckers—"

"Thousand dollars, Uncle Gav." I swear Finn's voice echoes from the vents in the room.

"You should pay for my curses, since it's your mother ducking fault." Gavin pulls out his wallet and hands it to Beckett to take out the cash.

My oldest brother counts out the hundreds loudly, then calls his son in. "Huck, it's all here!"

Finn darts into the room, snatches the cash, and nods at Gavin. "Pleasure doing business with ya." Then he's gone.

Liv just closes her eyes and shakes her head. Probably silently calling us a bunch of idiots. She wouldn't be wrong.

"Do you need help coming up with date ideas?" Aiden wiggles in his seat like an excitable puppy. "Because seriously, I am an epic planner."

I settle back against my chair and close my eyes. For a long minute, I replay all their comments and suggestions. I need to show Sara that I'm still the guy I was when we were just friends. That no matter what our label, she'll always be my girl. Regardless of how things progress with us, I won't get weird again. I need to open up to her. "Nah," I say, hit with the perfect idea. "I know exactly what I want to do."

CHAPTER 32

Sara

> Brooks: Can I take you somewhere tomorrow after the photo shoot?

OH SHIT. I forgot all about that.

> Me: Brooks just asked me to go somewhere with him after the photo shoot tomorrow. What do I say?

> Lennox: Um, yes?

> Me: I'm still really hurt about how he acted. Maybe it's best if we go back to being just friends.

> Lennox: Is that what you want?

Shit. Now not only do I not know how to respond to Brooks, but I'd rather avoid responding to Lennox. Because no, I don't think that's what I want. But maybe it's what's best for us both.

I flip back to his text and read it again. I spent the whole day watching movies with Josie and Ava. We ordered in dinner and had it delivered to the hospital, and it wasn't until Josie started dozing in the middle of our third movie of the day that I finally headed home.

For the first time in a week, I didn't obsess over Brooks or how he makes me feel. Okay, that's a blatant lie. I thought about him a lot. But at least I didn't have to suffer through being ignored and brushed off when I was hanging out with the girls.

Though he did explain the reasons behind why he was acting so weird...

> Me: I think I want to be more than friends.

> Lennox: Oh good! Then we can find out what his penis looks like.

> Me: Lennnn!!!!

> Lennox: Bet it's huge.

> Me: Speaking from experience with the Langfield men?

> Lennox: If he's anything like his brother, then you're a lucky, lucky girl.

A bark of laugher escapes me. Brooks is practically double Aiden's size in every way that's visible while clothed. It wouldn't surprise me if that applied elsewhere.

> Lennox: Wonder if he's pierced.

> Me: No freaking way.

> Lennox: Have you ever been with someone who is?

> Me: No. Have you?

> Lennox: <side eye emoji>

> Me: Lennox!

> Me: If he is, then he would have had to go months without sex, right?

Lennox: No way!

Lennox: Oh shit. I just looked it up. You're right. God, how do men do it?

> Me: Haha. I don't think men who actually get it are men who are actually getting it.

Lennox: LOL. I'm dead.

I lean back in my bed, heart feeling light for the first time in days, and type out a response to Brooks.

> Me: Sure. Work related?

Brooks: No.

> Me: Friend related?

Brooks: No.

Brooks: Dress warm and be prepared to smile, crazy girl. I miss you.

My stomach is a riot of butterflies as I step inside Bolts Arena for Brooks's photo shoot. The photos are for a campaign for sports apparel—mainly the kind that goes under his uniform. I'm already salivating at the prospect of how he'll be dressed. Tragically, the underwear campaign was before my time with Langfield Corp, so I wasn't around to witness the way he posed for the shots that ended up on billboards all over Boston.

When I spot Hannah standing by the ice and holding two cups of coffee, I make a beeline for her.

The tiny brunette breaks into a huge smile when I approach and holds out one of the cups to me. "Finally!"

"Thanks." With a grateful smile, I accept the coffee and take a sip. Despite my warm layers, the arena is freezing. The pumpkin taste dances on my tongue, pulling a moan from me. "Pumpkin. My favorite."

"Ha, that's what Brooks said when he gave me the coffees. 'Give this to my Pumpkin. She's my favorite.' How cute is that?"

I choke on my latte and have to cover my mouth to keep from spewing the hot liquid on my friend. "Brooks said that?"

Honestly, I can absolutely picture him saying it. To me. But to someone else? Especially after how surly he's been to just about anyone he's come into contact with lately? If he's—

Not going to get ahead of myself. We'll see how he is today.

But even as I tell myself to temper my expectations, giddy excitement rises. It only continues to grow when a loud laugh echoes through the cavernous space. When the sound hits me, it's like being pummeled with a shot of pure elation. His laugh is one of many things I've come to crave over the last few weeks.

I find him instantly. Wearing a dark blue robe, Brooks is standing at his full height in front of a small woman, still laughing.

With her back to me like this, it's impossible to make out her words, but she speaks again, and there goes that laughter that hits me like an arrow to the heart.

Only a second later, the shot of elation turns into one of jealousy. Who is this chick and why does he find her so funny? I'm the funny one.

Laugh at me, Brooks. Pay attention to me.

Hannah nudges me. "Ready to see your boy?"

That sentiment, *my boy*, unsticks my feet, and I'm moving toward him once again.

"We're going to put you in the sin bin. When you're in there, stand up, put your arms against the glass like you're looking out at the ice. Then we'll take shots of you from the front and the back."

"Ya know I've never been in there, right?" he says, his tone teasing, maybe even flirtatious.

You're about to be, buddy.

"Hmm. You are known as the good boy of hockey. Although I'd consider you very bad," the woman says.

I will cut the bitch.

Brooks's laugh is so damn jovial. "How so?"

"I gave you my number after the shoot last month. I know you say you don't date—"

Tamping down on the murderous rage threatening to make me do something stupid, I clear my throat.

Brooks looks up and over the woman's shoulder, and when he spots me, his face lights up like the arena's spotlight has been turned on him. "'Scuse me." He jogs to the edge of the rink and jumps the boards with ease. Then he's in my personal space, staring down at me.

"Morning, crazy girl." Without giving me a moment to reply, he dips low and presses his mouth to mine. "Hmm. You taste delicious."

Breathless, I take him in. It's hard to explain, but he's different from the Brooks of the last few weeks. The tension in his jaw is all but gone, and the dark circles under his eyes have faded. He's lighter.

I ghost my fingers through the scruff on his face. He's normally clean shaven, so this must be for the photos.

"You're...you." My heart lodges in my throat. I wish I could take the words back, because as soon as they escape me, I'm terrified that bringing attention to the change will force him to disappear again.

He smiles as if he completely understands what I mean, confirming what I already suspect. "Yeah, Sar. I'm me." He brushes a wisp of hair from my temple. "Let's get this photo shoot over with so we can move onto our date." When he says that last word, date, he brightens further, if it's possible.

"Date?" I tease.

Brooks brings his lips to mine in the softest of kisses and hovers there. "Yeah, Sara. Our first date." He pulls back a fraction. "You and me. Today. Okay?"

I bite my lip, loving the flirtatious way he keeps staring at it. "Okay."

Forty-five minutes later, Brooks is bare chested and wearing nothing but a pair of navy boxer briefs that hug his muscular thighs. He's got a hockey stick in hand, and I have to keep checking to be sure I'm not drooling.

His ass is like two bowling balls. How does this woman get any work done if all she does is photograph athletes? Fortunately she stopped flirting after the first time he tensed beneath her touch. Apparently she recognized that it's more important to get the athlete relaxed for photos than to make unwanted advances.

"I can't believe that is all yours," Hannah says beside me as Brooks smolders for another round of shots.

I lick my lips and let out a soft hum.

"Sar, can you come here for a second?" Brooks calls as the photographer ducks her head and clicks through the images on her camera.

I head for the ice, but before I get more than two steps, Hannah grasps my arm and tugs me back. "Give me your jacket and throw this on instead." She holds up a Bolts jersey.

Scrutinizing her with a frown, I take the jersey and stretch it out in front of me. Sure enough, there's a giant 13 on the back. Clutching it to my chest, I assess her, then turn and eye Brooks.

"Don't ask questions." Brooks waves me over.

I obey, though I make my way to him slowly, confused about Hannah's instructions.

"Put it on and sit on my lap, please."

He's still in the penalty box, which is appropriate, because he seems determined to get us both into trouble.

He laughs like he can hear my thoughts. "Come on, crazy girl. I want a picture."

As I pass her, the photographer is tinkering with the settings on her camera like she's prepping to take another shot. She doesn't seem surprised or bothered by Brooks's suggestion.

Me? I'm feeling the exact opposite. Though the closer I get, the more curious I am, and with every step, excitement replaces every other feeling. Just outside the penalty box, I pull the jersey on over my long-sleeve black shirt. It's several sizes bigger than mine, so it falls halfway down my thighs.

"It's kinda big," I tease, grasping the hem so I can tuck it into my dark jeans.

Brooks circles my wrist and pulls me onto his lap. "Leave it. It's mine."

The breath whooshes from my lungs at that simple statement. Blinking, I sit up straighter in his lap. "Yours?"

Beneath me, the man is practically naked. Even so, his chest is warm against my back as he holds me close.

"Yeah. I wanted to see *my girl* in my jersey. Have a problem with that?" He settles his warm palm on my thigh and doesn't wait for me to reply. "Ready, Monica?"

With a friendly smile, the photographer adjusts the lighting umbrella beside her, then she aims the camera in our direction.

"What are we doing right now?" My heart doesn't know what to do. It flips over itself, but then it lodges itself up high, making it hard to breathe. "What's this picture for?"

Brooks laughs and cuddles me close. "So many questions. Just smile for the camera. I want a picture of us. This is just for me."

The woman shoots shot after shot for what feels like an eternity but is probably closer to five minutes.

When she finally steps away, back to clicking through the photos on her camera's display, I prod at my cheeks. "Jeez. How do you do that for so long? It was starting to get hard to hold my smile."

Brooks caresses my cheek, one side of his lips tipping up. "Normally, they don't want me to smile."

"Right. They tell you to be all broody." I push my lips out, going for an exaggerated sultry expression, mimicking all his modeling poses.

He tips his chin up and barks out a laugh. "You should probably stick with your day job, babe. Speaking of which, do you have your phone?"

"Sure, why?"

He responds by holding his hand out, and when I give in and pull my phone from my pocket and set it in his palm, he taps on the camera icon. Then he turns it so it's on selfie mode and presses his lips to my cheek. The contact sends a burst of surprised elation through me, and I can't help but smile. A real one this time.

He pulls up the picture and tilts the screen so I can get a good look at it. It's absolutely adorable. I'm beaming at the camera, looking surprisingly good in his oversized jersey. His eyes are closed and his lips are pressed to my cheek, his hair wavy and pulled back, high-lighting his golden skin.

"You have the login info for the Bolts' Instagram page?" he asks.

My chest goes tight at his question. "Um, yeah. Why?"

"You trust me?"

I bite my lip and nod. Of course I trust him.

He slips the phone into my hand and lifts a brow, silently instructing me to sign into the account. Once I do, I give it back to him.

Those butterflies are back, fluttering like mad as I watch him pull up the photo and type out a caption.

Our goalie is finally sharing what's made him so happy lately. Meet Sara, public relations manager for the Bolts.

Brooks hits Post, then hands me the phone. "Now you're the face of the Bolts. Job is safe, Sar. Ready for our date?"

CHAPTER 33
Brooks

"WE'RE STAYING HERE?" Sara scans the ice, then looks back at me, her brows lowered in confusion.

Now that I've changed into warmer clothing, I'm ready to get this date started. "For the first part of the date, we are."

"Oh, you think I'm going to let you take me on a multipart date?" she teases.

I run my tongue along my lips and bite down on a smile. "That's not guaranteed?"

She laughs. "Maybe. We'll see how you do out on the ice."

I grin. "Then I got this in the bag. We both know the ice is my specialty." I pull her toward the bench and drop to my knees. "Sit. Need to get you laced up."

She's still wearing my personal jersey. It's taking everything in me not to drag her home so I can strip every other inch of clothing from her body and do all the dirty things that have been playing on repeat in my mind since the moment she pulled it over her head.

For once she doesn't sass me. Instead, she demurely sits in front of me and allows me to take off her boots. She keeps her hands clasped in her lap and watches with a shy smile as I replace them with skates. When she's laced up and ready, I lead her out to the ice to my personal place of worship.

"I'm not as good at this as you," she warns, wobbling a little.

I chuckle and pull her close, then I push off gently so we move at a slow speed. "Not planning on letting go. Don't worry."

For several quiet moments, we skate hand in hand. She shuffles her skates, allowing me to lead. Everything about this space relaxes me. The familiar smell of the arena—the lingering scent of the concessions mixed with a hint of industrial cleaner and that indescribable smell of the cold. The crisp air against my cheeks. The sound of our skates sliding across the ice as our blades sink into it and push forward, making it feel like I have a superpower, like I'm gliding through air.

And even more than the location, Sara relaxes me.

"So this was your big plan?" she teases, breaking the silence. "Take me ice skating so you can show off your skills? Newsflash, Brooks, I watch you on the ice almost daily. Consider me impressed."

There's my sassy girl. "No. Thought we could talk. Hoped maybe you'd let me ask you a few questions so we could really get to know one another."

She side-eyes me, her lips turned down. "What are you talking about? We've been friends for over a year. By now you probably know me better than anyone." She squeezes my hand. "You can ask me whatever you want. You know that, right? You always could."

I push off harder so we move across the ice a little quicker. "No, I couldn't." The lump lodged in my throat makes it hard to breathe, but I swallow past it. "I love everything you've ever shared with me, but there are questions I've never asked because I had to protect myself..."

She slips and almost goes down, but I've got a good grip on her, so I slow and steady her.

With a deep breath, she continues shuffling forward. "And now?"

"Now I know it's pointless. I don't know when I fell, Sar, but there is no turning back. Even if I get hurt, I'd rather know everything there is to know about my friend, my favorite person..." My stomach knots as I force the words out. "And if I'm lucky, maybe my real girlfriend."

She turns to me then, her smile soft. "If the date goes well, you mean."

"Yeah." I clear my throat. "I know I have work to do. I need to show you that the guy last week... He's not me." I'm still so angry at myself.

"I know that's not you, it's just..." She ducks her head, focusing on the ice in front of us. "It hurt. And I'm not sure I'm even ready to date for real again." She sighs. "But I'm not willing to lose you. So can we take this slow?"

My heart pangs in my chest. *What's slow when I want to give her forever?*

"How 'bout we start with a few questions?"

"Okay, but I get to go first." The smile she aims at me is bright. Shit. I'd give her anything when she looks at me like that.

"What do you want to know?"

"Tell me something no one else knows."

I pull her along beside me, trying like hell to think of something that would impress her. The first thing that pops into my head is so not impressive. She'd probably laugh her ass off, though, and I do love her smile. "This secret isn't really mine, but since you're cute, I'll tell ya anyway."

She bites back a smile and raises a brow, waiting for me to spill the details.

"Last year in New Orleans, the guys and I were out after a game. We'd had a few drinks and were playing Truth or Dare."

Sara covers her eyes with her free hand, totally trusting me to guide her. "Oh God. Do I even want to know?"

I laugh. "Maybe not."

She peeks at me between her fingers, then sighs. "Okay, hit me with it."

"War is the most competitive guy I know, right?"

"Yeah, I can see that."

"And Aiden is a shit-stirrer."

She giggles. "Right."

"During War's turn, he chose *truth*, but then he refused to answer Aiden's question. So Aiden dared him to get his dick pierced."

"What was the question about?"

"Smart girl. How'd I know that's what you'd focus on?"

She throws her head back and squeezes her eyes shut. "I don't really want to picture Tyler's dick, *so...*"

I cough out a laugh. "Hate to break it to you, but that's gonna be hard after this convo."

"Oh no." She squeaks. "Either way, I wanna know what the question was."

"Aiden asked him why he missed that event. The one that Ava was so pissed about."

"The one at the YMCA?"

"Yup."

"Why wouldn't he tell you guys the truth about that?"

I shrug. "No idea, but since he wouldn't, he got his dick pierced."

She barks out a laugh. "Oh my God. And you guys were all there?"

That's when I wince. "Like I said, we'd all had a few drinks, so we went with him. And like idiots, we kept playing the game. War, being the mastermind that he is, came up with questions he knew we wouldn't answer."

"What was yours?"

My stomach plummets then. I shoulda known she would ask that. "He asked when the last time I had sex was."

"And you wouldn't answer it?"

"Well, he phrased it a bit differently, I guess."

The crease between her brows deepens. "How did he phrase it?"

"He asked whether I'd been saving myself for you since we met."

Her mouth falls open, and she brings a hand to her chest. "What?"

Truth time. I take a deep breath and will my stomach to stop rolling. "I guess that could be considered my secret, since I didn't admit it that night."

Sara spins and grabs the front of my shirt with both hands. Her movements are so abrupt her feet almost go out from under her, but I grasp her elbows to steady her.

"Wait," she practically hollers. "Brooks Langfield, does that mean you have a *piercing?*"

I nod, blowing out a relieved breath that she isn't focusing on the fact that I haven't touched a woman since I met her.

And, well, a fuck ton longer than that.

"And Aiden and Tyler?"

"Yeah, we're idiots. I know." Despite how ridiculously sideways that night went, the memory of it is damn entertaining. "War and I had to, since we wouldn't give up our truths. Fucking Aiden did it because he doesn't like to be left out."

"Holy shit! You've got a bejeweled penis! The whole team has fancy peens!" she shouts.

With a chuckle, I slap a hand to her mouth. "Remember how I said it was a secret?"

She nods beneath my palm, so I remove it. Though I take advantage of the moment and drop a kiss to her lips.

"Have you seen theirs?" she whispers, her eyes the size of saucers.

I scoff and give her a grin. "We all shower together, Sar."

"Oh my God." She palms her forehead and groans. "That is so not an image I needed."

"Are you picturing all of us showering together now?"

She nods, her lip pulled between her teeth again. "And your bedazzled penises." The words are barely out of her mouth when she falls against me and cackles.

"Stop talking about my cock like it's a Lisa Frank art project." I squeeze her tight, holding in my own laugh and relishing the heat of her body against me.

She snorts, and her skates slip on the ice. "I can't."

"You're picturing them colored now, aren't you?"

She's laughing so hard she can't breathe.

I heft her a little higher, because with every laugh, she slides a little closer to the ground. "Fuck, Sar."

"I'm sorry." At this point, tears are streaming down her face.

She blows out an exaggerated breath and swipes at them. "Wait, you can't have sex after getting pierced. For, like, a while."

I squint at her. "You been looking this up?"

Without shame, she nods. She doesn't even look away.

Now that she's mostly calm, I take off again, pulling her with me and keeping my speed slow.

I probably don't want to know why she was researching care instructions for dick piercings, but I'm irrationally happy that she's curious rather than freaked out about it.

"The website I found said you couldn't have sex for quite a while."

"You worried 'bout having sex with me, Pumpkin?"

Her cheeks go rosy, and she stumbles forward. I pull her against my chest and bring us to a complete stop again. "Relax, I got it done last year. Completely healed now."

"Right," she breathes, avoiding eye contact all of a sudden. "And you don't have sex during the season."

That tongue of hers peeks out, sliding along her bottom lip, and I swear she moves in closer, her chest brushing mine as she inhales. Finally, she tilts her chin, and for a second, I get lost in her eyes. They're my favorite color, the lightest of blues, the color of ice.

Caressing her cheek with my thumb, I brush my lips against hers. "For you, I could make an exception."

Her eyes flare with heat, the ice of her irises suddenly a flickering blue flame. "I definitely think you should." Her flirty tone has the last bit of my control snapping. I push her back against the glass and kiss the hell out of her. Just like every time I touch her like this, I forget where we are. I forget that anyone but the two of us exists. That we might not be alone. And I get lost in Sara.

CHAPTER 34

Sara

"WHERE ARE YOU TAKING ME NOW?" I'm so intoxicated by this man I'm floating about an inch off the ground.

Brooks grins over his shoulder. He's practically dragging me along behind him on the top floor of the arena, a place I rarely visit. "Live a little."

"Oh, I don't know." I squeeze his hand. "Your idea of living is bedazzling your penis. I'm not sure I can keep up."

I still can't wrap my head around it, even if I'm beyond excited to see it. And nervous.

I haven't been shy about sex since college, but the idea of seeing my best friend's penis makes me feel like a teenager. Giddy and slightly juvenile. If he whips it out, I can't guarantee I won't point at it or call it pretty. I can't control my mouth when I'm around him. The most awkward things come out.

It's truly mortifying.

"You ever going to get over that?"

With a playful wince, I shake my head. "Probably not."

"Cool." He dips his chin. "I'll be prepared, then."

Slightly offended but mostly amused, I knock my shoulder against his bicep.

The grin he hits me with lights up my insides. God, I like him like this. If things were always like this...

Don't get ahead of yourself.

That reminder has me forcing my heart and my brain to rein themselves in.

We approach a solid black door I've never set foot beyond before, and Brooks holds it open for me. "Ladies first."

"Great, so if we get caught, I'll be the first one they see."

His boisterous laugh follows me into the room. "Pumpkin, my family owns the building. Who's gonna catch us?"

Bouncing on my toes, I spin to face him. "Beckett can be pretty scary."

That comment pulls a chuckle from him. "The man I made friendship bracelets with yesterday? Yeah, I'll take my chances."

My heart warms, and my lips twitch at that mental image. I like that idea a bit too much. Brooks and his grown-ass billionaire brothers sitting around a dining room table, surrounded by colored beads, making friendship bracelets. It's another perfect reminder of who he is. Of the Brooks he's always been. Of the man I'm kind of crazy about.

The lights in the room are off, but because of the big window overlooking the rink, the unfamiliar space is easy to make out. "What are we doing in the announcer's booth?"

He steps up beside me, his hands in his pockets, and scans the arena. "You asked me about my rituals a while back. I come here before every home game."

I turn and take him in, silently waiting for him to elaborate. God, he's so gorgeous. Tendrils of hair have escaped his bun since the photo shoot, and the scruff on his face makes the giant of a man look even more rugged.

"I visualize every potential play, as I've told you. I run through them up here. Kind of imagine the play-by-play as if the announcer is calling it. How I'll stop the puck in each scenario."

I can't stop the smile that forms on my face. "That's adorable."

With a huff, he side-eyes me. "Adorable?"

"Not what you were going for?"

"Not quite." His lips quirk. "But I'll take it, I guess."

"So why'd you bring me here?"

He turns to me, pulling both hands out of his pockets, and takes hold of mine. "Because I want you to know me. All of me. I'm obsessive and crazy focused when it comes to the game. I told you I've never dated during the season, but that's not the exact truth."

My heart rate kicks up, and I have to fight the urge to take a step back.

The gentle way he squeezes my fingers is a reassurance. He reads me so freaking well. "It's not a lie. Just not the full truth." His swallow is audible, and his Adam's apple bobs harshly. "I don't broadcast this, but I've never dated. Period."

This time my heart trips over itself. "Oh."

"For as long as I can remember, I've focused on nothing but being the best goalie, and before you, I never met anyone who could compete with the game."

The smile that overtakes me is so broad it makes my cheeks burn, and heat creeps up my neck and into my face. If this room were any lighter, I have no doubt Brooks would be able to see just how pink I've gone.

My voice quakes right along with my knees when I push the words out. "But *I* compete with the game?"

"It's a shutout, babe. There's no competition. For all these years, I thought that I had to pick. Between the game and a relationship. But not being with you didn't keep me from obsessing over you. I couldn't get you out of my head last year, and we still won the Cup." He rubs circles against my hand with his thumb, a little too quickly, like he's nervous. "So if you're open to it, I'd like to try being with you. For real. Instead of being my fake girlfriend, I was hoping you'd want to be my first real one."

"I'd be your first?" The thought makes it hard to breathe. How has Brooks never dated before?

"You'd be my first everything." He's so quiet, and his voice is filled with so much vulnerability.

Sincere green eyes study my reaction. They're swimming with a potent mixture of fear and hope. The tension in the air is almost suffocating.

"Brooks." It's hard to breathe all of a sudden. "Never?"

He sucks on his bottom lip and gives his head one firm shake. "No."

"Holy shit."

Dammit. I wish I knew how to respond in a way that would put him at ease. But he knows me. He shouldn't be surprised that I turn into a babbling idiot at moments like this. I clamp a hand over my mouth, hoping to stem the idiocy threatening to spew from me, but the words tumble out anyway.

"No one else has taken that bedazzled penis for a ride?"

He snorts, and his cheeks flame. I'm pretty sure mine match.

"Your pretty penis is all mine?"

Oh God. Someone stop me.

"Tell me it sparkles, and I'll drop to my knees right now."

"Are you done yet?" he teases. Even his ears are pink now.

I suck in a deep breath. "Yes, I think I am. Wait." I groan. "Nope. One more. Does it shoot actual pearl necklaces?"

"Sara!" His chest heaves with laughter.

I throw myself against his broad chest and cling to him, and we hold each other up as we dissolve into giggles. He smooths a hand over my back, calming me with his touch, and I snuggle further into his chest.

"Thank you for trusting me with another secret. I promise I don't take the fact that you're a virgin lightly. We can definitely go slow."

He drags his hand down to my ass and squeezes. "Never said I wanted to go slow."

My skin heats, and tingles shoot up my spine. I look up at him, my chin on his chest, and breathe him in. "Right. That was me."

"Mm-hmm." He lowers his head, casting his face in shadow, and stares down at me. His tongue slides against his lip again, making heat pool low in my belly.

I groan against him. "Why did I want to take things slow again?"

"Because my uncle stomped on your heart, and then I hurt you."

My lungs constrict, but I breathe through the ache. "Seb didn't hurt me, Brooks. But losing you—"

He splays his hands on either side of my neck, cradling my head and threading his fingers through my hair. "You will never lose me."

With a deep breath in, I allow that sentiment to settle between us. There is no nervousness when it comes to that anymore. I believe him. This man just bared himself to me. He spent the day showing me that I'm safe with him. He deserves to know he's safe with me too.

"I'd like to see the bedazzled penis now."

A slow smile spreads across Brooks's face. Still cradling my head with both hands, he tips forward and kisses me softly. "You're insane, you know that?"

"Certifiable. Now take off your pants."

"Sara—"

"Owns your penis," I decree. "Now show it to me."

His smile turns into a smirk, but he doesn't make a move to obey. I splay my hands on his chest and slide down his body, taking my sweet time kissing him as I go.

"Have you done this before?" I ask between kisses down his abdomen.

Above me, he shakes his head and grunts.

I'm a riot of emotions. Excitement and pride and ecstatic shock. It culminates into an unfamiliar sense of power. Because this man has been saving himself for me. Hell, he pierced his penis rather than admitting the truth to his friends.

I unbuckle his pants and grin up at him. "If you aren't going to help me, then you might as well get back to your ritual. Why don't you visualize what's about to happen? Ya know, give us a play-by-play. Maybe then you'll score just like we both know you want to."

"How is it that you can simultaneously drive me fucking insane and turn me on?"

"It's a talent. Just wait till you see what I can do with my tongue." I tug on his jeans roughly.

He laughs at my comment. It's gritty. Dark. It scrapes through me with a delicious friction that makes me squeeze my legs together.

His navy-blue boxers are sculpted to him, putting every inch of his erection on display. From here, I think I might even see the outline of his piercing. Gliding my finger up his shaft slowly, I hum, memorizing every inch. My pussy clenches when I find the piercing. When I continue up, I hit another, then another. My breath catches, and excitement thrums through me. "Three?" I tip my head back and lick my lips at the vision that hits me.

"Fuck, Sar," he grinds out, fisting his hands at his sides as if he's trying to keep from touching me.

"I'm going to suck your cock. I'd appreciate it if you weren't a saint right now. Touch me, Brooks. Be a good boy and grab a fist full of my hair and fuck my mouth."

His cock bobs, stretching the already tight fabric of his boxer briefs taut.

My core throbs. "You like being called a good boy?"

His jaw locks, but his eyes are hazy with lust. I'm drunk on it.

Sliding my fingers beneath the fabric of his boxers, I revel in the feel of his hot skin. I pull them down and moan when his heavy cock finally makes its appearance. In the dim light, the three piercings that make up his Jacob's ladder glisten in Bolts blue.

I try to hold back my smile but can't. "You take your loyalty to the team seriously, I see." I lick from the base of his balls right up to the tip and then press a kiss to where a bead of excitement has accumulated. The taste of him on my tongue pulls an appreciative hum from deep in my chest. "So good."

Finally, he settles a hand on my head, his broad palm warm against my scalp.

I open my mouth and suck him in. Holding him there, I look up and smile around his dick. In this moment, I understand the phrase about a person having hearts in their eyes. Because that is precisely how Brooks is looking at me. Like I own his damn heart.

I tickle the piercings with my tongue, and he grunts. "Fuck. I need to move."

Desire wells in me, and I moan around him. "Good. Then take control. Fuck my mouth," I dare.

He closes his eyes, and I swear a switch flips. When he opens them again, he's no longer looking at me like I'm a precious thing. Instead, his gaze is filled with nothing but feral need. The hand on my head snakes around until he's got his fingers threaded through my hair. Then, with a grunt, he tugs and makes a fist.

"Squeeze my leg if it's too much," he warns.

Despite the way my body thrums with desire, my chest aches with affection too. I like that I'm the first person he's experiencing these things with. That he's worried about being too rough because he truly doesn't know. I like experimenting together, but more than anything, I feel protective of him.

He's worried about hurting me, but what he doesn't know is that I like my sex rough. And I have a feeling that even though we all call him Saint, there's a wicked part of him that's been dying to come out.

Brooks has more restraint than most, but with this new information about his virginity, I'd bet just about anything that once he gets a taste, that restraint will snap. And I'm just the girl for him to lose it with.

The hard floor makes my knees ache, but damn if I don't love the way he towers over me. He's all strength and power, his thick cock sliding in and out of my mouth, causing me to gag every few thrusts, the metal rings rubbing against my tongue.

"You look so fucking good in my jersey, Sar."

Eyes watering, I stare up at him, all while I continue to suck him off.

"But you'd look even better spread out on my bed. Or riding my face."

I swirl my tongue along the edge of his shaft, right along his balls, eliciting a grunt from him. The sound sends my arousal kicking up a notch. Fuck, I'm already so wet for him. I cup his balls in one hand, grazing my thumb back and forth across them while I continue to work him over.

"Right there. Oh, fuck yes, Sar. I'm going to come if you keep doing that."

My stomach dips and liquid heat drips from me. Determined to send him over the edge, I double down on my efforts. I suck harder, gripping the backs of his thighs so that he can't pull away, forcing him to come down my throat.

He curses as his cock twitches in my mouth, and I moan around him. With one last lick, I drop back to my ass and grin up at him. And then, in my best announcer voice, with my hands cupped around my mouth, I whisper, "He shoots, he scores. And the crowd goes wild! *Ahh!*"

With a throaty laugh, he lifts me off the floor. Then he spins me and sets me on the table in front of the window. The kisses he places on my lips are soft, and so is the humming rumbling from him. But when he pulls back, there's a wicked gleam in his eye.

With one brow lifted, he points toward a button.

I squirm, my pulse racing. "That what I think it is?"

When he presses the red button, it illuminates. And when he speaks this time, his voice echoes outside the booth. He's turned on the audio system. That means his every word is booming through the speakers in the arena.

"Do me a favor, Sar." He pops the button of my jeans and lowers the zipper. "Narrate every little thing I do. And everything you want me to do."

With his fingers tucked into my waistband, he slides off my pants. "And if you stop..." He licks his lips and settles on his knees. Then he yanks me to the edge of the table. "I stop."

CHAPTER 35
Sara

AVA SHOWS up bright and early, armed with donuts, coffee, and a smile.

Brooks has practice with Fitz this morning, so he headed down to his apartment to get ready an hour ago.

I bring the steaming latte to my lips and hum. "You are officially my favorite person."

Ava laughs. "Thank Lennox for all of this. I'm just the delivery girl."

As if on cue, my phone buzzes on the counter. I scurry over and tap the screen, giddy when I see my best friend's name.

Lennox's smile is bright. "Good morning, lover! You know what time it is."

I smile into my cardboard cup and wave Ava into the living room. Silently, I point at the coffee table, instructing her to put the donuts down and relax.

Ava's literally the bright spot in any room. She's always dressed in soft colors. Never black. This morning is no different. She's decked out in nothing but cream, from her leggings to her crop top to the long cardigan layered over it. Her wavy red hair is pulled back in a messy ponytail, and her freckled face is free of makeup.

When she holds a pink glazed donut to her lips, I wince. If I was dressed the way she is, there's no way I could get away with eating a donut without staining the light fabric with icing. She's a brave woman.

"How was the date?" Lennox asks, pulling my attention back to her.

Remembering every moment of yesterday—from Brooks's heart-felt apology to him teaching me how to skate to his confession about being a virgin—leaves my smile wide. "It was amazing."

"Did you guys bang in the arena or something?" Lennox teases. I'm glad that, for once, she can't read me and figure out every little thing we did.

I desperately want to work through all the emotions whirling inside me, but more than that, I want to protect Brooks's privacy.

"We're taking it slow."

Lennox slumps against her bed and pouts. "I can't believe you still haven't fooled around with him."

"I didn't say that. He did go down on me in the announcer's booth. And he forced me to describe everything over the speaker," I admit, tossing her a bone.

"Shut up," Ava hisses, slapping the cushion beside her. "What if someone had come in?"

"Then they'd have heard Brooks score three times." The laughter bubbling out of me is light and loud.

Beside me, Ava goes pink, but Lennox is cackling. She's flat on her back with her legs in the air, kicking them in excitement.

"Okay, enough," I pant, slapping a hand to my chest. "We're making Ava uncomfortable."

"You're not," she insists. "But seriously, aren't you worried about getting caught? I mean, in the act?" She won't even say the word, and suddenly I'm wondering if Brooks is the only virgin employed by Langfield Corp.

Lennox, the hussy, barks out another laugh. "It's called cunnilingus, Av, and why are you acting all virginal? Please tell me you aren't saving yourself for War like Brooks has been saving himself for Sar."

My stomach drops and my mouth falls open. How the hell does the woman do that? I thought her supernatural talent was limited to positions. Not a person's lack of sex, period.

Lennox waves a hand. "Secret's safe with us. Even if your face hadn't just given it away, I assumed. When I dated Aiden in high school, Brooks was still a virgin. If the man held on to his virginity through college and then when women literally threw themselves at him when he was drafted, it's a given that he was until he met you. He's never dated, and the guy's a romantic. He wasn't just giving that shit up."

I'm speechless. Not that I have anything to say anyway. Protecting my best friend's secret and his privacy are my top priorities.

"I'm not a virgin," Ava says quietly, pushing a loose strand of hair behind her ear. "And the last person I'd have sex with, let alone give my virginity to, would be *Tyler Warren*."

The way she says his name, filled with animosity and distaste, makes me giggle.

"Talk about one person we all know isn't a virgin." Lennox sighs. "He's got that whole bad boy with a back story thing going for him, Av. And I bet he's amazing in the sack."

Ava gasps, her jaw going slack, and both Lennox and I dissolve into giggles at her reaction.

"Why do you put up with us?" I ask.

She shakes her head and huffs out a breathy laugh. "Someone needs to keep the two of you in check."

"True. Lord knows I'm not that person," Lennox admits. "So, how are we feeling about Seb now? Is operation make-him-quit getting anywhere?"

"I don't know." I slump back against the couch. "He almost ruined my relationship with Brooks, and I'm worried that Brooks will do something rash if Seb pushes him again." I pick up my coffee and take a slow sip. "Brooks has it in his mind that he needs to protect me. Like he thinks I'm heartbroken over Seb. But we were never like that. The relationship was so shallow. How could it not be when he insisted it stay a secret? We flirted in the beginning and fooled around a few times. But looking back? The only thrill I felt was because of the sneaking around. Not because of Seb. And that got old quick. By the time I found out about his wife, I was already over it. I just hadn't ended things because I was holding out hope for more. Like maybe if we could date out in the open, my feelings would grow. I guess I was still wishing he was more. And now that I know what more looks like..." I huff. "God, I can't believe I wasted any time on him."

Ava smiles. "It's like that saying. 'If he wanted to, he would.'"

"Yes!" I slap my thigh and sit up straighter. "That exactly. Finally experiencing what it feels like to be chosen, not daily, but hourly, by the minute, puts it all into perspective. Brooks is still upset that we fooled around in public, but it felt incredible to know that he wasn't embarrassed to be seen with me. To think that maybe he couldn't help himself. He had to touch me, kiss me, make me come."

The pink stain on Ava's cheeks moves to her chest, and she's focused on a spot on the coffee table in front of us now.

I cringe. "Sorry."

"It's fine." She shrugs. "I was raised that it wasn't okay to talk about this stuff. But believe me, living in this building has opened my eyes."

Lennox giggles. "And yet you still haven't boinked a single hot hockey player."

Ava's eyes widen and she pulls back. "How do you know I just haven't talked about it?"

With a scoff, I shake my head. "Don't even try it. She has this weird ability to tell when a person has had sex, down to position."

Lennox nods. "You can call me Madame Lennox."

That sends us all into a fit of laughter.

When we've settled again, I go back to my coffee. "I just want

Seb gone. More for Brooks than for me. This is Brooks's team. If you knew just how dedicated he is to the team—" I leave it at that and avert my gaze. Shit. If I'm not careful, Lennox will fixate on that comment and glean way too much information from it. I doubt she can see in my eyes that Brooks has a Bolts-blue Jacob's ladder, but I'd rather not test the theory.

Thankfully she's subdued, thoughtful. "He always was the most dedicated."

"I'm tired of Seb's comments, his stares, his attitude." A pit of dread forms in my stomach when I really think about how often he's hovering nearby. "I hate that he could be standing in the hall right now. That he lives next door. It's gross."

Ava's lips twist, and she hums. "You really think there's a chance you could get him to quit? Wouldn't it be better if Brooks went to his brothers and told them the truth?"

Lennox taps her finger against her lips. "Or maybe we just take things up a notch. The two of you need to be more in his face."

"Brooks won't use me as a prop." I fold my arms over my chest and let out a *humph*. I liked the games we played to piss Seb off. At first I thought it was ridiculous, but then it became fun.

Even so, I get why Brooks doesn't want to do it. He's focused on the two of us, and he wants our sex life to be for us, not for someone else.

But that doesn't mean I'm done fucking with Seb. I just need to go about it in a different way.

"So you do the dirty work," she counters, breaking out in a smile fit for a villain.

"No." Ava shakes her head. "Look at the two of you scheming. How did you survive college together? Did you have any voices of reason around? You must have had someone."

I raise a hand and grin. "That'd be me."

"Oh God," she mutters.

"What are you thinking, Len?"

She picks up her phone so she's centered on the screen. "You've already got the hat and the jersey. The whole sitting on his back while he does push-ups thing." She looks off to one side, then goes on. "You've fooled around in front of Seb. You've made sexy noises so loudly he's bound to have heard. But nothing seems to be pushing him."

I nod. "Right. That's my point. Nothing works."

"So you need to be more extreme. *More* over-the-top."

"I don't think so," Ava says, a worried frown marring her face.

"What if you dyed your face blue?" Lennox beams, like this is genius.

Rearing back, I scoff. "Um, what?"

"Okay, paint, then. Paint your face blue. Oh my God. Paint your whole body and streak across the ice!"

"Do you hear yourself?" Ava asks, her voice pitched high. "How in God's name would that help?"

I laugh, just imagining Seb's face if I did that. "I'd probably get fired if I ran across the ice naked. I'd probably slip and fall and end up with a concussion too. So I'm gonna go with a no on that one. Even though pissing off Seb does make me happy."

Lennox groans. "Ave, stop being so reasonable. You're ruining all my fun!"

Ava's grinning as she pulls her phone from her pocket. "I actually have to go. But seriously, do not dye your face. That is a really bad idea."

I nod, already entertaining another idea. Something equally loud, equally annoying, but a little less permanent or Smurf-like.

When the door shuts, I bring my phone closer and smirk. "Okay, Len. We're going to the store."

She bounces on her bed. "Yes. Okay, call me when you get there. I want to see your evil scheming in action."

Once we've disconnected, I pull on my favorite new beanie—the one declaring me Brooks's bunny—wrap a blue Bolts scarf around my neck, and slip into my leather jacket. Then I head for the door.

When I throw it open, I stagger back. Seb is standing on the other side of it, a brown box in one hand and the other poised to knock. His salt-and-pepper hair is a mess, like he's been pulling on it. He's in a pair of jeans and a black sweater. The look is casual for him, yet still a little too formal.

For a moment, I stare at him, confused about why he's here. He watches me in return, his face blank. But as he takes me in, sliding his gaze up to my hat, that dull expression morphs into a familiar scowl.

God, how did I ever find this man attractive?

The bluish gray of his irises makes him look like one of those walking zombies. Void of anything but misery. Both eyes are rimmed black from the broken nose he's sporting. The one he claims he got when he tripped and hit a dresser on his way down. I tamp down the elation that zaps through me at all the misfortune he's so obviously earned.

"Can I help you?"

He crosses his arms over his chest, his scowl deepening into a menacing glower. With a shake of his head, he scoffs. "Thought the charade was over."

My stomach knots. "Excuse me?"

"The charade. The revenge plan you and Brooks so obviously concocted when you found out I was married." He waves a dismissive hand in my direction, as if I'm worthless. As if his nephew couldn't possibly be interested in me. As if pity is Brooks's only motive.

But I know the truth about how Brooks feels. And I know how he makes me feel.

A full-on smile spreads across my face. "Guess I should be thanking you, huh? If you hadn't fucked up so royally, my best friend would still be convinced he had to be a robot like you. And I'd be missing out on the best relationship I've ever had."

With a growl, he pushes the box toward me. When I catch sight of the label, that elation is back. It's a package from an erotic online shop. I totally forgot that I'd ordered a bunch of dildos in my name and had them sent to Seb. I giggle and peer up at him. The box has been opened, so he clearly saw its contents. I am so immature sometimes.

The sneer on his face makes him look so ugly. "These little games of yours are pathetic. He's going to destroy his career. Is that what you want? He's playing like shit. Can't stop a goddamn puck to save his life." He takes a step closer. "You want to destroy him? Destroy his relationship with his family? You don't have much of one, but his means everything to him."

I should feel his words like the slaps he intends them to be. But Brooks's love doesn't leave room for them to land. Maybe Brooks was colder, angrier, off his game for a few weeks. But that wasn't because of me. That was because of the poor excuse for a man in front of me.

I set the box on the table in my entryway, then step out the door and pull it shut. He doesn't deserve another moment of my time. "Thanks for delivering my dildos, Seb."

As I side-step him, he takes a surprised breath. "You'll ruin him. You ruin everything you touch."

I laugh all the way to the store. I have every intention of ruining something, but it won't be Brooks.

Then again, maybe he and I are ruining each other. As we grow closer, I kind of hope neither of us looks like the person we used to be. I already feel stronger, and I'll do everything in my power so that Brooks can say the same.

But as far as ruining him? Yeah, I guess I will. I'll ruin him for every other woman.

Because Brooks is mine, and I won't give him up.

CHAPTER 36
Brooks

"SOMEONE'S IN A GOOD MOOD." War saunters into the locker room, his attitude cocky and annoying as hell.

"Oh, didn't you hear?" McGreevey tees it up.

Rowan, the asshole, joins in. "Our goalie is finally getting some."

I look from one guy to another, being sure to glare at them all.

War shakes his head. "Nah, that's not it."

Propped up against my locker, I fold my arms and roll my eyes. "Out with it already."

War smiles and shakes his phone back and forth in front of him. "It's because he's now *Sara's boyfriend.*"

Aiden swipes the device from him and studies my Instagram profile. I updated it last night while lying in bed with Sara. Did it to make her smile after a couple of asshole trolls commented on the Bolts' page about her being a flavor of the week.

First, I'm not like that, so it made no sense, and second, I want to make sure the world knows that I was the one who posted that photo to the Bolts' official page, not Sara.

I edited my bio and listed my status as her boyfriend, replacing what used to say *starting goalie for the Boston Bolts.* Then I forced her to airdrop the photo of me kissing her cheek and uploaded it with a caption that read *Instagram Official*.

The smile she wore makes all the ribbing I'll get worth it. We spent three days just hanging out. She'd go to work, and I'd go to practice, then we'd order food or make dinner together.

Inevitably we'd end up back in bed, naked and exploring one another, but we haven't taken things any further than we did in the announcer's booth. I'm in no rush. If I have my way, we'll have plenty of time for everything, and I want to savor each step.

My little brother nudges me. "Proud of you." For all of Aiden's bullshit, the kid loves love. He deserves it more than anyone too.

"Thanks. Now will you sing so they get off my back?"

With a laugh, he jumps up onto the bench, and after one deep breath in, starts his own rendition of the theme song from *The Fresh Prince of Bel-Air*.

"Men, I'd like to tell you a story all about how
The Bolts gonna turn this season around
It involves number thirteen
Standing right there
And the woman he calls Pumpkin that the rest of us call Sar..."

All around, the guys are hooting and hollering. A deep sense of satisfaction washes over me as I watch my little brother entertain us all.

He just might be right. I have a feeling tonight is the beginning of our comeback.

The chanting inside the arena as we make our way down the tunnel is louder than normal, more electric. Even the fans know tonight is gonna be our night.

I stayed at Sara's last night, so it's only been hours since I last saw her, yet as I hit the ice for warm-ups and I eagerly search the stands for her, my heart is thumping against my sternum. War skates up on my left and nudges me. Then he uses his stick to point toward the players' bench. There, in my jersey, is my girlfriend. But she's made one drastic change since I left her this morning.

"Fuck. Did she dye her hair blue?" War heaves a laugh.

I'm already skating toward her, with him on my heels. She's wearing the damn *Brooks's Bunny* beanie she loves so much, and beneath it, her hair is Smurf blue.

Before I can get to the boards, Coach is hollering at me. I tune him out and point my hockey stick at Sara. Then I drop to the ice to start my hundred. War circles me once and darts over to the bench. A minute later, he's depositing Sara on my back.

This might as well be an official part of the Bolts' warm-ups from here on out. Fans eat it up, and Gavin is all about it. Seb can fuck himself if he thinks this will stop anytime soon.

Once Sara settles on my back, the crowd starts counting. Her bright smile lights up the arena from every screen in the place. From here, even I can see her. I keep my focus fixed on her gorgeous face as I go, and I don't even feel the burn as I push up and down.

War helps her off as soon as I hit one hundred, then I haul myself up, snagging my stick on the way.

"What'd you do, crazy girl?"

She toys with the tips and tilts her head. "Like it?"

"As if you could possibly look anything but gorgeous." I brush a thumb over her cheek.

"Sebastian lost his mind when he saw it," she says with a conspiratorial giggle. "We're wearing him down, Saint."

All I can do is laugh. I'm not sure her hair color is going to push Seb to quit, but I do enjoy the enthusiasm.

"And now my hair matches your bedazzled penises!"

Beside me, War grunts and almost loses his balance. He rights himself, drops his stick, and puts his hands on his waist. "*Dude*, you said you'd never tell!"

Sara slaps a hand over her mouth, her eyes blowing wide.

"Fuck, crazy girl. Go watch the game before you cause more trouble."

"Good luck, Brookie—"

"Sara," I growl.

She grasps my jersey and pops up on her toes. With my skates on, I tower over her, so I bend at the knees until we're face to face.

"Be a good boy," she murmurs, her voice pure sex. "Bring me back to the boards, and I'll ride your face tonight."

I snap my mouth shut and stand to my full height. With one brow cocked, she smiles, waiting for me to lift her up. The girl knows how to get what she wants, all right.

The game isn't even close. Aiden, Daniel, and War run circles around Atlanta, and when the buzzer sounds, the arena is chanting *Saint, Saint, Saint*, because in the final seconds of the game, I landed in a split to block the puck, officially earning us the shutout.

The guys skate around me, slapping my back and jumping on me, and soon the chants turn to *Sara, Sara, Sara*.

When my teammates scatter, Aiden is in the middle of the ice. He breaks out into his rendition of the *Fresh Prince* theme song. This time it's about the win and the girl I can't wait to kiss.

We head back to the locker room to shower and change, a little rowdier than we have been in the last couple of weeks, knowing the press should be kind to us tonight.

McGreevey pats me on the back. "Keep playing like this, and we'll all be getting down on one knee and begging Sara to marry you."

Beside me, War practically chokes on his own saliva.

I only smile. The idea isn't half bad.

"Holy shit," he whispers when I don't reply to McGreevey. "Does she know?"

I toss my helmet onto the bench and get to work on my skates. "Know what?"

"That you're so fucking gone for her? Brooks, a week ago, you weren't sure if she had any real feelings for you. Now you're thinking about proposing?"

"You're proposing to Sara?" Aiden's voice is too fucking loud.

I shoot up straight and glare at him. "I'm not fucking proposing. You"—I point at War—"shut it. And you"—I point at Aiden—"let it go. We just started dating. I'm happy. Let me just be happy and leave it at that."

Aiden shrugs and disappears into the showers, but War's watching me with a frown. "We're going to Carolina next week."

"Yeah, and?"

"Is she going to introduce you to her family?"

My heart sinks, because she hasn't mentioned it. Sara is an open book in every respect, except when it comes to her family. I know she has a much younger brother, and I know she talks to him and her mom pretty regularly, but she's tight lipped any time I bring them up.

My family is part of almost every facet of my life. I couldn't hide them if I tried.

"Don't be a dick." I shuck off my compression shorts and head for the showers.

"I can't believe you told her about our piercings, man," War huffs. "Thought that was a sacred moment."

I cough out a laugh. "Sacred moment?"

"Yeah, I offered to hold your dick and everything."

"You guys are fucking weird." McGreevey gives us a dark look when we step into the showers.

I avoid looking at any of my teammates. Showering with a group of men isn't uncomfortable. I've been doing it since peewee hockey. Even so, we don't hang around and chat while our dicks are hanging out. It's more like *get in and get the fuck out.*

For everyone except War, apparently. "He told Sar about our matching dicks."

I snort as a slew of Sara's nicknames for them come to mind. And now I'm picturing Lisa Frank dicks.

Stop thinking of your teammates' dicks.

Pink swirls. Purple jewels. *Fuck, I can't unsee it now.*

"We should all get matching ones," Hall says, holding his cock like it's his most prized possession. Maybe it is. The kid is hung. I'll give him that. Easily the biggest here. That was a bit of a surprise, considering that he's about average size for a pro hockey player. Several of us have inches and muscle on him. Maybe that's why he's such a cocky son of a bitch. He's still new to the NHL and obsessed with hooking up with every puck bunny he meets.

"You wouldn't survive the healing process," I mutter.

War snorts. "I bet he can't go two nights without a bunny, let alone two months."

Hall *humph*s. God, he's such a kid. "Fuck you. You calling me a whore?"

"You got your nickname somewhere, Playboy," War taunts.

"It's because I make the plays, dipshit."

"Mm-hmm. Whatever you tell yourself so you can sleep at night." War always has to have the last line.

"How about you all shower without playing with your dicks?" McGreevey pleads.

That's a solid plan. I finish up, then head back to my locker to get dressed, smiling the whole way. Today's been a great fucking day.

The second we step foot into Sara's apartment, she practically drags me to her bedroom, her blue hair bouncing and her ass swaying seductively as she goes.

I don't know what's gotten into her, but the elevator doors were barely shut when she dropped to her knees. I had to yank her up before she could get my belt undone. There is at least one camera in that stainless-steel box because Gavin is a control freak who keeps tabs on all his players.

Before we've even hit her bedroom door, her jersey flies through the air, followed by her bra. When she spins around, her nipples peach and pebbled, and tweaks one while moaning my name, my cock strains painfully against my pants.

"God, is it bad that I love this contrast? You in a suit while I'm completely naked?"

I bite down on my fist and swallow a groan. She's absolute fucking perfection. "No, crazy girl. Pretty sure you naked is my personal heaven. I literally don't know where to start."

Her blue eyes dance, and her lips turn up in one of her mischievous smirks. That look means she's got plans for me. Fuck, I can't wait to find out what they are.

"I want you to sit right there and tell me what to do." Her voice is breathy, like she's already worked up just thinking of all the possibilities I could come up with.

"And I can't touch you?" I rasp, palming my dick over my pants and squeezing for a little relief.

She grazes her nipples with her fingers, her breasts hanging heavy, and heaves in a breath. "Not yet," she taunts. "You have to make me come first."

"That's my favorite thing in the world, Sar. Now you're just spoiling me."

She licks her lips and rubs her thighs together. "Be a good boy and sit down."

"Thought I was in charge?" I challenge her, though I do as she says, because being Sara's *good boy* is a high for me. I love pleasing her.

I drop to the bench in the corner of her room. It's one of those ornate pieces with a fancy French name my sister would no doubt know. Legs spread wide, I lean back, keeping my focus firmly fixed on the knockout in front of me. Her bare ass taunts me as she wanders into the bathroom. When she reappears, she's holding a small pink object.

"Edge of the bed," I command.

Her eyes flash with excitement, and a visible shudder works its way through her.

"Spread your legs and let me see how wet you are."

Without hesitation, she plops onto the bed and spreads herself wide. "Now what?" Her tone is so fucking seductive, her words oozing sex.

"Show me what you have to play with."

I unbutton my jacket and slide it off, then unbutton the cuffs of my shirt.

Sara holds up what looks like a rosebud. "It's for my clit. Think you can get me off quicker with your tongue?"

My responding laugh is like sandpaper. "Crazy girl, toys aren't competition. I'm going to use that to get you all worked up, and then I'm going to lap up every last drop of your orgasm."

"God, that's hot." She writhes on the bed, gripping the comforter with her free hand.

I undo the top button of my shirt and take in a deep breath. Then I work the rest of the buttons until my shirt hangs open. "Slide the flower against your pussy, baby. But don't you dare turn it on." I shuck my shirt and drape it over the end of the bench, then get to work on my zipper. I pull my cock out just as Sara arches into her toy, seeking satisfaction she'll never get from a silicone object.

"Look at you, worked up and desperate." I stroke my shaft and give it a firm tug. "Not nearly as fucking desperate as I am, though."

She moans as she rubs the pink toy against herself. "Please, Brooks."

"Turn it on, crazy girl. Let me see what my supposed competition does."

She holds the toy above her and presses a button. When she sets it against her clit, she practically bows off the bed. My body arches forward of its own accord. I can't stay seated any longer. I'm too far away from her, and my need to watch exactly what's happening is too great.

My pants fall to my ankles when I stand. I kick them off in a hurry, then settle myself beside her. When she cries out, I slide my palm over her mouth, silencing her.

Blue eyes grow wide as she stares up at me.

"These sounds are only for me. Your orgasm is mine. He doesn't get to hear it."

I'm over the games. I'm over sharing any part of her. And I need to know that she is too. I need to know this is about me. About us. That she's truly over whatever they had.

Her eyes go hazy with lust, and she writhes again.

I lift my hand and take in every feature of her beautiful face.

"Then you better stuff my mouth with something to shut me up, Saint, because when you're looking at me like that, with that massive cock in your hand, I can't be quiet."

Her taunts work. I laugh, feeling lighter knowing this isn't about him at all.

I slide up the bed and press the head of my dick against her lips. "This work?"

With a sweet smile, she kisses the crown. Then she circles her tongue around it, making me grit my teeth. "Not sure, but it's worth a try."

"Give me that toy," I demand.

She waggles her brows. "Get it yourself."

With a grunt, I haul myself over her and straddle her head.

She practically squeals, and with a squeeze of my ass, she sucks me into her mouth. And then when I fuck her face while devouring her pussy, only I hear her screams as she shatters beneath me.

CHAPTER 37
Brooks

"I'M surprised you let the girl out of your sight." War props himself up against the counter in my kitchen, beer in hand.

We're having the first ever Bolts team dinner, and I'm hosting. Not all the guys could make it, but there are enough of us that Daniel and War had to bring chairs from their apartments to seat everyone.

"And I can't believe you brought team dinners back. This is awesome."

Our dinners in college were nothing like this. Tonight, we've upped the fancy with tablecloths and candles, real forks and plates, and a whole selection of wine. We even have cloth napkins that Aiden spent an inordinate amount of time turning into bolts of lightning. Yes, the napkins are Bolts blue. I can't make this shit up.

My brother stands in the corner, shaker in hand, humming "La Cucaracha" while swaying his hips. "Who wants a cocktail?"

Daniel is the first to grab a glass of the neon blue drink. "This stuff is delicious."

With a shake of my head, I open the oven a couple of inches to check on the lasagna. When I note that the cheese has melted perfectly, I pull it out and pop the garlic bread in. By the time the lasagna is cool enough to eat, the bread will be ready.

I point to the lettuce next to War. "Make yourself useful and toss that salad?"

War chokes on his beer. A little dribbles down his chin as he pounds on his chest and coughs. "Guy's got jokes."

I shrug. "No, I really just want you to toss the lettuce."

McGreevey steps into the kitchen, glass of red wine in hand. "Smells fucking phenomenal. Becca is going to be so jealous." He pulls out his phone, leans in close to my masterpiece, and snaps a picture of himself grinning beside it. He taps out a text, then pockets the device again and sips his wine.

"You can take her a plate," I offer.

He laughs. "Nah. It's more fun this way. She taunts me with pictures of the things she makes for dinner while I'm on the road. It's only fair that I do the same for her."

"If I was married, those are not the kind of pictures I'd want my wife to send me while I was gone," War chimes in.

McGreevey licks his lips. "Oh, I get those pictures too. Not all of us are lonely with just our hand day in and day out."

I snort, and War glares at me. "Boy's not celibate for the first time in his life, and now he's judging me."

I fold my arms across my chest. "I'm not *not* celibate."

His eyes go comically wide, and I worry he's going to choke on his beer again. "Sara hasn't taken that virginity yet?"

The apartment goes dead silent, and War cringes. *Yeah, man.* His voice was entirely too loud.

"Saint's a virgin?" Hall asks, blue drink dangling from his fingers.

War sets his beer on the bar. "Shit." He meets my eyes, red faced and wearing an apologetic frown. "Sorry, man."

I shake my head and wave him off. "You're all making a bigger deal out of this than it needs to be."

"Dude, you're a thirty-year-old virgin." Hall nudges my brother, probably expecting backup.

Aiden merely shrugs, shaker in hand. "Guy's only ever wanted one girl. I think it's sweet."

My chest goes tight at the sincerity in his tone. "Thanks, bro."

Hall sighs, his shoulders slumping. "But you've got the glitter. Why would you get the glitter if you weren't going to use it?"

Aiden pauses his shaker. "Did you just say my brother's donkey dick's 'got the glitter'?"

"Did you just refer to his junk as a 'donkey dick'?" McGreevey mutters with a grimace. "Fucking Americans, you guys are weird as shit."

"Least we don't eat ketchup chips," Aiden chirps. He's the only person I know who doesn't like ketchup. "Crazy Canadians."

I snort. "You can't insult the Canadians. They gave us hockey."

He glares at me and shakes the stainless-steel cup he's still clutching for emphasis. "I had your back."

"Hey." I hold up my hands and laugh. "I'm not bothered that I'm a virgin. Neither is Sara. It'll happen when it happens."

"But, like, it's gotta be romantic, right?" Hall says, stalking toward me now.

"Um, no." I grab a beer from the fridge and point at the salad. "War, grab that." Then I hand my beer to Hall. "And you, take this. Aiden, get the bread. I'll grab the lasagna."

"What can I do?" McGreevey asks.

"Summon the guys so we can plan the great deflowering," Hall jokes.

"Ha ha," I mutter. I slip my oven mitts on, then follow them into the living room with the lasagna.

"Camden, what do you call a thirty-year-old virgin?" Hall teases.

Our second-line center shrugs. "Your sister?"

Hall scoffs. "Dude, that's out of line."

This guy. "And you're not?" I give him a pointed look.

"She's my twin sister," he says. "She's only twenty-three. And she'll be a virgin until she's fifty."

I roll my eyes as I place the food on the table. "You're insane."

"Don't anyone at this table even think about Millie like that." He points a finger at War, then drags it around the room, making sure to make eye contact with each of us. Then he sets my beer at the head of the table.

War rubs his hands together and sits beside me. "Okay, boys, we gotta strategize. How should Brooksy pop his cherry?"

"I don't have a cherry." I lean back in my chair and drop my fists to the table. "Also, I don't need your help."

Across from me, Camden is tapping away at his phone. "I looked it up. A guy doesn't have a cherry, *but*," he says, dragging out the word and grinning at me, "you *can* drop your Skittle."

War chokes on his beer again, and I slap him on the back. I consider cutting him off. Drinks seem to be a hazard for him tonight.

"Fuck," Camden says. "Some of these are ridiculous. Virgout. Cherry blaster—"

"Please stop talking."

"Where's your whiteboard?" Aiden is up and out of his seat in a flash and headed toward my bedroom.

"How many times do I have to tell you to stay out of my room?" I should have locked it before he got here.

The ass ignores me and disappears inside.

McGreevey grunts. "This'll be good."

"Enough out of you, old man," Hall volleys. "He doesn't need to be slapping the tims."

I sigh. "What the hell does that even mean?"

"Or playing with the ketchup." Aiden snorts, wheeling the whiteboard into the living room.

War pinches the bridge of his nose. "Playing with the ketchup?"

Aiden shrugs. "Canadians. What can I tell ya?"

"We don't play with the ketchup." McGreevey grunts. He shoves a big bite of lasagna into his mouth, then he points at it with his fork. "But I'd full mountie my wife if she could cook like this. Jesus, Brooks. You've been holding out on us."

War slaps me on the back. "Man can cook, and he's got a donkey dick covered in glitter. He'll do just fine."

I shake my head and pick up my fork. "Hope y'all enjoy the first and last Bolts team dinner."

CHAPTER 38

Sara

"YOU SURE YOU'RE up for this?"

I laugh at Brooks as he leads me toward Beckett's house. "They're kids. Why are you acting weird?"

Beckett and Liv have an ultrasound appointment, so we offered to watch the kids this afternoon. Later, we're having dinner with his family.

As we hit the top step of the porch, the door swings open, and Deogi comes barreling out, heading right for me. Before I know what's happening, Brooks's massive arms circle my waist, and he pulls me to his chest. If not for his quick reflexes, the dog would have taken me down the steps with him.

"Ducking snakes! I told you no more pets, Huck!" Beckett yells from somewhere inside.

Deep laughter rings out from behind us.

Brooks turns at the sound, taking me with him since he's yet to release me. Cortney is on the sidewalk, holding Deogi by the collar and laughing so hard his face is red.

Beckett's shadow darkens the doorstep. "Man Bun," he growls.

Cortney points at him and heaves in shuddering breaths. "That's for turning my hair blue. Told you I'd get even."

Beckett narrows his eyes at him, his jaw working. He's silent for a second, but then his eyes dart our way, like he's just now noticed us. With a heavy sigh, he steps back. "Don't worry, the snake was fake. You can come in."

Cortney follows us up the steps with the dog in tow. "Don't tell me he pranked you too, Sara."

I frown. "No, why?"

"Your hair's blue." He assesses me with a small frown, like he can't quite figure me out.

Brooks laughs and pulls me into his side. "She's my biggest fan."

I smile and fiddle with the ends. "He's right. This was intentional."

Cortney nods, brows raised. "I like it. Shows a real dedication to the sport."

Liv appears at the bottom of the stairs and smiles, one hand on her belly. "Thank you for watching the kids." Then she turns to Cortney, and her expression morphs into a scowl. "I expect better from you. You've witnessed firsthand the awful sounds my husband makes when he screams."

Brooks's deep chuckle rumbles in his chest. "Damn, I'm sad we missed that."

I fold my lips over to keep from laughing at my boss.

"Mom, are you ready for me?" Finn calls from somewhere upstairs.

Liv covers her mouth. "Whoops. Okay, guys," she whispers, moving in closer. "Act impressed. Finn has a new outfit, and he's been wearing it just about every day. I'm not sure it's better than the tutus over the camo pants, but it's easier to wash." She backs up to the stairs again and hollers up to the second floor. "Yeah, bud. We're ready."

The steps creak as Finn makes his way down. When he finally comes into view, Brooks and Cortney both make sounds in their throats, then immediately cover them with coughs.

In jean from head to toe, Finn wears the hell out of denim. A gold chain hangs around his neck, and he's rocking a pair of blue aviators.

Brooks is the first to recover from his coughing fit. "A denim suit. Looking good."

When Finn hits the bottom step, he leans back against the banister, folds his arms across his chest, and gives us what can only be described as a model pose, all serious face and chiseled jaw. For a six-year-old, it is impressive.

"I can have my people talk to your people. I'm sure they make it in your size."

Liv snorts. "Your people?"

Cortney throws a thumb over his shoulder. "I gotta get back home. Looking good, Finn."

"Thanks, Man Bun."

Once Beckett and Liv leave, Brooks and I load up the kids and take them to the arena, where Aiden and Gavin are already waiting for us. I'm camped out on the team bench, and all three men are skating in circles with Finn, Winnie, and Addie.

Finn begged Brooks to wear a jean jacket so they could match. Brooks tried not to look too relieved when he explained to his nephew that he didn't own one. Somehow Gavin caught wind of the conversation, and when we showed up at the arena, there was a brand-new denim jacket in Brooks's size waiting for him.

I try not to shake with laughter while I record a video of Brooks and Finn skating around the rink in their matching outfits. This is so going on the Bolts' Instagram feed today.

I've just tapped the circle at the bottom of the screen to end the recording when an incoming FaceTime notification pops up.

I immediately tap Accept when my brother's name flashes on the screen. "Hey, bud!"

Ethan's return greeting is a peel of laughter. "Holy crap. What happened to your hair?"

With my free hand, I sweep the end of my ponytail, making it swish. "Like it?"

"It's blue," he says, pointing out the obvious.

"Yup! Bolts blue."

Ethan shakes his head and grins. "That's something. What are you up to?"

I tap the screen and flip the camera so he can see the guys. The instant I do it, I'm hit with a wave of guilt.

Brooks is hanging with his brothers and nieces and nephews on the ice. It's a simple activity, but it's something my brother may never get to experience, despite how much he'd love it.

But my brother hates being pitied, so I raise my voice, maybe a bit too loud, to get their attention. "Say hi to my brother!"

Aiden and Gavin wave, as do the kids, but Brooks practically ices me when he comes barreling in my direction and then speeds to a stop.

With far more excitement than is appropriate for the situation, he shouts, "Hi! I'm Brooks."

My brother maintains his cool demeanor. It's a feat, considering this man is his favorite player. "Uh, hi."

Brooks clears his throat and studies me, his lip caught between his teeth. Then he looks back at the screen. Is he...nervous? He runs his hands through his hair, inadvertently messing up his perfectly done low bun. "I'm your sister's—uh..." He blinks at me, all awkward and adorable.

I cough out a laugh and tap my phone's screen so I appear on camera again. Then I wave Brooks over. "This is Brooks, my boyfriend."

My brother's eyes double. "Brooks Langfield is your *boyfriend*?"

The shyness seems to slowly drip off Brooks as he realizes my brother knows who he is. When he sidles up next to me, he stands a bit taller and wraps his arms around my shoulders. "That I am. I know hockey isn't your favorite, but if you wanted to come to the game when we're in town, I'd be happy to have tickets put aside for you. I'd love to meet you and your mom."

Ethan's jaw unhinges. "Uh...not my favorite sport?"

"I...um..." I sigh and try not to let the defeat I feel show. "I'm sure they'd love that."

"Yeah, we would," Ethan grins. "Now I get the hair."

Brooks runs his fingers through it and gives the ends a tug. "It's cute, right?"

"Yeah. I'm just surprised you did it now. Isn't your appointment tomorrow?"

"Appointment?" Brooks tips his head to one side and squints at my brother.

My stomach plummets at the reminder. "Oh shoot."

More like *oh shit*.

Shit, shit, shit.

Ethan's face falls, probably in response to the blatant despair written all over mine. I'm supposed to have my hair cut to donate to an organization that makes wigs for children. Yet I went and dyed it blue. I've been growing it out for a solid year. God, my stupid, immature knee-jerk reaction to pissing Seb off...

"Maybe someone wants blue hair?" Ethan offers. He's sweet to try to make me feel better.

"Yeah, maybe," I mutter, dropping my chin and avoiding Brooks's gaze. "Can I call you tomorrow, bud? We're babysitting right now."

Ethan nods. "Sure. It was nice meeting you, Brooks."

Beside me, Brooks smiles and runs his hand through my hair again. "You too. Looking forward to meeting you in person."

I hang up and keep my head down while I pocket my phone, but I can feel his eyes on me.

"Hey." He gently grasps my chin. "What was your brother talking about? What appointment?"

Fighting back tears, I let out a frustrated growl. I'm so angry with myself. And disappointed that I let my vindictive side get the best of me. I dyed my hair blue to piss off Seb without even a thought about what really matters. "I was supposed to donate my hair to charity tomorrow but now..." I tug at my blue hair, and a pang echoes in my chest where my heart should be.

God, how could I be so dense? *So selfish? I've been growing it for over a year...*

"Is mine long enough?" Brooks steps in front of me, his expression serious and so sincere.

I startle back a step. "What?"

He tugs on the tie holding it back and combs through it with his fingers, almost like he's showing it off. "Will mine work?"

"You'd cut your hair?"

He lifts one shoulder in an easy shrug. "Sure."

"But you love your hair," I argue. "Everyone loves your hair. It's, like, *you.*"

"Is it important to you?" He ducks his chin and scans my face.

"Your hair?"

With a sigh, he shakes his head, no doubt exasperated with me. "No, the donation. It seems like it's important to you."

Still protective of my reasoning, I school my expression. "Yes, but—"

He brings his forefinger to the underside of my jaw, forcing my mouth closed. "If it's important to you, then it's important to me."

Is he kidding me? I take him in, noting the sincerity in his expression and the tender care in his green eyes. He can't be real. How does a man like him exist? And how do I keep him?

"Are you, uh..." I stutter. "Are you saving yourself for, like, a special moment or night or something?" My heart pounds in my chest and my fingers itch to touch him.

Brow furrowed, he considers me. "What? No, all I need is you. Why?"

"Because when we get home, I'm really going to need to fuck you."

He laughs in response to my statement, but I'm not kidding. He's willing to cut his hair for me. Just because. He swooped in as my fake boyfriend that first night. *Just because.*

The man is too good. I'm so fucking turned on I can barely hold back from jumping him right now.

"Brooks, I'm serious. I've never needed someone the way I need you."

He leans in close and wraps his fingers around my neck loosely, holding me in place. "That, Sar. *That's what I've been saving myself for.* I've been waiting to find the woman who needs me as much as I need her."

I take a moment to admire him, to study every line of his face. And I know now, without a doubt, that I need him far more than he needs me. It's bone deep and dangerous. Carved into my very being. But I want it. I want him.

"Good, you've found her."

CHAPTER 39
Brooks

"YOU'VE FOUND HER."

Sara's words play in my head on repeat for the rest of the evening.

They echo steadily through my brain while I skate with my family. Only getting louder when we return to Beckett's house for a family dinner that both of my parents make an appearance for.

"You've found her."

When Beckett and Liv walk into the house carrying a small stack of pizza boxes, Sara's eyes meet mine, and I swear she's silently speaking those words again.

My brother's expression is blank, and his eyes are hazy.

"What's wrong with him?" Gavin asks our sister-in-law, grabbing the pizza boxes from Beckett. He sets them on the kitchen counter, then quickly turns back, brows lifted in question.

Liv glances at her husband, lips quirking up, and lets out a little hum. "We got some news at the doctor's office."

"Everything okay?" Sara perks up from her spot beneath my arm.

Liv nibbles on her lip and glances at her husband again. He now has his palms pressed flat against the counter and his head hanging between his shoulders.

My stomach sinks at his posture. "He really doesn't look okay."

Liv gives a wobbly smile, making me feel a modicum better. "We're having girls. Two of them," she squeaks.

Finn launches himself into the air, his gold chain hitting him in the chest with a *thwap* when he lands, and pumps his fist. "*Yes!* Still the only boy!"

Beckett's face is green when he looks up. "Period panties," he whispers.

Liv scoffs and slaps him lightly on the back. "Ignore him. He's got a little PTSD after living with all my friends. He'll be fine." She shuffles over to the cabinet and pulls a stack of plates down. "Beckett, pull yourself together. The twins won't get their periods for at least another twelve years. You'll be over fifty by then. Act it."

Beckett turns a horrified look in her direction, his hands still firmly planted on the counter, as if he needs it for support. "Kick a man when he's down, why don't ya?"

Gavin sidles up to him and squeezes his shoulder. "Come on, old man. Just think of all the hockey boys who are going to be begging to date your daughters."

Beckett lunges for him, and he hustles back, out of his reach.

A laugh bursts out of me at the scene, followed by a wave of warmth when Sara leans against me. I pull her in tighter to my side as we watch the disaster of a show that is my family.

I can't stop from tipping her chin up and lowering my mouth to hers. It's as if there's a magnetic pull between us getting stronger every day.

"You've found her."

It's after ten when we finally get back to our apartment building. Finn begged us to stay until he fell asleep, and then Aiden serenaded us with a moving rendition of "The Sound of Silence" by Simon and Garfunkel. He, of course, changed the words, but they were no less moving. Beckett, Gavin, and I hummed in the background. Liv and Sara stood in the doorway, soft smiles on their faces, recording the entire thing. I'm sure it will be on the Bolts and Rev's pages tomorrow.

I don't even fucking care. Spending the day with my girl has left me all warm and gooey, like a chocolate brownie with vanilla ice cream melting on top. If today's shown me anything, it's exactly what Sara said. I've found her.

The instant the elevator announces our arrival on her floor with a ding, I'm herding her through the stainless-steel doors, desperate to get her alone in the privacy of her home.

"Whoa! Look who it is!" Daniel is kicked back on the couch in the communal living area. He's accompanied by a group of guys all wearing sweats and watching a movie.

"Nice slippers," Sara teases with a laugh.

Hall lifts his feet and kicks them up and down, showing off gigantic *Elf* slippers. "Buddy's the man!"

"It's not even December." I roll my eyes at the guys, though I can't help but smile. I'm honestly surprised they're hanging at home and not out causing trouble on their last night before another ten days on the road.

War raises his brow at me and nods toward Sara. "You guys have plans tonight, or you want to join us?"

Sara's wide eyes and gaping mouth have me choking back a laugh. I'm glad to see she's just as eager as I am to get away from the guys.

I shake my head. "We're good. Enjoy the movie."

War tosses a piece of popcorn into his mouth and settles back against the cushions. "Eh, I don't blame you. Shiny toys are more fun. Just ask the playmaker."

"Stop teasing me with your glitter dick." Hall groans. "I get it. I'm not as cool as you."

"We need to move out of this place," I grumble, pushing Sara along.

She laughs. "I don't know. It's kind of quaint. It's like they're sending you off. Real teamwork there."

"Make sure you don't come back with your Skittles!" War hollers as we round the corner.

She unlocks her door, but before she steps inside, she turns back to me, her expression soft. "We don't have to do anything tonight."

That feeling in my chest from earlier squeezes tighter, washing away any thought of the idiots outside. Words she's not ready to hear dance on the tip of my tongue, but I swallow them down.

"It should be special." She slides her jacket off, avoiding my gaze.

"It's special because it's you." My voice comes out far stronger than I feel.

Sara hangs her jacket up and finally focuses on me. Whatever she sees in my expression has her smiling one second, and in the next, she's pressing me against the wall with one palm, lifting up on her toes and kissing me softly.

"Okay, give me a few minutes. Just um—watch Pacey or something."

I laugh and drop a peck to her lips. "You want me to cry the first time we have sex?"

A teasing glint sparkles in her eye. "Oh Saint, you'll definitely be crying, but there won't be any tears involved."

She disappears into her bedroom before I can come up with a cocky response. It's probably for the best. I'm a thirty-year-old virgin. I've got nothing to be cocky about.

You won't be a thirty-year-old virgin much longer, that cocky asshole inside me says. He sounds kind of like Aiden.

With a chuckle, I settle on her couch and turn on the television, though I don't turn on *Dawson's Creek*, despite Sara's suggestion. I prefer to watch it with her anyway.

I twiddle my thumbs for a solid twenty minutes, doing my best to tamp down on my racing thoughts, before she finally calls to me from her bedroom, her voice soft.

TV turned off again and remote put back in its place, I wipe my hands down my pants and heave myself up. As I amble slowly toward her room, I focus on breathing steadily, trying to get my head on straight.

The instant I push open the door, I know it's no use. This girl is my undoing. Sara is perched on the bed in nothing but my jersey, wearing a coy smile, her blue hair highlighted by the soft glow of the candles she's strategically lit throughout the room.

"You're gorgeous." My voice is nothing but a rasp. She's stolen the air from my lungs.

"And you are everything I've ever wanted." There's a vulnerability in her tone. A raw honesty.

God, I like her unscripted like this. The crazy girl who owns my heart. My life changed the moment she entered it, and it's about to change again. Not because of sex. Not because I'll no longer be a virgin. But because after tonight, there'll be no denying it. She's the one.

I clear my throat to once again rein in those rambling thoughts, then pull my shirt over my head.

"God, that's hot," she murmurs.

When I look up from where I've draped my sweater over the bench, she's sliding her fingers close to what I now can see is her bare pussy.

"What is?" I get to work on my belt next, but I can't tear my focus from her.

"The way you took off your sweater. With one hand. Fuck. Brooks, do you have any idea how gorgeous you are? All you have to do is breathe, and I'm ready to combust."

I smirk, and pride rises in me. It's nice to hear that she's as obsessed as I am.

"Oh yeah? What are some of the things you like?" Fully naked now, I stalk to the bed and kneel beside her.

She watches my every move, rubbing soft circles against her clit. Rather than wait for an answer, I grasp her hips and slide my jersey up her torso a bit so I can have a better view of what she's doing.

"I like when you fuck me with your tongue."

"What else?" I stretch out on the mattress and motion for her to settle that sweet pussy on my face.

She doesn't disappoint. *She never disappoints.* Clutching the hem of my jersey in one hand, she straddles me and lowers her ass to my chest.

I grip her thighs and pull her to my lips, where I torture her for a bit, getting her so wet and worked up she's grinding on my face.

"Your cock, Brooks. I need it. Please."

I circle her clit with my tongue one more time and give it a nip. Then I drop my head back and take in the gorgeous woman on top of me, her trembling thighs and heaving chest and her pink cheeks. "Condom?"

Sara's blue eyes hold mine as she looks down at me. "Only if you want it. I'm on birth control."

A guttural sound starts low in my chest and rumbles out of me. "Fuck."

She smiles as she shimmies down my body, and I see stars when she grinds her hot, wet lips against my hard length.

"I want to feel all these piercings inside me, Brooks. Will you let me do that? Will you let me ride you while you're completely bare? Let me feel every inch of you?"

Her teasing tone has my cock weeping. I grasp her hips and hold her in place. "Are you sure?"

Sara's lips tip up in a soft smile, all hints of teasing gone. She leans down and brushes her lips against mine. "Please, Brooks. It will be a first for me too. And I get to experience it with you." She brings her mouth to mine again. "God, I feel like I'm the virgin. You. This relationship—this is a first for me."

The underlying meaning is clear. It's not about the sex. It's that we're making love. Tonight is a first for her, because there isn't another person in existence that either of us could share this connection with.

The physical may feel incredible, but it's the pull between us, the tether that connects us, the deep friendship that gives our relationship such a firm foundation. The trust, *the love.*

I don't need to give her a verbal confirmation. The way I kiss her back is answer enough. Our tongues dance, the moves choreographed by some greater power, as she positions me. Then she deepens the kiss and lowers herself over me slowly.

"Fuck." All the air escapes my lungs as her hot heat squeezes me like a vise. It's otherworldly, spine tingling. When I bottom out, filling her completely, every nerve-ending in my body ignites.

"Yes, Brooks. Oh fuck. That feels—you feel. Oh my God."

Her rambling thoughts pull a chuckle from me, but then her pussy squeezes me, and I hiss in a breath. Her hands are in my hair, tugging, pulling it so taut I have to angle up into her mouth to ease the burn. "I'm going to fuck you now," she murmurs against my lips.

I snag the hem of my jersey and pull it over her head. "Need these." Curling up, I suck one nipple into my mouth. Her responding gush warms me further, and I almost lose it. Damn. My girl loves when I play with her nipples.

She throws her head back and babbles incoherently again, but then she snaps her spine straight, presses a palm to my sternum, and pushes me back. Eyes locked with mine, she begins to ride. Her tits bounce, then her head falls back again, and she sends me hurtling into a new type of pleasure. *What the fuck is this perfection?*

Sara is in total control, riding me, moaning my name. Every single second is nothing but bliss.

"Your bedazzled penis is officially my favorite toy," she gasps out.

I give her ass a light tap. "Sara."

She lets out a breathy laugh. "It's perfect, Brooks. You're perfect. I fucking—God, it's like you were made for me."

Her movements get more frantic, more frenzied, and my vision gets hazy. Every sensation, every emotion, blends together, sending me into sensory overload or some shit like that. I'm on the precipice. I'm going to come so damn hard I might black out.

"Need you to come, crazy girl." I press my thumb against her clit.

"Yes, Brooks." Her screams get louder. "You're such a good boy."

Her praise does it. I fucking explode inside her. In response, her pussy clenches down, milking my orgasm from my body.

"Yes, Brooks. Fill me up. Let me have it all." She slumps against my chest and holds me tight as I continue to jerk inside her, her soft whimpers and moans of pleasure a seductive soundtrack to the moment.

I settle a hand on her back, pressing in deep, reveling in the feel of her, the way she envelops me, the way she's draped over me. And in that moment, I can't not say it. Maybe it's the hormones, or maybe it's her death grip on my cock. Regardless, the truth comes spilling from my lips.

"I love you, Sara."

My admission echoes between us. Her breath hitches, but she doesn't pull back, and she doesn't tense.

She doesn't need to say it back. I just couldn't hold it in any longer.

"I've known it for a while." I glide my fingers gently over her bare back. "We promised one another the truth, and that's mine. I love you, crazy girl. I'm crazy in love with you."

Hands pressed to my chest, she lifts up and fixes her blue eyes on me. They're glistening and filled with a mixture of surprise and what I'm almost certain is love. "Will you come to my mom's house this week to meet my family?" She worries her bottom lip between her teeth. "My brother is actually a huge fan."

With a low laugh, I relax against the mattress. This is big for her. I'm not disappointed that she didn't say it back. She's opening up, and that's so much bigger than words. She doesn't need to say them, because I feel them enough for the both of us. And we've got time.

"Oh yeah? A fan of me?" I tease her, squeezing her sides.

A warm, relieved smile spreads across her face. She's not ready to say more, and I won't push her on it.

"I wouldn't say he's your number one fan, but you are his favorite player."

"Who's my number one fan?"

She licks her lips and dips lower. "Me."

Still inside her, and happier than I've ever been, I smile. "Yeah, crazy girl, I'd love to meet your family."

CHAPTER 40

Sara

> Me: Tell me I need to leave the bathroom.

> Lennox: You need to leave the bathroom.

> Lennox: Unless there is like a murderer outside the bathroom.

> Lennox: Or a python waiting to eat you.

THE WAY the dots dance on the screen signals that she's got another horror story coming.

> Me: There's no murderer or python or anything else. I'm just freaking out because I'm taking Brooks to meet my family this morning.

> Lennox: Oh. Trying to decide if you can go long enough without stripping and begging to feel his piercings again?

Lennox: Maybe you can slip into the
bathroom at your mom's house and get in a
quickie with his bedazzled penis.

> Me: Lennox! I have no idea why I tell you
> anything.

Lennox: HAHAHA. Because I'm amazing
and you love me and no one else would
understand your crazy obsession with your
boyfriend's bedazzled jewels.

> Me: He doesn't have bedazzled jewels.

Lennox: Fine. But wouldn't that be
amazing? I mean, shiny balls. I feel like he
really missed the ball on that one. Ha. Get
it. Missed the ball?!

> Me: I'm officially telling you nothing from
> now on.

I flush the toilet and turn on the faucet, even though I didn't go to the bathroom. Not sure what's more embarrassing: my boyfriend assuming I spent thirty minutes on the toilet, or my boyfriend discovering that I'm hiding from him and all the emotions bubbling up inside me.

Since Sunday night when Brooks gave me his virginity and then told me he loved me, I've been a messy bundle of nerves.

Brooks is kind and good and a freaking beast in the bedroom. Seriously, he's the best I've ever had, and it only partially has to do with the bedazzled penis—and I had to go and be the first woman he ever slept with. Now he's got high school–level feelings for me.

I don't want high school–level feelings. I don't trust them. It's possible he only said those words because of the sex. Now that he's slept with me and realized how amazing sex is, will he wonder what it would be like with someone else?

I won't be able to handle that. Losing him after experiencing perfection with him would destroy me. I have very un-high-school-level feelings for Brooks. I like him. A lot.

He can't possibly *love me* love me, though. He doesn't know what else is out there, so how could he?

I'm spiraling. And now I'm hiding. If I don't hide in here, I'll probably blurt this all out and then tell him I really, really love him, not just high school–level love him, and he'll go running for the hills.

Or toward the actual puck bunnies. Not just a woman who wears a hat that declares her as one.

His *only* one.

Brooks knocks on the door. "You feeling okay?"

And now he thinks I've got an upset stomach.

Shit.

Literally.

"I'm fine. Just—"

Just what? Freaking out because sex with Brooks is the best of my life? Because the man on the other side of the door is the best man I've ever met, and I'm so scared he's going to realize I don't deserve him?

Yes. That's exactly it.

Heart pounding in my chest and stomach churning so violently I might actually have to spend another thirty minutes locked in the bathroom, I force myself to open the door.

At the sight of him, some of my anxiety ebbs. He's standing close, hands in his pockets, hair loose and wavy around his chiseled jaw—because, oh yeah, the man cut his hair and donated it to charity, *for me*, then posted about it on social media and challenged every other guy in the league to do the same—and green eyes glassy and swimming with worry.

I fucking melt. How could I not? He's perfect, and he's mine.

"I'm freaking out," I confess.

His responding smile is knowing. And it's kind, and understanding, and perfect. Just like he is. "C'mere, crazy girl." He opens his arms to me.

With a frown and a *humph*, I step into his embrace. The second we connect, I feel lighter.

He bands one arm around me and smooths the other down the back of my head. I love when he does that.

"Tell me what's going on."

"I really like our sex and I really like you and what if you get bored with me because you can't only ever want to have sex with me and you high-school love me and I didn't love high school and I really like your penis and no one else is ever going to compare but for you I don't have a bedazzled anything—I guess I could bedazzle my vajayjay but I don't really love needles and would you even want that?" The words float out in one long, incoherent sentence. That's what I do. I spill all my thoughts to him all the freaking time, like an insane person.

With a tug on the ends of my hair, he forces my head back. When I begrudgingly look at him, he's not smiling. He's not laughing at me. There's no teasing humor in his expression. And he most certainly doesn't seem annoyed by my ridiculous monologue. No, his face is marred with a concerned, thoughtful frown.

"I don't high-school love you. I *love you* love you." Now he's smiling. It's soft and kind. "What else? Oh right, your vajayjay is perfect. No bedazzling necessary. And Sar, I waited years to find the person I wanted to give my virginity to. I could have gone out and screwed around like the other guys, but I chose to wait for perfection. And I found it. Now that I have it, why the fuck would I want to test it out with anyone else?"

"But what if you do?" I whisper, though my concerns are seriously waning. The way he's holding me, the way he's caring for me, force them further from my mind by the second.

Brooks presses his lips to mine. Then he kisses my cheek. Then he moves to my chin and up to the sensitive spot below my ear. "I'm in love with you, crazy girl. Trust me to love you."

"But what if you only think you love me because of the sex?" My voice is void of any real concern.

Brooks tips my chin up and waits for me to focus on him. "I know that for you this all seems new. These feelings, my obsession, my love. I can understand why you think that my feelings for you could be high school–level shit. But I've spent a year getting here. It didn't happen on Sunday night when I sank inside you. I knew I loved you when I claimed you as my girlfriend. I fell in love with you while we sang Lake songs in my truck on the way to the beach this summer. When we made fajitas and watched *Dawson's Creek* on that Wednesday night when you spilled tequila all over my lap. The day you got poked in the eye with my 'massive dick' and ran around my apartment like a crazy person."

My heart squeezes so tight it aches. "It really is a monster of an appendage."

He chuckles and caresses my chin with his thumb. "I'm in love with you. I have been. I'm in love with who you are, the way you make me laugh, the lightness that hits me when I'm around you. You're my favorite person in the world. If we'd never kissed, if we'd never had sex, I would still love you."

The vise that's been clamped around my chest loosens, and I let out a light sigh. "But the sex is a nice bonus, right?"

With a deep laugh, he moves in until our lips are only a breath apart. "Yeah, crazy girl. The sex is definitely a nice bonus. But it's only this good because it's with you. Because you're the woman I'm crazy in love with. I don't need to test that out to know it's true."

"It's true, you know." I pull back a little, my confidence growing. "No one else would be as good as me."

His resounding laugh is silenced when I crash my mouth to his. We're going to be a little late to meet my family.

"Now who's the nervous one?" I tease as we stand outside the door to my mother's apartment.

"I just—" Brooks straightens and stares me down. "I've never met a girlfriend's family before."

My heart flips over in my chest. Because he's never had a girlfriend.

I squeeze his hand. "They're going to love you. It's just my mom and Ethan." I take a deep breath and search his face. "Ethan has MS."

Brooks's broad shoulders lower, and suddenly, instead of me easing his nerves, he's the one comforting me. A squeeze of my hand, a palm slipped around the back of my head. Then he's pulling me close until his lips land on my forehead with a gentle kiss.

Is this what it'll always be like? Us being there for one another. Us as a team? Because that's what it feels like.

"It's one of the many reasons my job means so much to me," I admit. It's time to give him this piece of me.

He deserves to have more of me than anyone else. My worries, my concerns, my truths.

I take a deep breath and swallow past the lump in my throat. "It's just Ethan and my mom and me. We don't have a big family like yours, and we never had much. My mom works herself to the bone every day for Ethan. My job makes it possible for me to help her pay for his care. It means he can have more than I ever did."

"You're an amazing person, Sar." His words are soft, but his gaze is intent, heavy with meaning. "Thank you for bringing me to meet them." He leans in and kisses me softly. "Thank you for opening up to me."

Stronger than either of us were moments before, we smile at one another.

"Ready?"

He nods and turns toward the door. "Ready."

The apartment hasn't changed since the last time I was here. Pillows with sayings like *thankful and blessed* adorn the second-hand brown couch my mother bought when I still lived at home. The beige recliner in the corner is worn, and the wall behind it is covered in photos that span my entire life. The scents of crisp apple pie and fall hit me as I step farther into the room, and the sound of my brother's cheers make me smile.

"He must be playing Xbox," I tell Brooks, gently leading him through the open space, going in search of my family.

The apartment is small. Two bedrooms, a kitchen, and a modest-sized living room. Since he moved from a crib to a regular bed, my brother has had his own room. For years, my mom and I shared.

It's not glamorous. It doesn't resemble Brooks's life in any aspect. But it worked for us. It still works for them.

My mother pops out of the bathroom with a surprised squeal. "You're home!" She lunges at me and wraps me in a tight embrace. The feel of her arms around me is a comfort, and I immediately sink against her. We're about the same height and build. Her hair is the same blond color mine was until a few days ago, and she has it pulled back in a ponytail.

I squeeze her once more, then pull away. "Mom, this is Brooks, my boyfriend."

Brooks holds out his hand and smiles.

My mother beams back at him. She's practically glowing when she gives me a quick assessment, but then she's focused on him again. "It's so nice to meet you, Brooks. We've certainly heard a lot about you."

His responding grin is boyish and almost shy. "Thank you for having me over. It's nice to finally meet Sara's family."

"Sar, why don't you go introduce Brooks to your brother, then come help me with lunch?" my mother suggests. "I'm sure you two don't have a ton of time before the game tonight."

"No rush, ma'am."

My mother swats at the air between her and Brooks. "Don't ma'am me. Makes me feel old. Call me Nancy."

"All right, Nancy." He gives her a sheepish smile and a nod, but I'm already dragging him down the hall in search of my other favorite person. "She's nice," he says softly.

I stop outside my brother's room and knock.

"Come in," he shouts.

The moment I open the door, my inner lunatic emerges again, and I dart for Ethan. I tackle him and squeeze him tight, drowning in relief and excitement at seeing him after months apart.

"Jeez, Sar. Let me breathe!" he teases. But when he drops the controller and swivels in his gaming chair so he can throw his arms around me, I know he's just as excited to have me home as I am to be here.

I sigh and squeeze him tighter. "You look good."

He stiffens in my arms, probably spotting Brooks behind me, and wriggles free of my hold. "Holy crap," he mutters out of the side of his mouth. "You're really dating Brooks Langfield."

Brooks's bellowing laugh from the doorway makes me smile and sends my heart soaring. "Believe me, I'm amazed she agreed to be my girlfriend too." He steps into the room and nods toward the screen. "That NHL 22?"

Ethan's smile splits his face. "Yeah."

"Have another controller?"

"You play?" my brother breathes, his brows in his hairline.

"Not as often as I'd like, but yeah, I think I can keep up."

Ethan laughs. "We'll see about that."

With that, Brooks is taking the proffered second controller and settling on the floor beside Ethan.

I've essentially been dismissed.

"I guess I'll go help Mom with lunch." I throw a thumb over my shoulder and back toward the doorway.

Neither of them so much as acknowledges me. They're both 100 percent focused on getting Brooks set up.

At the door, I rest my head on the frame and soak in the sight of them for a moment. My brother may not be able to do all the things the Langfield kids can, but the instant Brooks met him, he found a way to bond with him. I shouldn't be surprised. Even so, it makes my heart all gooey.

"You're very smiley," my mother says as I enter the kitchen.

I am, in fact, very smiley. My heart is still melting, and I'm pretty sure I floated my way down the hall to get here.

"Ethan looks good." I sidle up beside her.

She's standing at the counter, plating an absurd amount of food.

With a frown, I take it all in. There's chicken and side dishes and rolls and even a plate of cookies. "Is someone else coming over for lunch?"

"You're dating a big hockey player. He needs to load up on carbs before the game."

With a laugh, I rest my head against my mother's shoulder. "That's very cute of you."

"Your brother is so excited to go to the game."

I warm at the thought. "I'm glad you guys are coming. It'll be fun."

"And things with Brooks..." She picks up the platter of chicken, but she doesn't move. She just tilts her head and takes me in. "Are they serious?"

"I think so."

Her eyes go wide. I've never had a serious boyfriend, and I've certainly never brought a man home to meet my family. I'm fiercely protective of them.

With a nod, she takes the platter to the table. "He better be good to you."

"He is, Mom." I pick up the basket of rolls and follow. "He's one of the good ones."

With a nod and a small smile, she leans out into the hall. "Ethan, time for lunch." She shuffles to the fridge and pulls out a jug of lemonade, then returns to the table. "I'll probably have to call him four more times before he'll really hear me. He gets so lost in the game."

As we're plating the food a minute or two later, Brooks and Ethan appear. Of course this perfect man would turn off the game the moment he's beckoned.

"This looks great," he says, gripping my waist.

"You have a lot of work to do tonight, so eat up." My mother motions for us to sit.

Brooks pulls out my chair and waits until I'm seated before pushing it closer to the table. Then he presses a kiss to the top of my head and settles beside me. He places his napkin on his lap, and with one hand wrapped around mine, he uses his fork to cut into his chicken with the other, as if he can't possibly let me go.

It's adorable.

"What's it feel like out on the ice?" Ethan asks, his tone wistful and a little sad.

"Feel like?" Brooks scans the room for a moment, really considering the question. "It's a lot like what I think flying feels like. If you close your eyes while you're gliding."

Ethan closes his eyes, almost as if he's visualizing it, and Brooks squeezes my hand.

My little brother opens them again, picks up his fork, and gives Brooks a small smile. "Cool."

"So, Brooks," my mother says, "tell us about your family."

Lennox: Did you ever leave the bathroom or should I summon your mother to come get you?

Me: Haha, you are so funny. We're at the game now.

Lennox: Aw. How did Saint Brooks do when he met the family? I'm sure your mother loved him. He's got a face a mother would love.

Me: <eye roll emoji> He's got a face everyone would love. Literally. He was the Bachelor of Hockey for Sports Illustrated last year.

Lennox: And now he's all yours. Smoochie face.

Me: You know they have emojis for that, right? You don't actually have to write out the word.

Lennox: Crying laughing you're so funny.

Me: <crying laughing emoji> see? There's one for that too.

Lennox: Go watch your boyfriend. I heard he's pretty good on skates.

Me: Ha. Love you bye.

Lennox: Love YOU!

"Brooks really went all out, didn't he?" my mother says, tugging on her blue Bolts toque. She's also wearing a brand-new jersey.

My brother is decked out in a jersey emblazoned with the number 13 as well. He's beaming so brightly I swear there's a spotlight set on him. We're standing behind the plexiglass, watching the guys warm up. His eyes are huge, and he hasn't stopped bouncing since we stepped foot in the arena.

"Do you see the Leprechaun, Sar?" He tugs on my shirt and points at Aiden.

With a laugh, I wave at Aiden. He flashes me a grin and waves back, officially making my brother believe I'm the coolest girl he's ever met.

"I can't believe they all know you," he says, his tone filled with awe.

I muss his hair. "I am the coolest."

He shrugs me off and points to Brooks. "Look, he's skating toward us."

He sure is, and I can't contain the smile that takes over as I watch him approach. I'm fan-girling just as badly as Ethan is. No matter how many times I see Brooks play hockey, I'm enamored by him. Captivated. That extends to his every move off the ice too. Though when he's in this setting, his cockier side comes out, and damn, is it hot.

As he gets closer, those green eyes dance, making my stomach flip, and a smile tugs on his lips. "Hey, Sar." Even the way he says my damn name makes me swoon. "Bring Ethan to the bench for me."

My mother and Ethan turn to me in unison. My mother is biting down on her bottom lip, nervous. Ethan's eyes are bright and curious. Since the moment they met, he's hung on my boyfriend's every word.

I guide him to the gate and wave to the staff, making sure my employee badge is visible, since this isn't our home arena. Once they've waved us through, I lower myself to give my brother instructions. "Stay back and out of the way. The guys are all in skates. They'll crush your toes if they step on you."

Ethan's eyes are wide as he gapes at our surroundings. The huge hockey players preparing for the game, the coaching staff talking in whispered tones to one another, the guy out on the ice barreling toward the boards—the same one motioning for me to bring my brother closer.

"You want to fly, Ethan?" Brooks hands his hockey stick to one of the staff and holds out his gloved hand.

"You sure about this?" I ask, shuffling closer so Ethan can't hear me. "Seb might lose his mind."

Brooks shakes his head. "Even he's not that much of a dick. Come on, take my gloves and help your brother over."

I yank the glove off his right hand, then he tears off the left. With them tucked under my arm, I wave Ethan closer.

"What do you say?"

He doesn't hesitate. With all his might, he throws a leg over the boards. He wobbles back, but I steady him. When he's upright, Brooks scoops him up under the arms, then instructs him to stand on the tops of his skates.

"All right, Ethan. Time to fly." With a wink at me, Brooks pushes off, and then they're flying.

I cover my mouth and will my heart not to leap right out of my chest as my two favorite guys maneuver around the ice. Every one of our guys out there circles the pair, and Brooks starts pointing like he's introducing them all to Ethan. Then they're taking off again, the whole group staying in a circle formation and gliding together.

"If he fucking falls with that kid..." Seb mutters.

"They could skate blindfolded." Fitz laughs. "They're fine. Sar, you want to get out there? I can get a picture."

"No." I shake my head, unable to take my eyes off the ice. "But good idea." Phone in hand, I tap the screen and hit record. Not for the team. Not even for me. This is for Ethan. His face is so bright, and his cheeks are rosy from the cold. God, he's never looked happier.

When Brooks brings him back to the bench, my throat is so tight I can't speak.

"That was amazing!" my brother yells.

Once Ethan is on his feet on my side of the boards. Brooks hovers so close his skates tap the barrier between us. He grasps me by the neck and ducks low so our mouths are a breath apart. "Enjoy the game, crazy girl. I love you." Then he kisses me. It's quick and chaste. When he pulls back, he shoots me a wink and snags the gloves I still have tucked under my arm.

He's skating away and getting into position before I can process the significance of what he's just done for me and for Ethan. Before the impact of those last few words he spoke can register.

It isn't until he's in place that the way he said I love you sinks in. The phrase left his lips like it was second nature. Like he'd easily say it every day for the rest of his life. Like he truly loves me.

In a daze, I clasp Ethan's hand and guide him back to where my mother is standing at the glass, beaming just as brightly as my brother.

"That man is something special, Sara."

I nod woodenly, still at a loss. He is special.

And so much more. He's my best friend. The man who does whatever he can to make me smile. There's no ask too big. No favor too much.

He finds out I was supposed to cut my hair for charity and can't, so he cuts his and dares the league to join in. The challenge has gone viral. *He did that for me.*

My brother asks what it's like to skate, and rather than just describe it, Brooks brings him out to experience it for himself.

He's the best person I know. And he loves me.

For the past year he's spent his nights beside me on the couch, watching every rom-com ever put out on VHS. He's humored me and let me cry on his shoulder during season after season of *Dawson's Creek*. He took me to a Lake Paige concert and snuck me backstage to meet her. He makes dinner for me and laughs at my insanity.

I think maybe he's always loved me.

And maybe I've always loved him.

Oh shit. I love him.

I *love* him.

My heart pounds out a rhythm in my chest. One that feels a lot like *I told you so.*

I have to tell him.

"Mom." Emotions swirl through me as my chest tightens, the ache almost unbearable. My heart is about to beat out of my damn chest if I don't say these words aloud. I grip her shirt and pull her back toward the ice. "I have to tell him."

"Tell who what?" When all I do is gape in response, she points at the box where we left our things. "Honey, our seats are over this way."

"You go." I release her. "I'll be right back." Taking the stairs two at a time, I dodge fans locating their seats and run toward the ice. We're seconds away from the puck drop, and the music is already playing. The guys are lining up, so I push myself faster.

I have to tell him.

Arms in the air, I wave them wildly as I dart for the glass. Brooks doesn't see me. He's in the zone, settling into his position, knees turned inward, head tucked, completely focused on the players at center ice.

"Brooks!" I shout, desperate to get his attention before play begins. "Brooks, wait!"

He doesn't hear me. The music is loud and the fans are still milling about and getting settled in, but I don't stop calling his name. My sole focus is getting these words off my chest.

I practically slam into the plexiglass, pounding my fists against it and screaming like a lunatic. "Brooks!"

At center ice, Tyler swivels, ignoring the ref moving to the center line, puck in hand.

Aiden straightens next, eyeing Tyler. When he spots me, I point to Brooks, tapping my finger harshly against the glass, desperate to communicate that I want his attention.

When McGreevey spots me, he taps his stick on the ice to get Brooks's attention. Once he has it, he points his stick at me.

As if in slow motion, Brooks turns in my direction. The moment his eyes lock on me, I freeze.

Oh God. What do I do now?

The entire team is now staring at me. Their opponents too.

Brooks leaves the crease and skates toward me. I can't make out his features beneath his mask, but his shoulders are high and his posture is rigid in concern.

"Thirteen, get back in position!" Seb yells.

The ref blows a whistle.

Fans scream in surround sound.

I'm not sure if they're booing or cheering. The buzzing in my ears from the adrenaline rush makes it impossible to tell.

Brooks stops with his face inches from the glass and peers down at me, green eyes filled with worry as he catalogs every inch of me. Like he's truly afraid something has happened to me in the few minutes since we parted. "You okay?"

"I love you." The words hurtle out of my mouth.

Brooks blinks and holds his gloved hand up to his ear. "Come again?"

"I love you!" I scream it this time, hands splayed against the glass. "I love you so much, Brooks Langfield. I'm in love with you. And it *is* a high school kind of love. It is. And I'm glad it is, because it's the kind of love that's usually only possible before you've had your heart broken. The kind you believe is forever.

"A Pacey and Joey love. Like with the painting on the wall. Before they broke up. But we won't break up, because we know better and we don't need all that drama. And I love you."

I tip my chin up and laugh. The love I have for him makes me effervescent. Like I might just float up to the rafters. And it feels so damn good to finally tell him.

"It's a good love too." I clutch my hands to my chest, savoring the way my heart aches. "Innocent and pure and good. Because that's what you are. You're a good person, Brooks. The best. And I'm in love with you."

He tears his gloves off and slaps his hands to the glass. I hold mine up to his.

"I heard you the first time, crazy girl. Just wanted to hear you say it again."

I shake my head, smiling so wide my lips might crack. "I love you."

He drops his helmeted head against the glass. "I love you too." He lets out a long, almost relieved breath.

The whistles blow again, and he jumps. He whips his head around, then turns back to me. "I gotta game to play, but maybe we can talk about this later, yeah?"

Elation flows through me, but it's instantly replaced by trepidation. Because suddenly I realize the entire arena is watching us. Our images are magnified on the Jumbotron. The refs are going ballistic. So is Seb, along with the coaches from the other team.

"Shit. Are you going in the sin bin?"

Brooks is smiling wide as he picks up his gloves. He shakes his head and skates backward toward the net. "Worth it," he shouts.

Tyler is already headed toward the penalty box. McGreevey's daughters never schooled me in the protocol for when a goalie delays the game, but I learn quickly that in place of Brooks, one of his teammates must sit for the penalty.

Tyler waves at the crowd as he takes one for the team, quite literally.

I mouth an "I'm sorry," and in response, he points to me, then presses his gloved hand over his heart.

On my way to my seat, while my heart is still pounding and a thrill zips up my spine, my phone vibrates in my pocket.

It's a text from Lennox.

> Lennox: Shocked emoji. Swooning emoji.
> Proud of you emoji.

I smile as I climb the concrete steps. Some of the fans I pass cheer, but most are Carolina fans who are sure to boo loudly. Even so, I hold my head high, feeling awfully proud of myself too.

And happy. So damn happy.

CHAPTER 41
Brooks

"WERE THE GUYS PISSED?"

Sara and I spent a little time with her family after the game. It wasn't enough, but the day had been a long one for her brother, and on a selfish level, my sole focus was on getting Sara alone.

One step inside the hotel room, and I'm stripping out of my suit and giving Sara instructions to get in bed in nothing but her underwear. If she's completely naked, I'm afraid I'll get distracted, and I really want to talk to her before losing myself inside her again.

I swipe a wisp of hair from her pretty face. The blue is fading bit by bit. It's a muted tone now rather than the bright Bolts blue. "Don't care."

She snuggles closer and huffs a laugh. "That's not what I asked."

With a kiss to her lips, I nuzzle into her neck. "Say it again."

Sara shifts back and looks me in the eye, giving me a coy smile. "That's not what I asked."

Sassy thing. I pinch her ass, pulling a squeal from her, then hover over her body, propping myself up on one elbow. "Say. It. Again."

Warm hand pressed to my heart, she murmurs, "I love you, Brooks Langfield."

God, it's the sweetest thing. Those words from her mouth. The way she beat on the glass to get my attention. Even the penalty. I'd endure a thousand of them to hear her tell me she loves me.

"I love you so much, crazy girl."

"Oh," she breathes, teasing. "Is that my given name now?"

"I love you so much, *my* crazy girl."

She giggles. "Much better. So, are we ever going to take off all these clothes?"

My pulse picks up, but I can't help but tease her right back. "All I'm wearing is a pair of boxers."

The frown she gives me is full of mock disapproval. "Exactly. Too many clothes."

With one finger, I slide the strap of her tank top over her shoulder, then slip in close to kiss her neck. While my lips ghost over her sensitive skin, I cup one breast. "True, I need these nipples in my mouth."

She arches into me and moans. "I'd really like that."

"What else would you like?"

"Your cock in my mouth."

Fuck. *This girl.* How the hell did I get so lucky?

"Anything else?"

I kiss down her neck and pull on her top until her breasts spill out. Then I swirl my tongue around one nipple, then the other, channeling all my patience while I wait for her to tell me every desire she has.

"Your mouth on my clit."

I smile against her supple skin, then pull back. "My favorite place." Eyes fixed on hers, I slide down her body, pulling her panties with me as I go. "Anything else?"

I lick my lips, salivating, and press a delicate kiss right where she wants me. Then I dive in, swirling her clit and giving it a good suck.

The sigh that escapes her is needy. "I want you to fuck my ass."

My already hard dick presses painfully against her leg. I pause, keeping my mouth on her pussy, and peer up at her. "You do?"

With a thick swallow, she tilts her chin so her eyes are locked with mine. "Yes. I want to feel you everywhere, Brooks."

My heart clenches, and I freeze. "I don't want to hurt you."

The smile she gives me is soft and sweet. "Don't worry, I'll talk you through it. First, you're going to lick me until I come." She scrapes her nails along my scalp, sending a shiver through me. "After that, you're going to finger my ass and lick me there until your cock is so hard it's begging for me to let you in."

She pauses and lets the words settle between us. Then she licks her lips and tugs at my hair.

"Then I'm going to teach you how to ease that cock inside me, and you're going to feel a kind of pleasure you never knew existed."

I have to fight the urge to flip her over and pound into her at the image she paints. "Holy fuck."

"Do you want that?"

My heart races and sweat slicks down my spine. "Yes."

"Good boy." She grasps my hair and wraps her legs around my neck, forcing me to pleasure her.

Impossibly hard, I press my dick into the mattress, seeking relief, all while swirling my tongue and fucking her with my fingers.

"Yes, Brooks. So good. Right there." She bows off the bed. "Fuck, I love the way you're grinding against the bed. Pleasuring me turns you on, doesn't it? You need to come so bad you don't know what to do with yourself, don't you?"

I can't stop to respond. My tongue refuses to release her.

"If you take my ass like a good boy, I'll even play with yours."

My ass clenches in response, but I don't let up. I never thought I'd be into ass play like that, but the way Sara talks, the way she tastes, is hypnotic. I'll let her do whatever the fuck she wants to me.

"You like that?" she says with a surprised lilt. "You want me to play?"

"Fuck, Sar. I love when you play." I curve my finger just like she likes, and she shatters in my arms, squirting just like I like, right into my mouth. "You taste so good."

"There's lube in my suitcase." She goes limp against the bed, coated in a sheen of sweat, her chest and her cheeks rosy.

I'm so wound up I stumble and see stars when I launch myself off the bed. But I power through, and when I have the bottle in hand, I slide my boxers down and kneel on the bed. "What position works best? From behind?"

She bites down on a sexy smile. "Why do I love this so much?"

"What?"

"It's endearing." She presses a hand to her heart. "The way you trust me. The way you listen."

I frown. "Why wouldn't I? I want you to enjoy this. And you know what you're doing. I don't."

Sara leans up on her elbows, her hair cascading around her shoulders. Her nipples are pebbled, her chest heaving. "Because most men don't listen. I love that you do. I love that you're not intimidated by my experience."

Desperate to touch her, I drop the bottle of lube onto the mattress and climb over her. "Not intimidated at all. You make me feel so damn good, Sara. I want to do the same for you." I take her lips in a gentle kiss.

She nips at mine in return, turning the interaction playful. "Let's do it this way." She pulls back. "I want to watch your face as you sink inside me. Want you to see just how much I enjoy that perfect cock inside my ass. And this way, you can finger me while you fuck me, and I play with my clit. How does that sound?"

A bolt of lust rushes through me. "Fucking incredible."

I kiss her again, and the simple peck turns into more. Mimicking the movements of my tongue, I grind against her and slide inside her, coating myself in her arousal. She's soaking wet and warm and so damn tight around me. "God, I could live inside you."

She smiles and snags the lube I threw onto the bed beside her. "Sit up and use this." With one elbow planted on the mattress, she uses her free hand to slide off her top. It's still bunched around her waist, exposing her tits completely.

With the bottle in hand, she pushes on my abdomen until I pop out of her.

"You're so fucking beautiful, Sara."

She smirks. "Why? Because I'm naked, I've got your cock in my hand, and I'm about to teach you how to fuck my ass?"

"No." I cup her cheek and caress her soft skin with my thumb. "Because you're mine."

She sucks in a surprised breath and blushes. "Okay, Romeo. Let's do this."

My responding laugh is cut short when she drizzles lube around the head of my cock. The cold liquid teases my nerves. When she circles my dick and squeezes, the chill turns to a heat so intense my insides ignite. And when she lines me up where she wants me, the inferno blazes.

"I'm pretty wet, so slide in easy while I play with myself."

Beneath me, she slips her hand between her legs, and I follow her instruction, easing my cock into her tight hole. All the while, I watch her fingers circle her clit, letting the visual fuel my need for her. Her stomach tightens as I breach the first inch, and her lips part as she lets out a moan.

I tense, ready to slide back out. "Does it hurt?"

"No." Her lashes flutter, and she smiles up at me. "I love anal. This feels so good."

For the record, I officially love anal too. And not just because she's squeezing me so tight I can barely breathe. But because in this position, I can bury myself inside her and watch her play with herself. My gorgeous girlfriend who takes care of me. Who asks for what she wants. I love that about her. I love her.

I sink in another inch, and she lets out a loud whimper.

"Yes, Brooks. Fuck me, please. I want you to fill my ass with your cum. Be my good boy."

Gripping her thighs, I dig my fingers into the soft flesh and hold her open, then I do exactly as she asks. I slide in and out of her, watching as her tits bounce. It isn't long before my balls go tight. "I need you to come, crazy girl. What do you need?"

"Your fingers," she pants, working herself faster.

Happy to please, I spear her with two fingers and curl them just how she likes. I can feel myself through the thin wall separating my fingers and my dick. With the intrusion, she gets tighter, pushing me even closer to the edge.

"*Yes,*" she shouts, clenching down on me.

"That's my girl." Taking the cue, I pick up the pace, pounding inside her. "Squeeze me, crazy girl. Make me fill that hole until you're dripping. Look at you. You love this. You're panting and greedy, all because my cock is in your ass."

"Yes, Brooks. I love it."

I bat her hand away and slap her clit, and she shatters beneath me again, her second orgasm blending with the first. That's all it takes to prompt mine. I close my eyes and clench my jaw as I unload inside her.

When I open my eyes, she's watching me, jaw slack and her blue eyes hazy. "That was..."

I suck in a breath. "I know." Gently, I slip out of her. With a soft squeeze of her thigh, I hop off the bed and head to the bathroom.

When I return with a damp washcloth for her, she's already walking toward me. "Shower with me, baby." She grasps my hand and leads me back into the bathroom.

Once the water is running, I pull her into my chest and hold her while we wait for it to warm. The steam that billows out and surrounds us calms my muscles and my pounding heart.

"I could fall asleep in your arms," I whisper, dropping a kiss to her forehead.

Sara looks up at me, her gaze trusting and sure. "Promise?"

Without hesitation, I brush my lips to hers. "For the rest of our lives."

CHAPTER 42
Brooks

Sara: Meet me in the laundry room.

Me: Why does that sound dirty?

Sara: Because I'm me. But seriously. I'm all by myself. This place is creepy.

Me: Be down in five.

Sara: Great. I'll just sit on the dryer and wait.

Me: Sara.

Sara: What?

Me: You better not be naked when I walk in there.

Sara: Oh. Hmm. But all my clothes are wet.

Me: Crazy girl, if the guys walk in and see you, I can't be held accountable for what I'll do to them.

Sara: I put a sign up. The laundry room is closed for the next thirty minutes. Hurry Brooks. Don't want me to get wrinkly.

Me: Why would you get wrinkly?

Sara: Because I'm wet!

Me: Get me out of here now.

Sara: Is there a problem, Brookie?

Me: You can't jam a fucking plug in my ass while giving me a blow job and then expect me to sit through a press conference. Get me out of here.

Sara: Can we watch Christmas movies?

Me: Of course. When?

Sara: December

Me: When?

Sara: I said what I said.

Me: Just downloaded the Hallmark app. Think we'll be set for December.

Sara: I love you.

Me: Chinese takeout and The Holiday lined up for tonight. You want me to pick up anything else on my way back to the hotel?

Sara: You're my favorite person.

Me: Didn't answer my question, crazy girl.

Me: But you're my favorite person too.

Sara: My brother is here! Brooks! What did you do? My brother is here!

Me: Love you, crazy girl. I'll be home to pick you all up soon. My brothers are excited for your family to join us for Christmas.

Sara: You are the best person in the world! Just so you know. I'm crying. And you are so getting lucky tonight.

Me: I'm lucky every night, Sar. Merry Christmas.

Sara: So hear me out. You, me, a bottle of bubbly, and a hot tub at midnight.

Me: You don't want to go to the party? Rumor is that Lake will be there.

Sara: Honestly, I just want to be alone with you.

Me: Where do you want to go for Valentine's day?

Sara: hmmm. I mean I love Italian.

Me: So Italy?

Sara: <smacks face emoji> Brooks Langfield, you are too rich for your own good. I meant an Italian restaurant. Although now that I'm thinking, I kind of want steak.

Me: Plane will be ready to take us to New York at six.

Sara: New York!

Me: Lennox is meeting us for dinner. You're welcome.

Sara: Oh my God! You are literally the best.

"Good Morning, Boston. I'm Eliza."

"And I'm Colton. And this is the Hockey Report. How was your Valentine's day, Liza?"

"Better than you can imagine."

"Oh yeah? Hot date? Wait, don't answer that. I really don't want to know about my sister's dating life."

"Ha ha. Hilarious, Colton. He knows I'm embarrassingly single, folks."

"How is one embarrassingly single?"

"Embarrassingly single is the kind of single when you stay home alone and order takeout, yet still feel like you were out on a date because you watched the live posted by Brooks Langfield's girlfriend, Sara, and her best friend, Lennox."

"Oh, I might be that kind of single, then too."

Eliza laughs. "To be fair, I'm fairly certain all of Boston was watching. The minute they went live, I was sure Lennox was holding the camera and that Brooks would drop to one knee."

"They've only been together a few months."

"So? They're perfect together. It's clear how much he loves her. It's *the sweetest thing ever. And did you hear his nickname for her? Crazy girl. Ugh, I can't. It's so cute."*

"Are we going to talk about hockey today? The Bolts are looking great, in case you were wondering."

"You're the one who asked about my Valentine's Day..."

CHAPTER 43
Brooks

Sara: I'm mad at you.

Me: You're mad at me?

I SMIRK. This'll be good.

Sara: Yeah, I'm mad at you because you don't give me phone sex.

I cough to cover up my laugh. War snaps up straight beside me, so I spin so he won't see my phone.

Me: Phone sex?

Sara: I'm sitting with Becca. She says she gets phone sex when the team is on the road.

This time, I laugh out loud, leaning against the lockers and shaking my head. War takes this moment of weakness to snatch the phone from my hand.

His eyes go wide, then he snorts as he scrolls through her commentary. "Oh, she's typing again," he warns.

I grab it back just in time to see the dancing dots turn into a message.

> Sara: And don't even come at me with the nonsense that I travel with you. I DESERVE PHONE SEX.

My chest rumbles, and I can't wipe the smile off my face.

"What'd she say now?"

War grabs for the phone again, but I bolt upright and hold it to my chest.

"Come on, man. I want to smile. Let me smile."

Still clutching the device, I shake my head. "Get your own girlfriend."

This has been the status quo for the last few months. Pure happiness. Smiling. The team is playing as well as we did last year. Life with Sara is amazing.

We travel together, and when we're in Boston and not at the arena, we're wrapped up in one another. Cooking together, making love. We finished every season of *Dawson's Creek*, and I'm not afraid to admit that I was fucking sweating at the end when I worried Joey might actually pick Dawson. If she had, it would have totally ruined Sara's declaration of love.

But like Joey and Pacey, Sara and I are forever. Best friends and everything else.

Sebastian's a nonissue these days. I barely speak to him when on the ice, and I never speak to him off it.

I surprised Sara by flying her family up for the holidays. If I have it my way, we'll spend every Christmas with both families under the same roof. While they were in town, we made sure Ethan got to experience another Bolts game. The smile affixed to Sara's face the whole week they were in town was priceless.

Liv gave birth to the twins two weeks ago. We all breathed a sigh of relief when Beckett didn't immediately start calling them Thing One and Thing Two—or even worse, Girl One and Girl Two.

June "Bug" and Maggie "Mae" were born prematurely but spent less than two weeks in the NICU. Now they're the center of Beckett's world, right alongside their older siblings and Liv.

Late February in hockey means we've all got our heads in the game. Playoffs are around the corner, trade deadlines are looming, and now is when the exhaustion can easily set in if we're not careful.

We're facing New York at home tonight. It may be late in the season, but there isn't even a hint of exhaustion in Boston. We're hungry for another cup.

Aiden jumps up onto the bench and belts out "Bolts' Paradise," his unique version of "Gangsta's Paradise," by Coolio. When he's done, we head out of the locker room, focused and with our blood pumping, ready to kick New York's ass.

The chirping starts early. Vin is in Aiden's face from the moment the puck drops.

Aiden tries his best to brush it off, but he gets aggravated quick. War tries to interject, slicing his stick between them multiple times, but it's like Vin and Aiden don't even see him.

My little brother doesn't fight, so whatever that ass is saying to set him on fire must be bad. McGreevey and Parker are pure muscle tonight, keeping New York's offense out of the crease and making my job slightly easier.

It isn't until the third period that New York gets even close to my net. Naturally, it has to be Vin. The cocky motherfucker comes at me, but McGreevey is on him, and when he steels the puck, instead of chasing after him, Vin allows the center and winger to duel it out.

"How's the girlfriend?" he yells at me.

I keep my focus on the puck and the puck alone rather than acknowledging him. During the game, not even Sara can pull my focus. I'm certainly not going to let this asshole do it.

When I don't reply, he skates closer. With a huff, I push him back out of my net. What the fuck is this guy doing? Is this a play?

Refusing to let his antics get to me, I keep my attention fixed on the guys who are still fighting over the puck in the corner.

"You think I can have a go at her?" he jeers.

I grind my teeth and bite back a growl.

Ignore the motherfucker. He's not worth it.

The puck breaks free, and Parker sends it to Aiden, who's hustling down to New York's net.

"Game's over there," I taunt, repositioning.

Instead of hauling his ass toward the action now that his net is in play, he sticks far too close to me.

"Come on. Just a taste. It's a family rite now. First it was Uncle Seb, then you. I'm sure Gavin'll be itching to hit that soon. It's only fair that you let me test her out before that."

It's not his taunts that get me. Guys will say all kinds of shit to rile the goalie. It's not even his nasty insinuations. It's his knowledge of the history between Sara and Seb. The only way he'd know is if my uncle told him.

Why the hell would he go around talking about her like that? Did he really tell his asshole nephew, of all people, that he cheated on my aunt and slept with my girlfriend?

Something deep inside me snaps. My vision goes red, and rage takes over. I heave him forward, out of my way, and skate for the bench, pushing off the ice with all my strength.

As I approach, the eyes of every coach are bugging out. They're hollering and waving, and then the refs are blowing their whistles like crazy.

But when I set my sights on my uncle, the chaos disappears and time ceases to exist.

Anger floods my blood, a dark poison taking control, spurring me on and pushing me forward. Strangling any logic out of me until all I want is my uncle's blood dripping from my fists. I drop my stick and toss one glove to the ice, then the other, flying toward the Bolts' bench. My helmet gets tossed last. In one fluid movement, I hop the boards, the weight of my gear not even a factor.

"You motherfucker!" I roar when he's within swinging distance.

My uncle doesn't have time to block the first hit. In fact, his eyes go wide like he didn't expect it at all. He topples to the ground under the force of the blow.

I don't stop there. I climb on top of him, the tips of my skates digging into the flooring and my vision tunneling.

"Fucking her over wasn't enough?" I land a punch to his nose, relishing the way it crunches under my fist. "Lying to her wasn't enough?" A hit to his jaw. "Cheating on Aunt Zoe wasn't enough? You had to go run your mouth to fucking *Vin* about your affair with Sara?" With every word, I hit him harder. My vision has gone dark. All I can see is a blur of blood and flesh beneath me.

A flash of blue appears, and cool skin presses against my cheek. Then there's a hand on my arm, holding it back. The sweet scent of pumpkin spice envelops me with another cool compress. This one on my other cheek, pushing, forcing my head to one side.

"Brooks, baby. Brooks, calm down. War, I think he's going to pass out. He's not responding."

It's the panic in her tone that shakes me from my haze. "I'm okay," I mutter, pushing back onto my haunches, blinking the world back into focus.

"Holy fuck." War is at my side now too.

Gavin is the next one I spot. His eyes are wide and horrified. He's dressed in his usual suit, kneeling beside the medics, who have also appeared. Both are bent over my uncle.

"The fuck did you do?" My brother's voice is just as unrecogniz-able as the bloody man laid out before me.

"Help me get him up," Sara begs. She's still in front of me, her hands on my face, but she's pleading with War.

I don't move. "It's me or him, Gavin."

"Get him out of here," he says to Sara, his lips curling. He keeps his gaze averted, turning back to Seb.

Sara stands and yanks on my arm. "Please." Her voice cracks, garnering my attention.

I tip my head up, still stunned. Her eyes are glassy, and tears run in rivulets down her face.

The refs are heading my way, ready to toss me from the game. That gets me moving. With my skates still on, I haul myself up and grab Sara's hand. Then I lead her to the tunnel. The noise in the arena is deafening. Screams and cheers and boos follow us as we walk right out of the arena. I don't stop to change. I don't grab my things. I pull off my skates and I don't look back at the place I may never set foot inside again.

CHAPTER 44
Sara

"*WHAT DO you think the Bolts will do now?*"

"*I'll be honest, Bob. Without Brooks, I'm not sure the Bolts can pull it off. Team morale will likely plummet. Can't imagine a coach sleeping with his player's girlfriend will bode well for anyone, either. But things are looking even worse for the Langfields. Remember, Lukov is his uncle.*"

"*Thank God the holidays are over. Oh, to be a fly on the wall at dinner next Thanksgiving.*"

Brooks snatches the remote from the cushion beside me and hits the power button. "I told you not to watch this garbage."

I haven't moved from this position since I woke up. What better way to start my day than by enjoying my coffee with pumpkin spice creamer while watching the entire city of Boston decimate my reputation?

With my head lowered, I let my hair fall around my face like a curtain. The embarrassment that eats at me now that the entire world knows about my affair with Seb has left me perpetually red. As if I'm walking around with it tattooed on my forehead. Might as well stitch a scarlet *A* to my shirt.

Adulterer.

Destroyer of the Boston Bolts franchise.

Slut.

Every social media outlet is flooded with comments, and none of them are pretty.

Brooks hovers over me, dressed in a pair of blue Bolts shorts and nothing else. His hands are purple from the fight, and his eyes are sunken and rimmed red. He barely slept last night. Neither did I. So I noticed how many times his phone buzzed and how many times he disappeared into the bathroom and turned the water on so I couldn't hear his side of the conversations. That alone doesn't bode well for me.

War dropped by with his wallet, his keys, and his phone last night, but he didn't linger. Brooks's list of notifications was out of control already, and it's only gotten worse since then.

I duck my head again, wringing my hands in my lap. "What else am I supposed to do? I don't have a job." My stomach roils so violently I worry I'll be sick. I love my job, but that's the least of my concerns. Without it, I'll lose my home. Without it, I can't pay for my brother's medications. Without it, I can't stay in Boston.

Not that anyone in Boston would hire me after this. There's no point in putting off the job search in North Carolina.

As much as I don't want Brooks to see how absolutely wrecked I am, I can't stop myself from peeking up at him. The man I love. The man I thought would be my forever.

Without this job, can we make it? Being apart for days at a time during the season is one thing, but if we're forced to live states apart even when he is home, I don't see how we can survive.

Not to mention the trolls. If they could climb out of my phone's screen to protect Saint Brooks from Slutty Sara, they would. Better yet, they'd stick me in one of those contraptions they used to shame people in olden days. They'd leave me there with my head and arms hanging out and throw apples at me. Or maybe pie. Probably penis-shaped pies. Because they're mean, and I'd deserve it. Slutty Sara deserves to be penis pied in the face.

"You're not going to lose your job."

"Easy for you to say. They *can't* fire you."

Brooks scoffs. "Pretty sure Gavin would like to. *And* he has that power. But they aren't going to fire you. You did nothing wrong." He steps in front of me and hauls me to my feet. "We'll talk to a publicist. We'll set the record straight." With a huff, he drops down to the couch and pulls me onto his lap. "It's been *one* fucking day. I'm not going to let him ruin us."

I snuggle into his chest. "I don't want to be penis pied, Brooks. But if they do, make sure it's blueberry. Red isn't my color."

His chest rumbles beneath my cheek as he pulls me in tighter. "Crazy girl, I'm not even going to ask."

"I'm serious." My lips quirk a little, despite my best efforts.

"What about boysenberry? Or peach?" He kisses my forehead. "Ooh. Pumpkin would be perfect."

I smack his chest lightly. "No one uses pumpkin in a penis pie."

Brooks chuckles. "My bad."

Reluctant to break our connection, I pull back and suck in a breath. "I should probably shower and get dressed. Maybe work on my resume."

"They're not firing you." His brows are pulled low, and that surly frown I haven't seen in months has returned. "I'm serious, Sar. It's not happening."

"Even if they don't, how can I stay here? The whole city hates me."

Fingers digging into my chin lightly, he forces me to look at him. Tormented green eyes study me. "I will fix this."

It's a relief that he isn't offering to pay my way. He isn't asking me to move in, and he isn't offering to help with Ethan's medical bills either, thank God. It would destroy me if he did. I'm too prideful.

Eventually, I want to live with Brooks. I want to rely on him, and I want him to feel the same about me. But not like this.

Throwing money isn't Brooks's style, which only makes me love him more.

Just as that thought brings me a modicum of peace, both our phones light up on the table in front of us, and my heart is in my throat again.

Liv's name appears on mine.

> Liv: We're going to handle this. You know the drill. Keep your head down for a few days and let me do what I do best.

A tremor of relief works its way through me. Liv is a master fixer. Time and again, she's done it for Beckett, for the organization. Hell, she did it for herself when her life blew up. If anyone can find a way to get the press on our side, it's her.

But beside me, Brooks's shoulders are slumped and he's wearing a defeated frown. He offers me his phone.

> Gavin: Be at Langfield Corp at 10 A.M. Aunt Zoe has called a board meeting. Don't even think about bringing Sara.

A penis pie to the face is sounding more likely by the second.

CHAPTER 45
Brooks

THE WALLS of Langfield Corp have never intimidated me. Unlike my brothers, I've spent very little time in this building. While Aiden and I were playing peewee hockey, Beckett and Gavin were earning MBAs and being groomed for this office.

For as long as I can remember, the plan was for each of them to take over their respective teams. While scouts were watching me play in high school, Gavin, who's ten years older than me, was already working his way up the ladder.

Running the Bolts organization was his destiny, and playing for them was mine.

Yet, as I step into the building, I know that if he tells me he's firing Sara, I will not be returning to the team I love.

And I doubt I'll walk these halls again.

It's Sunday, so the building is quiet. Good. The fewer people around for this shit show, especially those who don't share our last name, the better.

My heart gallops, and my breathing goes shallow as I stand outside the conference room.

When I've finally garnered all the courage left inside me after last night's nightmare and the dozen phone calls I've dealt with in the last twelve hours, I open the door and force myself to cross the threshold. The first person I lay eyes on is my aunt, and my stomach sinks at the cold, hurt look on her face.

She and I have always been close. She made it to every one of my games when I was in high school, traveling with Seb all over New England to make sure I could always look into the stands and find a familiar face. No matter the weather conditions, the long car rides, or the early ice times, she never complained. She sat in the stands and cheered. She showed up.

Frozen, I simply stare, unsure of what I can even say to her. I didn't cheat. I didn't lie. Not intentionally, at least. My only fault was that I tried to protect her. Though, in the end, all I did was hurt her.

She looks away first, turning her chair so she's facing the window. Her back is to me, but she swipes at her face, and her shoulders shake when she pulls in a harsh breath.

Gavin is here too. His face is gaunt and his eyes are sunken. Like he's aged years in the last sixteen hours. He clears his throat. "Thanks for coming."

Beckett nods at me from the chair beside Gavin. His contemplative expression gives me a modicum of relief. When he's angry, the whole world knows it. He looks more tired than anything. Between his newborn twins and the shitstorm I created, he was probably up all night.

My father motions to the seat beside him. His expression is unreadable.

"Aiden coming?" I ask.

He furrows his brows and picks up his coffee cup. "Why would Aiden be involved?"

"From the look of things, this seems like a family meeting. Shouldn't he be here?"

My aunt whips around, her face a mask of fury. "His girlfriend didn't sleep with my husband."

The heartache I felt for her when I arrived is suddenly overshadowed by frustration. "Mine didn't either."

Her eyes go wide, but she purses her lips and pulls her shoulders back. "If that's the case, then how do you explain what happened yesterday?" She raises her brows. "And why did my husband admit to it last night? He told me everything. How he was trying to protect you from her. How she seduced him."

"Hold up." Gavin sits straight in his chair and holds up a hand. "Seb is a grown man, and Sara isn't here to defend herself."

"Did she or did she not sleep with my husband?" My aunt's green eyes, so much like mine, darken as she glowers.

Pinching the bridge of my nose, I let my shoulders sag. I can't sugarcoat this part. "She did."

She stands, sending her leather chair rolling back and hitting the wall with a loud *thwack*. "I want her gone." With that, she strides for the door. When she reaches me, she pauses and lays a hand on my shoulder. "I love you, Brooks. I've always considered you mine." She swallows thickly and lowers her face so she's looking me in the eye. "But asking me to deal with a woman who slept with my husband is too much. Dump her." Based on her comments thus far, I expected her to be angry or vindictive, but her tone is desperate, and every line on her face is etched in pain.

It breaks my heart. I reach for her hand and squeeze. "She didn't know he was married."

"I don't care." Another tear slides down her face. "I can't be anywhere near her. She needs to go." Pulling her shoulders back once more, she clears her throat, and then she walks out of the room, taking the last vestiges of hope I've been clinging to with her.

I turn to my father. "You can't fire her."

He looks just as helpless as I feel. "She owns half the company, Brooks."

I scoff. "Of course this is about business."

It's always about business with my father. Never has he put us kids first. He threatened to revoke Beckett's title if he didn't find a wife. He was able to spin it in his favor when he chose Liv and they actually fell in love. But even so, Beckett's best interests weren't even on my father's radar. All he cared about was Langfield Corp. How Beckett's reputation affected profits. How the media portrayed our family. That's all that matters to him.

"Seb is her husband," Gavin grits out. "It's not about the fucking game. I could give two shits about any of that. We have so much goddamn money that every one of us could retire today and never spend it all." He steeples his fingers in front of him. "This is about family. *Your* family. The people you kept in the dark. I can't count how many times I asked you what was going on with you and Seb. You refused to admit there was a problem until you blew up on national television and broke Aunt Zoe's heart in the process. It was selfish."

"Yes, *I* was selfish." I pound against my chest. "Me." I swallow down the urge to smash a fist into the table. My hands are damaged enough. "Not Sara. Me. So if you want to punish someone, then fire me. But she keeps her job. I promised her."

Gavin's jaw clenches. "Newsflash, Brooks—you don't own the goddamn team." He points at my father. "He does. And you don't have the authority to make managerial decisions." He pounds against his own chest. "I do. And you weren't the one who had your heart trampled all over on national television." He nods at the door. "*She was.* All because of what? Pride? Is that what this is about? This isn't like you. You're not like this."

"Because I wanted a goddamn shot!" I shout, my anger getting the best of me.

Beckett stands and rounds the table. Silently, he sits in the chair beside me and rests his hand on my knee.

I nearly jump at the unexpected touch. Then I blink at him, my often stern and cold older brother, baffled at the way he offers such gentle support.

He's focused on me, his face a picture of calm. "A shot at what?"

Regret and disappointment spiral through me. They're right. Going after Seb the way I did was selfish. I'll own that. But if I could rewind the clock and take it back, I wouldn't.

"At being with Sara." I look from Gavin to my father, then back to Beckett. "I wanted her, and I didn't want to hurt Aunt Zoe. I knew if she found out about Sara, then I could never have her. You would have sent her back to North Carolina in a heartbeat, and I would have lost her. I couldn't lose her. I *can't* lose her."

Beckett nods. "We're not sending her back to North Carolina."

My father slides back from the table. "That's not your decision."

Beckett glares at him, but it's Gavin who speaks. "It's my decision." He runs a hand down the front of his shirt, smoothing the fabric. "I have managerial power. She works for me. Thank you for coming in." The nod he gives me is all business. There isn't a hint of brotherly affection in his posture. "Expect an email regarding your suspension and the upcoming board hearing. Go home."

I don't move. All I can do is gape at the robot masquerading as my brother who's sitting across the table.

Beckett squeezes my arm. "Come on, I'll ride down with you." He stands and waits for me to collect myself. Then he guides me out of the office and toward a black town car out front. All the while, I can't help but feel like the world is upside down. My funny, outgoing brother holds all the cards, only he's been replaced by a cold, angry doppelgänger.

"I don't know if I can forgive him if he fires her," I admit to Beckett.

He nods thoughtfully, watching the scenery out the window as his driver heads toward my apartment. "Give him time. He'll make the right decision."

Beckett's confidence doesn't ease the dread that sits like a lead ball in my gut.

"If he doesn't, just remember that it's not because he doesn't love you. Running a multi-billion-dollar company, shouldering the responsibility for decisions that could affect hundreds of employees, can be a challenge. We can't always put ourselves or our family first. Sometimes we have to sacrifice to do what's best for the whole. Either way..." Beckett shakes his head. "Just focus on Sara. Talk to her.

Work with her. Don't do what I did and try to fix it on your own. That was my mistake with Liv. I tried to make things right without her input, and in turn, I left her thinking I didn't care about her." He gives me a half smile. "Liv trained Sara. She's a smart girl. She'll land on her feet. Stand by her side. Hold her hand when you leap, and you'll both be just fine."

I stare at my brother in awe as we arrive at my building. "You're really fucking smart now that you married, Liv."

Beckett grins. "Tell me about it. Best ducking decision I ever made."

I laugh for the first time in what feels like days.

Beckett shocks me again by leaning in and giving me a hug. We don't do this nearly enough, but in this moment, I vow to make it a regular thing.

"Thanks, Beckett."

I can hear the ruckus from the hallway outside my apartment. *What in the hell?* When I push my door open, I come face to face with the entirety of the Bolts' roster. They're spread out, taking up every inch of space between my kitchen and living room.

"Look who finally decided to show up for team dinner," War crows, sauntering out of the kitchen carrying a tray.

"Don't remember inviting you guys over." I frown. "Not trying to be rude, guys, but now's really not a good time."

Aiden holds up a pitcher of yellow liquid and shakes his head. "It's always a good time for tacos and margaritas."

"Tacos?" I eye the packages War is doling out. "Is that a Taco Bell wrapper?"

War grins. "The only thing the Americans do right. Fake meat in a crunchy chip."

My stomach rolls, and I fight back the urge to gag. "Don't call it fake meat."

McGreevey unwraps his taco and takes a giant bite. "I think it's delicious. Now," he says, talking around the food in his mouth, "sit down, and let's figure out how the hell you got yourself suspended."

Hands pressed to my face, I let out a groan. "You guys shouldn't be here. Coach is gonna lose his mind."

War shoots me a devious smile. "Wasn't that the plan?"

"Huh?" Parker eyes his taco with a suspicious frown. His wife is a health nut, so I doubt he's had Taco Bell in a while. His stomach may not be too happy with him for giving in and going with the crowd tonight.

"Come on, Saint." War tosses the tray of remaining tacos onto the table. "Sit down and tell everyone about how our coach is a sleazeball who lied to Sara and conned her into sleeping with him. Then we want to hear all about how you came to the rescue as her fake boyfriend."

Aiden gasps, his eyes bulging comically. "Seriously?"

I drop my head back and curse at the ceiling. "What the fuck, War?"

"We're a team," he says with a shrug. "Teams stick together. Your teammates have your back. Everyone here agree?"

The room erupts with shouts in the affirmative, but my shoulders feel tight. That was Sara's secret. Sara's private life.

War steps up next to me and pushes me toward my seat. "You've tried to handle this on your own. That went epically wrong. So let us help you make it right."

I sigh and scan the faces around the table. No one looks angry. No one's said a bad word about Sara since I arrived. They're not balking at War's explanation. They're all just here. For me. Showing up like a team does and, well, eating slightly cold fake-meat tacos.

"I don't know what to do." I slump forward, resting my elbows on the table. "I think they're going to fire her."

War shakes his head. "Not going to happen."

Aiden holds up his taco, spilling lettuce all over the table. "Absolutely not."

"I don't know what else to do." I turn to War, who's taken up residence in the seat beside me. "Where is she, by the way? She wasn't here when you got here?"

"She said she had to run an errand and that she'd be back later tonight." He leans over and opens the fast-food wrapper in front of me. "Eat a taco. It'll make you feel better."

McGreevey shakes his head as he grabs another one. "It won't, actually. But do it anyway."

Resigned, I pick up the damn taco and take a bite.

Aiden hops up and darts into my bedroom. A moment later, he's wheeling in the damn whiteboard again. When he turns it around, it's been cleared off, and at the top, in bold letters, he's written *Operation Get Rid of Coach and Keep Sara*. "Okay, boys. It's time to brainstorm."

CHAPTER 46

Sara

ALONE IN THE APARTMENT, it didn't take long for all the voices to get to me. The commentators, randos spewing BS on TikTok, sports fans, even religious zealots. The speculation was wild. But every one of the people talking about the events of last night agreed on one thing: I'm the problem.

Some thought Brooks was wrong for attacking his uncle. Many agreed that Seb was wrong for sleeping with me when he has a wife at home. Naturally, money and the evil that comes along with it could be blamed. According to several folks online, everyone involved is too rich to have true morals. They obviously haven't done a deep dive into my past.

In the end, each believed that I was at the center of it all. I'm the home-wrecker.

There's no way around it. In the end, the Bolts will have to fire me to appease the critics and fans alike.

I shouldn't be here. The babies have only been home for a matter of days. And despite her earlier text, I'm sure Liv's husband has instructed her not to get involved in my drama.

Gavin and Beckett are a team. They're extremely close, and if

Gavin doesn't want me at Langfield Corp, then I'm confident that Beckett will back him up.

Yet I find myself on her doorstep anyway. Sunglasses on, hood pulled up over my hair, head down so no one will recognize me.

The last thing I need to do is fuel the media fodder.

When Liv opens the door, spit-up dripping down her shirt and a crying baby in her arms, looking all sorts of disheveled, my heart sinks.

"I shouldn't have come. I'm sorry."

But before I can make it down the steps, she's reprimanding me, mom voice and everything. "Sara Case, don't you dare make me chase after you with a newborn in tow!"

I sigh and turn around. Though I do a quick scan of the street, hoping no one was close enough to hear her shout my name. "I'm sorry."

"And don't apologize. This is what family is for. Get in here." She holds out her arm.

Tears sting my eyes. It takes everything in me to keep them from falling.

"Dyl, can you take Maggie for me?" she hollers, disappearing inside.

I trudge up the stairs and toe off my boots in their entryway. The house is warm and smells like cookies.

Liv gives me a kind smile. "Dylan and Winnie have been baking. June is fast asleep, but this one? She's a clingy mess, just like her father." She grins down at Maggie. "You're a little needy one, aren't you, baby girl?"

My mood instantly lifts at the sight of her daughter's chubby cheeks and puckered lips. It's a fact. It's impossible to be sad while in the presence of a newborn. "She's beautiful."

"She is." Liv straightens. "Let me drop Ms. Needy off with Dylan in the kitchen. Go relax on the couch. I'll be there in a second."

In the living room, I wander along the perimeter, taking in the pictures on the walls. A photo of Liv and Beckett from their wedding in Vegas sits on the mantel. Her cheeks are rosy and her eyes are glassy, but her smile is blinding. The way Beckett looks at her, the complete and utter devotion he wears like a badge, makes my heart pang. It's obvious he was smitten on their wedding day. And that hasn't changed.

Beside that photo is one of Finn. He's wearing one of his signature tutus, and he and Beckett are dressed in matching Revs jerseys. Another one showcases all five of them: Finn, Beckett, Liv, Winnie, and Addie. They're smiling at the camera while they stand in front of this brownstone. If I'm not mistaken, it's the day Beckett surprised her with the keys and told her he'd purchased every house on the street so she and her friends could live near one another without having to live *with* one another.

A photo of the four women is next. Liv and her three best friends are posed in front of the original brownstone a couple of doors down. I tear up as I take in the details. God, I miss my friends.

There's so much love in this house. So much love in Brooks's family. And they're all going to hate me.

Why did I come here?

I turn, ready to bolt out the front door before Liv can return, but Finn saunters in, foiling my plan.

"Hey, Auntie Sar. What are you doing here?"

Finn's hair is slicked back, and even though it's overcast and thirty degrees outside, he's wearing his aviators. I can't help but smile.

"I thought I'd stop by to see the new babies and say hi."

Finn turns in a circle. "Uncle Brooks come with you?"

"No." I shake my head, working to hide the way my heart cracks at the sound of Brooks's name. "He had a meeting today."

"Oh, Bossman had a meeting too."

My stomach tightens. I'd bet anything he's at the same meeting as Brooks. They're probably sitting around a conference table deciding my future as we speak.

Finn steps closer. "When's Ethan coming to visit again?"

"Oh, um, I don't know, actually."

"Bossman says family sticks together. Especially us boys. There are so many of you girls, so you need to bring him around again. We need all the boys we can get."

A warm affection for this little boy fills me. "That's sweet, but Ethan isn't really part of your family. Maybe we can FaceTime him in a little bit, though."

"What you mean he's not my family?"

"He's my brother. You know that, right? And I'm not *really* your aunt."

Finn scrunches his face up and tilts his head to one side. "So? Auntie Dylan and Auntie Shay and Auntie Delia aren't really my aunts either. But we're all still family."

"Agreed," Liv says from the doorway, observing her son with a wistful smile. "Finn, go get your stuff together. Uncle Gavin is going to take you to the park."

"Yes!" Finn pumps his fist. "Uncle Brooks is right, Auntie Sara. You are a crazy girl. Gavin isn't really my uncle either, but he's still the best one I got." With those parting words, he darts out of the room.

Liv settles on the couch and waves me over. "He's right, you know. We're all your family."

"How could you possibly still feel that way?" I settle in beside her. "After everything you know—"

She clutches my hand, silencing me. "What I know is that my friend is hurting, and that's the only thing that matters."

I lower my head and pick at the fabric of my leggings. "I wouldn't be so sure. Right now your husband and Gavin are probably arguing with Brooks. I'm destroying this family." The tears I've been holding back well at the mere thought of causing a rift between the guys.

Liv shakes her head. "Brooks is a big boy. As are Beckett and Gavin. They're all responsible for their reactions and how they handle this." She dips her head, catching my eye. "I know you. Whatever happened between you and Seb, there's got to be more to the story."

I break down then, and the tears escape in earnest. Sniffling, I shift to face her. And then I tell her everything. I tell her about how my relationship with Seb started. About how he told me he was divorced and about the moment I discovered the truth.

"Brooks just stepped in without knowing the details of what had gone on between you two?" Liv asks, her brows arched high.

"Yes." I wring my hands in my lap. "He's the best person I know. And it may have started off fake, but it's real now. I'm in love with him. But I won't let him lose his brothers. Or his career. Not because of me." With a long breath out, I cover my face with my hands. "Seb was right. I'm going to cost him everything."

Liv grasps my wrists and tugs my hands away, shaking her head fiercely. "I can't promise anything when it comes to Brooks's career. I can't even make promises regarding yours. But we can talk out our options. Make a plan. That's what you and I are good at."

She offers me a soft smile that I can't help but return.

"As for this family? The relationships between the guys? I *can* promise those will not change. They have something special. *This family is something special.* And you are a part of it because Brooks loves you. It's that simple. We don't turn our backs on one another. No matter what. Blood doesn't matter. *Love matters.* And, Sar, we all love you."

I'm still trying to wrap my head around the love and devotion she's describing when the doorbell rings. "That'll be Gavin here to pick up Finn." Liv slowly rises from the couch. "I'm going to go check on the twins. Why don't you get that?"

My stomach lurches at the thought of facing him, but I trust Liv. And she's right. This family is special. If nothing else, Gavin should hear the truth from me.

My whole body is rigid as I make my way to the door, but I fill my lungs and force myself to pull it open.

On the other side, Gavin's tired smile falls. "I haven't made any decisions yet, Sar."

I nod as I move back so he can enter. "I'm not here to sway your decisions. Well, not much at least. Just—" I take another deep breath. "You deserve to know the truth. And I'd really like the opportunity to tell you my version of it."

With a sigh, Gavin points to the bar in the dining room. "Will I need a whiskey for this?"

I shrug. "We probably both will."

"*Good Morning, Boston. This is Colton, and I'm here with my sister Eliza to bring you the Hockey Report.*"

"*Thank you, Colton. We've got some exciting news. Obviously, we'll be chatting about all of this week's games. But first, I want to make sure our listeners know to tune in again tonight. We'll be live with an exclusive interview that you don't want to miss.*"

"*You're right, Eliza. I really don't think anyone will want to miss this. Our favorite player was suspended for attacking Coach Lukov, making this week a tough one for Bolts fans.*"

"*The news of the suspension was shocking, but before we jump to any conclusions, let's wait and see what happens tonight.*"

"*Way to keep them guessing, sis.*"

Eliza laughs. "*Little edging never hurt anyone.*"

"*Oh God. Please don't ever say that again.*"

CHAPTER 47
Brooks

FOOTSTEPS ECHO off the concrete walls and floor as my teammates follow me through the tunnel toward the ice. Before hitting the crowded arena, I turn around and look everyone in the group in the eye. It's a humbling moment. Every one of these guys is here to support me.

"You don't have to do this—"

War holds up a hand. "We all know. We're awesome. Everyone wants to get matching penises to celebrate, and you love us. Now turn around, Saint. Let's go show Boston what it means to show up."

"Yeah!" Hall hollers. "To matching penises!"

Dropping his head with a chuckle, Aiden holds up his hand. "To brotherhood."

"To doing the right thing." McGreevey takes a step closer. "To protecting our girls. To consent!"

The sheer number of cheers to that sentiment, along with the volume, rattles me. This isn't just about me. It's not about my suspension. We're doing this because of what Coach did to Sara. Every one of these guys was disgusted when they learned how he used his position of power. How he lied. Threatened her career. Manipulated her. How he stole her ability to make her own decision by deceiving her.

I swallow thickly, heart lodged in my throat. "I've never been prouder to be a Bolt than I am right now."

War claps my shoulder and pushes me forward. So I go, and I lead my teammates into the arena. Every one of us is dressed in a game-day suit. The cavernous space is cold and chaotic. The fans go crazy when we emerge, but the cheers quickly turn to gasps and frustrated shouts about our lack of gear. Without a doubt, every eye follows us as we approach the bench.

The game starts in an hour. The guys should be geared up and on the ice by now. The coaches are clustered together, each studying their iPads. Not one of them notices us, so I clear my throat to get their attention.

When heads pop up in response, I fill my lungs with a deep breath of cold air and let it out again, steeling my resolve. "So long as Sebastian Lukov is the coach of this team, we won't be on the ice."

The men in front of us blink, and Sara pops up behind them. She's wearing a confused expression and my Bolts jersey. "What are you doing?" she mouths.

"None of us will be suiting up until you remove Brooks's suspension," War demands from beside me.

Aiden steps up to my other side and grasps my shoulder. "I'll never play for you again."

I suck in a harsh breath at his words, and damn if tears don't prick the backs of my eyes.

My brother is the best center in the league. Hands down, there is no competition. Yet he's willing to put what will likely be a hall-of-fame career on the line for me.

Sara has tears in her eyes when she puts a hand on Coach's shoulder. He still hasn't looked up. His head is bowed over his iPad, and he's got a Bolts hat pulled low, probably to hide the nasty bruises I left all over his face.

But then he looks up, and instead of the ice blue irises I'm expecting, I'm met with a pair of brown eyes I'd know anywhere. Surprise hits me like a shot of electricity when the man beneath the bill smirks.

"That so?"

Gavin is literally the last person I expect to be standing before me wearing a smile.

And in a hat...

This man lives in expensive suits, and his hair is always perfectly styled. He owns the team, for fucks sake. What is he doing down here on the bench?

"Gavin?" Aiden's voice goes up an octave, like he's been kicked in the balls.

"What are you doing here?" I can't help the terse tone. After the way he talked to me the other day, it's hard not to be angry with him.

Gavin smiles at Sara. "Turns out your girlfriend is a great communicator. It's amazing what can happen when two people talk rather than yell. She and I bumped into one another, and when she politely asked me to hear her out, I obliged. Then she laid out all the facts. From there, I fired the asshole you all refuse to play for."

"This is a bit anticlimactic," Hall grumbles.

"Does this mean we should get dressed?" one of the second-string guys asks from the back of the crowd behind me.

Gavin stands and folds his arms across his chest. "You think?"

"Wait." Aiden narrows his eyes at Gavin. "Who's our coach?"

Our big brother merely grins. "You're looking at him. Now go put on your uniforms before I make you all drop and give me a hundred."

The guys clear out pretty quickly, but War and Aiden stay by my side.

Heart pounding, I take a step closer to my brother. "You're not messing with me, right?"

Gavin presses his lips together in a firm line. "I wish you had come to me when you discovered what Seb had done." He looks back at Sara. "I wish *one* of you had come to me." He tucks his iPad under one arm and adjusts the brim of his hat. "That bullshit has no place here, and so I did what any good boss would do."

"Wait, what about Aunt Zo? I thought she—"

My brother holds up his hand. "I went to see her after I left Beckett's last night. She's not happy, obviously, but she loves you. It will take her time to get past what happened, but in the end, she wants you to be happy, and she knows your girl is a big part of that. She told me to tell you she loves you and that Sara's job is safe. She also turned over her interest in the team to me. After I promised her that I'd fire Seb." He smiles at that last remark.

"I'll go see her after the game. Try talking to her again."

Gavin shakes his head. "She's on her way to Paris. She's going to spend some time with Sienna until things die down here."

It feels wrong to feel so relieved when her entire life fell apart, but I do.

"She knows you were trying to protect her, Brooks. She gets it. But she's gotta nurse her wounds. Her decades-long marriage is over. It's a lot to move past."

Beside him, Sara is crying, her cheeks streaked with tears.

When I realize, I lunge for her and pull her into my arms. "Why are you crying, crazy girl?"

"The guys were willing to sit out of the game? That was—" She shakes her head. "Brooks, look at what they did for you. I'm just emotional, is all."

With the pads of my thumbs, I swipe at her tears. It doesn't do any good. They keep flowing as she heaves in shaky breaths.

"They did it *for you*, Sara." I bend at the knees and catch her eye. "They didn't suit up *for you*. They did it in solidarity along with me, but we did it all *for you*. You're a part of this team, crazy girl. Without you, none of us would have played."

"First Beckett, then you. Do none of you believe in talking things out?" Gavin grumbles. "God, do I have to do everything?"

Sara laughs through her tears and turns in my arms, finding Aiden and War. "Thank you guys so much."

"Can I have a hug?" Aiden holds his arms out and ambles closer. "I'm a hugger."

War stays back, fist pressed to his mouth, laughing at my little brother.

"Oh, you're not getting out of this." I grab War by the lapels and pull him in. Then the four of us hug it out.

"Get in here, Gavin. We need a celebratory hug," Aiden croons. "And then I need to come up with a song. I didn't think we were playing, so I don't have one prepared. What are your feelings on Ariana Grande? You seem like an Ariana Grande type of coach."

Gavin frowns and takes a step back. "What kind of nonsense is he spewing?"

I laugh. "See what happens when you insist on talking?"

Sara peers up at me, still locked in our four-way hug. Her eyes are rimmed red, but they're bright. I release the guys and loop my arms around her, soaking in the warmth of her body and the peace that washes over me when I know I've got my girl—my crazy girl, my best friend, the center of my universe—wrapped up tight in my protective hold.

"I love you," I whisper.

Beside us, Aiden starts to sing.

Sara closes her eyes and laughs into my chest. "I love you too, Brookie."

"Good Evening, Boston. Eliza here with my co-host, Colton, for a special edition of the Hockey Report."

"Thanks, Eliza. Are you as excited as I am about our special guests?"

"Of course, Colton. I told you the edging would be worth it."

"Please stop saying things like that in public. Actually, for the sake of my sanity, please stop saying things like that period."

"Oh," Sara squeals. "I love a good edging."

Brooks chuckles. "She really does."

"Thank you." Eliza huffs a laugh. "For those out there who don't recognize these voices, let me make quick introductions. Colton and I have the honor of visiting with Boston's own Brooks Langfield tonight, as well as his girlfriend, Sara Case. Thank you both so much for joining us."

"Thanks for having us. We love your podcast," Sara says. "And we appreciate the opportunity to set the record straight regarding our relationship."

"Before we get to that, we need to talk about that goal, Brooks," Colton prods.

Sara giggles. "He's not normally so excited when a puck makes it into the net."

"Of course he isn't, since it's his job to block them," Colton says. "But those last ten seconds of the game against LA were impressive. We'll be watching replays for years to come. Not only did Brooks block a slapshot, but before the guys could get down to the goal, he lined it up and shot it straight across the ice and right into LA's net."

Sara laughs. "It was epic."

Even to the fans listening, it's obvious Brooks's sigh is a mix of exasperation and fondness. "Sara's excitement has very little to do with the goal. At the beginning of the season, her best friend declared that because we were dating, I'd have such good luck that I'd score a goal this season. Now the two of them think she's a psychic."

"Better than being a psycho," Sara teases.

"Oh, you'll always be my crazy girl, Sar. Even if your best friend thinks she's psychic."

"Sounds like the two of you have a lot to celebrate," Eliza says. "Your teammates were certainly excited. It looked like the entire team jumped on you at the end of the game. But then, Sara, you ran out onto the ice to congratulate Brooks. What was that moment like for you?"

"I wouldn't say she ran out onto the ice. She skidded on her ass across the ice is more like it." Brooks chuckles.

"Shut it, mister, or I'll tell them all about your Lisa Frank obsession."

"Sara," Brooks warns.

"I loved Lisa Frank when I was a kid," Eliza chirps. "All the purples and pinks. Oh! And the sparkles."

"Oh, Brooks is a huge fan," Sara teases.

"Anyway," Brooks grumbles. "Was there a question in there somewhere?"

"Oh, yes," Eliza says. "You ran out to him and he picked you up. Then the two of you clearly had a conversation that made her smile even more brightly. Would you share with us what you talked about?"

Sara lets out a light laugh. "You caught that, eh?"

"I think all of Boston caught it," Colton chides. "It's trending on social media."

"I asked her to move in with me," Brooks says proudly.

"And I said yes."

"Congratulations! You heard it here first, Boston. Brooks Langfield is a taken man. First Beckett, now you. How many more Langfield brothers are there? Two? Do you think love is in the air for either of them?"

Sara sighs. "I have my theories. I'm not ready to share them, but I will tell you that whoever they fall in love with better be fabulous, because Beckett's wife, Liv, and I are awesome."

Brooks's responding laugh is full of pure affection. "Okay, crazy girl. Let's go home."

THE END

EPILOGUE

"I HAVE to sing for my food." Aiden pushes his chair back and stands, then he clears his throat and starts his vocal warm-ups. "Do, re, me—"

"No. You really, really don't." From the head of the table, Gavin snags Aiden's arm and pulls, but Aiden yanks free and shuffles away.

I'm using all my willpower to hold back a laugh, but when Brooks side-eyes me with a smirk, I snort.

It's been like this since we moved in together two weeks ago. Effervescent happiness every moment of every day. Waking up to this man is like waking up to a fresh cup of coffee with pumpkin spice creamer. Kissing him, doing life with him, whether it's hanging in the laundry room while we wait for our clothes to dry or doing the dishes side by side or having sex in every slightly public place we can find, it's the most fun I've ever had. Because I'm doing it all with him.

Tonight is no different. Gavin summoned us all to his new apartment. He moved in to Seb's old place when he took over as coach. It's important to him to be available to the guys. His hope is to build solid relationships and deepen trust by being here with the team. And in line with that, he's hosting tonight's team dinner. Though I think he's regretting his decision to do so now.

I planned to stay home so the guys could bond, but Gavin insisted I come. According to him, I'm part of the team, so I'm required to be at the dinners. It's my first one, and I'm not going to lie, it's a riot.

Gavin glares at Brooks and me as Aiden begins a rendition of Ariana Grande's "thank u, next." As always, he's changed the words. This version is all about all of the coaches he's had over the years and how thankful he is to have Gavin now.

It's absurd and ridiculous, and I love every second of it.

When we arrived tonight, a torrent of unease washed over me. But once I stepped inside and got a good look around, it dissipated. The apartment is almost unrecognizable.

Gavin had it painted, and he replaced all the furniture. The walls are decorated with sports memorabilia. Rich mahogany furniture fills the space, along with oversized leather couches with recliners on either end.

The only thing that seems out of place is a baby grand piano that sits in the corner, almost hidden. I had no idea Gavin played.

This is the only unit in the building with three bedrooms. It's a little much for a single guy, but Brooks was thrilled when he took it. Now when Aiden and Jill fight, Aiden can stay here rather than with us in our one-bedroom apartment.

When the doorbell rings, Gavin practically jumps out of his seat and darts for the door. He's no doubt desperate to get away from the table and Aiden's singing.

"Sar, if this is another one of your packages, I'm going to start charging you delivery fees."

I giggle, and beside me, Brooks chokes out a laugh. Back when we were trying to get Seb to quit, I scheduled regular shipments of various sex toys to be delivered. Yes, I went a little overboard. Once again, my vindictiveness took over. I've called the company to cancel the autoship, yet they continue to show up at Gavin's door like clockwork.

Brooks is giving me a wicked grin. He's likely hoping it's exactly what Gavin is complaining about. Because we've made sure to test out each one. It's certainly made for a fun time for me.

"The last time I called, they swore the deliveries would stop," I say.

Gavin opens the door and scans the hall. He steps back, like he's going to shut it, but then he bows his head, and his entire body goes rigid. "Sar, *seriously?*"

I frown at Brooks. "What the hell did I order now?"

He shrugs and pushes his chair back. I follow his lead and shuffle behind him to the entryway.

Gavin hasn't moved an inch.

I peek around him, and when I spot the package that has him struck stupid, I gasp. "Aw, it's a baby!"

Gavin glares at me. "I see that. Why in the hell would you have a baby delivered to my apartment? Your kinks are getting out of control."

I cough out a laugh. "I did not deliver this beautiful little girl to you." I bend at the waist and scoop her up, car seat and all. She's much bigger than Liv and Beckett's twins, with good head control and chubby, rosy cheeks. As I examine her more closely, she watches me with the most beautiful brown eyes. Her hair is dark, and she's bundled up in a cozy peach sweater set. "Aren't you beautiful," I coo as I undo her car seat straps. She wiggles her arms and legs in excitement, all the while sucking on a pink binky. "And what a good little girl too."

Brooks snags the diaper bag from the hall and pulls at the card that's sticking out. "Looks like there's a note."

Gavin blinks at him. "Well, fucking open it."

"Gavin," I chide. "Has Finn taught you nothing?" I turn to Brooks and lift one brow. "What he means is *ducking* open it."

With a palm to his forehead, Gavin sighs. "Ducking A."

Brooks slides the card out, and his eyes go wide as he silently reads it.

"Out loud," Gavin grumbles.

Brooks holds it out to him. "No way am I being the bearer of that news. Read it yourself."

Gavin scoffs. "This family and their inability to talk. Fine, I'll do it." A little more aggressively than necessary, he snatches it from his brother's hand. "*Coach*," he starts and points to himself. "Guess that's me. *I can't do this. I know you said it's over and we couldn't be more— but she's more.*" His voice trembles as he continues. "*Too much for me. Meet Viviane, your daughter. You have more than enough resources to help her. So keep her or put her up for adoption. Either way, I can't do this.*"

The letter drops to the floor. Gavin's face is stark white, and he sways where he stands.

I'm at a loss, my heart in my throat. Beside me, Brooks roughs a hand down his face and shakes his head.

"Gavin," I say softly.

He looks at me and then looks at the little girl in my arms again. And then he takes a deep breath and reaches for her.

"Viviane," he breathes, as if he's testing out her name. He swipes a thumb over her peach outfit. As he does, the bracelet he's worn for months peeks out from his sleeve. Each of the guys has a dozen friendship bracelets by now. Winnie is obsessed. But this one is a constant fixture. The block letters spell *Peaches*.

What are the chances...

"Hi, baby girl." Gavin's voice is so low it's almost inaudible. "I—" He clears his throat. "I'm your—*dad*."

Want to read about Gavin's life as a single dad? Pre-order A Major Puck-Up here.

ALSO BY BRITTANÉE NICOLE

ACKNOWLEDGMENTS

We are officially in our Hockey Era and I am not sad about it. This book was SO much fun to write. Thank you to my amazing readers for trusting me to bring you angsty billionaires, possessive serial killers and singing hockey players. The fact that you devour whatever my squirrel brain decides to work on next means I have years of stories to tell.

This book would not have been possible though if not for some really amazing people. Sara, my day one hockey lover. This entire series only exists because of you. Happy Birthday my girl. Pretty sure Brooks will be a hard present to top. Your dedication as not only my pa, an incredible formatter, social media manager and basic Brittanee whisperer is not lost on me, but more than anything it's your friendship that I rely on day in and day out to get me through this life. Thank you!

To my work wife Jenni who beta reads, listens to my random thoughts, deals with my insanity and tells me we can say yes to everything because money comes back, I love you!

To my lovely editors, Beth and Brittni. You make my books better every single time. I will never stop singing your praises.

To my Book Babes and Swoon Squad, my street team, every release gets better because of you! I am always in awe of your friendship and support.

To my beta readers, Becca, Anna, Anna, Torie, Jenn, and Andi, thank you for all of your help in making this first hockey book of mine exactly what it needed to be. And for all your comments in the documents, they always make me laugh.

To Amy who constantly makes me amazing things for my readers, whether it's mini books, bracelets or jerseys, you spoil me. And for your friendship, you are one special gal!

And to my amazing readers, thank you for all of your messages, your Tiktoks, your dms, your posts and your rants. There is nothing I love more than hearing from each of you how a character affected you, or a storyline made you laugh. I love your reviews, your anecdotes, and the notes you send to me.

If you want to follow along on my writing journey and have sneak peeks into all the characters in Bristol, follow me on Instagram, join my awesome Facebook group, sign-up for my newsletter and follow me on TikTok.